The man levitated in the air on invisible strings. Guards and prisoners moaned and cried out. Some covered their faces, some watched in fascinated horror.

Only Johan remained impassive. Drawing his fingers together in the air, he steered the levitated victim across the room, out a yawning window into the night air—then opened his hand.

Screaming, the man dropped into blackness. A sickening crunch, as of an insect crushed under a wooden shoe, carried faintly on the night air.

Experience the Magic

Artifacts Cycle:

THE BROTHERS' WAR
Jeff Grubb

PLANESWALKER
Lynn Abbey

TIME STREAMS
J. Robert King

BLOODLINES
Loren Coleman

Masquerade Cycle:

MERCADIAN MASQUES
Francis Lebaron

NEMESIS
Paul B. Thompson

PROPHECY
Vance Moore

Invasion Cycle:

INVASION
J. Robert King

PLANESHIFT
J. Robert King

APOCALYPSE
J. Robert King

Anthologies:

RATH AND STORM
A MAGIC: THE GATHERING
Anthology
Edited by Peter Archer

THE COLORS OF MAGIC
A MAGIC: THE GATHERING
Anthology
Edited by Jess Lebow

THE MYTHS OF MAGIC
A MAGIC: THE GATHERING
Anthology
Edited by Jess Lebow

Ice Age Cycle:

THE GATHERING DARK
Jeff Grubb

THE ETERNAL ICE
Jeff Grubb

THE SHATTERED ALLIANCE
Jeff Grubb

Legends Cycle:

JOHAN
Clayton Emery

JOHAN

LEGENDS CYCLE • BOOK 1

Clayton Emery

Johan
Legends Cycle

Distributed in the United States by St. Martin's Press. Distributed in Canada by Fenn, Ltd.

Distributed to the hobby, toy, and comic trade in the United States and Canada by regional distributors.

Distributed worldwide by Wizards of the Coast, Inc. and regional distributors.

Made in the U.S.A.

Cover art by rk post
Cartography by: Rob Lazzaretti
First Printing: April 2001
Library of Congress Catalog Card Number: 00-103748

9 8 7 6 5 4 3 2 1

UK ISBN: 0-7869-2611-2
US ISBN: 0-7869-1803-9
620-T21803

U.S., CANADA,
ASIA, PACIFIC, & LATIN AMERICA
Wizards of the Coast, Inc.
P.O. Box 707
Renton, WA 98057-0707
+1-800-324-6496

EUROPEAN HEADQUARTERS
Wizards of the Coast, Belgium
P.B. 2031
2600 Berchem
Belgium
+32-70-23-32-77

Visit our web site at **www.wizards.com**

Dedication

To Hector and Sharon,
Lords of the Jumpgate.

Jamuraa
N
E
W
S
Great Wall
River Toloro
Tirras
Eflavra
Palmyra
Desert of Sukurvia
Bryce
Enez
Shaibara
Craggy Coast
Bay of Pearls
Sea of Serenity
0
1000
Miles

Chapter 1

The harsh sound of snarling and growling carried on the thin, cool desert air and disturbed Hazezon Tamar's meditation.

The wizard opened one hazel eye and peered about. He sat alone on a prayer rug amidst folded ridges of sand and shale as yellow as amber. His horse, caparisoned with an embossed saddle of dark red leather and many small silver bells, tossed its head and snorted. The mage had faced south for his trance, for he believed all good things came from the south, including blessings. But the wind blew from the north, as always, and brought the sounds of a dogfight or lion brawl. Hazezon saw fierce Osai vultures kiting down behind a ridge.

Clambering to his creaky knees, shedding sand, Hazezon caught the reins before his horse bolted.

"Where vultures land, misery dies, eh, Belladonna?" Hazezon spoke to his horse for company, for he was normally a gregarious man, and like all mages, both curious and superstitious. Swinging astride his ornate saddle, he continued, "Let us leave the desert spirits to their own devices and see what creature so pitifully lies down. One should never ignore a nudge from the unknown."

Belladonna was a gray gelding that, like its master, was no longer fast, but even tempered and capable, and able to haul extra weight. Hazezon was a man of middling girth and advancing years. His last wife had cursed him as a "fat-bottomed potion peddler." His stomach rumbled in agreement. Fasting was a component of meditation, and he'd skipped his breakfast of figs, eggs, and brown rice. His skin was as dark as tanned leather and was covered with a white mustache and beard. Hazezon wore the traditional garb of Jamuraa's desert seacoast: a loose robe of pale brown deftly embroidered, a keffiyeh or head scarf of white as befit a ruler, and a multicaped cloak of amber stitched with gold thread. A brass-hilted scimitar was shoved through his sash, a trapping of office. Hazezon Tamar hadn't struck anything with a sword for almost two decades. His weapon was his mind.

Tracking vultures atop a rise, Hazezon found a crowd of desert dwellers attending a single death. At the outermost ring hopped scruffy Osai vultures with naked heads as red as dried blood. Inward circled hyenas, thick-shouldered and strong-jawed and brutish, that barked and snarled. Closest to the disturbance padded a pride of tawny lions. Two males watched as a quartet of lionesses snapped at a figure not yet dead.

Hazezon found the figure strange. Refusing to die, it hunched on all fours with hands and feet drawn in so they couldn't be bitten. Yet the man—if a man—had odd contours, the back very long but the legs and arms short, a stunted giant. Too, the curve of the limbs was queer. Hazezon could see little, for the mystery man was wrapped in rags of burlap faded by sun and shredded by long travel. Yet rents in the rags showed Hazezon a burning gold and black tiger pelt. Since tigers were uncommon along the Bay of Pearls, Hazezon knew the stranger had come far. Yet why cross the desert? And how alone, with neither horse nor camel, and no retainers or baggage save a few crude gourds to hold water?

"Truly, Belladonna," said Hazezon to his horse, "the fates wished we witness this spectacle, for an odder man have I seldom seen on the sands of Sukurvia. He shows spirit, if he isn't an apparition, for beyond endurance he seeks to preserve his life even as the lions strive to take it. Can we turn away from a vision sent by spirits? Hardly. Steel yourself, my pet."

Taking a firm grip on the reins, Hazezon booted his horse. Instantly the obedient Belladonna bolted into a charge down the ridge, silver bells jingling. Hazezon warbled a war cry that rang in the desert air and brought every scavenger's head swinging around.

"Ho! Get on! Begone, sons of nine thousand devils! Take flight before Hazezon Tamar! Your ruler commands it! Git!"

Tall horse and cloaked rider thundered down the slope, hooves clattering on stones and shouts filling the air. Vultures flapped and croaked and beat the air so black feathers pinwheeled. Hunched hyenas gurgled and slunk away, but only to sheltering boulders. The lion pride snarled and curled their muzzles, and padded aside, ready to trot off, until their chief, a scarred lion with a bushy black mane, coughed and roared.

Hazezon had hoped his surprise rush would banish the beasts, but Belladonna planted four hooves and halted so hard the rider almost pitched from the saddle. As Hazezon fumbled to keep his seat, the king lion snarled, bunched its haunches, and vaulted from a standing start a full dozen feet. As the tawny meteor rocketed close, Belladonna shied, sidestepped, and almost stumbled. Rocked by his horse, only Hazezon's wild scrambling and cursing kept him astride. The four lionesses had left the crouched mystery man and padded in a file, as regular as soldiers on parade, to surround Hazezon. He'd misjudged the lions' hunger, or arrogance. The leader squatted to spring on the horse with long cruel claws.

"Impudent cat!" spat the man at the lion. "You rule a pride, but I command to the horizons! Take this! *Eneta . . . hala . . . hashana!*"

Conjuring with just one hand, Hazezon blew across his palm, and a rime of frost engulfed his flesh to the elbow. An easy spell in the desert's winter. A fog of swirling ice crystals puffed from his hand and splashed like sea foam into the lion's face. Curled muzzle, yellow teeth, and black claws were frosted white as fresh paint. Even the lion's eyes fogged so it was blinded. Its attack stalled. Clawing at its face and sensitive nose, the king whined like a tormented kitten. Coughing frigid air, the lion backed away, crumpled on one haunch, coughed, and fled. Instantly the lionesses broke off their attack and bounded after their master, tufted tails flapping like snapped ropes.

Hazezon tugged his tunic and capes aright and snorted, "So does magic triumph over might." Yet the mage didn't revel in victory, for with the lions gone, the hyenas began to circle. Their low-slung jaws that could crush bones made them as dangerous as the lions. Best the rescuer finish his rescue and move on.

Wrapping the reins around his fist, Hazezon hopped from the saddle beside the hunched and mysterious figure. In the excitement, he'd forgotten the victim's queer contours. His horse hadn't. No sooner did Hazezon hop down than Belladonna reared, whinnied, and tried to bolt, almost yanking the master's arm from its socket.

"What bewitches you, besotted son of a mule? Desist and stand fast, lest we feed the hyenas their supper!" Hazezon caught a rag-wrapped shoulder to get the man's attention. "Friend! Best depart! Come, quickly—*Tower of the Tabernacle!*"

Exhausted, the stranger collapsed, so Hazezon held a shred of rags. More of the orange-gold tiger hide was exposed, and a great swath of snow-white chest. The furred face was a riot of black and gold stripes with two amber eyes, like sun on a summer sea.

The stranger did not wear a tiger pelt, Hazezon learned, but rather owned one. Had been born in one.

"Great Defender!" Stunned, Hazezon dropped the rags as if afire. "A tiger in man's garb? How can such a thing *be?*"

"Not—tiger." The alien voice croaked a barbarous accent. Amber eyes, gleaming with intelligence, appealed for help. "Tiger man."

Belladonna whinnied and shied so hard Hazezon was jerked onto his rump and dragged half a dozen feet. Only by iron will did he retain his grip on the reins, for to lose them would cost his life. Staggering up, shedding dust, Hazezon tried desperately to think as his horse jittered and hyenas closed. Their evil black eyes glimmered beneath their spotted tufted heads, and their tongues lolled over curved fangs as if grinning. They stank too, as rank as a burning garbage pit. Best, the wizard thought wildly, to saddle and ride, yet the urgings of the unknown were not to be discarded. Who knew what greater disaster might befall Hazezon if he left this fabulous and unknown creature to die?

In the end the tiger man's actions decided, for the ragged figure crawled toward Hazezon as the only refuge. Custom alone dictated that a stranger in need be aided, and Hazezon adhered to custom as diligently as to superstition. Dragging his horse close, Hazezon grappled the ragged figure—long as a sea serpent and as heavy as a chest of gold, he seemed—and boosted him up across the saddle cantle. Belladonna whistled fit to panic as hyenas rushed.

"*Ona . . . orashan . . . mourtan!*" barked Hazezon, quickly scooping air in a broad circle.

Where his hand pointed, sand and rocks leaped as if spanked by a giant broom. Dust and pebbles boiled in a cloud that peppered the hyenas' muzzles. Blinded and sneezing, the animals rocked back and turned away. Some ran in panic, and two crashed together.

Before they could clear their eyes, Hazezon vaulted to the saddle, swinging one leg wide over the tiger man, and roared, "Ride, Belladonna! For the stables! Go!"

Terrified, the horse launched headlong and straight. The magic dust cloud had churned higher than a man's head, and the horse's plunge split it like a curtain. Hazezon glimpsed a large brown shape hurtling for his horse's throat, a hyena jumping blind. Whipping his scimitar from its scabbard, with more instinct than practice, Hazezon swept the curved blade amid the curtain of dust. Keen steel cut flesh. A hyena yelped and rolled away, and Belladonna burst free of the dust cloud into the clear desert air.

Hazezon rammed home his heels. The horse couldn't gallop for long with this much weight, but a half-mile should see them free of the hyenas' threat. He inhaled a deep breath of the desert air, dry and clean, austere but scented with sage and spice and a hint of exotic mystery.

"We'll get to safety, then talk, you and I!" Hazezon called over his shoulder. "We have much to tell, eh, tiger man?"

No reply. Hazezon risked a backward glance as his horse drummed over ridges of rock and sand. The tiger man's head hung as slack as a fish in a net, thumping on saddle leather. Yet one clawed hand, or paw, clutched the cinch so tightly that, even unconscious, the strange being would not slip off.

"You'll survive," said Hazezon, "if thirst and lions and hyenas can't kill you, and me too, for all my fat bottom and soft ways."

Chuckling at his luck and skill and glad to be alive, Hazezon Tamar steered his horse down into a twisted gully that led to the coast.

* * * * *

"Friend, what burden do you fetch from the desert?"

"Oh, sister. Uh, nothing that need concern you, if I may be so bold."

Hazezon halted. He'd led his nervous mount down a low wadi toward the Bay of Pearls. He always climbed this wadi as a path to the desert because it kept him off the skyline and disguised his desert visits. Hazezon Tamar ruled the city-state of Bryce, and although he ruled a peaceable community, he had enemies to be avoided, especially unaccompanied on desert trips. Regularly, Hazezon visited the desert to meditate, to think and study, and to improve his magic lest he forget it. Such studies fared poorly with retainers lolling nearby, fidgeting and shuffling and gossiping. Hazezon had talked to his horse to calm it from its strange and feral burden. Distracted, Hazezon was startled to meet another striding toward the desert.

The stranger was a druid. A short woman clad in dun robes and patched sandals, she sometimes came to Bryce to trade jade and malachite and garnets for provisions, then always returned to the desert with her meager satchels and water gourds. How this lone small woman survived afoot in a torrid desert rife with wild beasts no one could guess, though they suspected her magic must be powerful. No one knew her name. The merchants called her Stone-Bringer.

Naturally a courteous man, Hazezon stopped to talk, despite wanting to avoid the spooky druid. Thorn bushes and cedars with their strong resinous smell and jagged rocks hemmed in the trail, so he had no choice. Druids were a special breed, more than mere servants to the cryptic spirits of the desert.

Now Hazezon stammered like a child caught stealing berries. "This is a . . . vagabond I found collapsed in the desert, Your Worship. I must get him to water. . . ."

"I see." In the direct way of druids, much curiosity and no manners, the small woman drew back the stranger's rags. If surprised to see a tiger man, she gave no sign. Her face was burned black by sun, her hooded eyes as pale as milk glass. Hazezon wondered if she were mad. She announced, "Not dead, just sleeping. Exhausted and dehydrated. Strong."

Stone-Bringer examined the unconscious beast man from head to foot, just as Hazezon had done lashing him down lest he fall. More tiger than man and as heavy as a horse, he was nearly seven feet tall. His elongated fingers and toes were half the length of a man's and ended in claws as thick and black as shards of flint. He wore a simple harness decorated with a curious bronze buckle and a breechcloth of goatskin painted with a rude pattern of green and black triangles. He carried only empty gourds for water and a long knife of bronze. The rags were not burlap, but rather, the druid identified, the inner bark of a tree pounded soft.

"A clue to his origins," said Hazezon, trying to be helpful. This starry-eyed druid unnerved him.

The druid asked where the tiger man was found, but Hazezon could give only distances, for the desert held few landmarks.

"He may as well have dropped from the sky. I've read many an antique tome and heard stories of wolf men and horse men and even bird men, but never a tiger man, have you?"

To Hazezon's irritation, the druid answered obliquely.

"There are other planes and other worlds we can't touch, though they touch us."

"Well, yes . . ." Hazezon watched as the druid stroked the tiger man's muzzle and pried open an eyelid. "Planeswalkers were common before the glaciers and great floods, they say, but magic was young and strong then. What's that to a half tiger or me?"

"You would tap the mana of the spheres," said Stone-Bringer. "You seek to glimpse the ancients' time-lost secrets, to attain new heights of self-empowerment through magic."

"Uh, y-yes." Hazezon was startled. "But every magic handler craves new parlor tricks. Magic and mana are like gold. You can never have too much."

"How much we want. How much we ignore what we have." The druid might have chuckled as she studied the creature's ears.

"But to get back to this—man thing." Tired and irritated, Hazezon was curt. "Whence comes he, do you suppose? Is he a unique creation, a sorcerer's toy? Or from a community of cat folk? And where could they be? Jungle? Or the mountains?

No one inhabits the eastern deserts—no, wait. Rumors speak of oases in the far east. Do you know—"

"He comes from a threefold place," interrupted Stone-Bringer. The horse stirred as she cradled the tiger man's great striped head to her bosom and closed her eyes to concentrate. "From sand and fern and water. Threefold, three things made one, yet each separate. I wonder if . . ."

Hazezon waited, but the druid fell silent. Time dragged. Hazezon wondered why she cradled the tiger man's head. Surely this unknown creature, like a figure stepped from a legend, had been sent by the fates. Anyone could see that. The question was why? What should a man, or mage, do—

Hazezon froze as the druid began to sway, as if blown by unfelt winds. She keened, a low moaning noise that gave the watcher gooseflesh, then huffed as if she'd run ten miles. Words spilled from her mouth.

"Hunnnn . . . Threefold. Hunnn . . . Makes one, two, and none. None, one, and two. 'When none meets one, only two shall remain.' "

Abruptly the druid let go of the tiger man's head, so it thumped on the saddle. She shook herself, milk-glass eyes staring, and asked Hazezon, "What did I see?"

"S-see?" Hazezon wanted to run, leaving horse and stranger if need be. He'd been too rattled to grasp much meaning. "Uh, you said, 'none, one, and two.' When they meet, uh, only two remain."

"Oh, yes. The prophecy of None, One, and Two." The druid might have discussed marketplace gossip. "This tiger man is an instrument of prophecy. Guard him well, and luck will be yours. Fail, and he'll bring you destruction."

Hitching her satchels and water gourds, the druid turned and strode up the gully.

"Luck? Destruction? Wait!" Hazezon's curiosity overcame his unease. Dropping the reins, he trotted after. "Wait! Can't you tell me more? Is he good luck or bad? What should I do?"

"Luck evens out over a lifetime." The druid marched as she lectured, so Hazezon wanted to grab her arm but didn't dare. "Yet a man might steal luck by winning favor from the fates. Your man creature is of three parts, thus holy. The prophecy too is three parts, so linked. When the three are made one, some will prosper, and some will die. As always."

"But that's—" Hazezon gasped, wanting to say "useless." "Very vague and, frankly, not very helpful."

"It is not our mission to help." Stone-Bringer mounted rocks in a narrow cleft that left Hazezon stranded. "We interpret. Mortals fulfill. See to it."

"Yes, sister, of course. Gladly. But to what purpose? I fail to grasp—Are we—Bryce is attacked intermittently by Tirras. Will the tiger man aid us—"

"Ah." Stuck by a thought, the druid nonetheless kept walking. "Tirras attacks Bryce even now."

"*What?*" Hazezon gaped like a fish out of water. "*Now?*"

Pausing, Stone-Bringer pointed south by west. "Yes, now." Then she slipped away, up the path toward the desert.

Dashing back to his horse, Hazezon jerked the reins and jogged down the defile, puffing and wheezing. A few hundred feet of rocks dropped away to show foothills and orchards and fields. Beyond, the Bay of Pearls glistened like a restless sapphire. Bryce was brown kernels of stone clinging to the shoreline, much hidden behind a tall stone wall split by the many fingers of the glittering River Toloron. At several points behind the wall, evil black-gray smoke rolled upward.

Heedless of Belladonna's plight, Hazezon Tamar mounted and kicked savagely to gallop to the defense of his city.

Hazezon screamed at the sprawling vista, "Johan! May your twisted body be blistered by a thousand boils! Damn you, evil erstwhile emperor!"

Then he ran out of breath as horse, rider, and mysterious stranger pounded the trail.

* * * * *

Far to the north . . .

"They're here, Emperor."

Johan lifted his horned head and fixed baleful eyes on his chamberlain. The man was short and round but dignified in gray hose and a belted red tunic painted with Johan's four-pointed star. Johan had never learned the chamberlain's real name, but called him Hands, for so he used him, as another set of hands.

Rising, Johan left a table littered with colorful gimcracks. All were different and all magical, though the mage had yet to learn their functions. A horn covered with veins or glyphs was chipped around the mouth. A ring bore a broad face like a miniature painting, except the image could not be discerned, for it squirmed before one's eyes. A ball was faceted like stained glass, emerald green. A red shield was carved with a face in torment, as if a lost soul were trapped within its iron rim. A helmet had curled ram's horns. A hammer forged of steel had been indented with giant fingerprints. More lay waiting: a spoon, a silver disk, a bone dipped in bronze, a dried toad, some rods and wands, and more. The mage kept them nearby as toys to distract in idle moments. Certainly he didn't need their power, for he had power enough to level a mountain range.

The room Johan paced was unending, more than a quarter-mile long, as irregular as a snake's track, carved into the face of a mountain. Walls and floor were smoothed stone while the ceiling contained cracks and crevices and the odd stalactite. Windows, waist-high and square, honeycombed the undulating outer wall. By day, the view would reveal scraggy plains verging on deserts, a vast wasteland that rolled six hundred miles south to the Sea of Serenity, but tonight the winter sky was black and chill and awash with crystalline stars.

This was the mountain stronghold Krieghelm, a castle carved into the very face of a granite mountain, so that turrets and battlements and staircases merged with naked stone. Krieghelm reared above the sprawling city of Tirras here in the north, and from the highest tier of the granite castle peeked the never-closed windows of the north's ruler, Johan.

Now, by night, the sky seemed to pour into the wizard's chambers for the windows had neither glass nor oiled paper nor shutters. Johan apparently didn't feel cold, for the room was never heated except for meager candles to give light. The chamberlain, called Hands, shivered as he waited at the door, his breath frosting and fingers growing numb.

Scuffling sounded in the hallway, then a blow and a yelp, and Johan's foot guard tramped in dragging three prisoners. The six soldiers wore leather helmets and gray tunics painted with the red four-armed stars. The three prisoners wore work-stained smocks and rough shoes, short knives, knapsacks, and cloaks or blankets. One man carried a caulking hammer in his belt, one a mason's hammer, and the third a long polished stick and the leather bracers of a rope walker.

Hands the Chamberlain said, "You cared to interview three travelers from the south, Your Majesty. These men arrived just before the gates were closed at dusk."

The prisoners shivered in the icy room and at the fearsome emperor. Johan, emperor of Tirras and the Northern Realms, was tall, with fire-ruddy skin and so many tattoos he was striped like a tiger. He wore a purple robe of some exotic lizard skin that swept the floor and gaped at his breast, which was also riddled with tattoos, as were the backs of his hands. Most disturbing to the prisoners was where the purple robe bunched around Johan's neck and his head. Twin horns curled downward from his brow. Onlookers might assume the horns were sewn to the robe, until they saw another horn jutting from the man's chin. That small horn and a black **V** between his brows gave him the appearance of some ancient dinosaur reared on two legs. His black eyes glistened like nothing human.

Johan's eyes never blinked as he studied the prisoners. He paced back and forth silently, robes whispering, his bare feet seeming to glide over the frigid stone floor.

The prisoners were pinned at the elbows by two brawny soldiers, but the mason bobbed his head respectfully and said, "Uh, sir. Milord, or Your Majesty. We've come to Tirras seeking work, sir. We heard on the docks of Yerkoy you're building—"

"No doubt you heard plenty." Johan didn't look at the men as he paced back and forth before the night-black windows. "No doubt you serve as spies for Bryce."

"Spies?" chirped all three men.

Johan waved a tattooed hand. "Ease your suffering. Tell me what defenses Bryce has amassed and what my troops can expect."

The mason spokesman shook his head like a poleaxed steer. "M-milord, it's true we passed through Bryce, but we only stayed the night. We took a barge to Palmyra—"

"Liar." Still Johan didn't look, only paced like a caged tiger.

"M-milord?"

Johan's hand flicked as if brushing away a fly. The mason jerked. Johan's foot guard let go of his elbows. The prisoner gargled as if strangling, then clapped a hand to his throat. His right hand had changed. His fingers grew pointed, longer. Two fingers shriveled away. The skin grew glossy, then turned dark and hard and mottled with knobs. The mason screamed to see the transformation that now afflicted his whole arm.

No longer an arm, but an insect's claw.

The mason pushed his twisted arm away with his other hand, but it too changed. The man writhed and twisted and fell as his feet and legs were transformed. Buds swelled and burst on his forehead, as if beetles bored outward from the flesh, and two antennae sprouted. His jaw elongated. He grew mandibles like a praying mantis's. The change wracked his body so cruelly he screamed and thrashed as if afire. His two companions and Johan's guards backed away in awe and fear.

The man levitated in the air on invisible strings. Guards and prisoners moaned and cried out. Some covered their faces, some watched in fascinated horror.

Only Johan remained impassive. Drawing his fingers together in the air, he steered the levitated victim across the room, out a yawning window into the night air—then opened his hand.

Screaming, the man dropped into blackness. A sickening crunch, as of an insect crushed under a wooden shoe, carried faintly on the night air.

One prisoner sobbed into his hands. The other only stared pop-eyed at the emperor from whom they'd innocently sought work. Johan pointed to the next prisoner.

"You. Tell me what war preparations are laid in Bryce."

"M-m-mi—" The man couldn't speak for terror. Wildly he looked about for escape, but six guards blocked him like a gray wall. "I—I—"

"More lies." Johan hooked a hand in the air as if catching dust.

The staring worker was hoisted off his feet as if by ghosts. Soaring headfirst, he flew out the window in a long shallow dive for the rocks far below, screaming the while.

"You," said Johan.

His mind clarified by imminent death, the last victim stopped sobbing and babbled, "Milord, we saw soldiers on the docks. They had boats and were loading sacks, must be flour or corn meal, across a canal. Some were tearing down buildings over a bridge, maybe so no one could shelter behind 'em. Some were drilling, I remember that, marching through the streets with spears. Some rode horses with sabers. We aren't spies, milord, just simple tradesmen who take no side in any war, and that's the truth! I swear it!"

"Tell me." Johan's hooded black eyes flickered like cold fire.

The man yammered on and on, babbling until he was hoarse, desperate to recall and recount any military preparations he'd seen. After an hour he gasped for breath, out of ideas.

"There was—No, I told that a'ready. The soldiers—Barges full of rocks—no. That's—that's all, milord."

"Very good." Johan did not sound pleased, just eternally icy as his chamber.

The man sagged with relief, wiping his brow from his brush with death. He suddenly shouted as his feet kicked air, windmilling, for he floated inches above the ground. He let out one squawk as he was wafted to the window. Yet, when Johan's fingers opened he didn't scream. He simply fell in silence as if his heart had died already.

Standing at a frost-rimed ledge, Johan reflected on what he'd been told then decided it amounted to nothing. Yet the interrogation had gone well. By accusing the first two of lying then instantly killing them, he'd shocked and sharpened the wits of the third man, who'd spilled all he knew. Johan had then killed the third rather than release him, for such a terrified peasant would do little work, and he'd only spread rumors and terror among the Tirrans.

Likely such brutal tactics wouldn't fool a die-hard spy, Johan concluded then murmured to himself, "Still, no knowledge is wasted, and I can't know too much about Bryce if I'm to rule the city. . . ."

Chapter 2

"Are you an officer?"

Hazezon vaulted from the saddle and stood gasping, hanging onto the pommel. At an intersection just within the city walls, smoke rolled by in eye-stinging billows. Men and women trotted past with spears and buckets. Grandmothers herded children wrapped in their skirts against the smoke. A camel snorting in fear lumbered one way then reversed and dashed off. The buildings were mostly adobe, one or two stories, and the roofs tile, so were unlikely to burn, but plenty else could: cordwood, carts, haystacks, garbage, palm trees, cacti, century plants, canvas awnings, tapestries, and more. It seemed strange that the city he loved, with its homey smells of cinnamon and cooking oil, sea salt and mud flats, park flowers and privies, could be laid open to rape by foreigners.

The city ruler demanded, "Captain, what's happening? How many enemies?"

"It's nine devils' work to know, milord." The captain, a young man with a neat beard, bathed his scorched face at a public fountain whose surface was dappled with ashes. On the lip of the pool lay a scimitar stained with blood. As a militia captain, he wore no uniform, just a tradesman's loose tunic, baggy pants, and a turban coming unwound at the back.

Only his blue sash marked his rank. Smoke smudged his face and arms. "They set fires more for panic than destruction, I think. The fires were set at different points around the city, so we run every which way trying to douse them. Meanwhile Tirrans kill as they will and break doors in the marketplace after loot."

"Who leads the fight?" Hazezon's nose ran from exertion and smoke. His horse, Belladonna, hung his head and sobbed for breath, foam dripping from his tongue, even as he slurped noisily at the fountain water. The master had to yank the horse's head away lest he bloat. The tiger man still hung as limp as a sack of salt. "Where are my generals? Where are the soldiers?"

"Ringing the marketplace is my guess, milord—"

"Hoy, grab the bloated one!" blared a voice. "He'll have money!"

The two Brycers turned as a quartet of Tirran marauders rushed them. In gray tunics painted with four-pronged red stars and boiled-leather helmets trimmed with fur, they carried short swords or maces and round shields again painted with Johan's blazon. One wore red-painted cow horns on his helmet, a sergeant's badge. One man was bigger than the rest, with a broad flat brow overhung by shaggy hair and tusks denting his upper lip. The four laughed as they rushed the two townsmen.

Bryce's militia captain howled and leaped to the attack, swinging his scimitar overhand in a glittering arc. He would have split a foe's head to the collar, except he was outmatched. Two Tirrans split, dashing apart so the captain had to turn. As he slashed, clipping the edge of a shield, the nether attacker struck the captain's ribs with a mace. Winded, in agony, the captain whirled only to have his feet kicked out from under him. The first man rammed a sword straight into the captain's neck, and blood gouted as he died.

The attack came too swiftly for Hazezon to formulate a plan or jump back-to-back with his captain. Enraged by this callous assault on a citizen, heedless of his own danger, Hazezon churned both hands in the air as if stirring an invisible cauldron.

Three steps from death by twin Tirrans charging with swords, Hazezon bawled, "*Volaran . . . enet . . . zapran!*"

Gloating lust faded in the Tirrans' eyes as their running feet left the ground. A miniature tornado plucked the soldiers off the ground as if blown by a sky god. Howling, the men spun in dizzying circles. They rose as high as the rooftops. Still the mage stirred the air with arcane magic. Barely able to see through stinging dust, Hazezon managed to steer the desert dervish to sweep up the two Tirrans who'd killed the captain. Within seconds the stunned men were snatched off the ground and spun so hard they lost their weapons. A sword whizzed by Hazezon's head and whapped Belladonna's rump. The poor horse was so thirsty he continued to slobber at the fountain, ignoring the murderers and odd weather.

As Hazezon hoisted his hands higher, the dervish elongated like a pillar of smoke, higher than treetops, and inside it went four screaming Tirrans.

Abruptly Hazezon clapped his hands, and the humming dervish vanished.

The marauders were flung to all points of the compass. One man struck a building and crashed limply to the dirt. Another smacked his head on the stone plaza and broke his neck. The other two crashed on their backs and moaned from broken bones and dizziness. Even as Hazezon smugly dusted his hands, Bryce citizens who'd cowered in alleys dashed up, snatched their men's swords, and dispatched the moaners.

"Tell me now who's fat!" boasted Hazezon.

Yet the ruler of Bryce could hardly stop the Tirran's tyranny man-to-man. He had to reach his palace to organize a defense. He turned to Belladonna, but the slobbering brute was blown. He'd founder and die if ridden farther. Reluctantly, Hazezon drew a short knife to cut the tiger man loose and relieve the horse of his pressing weight.

"Jewels of Jasmine!" Hazezon stopped short, for the creature stirred. Great clawed hands flexed feebly, yet each flick severed a hank of taut rope. With a slither and splash, the tiger man flopped into the fountain.

"What—tiger man, what do you?" Shoving Belladonna aside, Hazezon grabbed the tiger man's head lest he drown. The massive striped body and sodden rags almost filled the pool. A paw as big as Hazezon's head pushed his hands away.

Almost bubbling from the water came the barbarous croak. "Leave me. Let me—soak."

"V-very well." Hazezon wrung his wet sleeves. "I must direct the city's defense. If you see men painted with four-pronged stars, run."

"Mercy of the Mothers!" A woman shrilled at Hazezon's elbow.

A jittery crowd had gathered around their leader. Anxious eyes looked in all directions, but too at the monster filling the fountain pool.

The woman screamed, "A tiger loose in the streets! Help —"

Hazezon rudely caught her elbow to stem panic. "Madame, this is a tiger man under my protection. I, Hazezon Tamar, your ruler! Citizens, attend me! Guard this tiger man well! He can speak and think as we do and is sent by the fates to aid us! You, you, and you, I charge to escort him to the palace! Understand? He is my personal guest and not to be harmed! And you there, take care of my horse."

Confused citizens, some bloody, all worried, agreed, eager to follow orders and regain stability in their lives. Tame talking tigers were the least of their troubles.

An old man rasped, "If he goes unharmed, milord, he may be alone. Tirrans overrun the city to slaughter every man, woman, and child."

"No," pronounced Hazezon. "I doubt that. True, they strike hard and steal, but never have they slaughtered in the past. Tirras is a plague like locusts, come in small parties under cover of smoke, but we can weather them if we keep our heads! Stay together, take refuge, discourage looters, and protect the children, and our worthy militia will drive the Tirrans off. This I promise, if you act sensibly. Now I must go."

Leaving citizens, Belladonna, and tiger man, Hazezon trotted off through the haze for his onion-spired palace.

Inwardly Hazezon cursed, and doubted his own speech. For one thing, there was an infernal amount of smoke. Houses were built of adobe clay, and roofs were tile by his own special orders to minimize fire hazard, yet buildings did burn. No doubt some of this mischief had to be magical, with Johan's lesser sorcerers either casting fire spells directly or else handing out potions of infernal flame. Burning buildings might have seemed trivial while his people suffered and died, but never before had Tirras sown this much discord. Despite his bold words of moments ago, Hazezon Tamar feared many of his citizens would die.

Bryce was nicknamed the City of Bridges, or the City of Canals, because the River Toloron splintered as it fed the Bay of Pearls. After many attempts by city engineers to force the river into set channels, they'd finally given up and simply bridged the many fingers of water. Thus Bryce was picturesque, as beautiful and delicate as spun glass, with arching stone bridges and intersecting canals, but spread out and shot full of holes that made it impossible to defend. Hundreds of hostile Tirrans could find hundreds of easy entry points.

Bryce had grown soft in recent years, same as its ruler. Once a haven for pirates and "sand bandits," the city allowed its aging founders to prosper until their wealth was an embarrassment and their children saw no need to go raiding. As freebooters built dynasties, Bryce evolved from a rough-and-tumble cutthroat hideout into an open-air market with low tariffs and piddling corruption, the most tranquil seaport along the contentious Craggy Coast. Reformed pirates hated practicing pirates, and after Bryce hanged a few wild buccaneers, life settled into a dull contentment of counting coins and flaunting wealth.

Then the circle closed. Being both rich and soft, Bryce became the target of raids. Not, this time, from the water, for Brycers recalled pirate tricks, but from far inland, across the sinister and inhospitable desert of Sukurvia.

In past years, distant Tirras amid its jumbled mountains had grown from an annoying pest to a downright threat. Four hundred years ago, the glaciers that towered over the land were magically evaporated by some archmage's caprice. Almost wiped out in flash floods, the hardscrabble hill tribes of Tirras who survived found all their topsoil washed into valley bottoms, which proved fabulously fertile. As food became plentiful, so did children, and Tirras's population exploded. Yet the landlocked city-state had little room to expand. To the north and west loomed forbidding mountains. To the south and east stretched the sun-blistered desert. Only a single thread connected Tirras to the south: the River Toloron, and at the mouth of the Toloron lay Bryce.

So, every year during Hazezon's long life, in spring and fall, the river bore boatloads of battle-ready Tirrans to raid Bryce. Landless young men and women, increasing every year, who were unable to farm or fish or harvest timber, had become a ready-made army for any leader aspiring to conquer the southlands.

"And Johan, may a thousand weevils infest his hair, is just the man." Hazezon puffed as he crested another bridge.

Resting, he surveyed the city from this limited vantage point where the smell of sea salt and mud flats and eel grass and old fish tickled his nostrils. Built on stilts and rocks and flats, Bryce stood little above sea level, and some quarters flooded when the wind shifted south. Now the wind pressed from the north, same as the invaders, so smoke blew out to sea. From here Hazezon saw all the fires had been set below the north wall. Clever, he admitted. The smoke swept across the city and drove the populace to distraction. Under the murky cover, raiders could glide their boats down the fingers of the Toloron and infest the city at its heart. Even should the fires do little damage, the city militia would be spread all over. Bryce had only twelve thousand souls and a tiny standing army. Her main defense was the militia, where every able-bodied man drilled regularly. But citizen-soldiers were a poor match for able young warriors hot for blood and glory. Even as Hazezon watched from his bridge perch, a handful of Tirrans in gray and red spilled from a warehouse along a canal, their sword blades red and their arms full of pilfered rugs, casks, furs, and other booty. No opposition greeted them.

Sipping air, Hazezon trotted for his palace. It wasn't a grand place, for ex-pirates were stingy with taxes. A former hall of a family gone extinct had been dressed up with unneeded columns and topped by onion spires, the whole painted a flat white, and the walls decorated with murals of sea adventures. Beside being the city's center, it had become a museum, or mausoleum, for odd bric-a-brac and junk donated by citizens too cheap to have it hauled away. Rubbing his smarting eyes, Hazezon noted the palace guards had deserted their posts, but perhaps they helped fight marauders. Staggering and winded, the ruler of Bryce grabbed a wall as he passed into the dark cool depths of the palace. He hoped a servant would greet him with a draft of spiced wine and some honey cakes with jam. After a year's worth of adventures in one afternoon, Hazezon craved refreshment.

Something was wrong.

There were no guards, no servants, no scribes. The front hall, a small receiving room of stone floors and pale pine walls, was empty. Stifling his panting, Hazezon cocked an ear. On tiptoes he crept down a short corridor to the main hall. This high-vaulted room with windows at either end, designed for entertaining, was jokingly called Tamar's Throne Room. It was cluttered with queer totems of obscene spirits, faded tapestries, old war banners, and other litter. The place was rarely quiet, for the city's bookkeepers and scribes chattered endlessly. Peeking, the city's ruler saw the long ink-stained tables were unattended. Parchments and scrolls skittered across the floor.

From another corridor Hazezon heard a crash, then a coarse laugh. A bad sign. Holding his breath, Hazezon tip-toed backward.

Too late. A Tirran soldier, a dwarf, waddled into the hall lugging a stone bust of some long-dead citizen. Hazezon had the inane thought that a ninety-pound bust of a stranger was damned poor loot. Then the soldier spotted him. The dwarf tried to yell, juggle the bust, and pull his sword out at the same time, fumbling it. The bust smacked to the floor, shattering a heroic and venerable nose. The dwarf's yell brought more Tirran voices echoing through the violated palace.

"Jabber-jaw!" snapped Hazezon. He debated whether to run or fight. Neither choice appealed. Then two more Tirrans darkened the corridor behind him.

A dozen clustered around his person. Hazezon noted their mixed ancestry. Most were sturdy hill men, blond and broad-shouldered, used to hard work. Other hill tribes had joined them: dwarves; a few coarse brutes with dusky casts and pug noses, either orc or ogre-blooded; a frail male halfling no more than belt-high; and three barbarians from the farthest north, dim creatures of cold climes, big and burly with short tusks and thatched hair. The last carried iron-headed clubs, though most carried swords, and a few had crossbows and quivers. No matter their shape, all the soldiers wore the gray tunic with four-pointed red star. Oddly, their uniforms worried Hazezon the most. Hill bandits and nomads and pirates wore whatever they chose, but these were true soldiers under military discipline. Johan, Hazezon now understood, had finally transformed his polyglot populace into a conquering army. Disorganized Jamuraa would lie at his feet ready for rape.

Surrounded, Hazezon tried to bluff. Imperiously he called, "This building is the civic heart of Bryce! Soldiers are forbidden here by custom and law! Begone, lest Johan learn you've violated a diplomatic pact and tarnished his chances for a peaceable negotiation!"

For a moment Hazezon hoped it worked. Soldiers were used to obeying orders. Halfling, barbarians, dwarves, and humans looked to their leader.

"You are Tamar, sir? Pasha of the city?" The sergeant sized up the enemy. Hazezon's official title was Tetrarch of the Free Realm of Bryce, but he went by many titles, including governor, lord paramount, suzerain, and the old-fashioned pasha.

Smirking, the sergeant touched his halberd to an awkward statue, some octopus-whale fetish, and tipped it over. The barbarians stumbled back as green stone smashed on the floor. The sergeant said, "Tirras has declared war on Bryce, sir. There'll be no negotiating, only surrender. Our orders are to seize the city and its leader. Take him!"

Outright war was news to Hazezon, but he acted before the soldiers rushing from behind could pin his hands. Popping his palms together, he snapped, "*Ana corsu efret!*"

Instantly Hazezon stood ten feet closer to freedom, having swapped places with a soldier behind him. One man still charged headlong to grab his comrade. Confused, the two crashed like crates of dishes.

Hazezon whirled and raced for the front hall. Something whacked his legs like a ship's boom, and he spilled headlong, skinning his hands on the stone floor. Scrambling to his aching knees the mage discovered a barbarian had hurled an iron-wrapped club at him. The halfling, as quick as a rabbit, hooked Hazezon's hand with a tiny foot so he sprawled again. The halfling flashed a dagger with a wicked needlelike taper. The sight of sharp steel froze Hazezon momentarily, but as ruler of Bryce he had the city's welfare to consider, not just his own life. Gambling, he flung out an arm and upset the halfling so the flying dagger struck the wall.

Over the sound of pounding feet, Hazezon scooped air behind him, silently pulling the mana to him.

With a broader cast of the whirlwind spell, the charm billowed through the room so parchments and tapestries exploded into flight. Oncoming soldiers yawped as spinning papers slapped their faces, and they coughed and sneezed as chalk dust blew about.

Hazezon couldn't harm his enemies with such trash, but hoped to fluster them and escape. Yet a jolt of pain ripped through his leg, lame from the barbarian's hammer blow. He then felt a stab of despair, for the double doorway was but a short jog away. Cursing, he scrabbled on his hands and knees and frantically tried to think of another spell. In the desert he might summon down lightning, or hurl rocks and boulders in a dervish, or turn sand to quagmire, but he was hampered indoors and within the city walls.

Panic clarified his thoughts as rough hands yanked his cloak. Desperate times called for dangerous spells. Still on one knee, he swiped one hand across his fingers as if striking flint and steel. As he moved he witnessed the spark growing to flame.

Soldiers yelped as Hazezon Tamar was wreathed in a blazing halo of flame. Men stumbled back, one batting fire from his hands. Hazezon grabbed the wall for support and pulled himself erect. He blinked, eyes watering, for the sheath of fire burned only an inch from his body and clothes. Sweat popped from his brow. Hurriedly he clawed and limped along the wall, for this spell would consume him if worn too long. If he could just get outside —

"Plague take him!" called the sergeant. "Kill him! Feather him full of crossbow bolts!"

Shambling along the wall, suffering his wounded leg and the searing heat of the magic immolation, Hazezon Tamar prayed they'd miss, or at least strike true and kill him. He was too old to brawl with hardy youngsters and then sustain torture at the hands of Johan's executioners.

Behind him a woman barked, "Clear aside!" probably so she could get off a straight shot. Oddly, Hazezon thought of Adira, called Strongheart, and wondered how she'd receive news of his death.

It was hard to tell with flames swimming before his eyes, distorting light and sight, but Hazezon thought the double doors were eclipsed. A rescuer? No, just a trick of his old eyes.

Suddenly a huge loping shape of black and orange stripes like living fire galloped straight at him. The mage ducked as the inhuman shape vaulted high over his head—

—and burst amid Johan's howling soldiers like a thunderbolt.

* * * * *

Far away, in the mountain hold of Krieghelm, an oily voice asked, "Care for mint tea? Tell me, if you please, have you visited Bryce lately?"

Johan of Tirras again paced his bleak mountain lair, but the cavern was less frosty, for he'd ordered iron braziers lit in this portion of the unending room. Too, he'd laid a table of tea and bread and sweetmeats for his guest. He'd even cloaked his appearance to an average, if bony, bald man in a monk's robe. Johan wanted to appear ascetic and scholarly, yet gracious. A clever man, Johan could be charming when it served his purpose.

Yet his hospitality was wasted, for his guest was a druid plucked from the desert and ushered into the mountain stronghold of Krieghelm by four guards. The man was solemn though young, with hair and beard bleached pale by the desert sun. He carried only a thin blanket roll and a few oddments of bone and bronze, and two gourds for water. Despite his poverty, he took none of Johan's fine food or tea or wine. Though he sat patiently, the druid's gaze lingered on the wide open windows where the distant desert showed only as a yellow crease on the horizon.

"There is little news from Bryce, but much from our desert," pronounced the druid.

"No news from Bryce?" asked Johan seating himself. "Not even that Tirrans overrun the city?"

"Oh, that." The druid dismissed the affairs of men. "No, the news comes from the east. A wanderer was found. A man and not a man. He may fulfill the prophecy of None, One, and Two."

"A traveler who's not a man is a harbinger of legend?" Puzzled, the drab-robed wizard sat up straight on his stool. The two men sat at a round table while Johan's foot guard lingered by the door. "What prophecy?"

"The prophecy of None, One, and Two is ancient." The druid lectured, one of his tasks. "It predates even the Ice Age. Some meaning has been lost in time, but a threefold being heralds the time of prophecy. A threefold being *is* None, One, and Two."

"How?" asked Johan.

"The being is none, because he or she is not of this world. He or she is one, a whole person, and two, of two distinct races. My master compared the buds in springtime."

"What?" Johan's voice was sharp. Was this rubbish or reality?

Unperturbed, the druid explained, "Within the winter branch is naught but memory: None. From none comes a bud: One. The bud blossoms, becoming two. From the blossom comes fruit: Three grown from none. The fruit falls, leaving none but memory again."

Johan waited, but the druid just sat with his chapped hands in his lap. Finally the mage asked, "And this not-man—how so is he not a man?"

"The man is half a great cat, orange and white with black stripes."

"A tiger man?" Johan didn't know whether to believe or not. Would a druid lie? Certainly, thought the emperor, everyone lied to get what he or she wanted. "Who found him in the desert? Whence came he?"

"He came from the east—"

"The east is a wasteland!" Johan snapped. "It's the end of the world, the hottest part of the desert, nothing but sand and great worms that breach the surface and swallow camel trains!"

"True," said the student of Citanul. "Nevertheless, he came from the east. He was found by Hazezon Tamar and taken to—"

"Hazezon Tamar!" Johan spat. The one person, or one of two who might stop his invasion of the southlands—and here he was sounding like a blister-brained druid himself, thinking in ones and twos. As superstitious as any mage, Johan groused, "Surely it can't be coincidence that a creature of prophecy should be found by the ruler of Bryce! But what does it mean?"

Silently Johan brooded, having answered his own question. Even fate conspired against him, calling cosmic forces to converge. It meant a long hard road to conquer the southlands. "Wait, when was this tiger man found?"

"Yestereve."

Johan scoffed. "How many hundred leagues distant? Yet you know it the same day?"

"The desert told me. When the fog lifted on the first stage of prophecy, even the snakes sleeping under the crimson cactus became aware." The druid shrugged, uncaring if Johan believed or not. "There's more. The prophecy states that when None and One meet, only Two shall remain."

"None, One—nothing!" Johan shouted. Striding to a lone podium, he caught up a huge heavy book with covers of leather cracked and fading. "Do you know what this is?"

"A book," dismissed the druid. Druids passed on their arts and lore verbally. Likely the man couldn't even read.

Snorting with disgust, Johan waggled the tome under the druid's nose. "This is the *Anvilonian Grimoire*. An artifact of the ages, a treasure to any mage in Dominaria. Every enchantment and mystic pronouncement known lurks in these pages, so it's said, albeit the passages are so dense and convoluted it beggars one's sanity even to skim them. I have studied this volume until my eyes fail and my brain blisters. Never have I glimpsed any prophecy of None, One, and Two!"

The druid didn't even shrug.

Binding his temper tightly, Johan plunked the book back on its podium. He persisted, for he wanted this man's knowledge to flow freely.

"Tell me then. If this tiger man is None, who's One and who are Two?"

"That has yet to be revealed." The druid rose to go, settling his water gourds on their ratty woven strings. "If you'll excuse me, I wish to return out of doors."

"I shan't excuse you." Johan's false face was as ugly as a block of chiseled wood. "Best you tarry in my dungeons. My executioners will learn more. Guards!"

Like clockwork soldiers, four guards clamped hands on the druid's biceps and wrists. The man stood still, only his lips moving.

"Take him to the dungeons, no, the west tower. He can pine for the outdoors and freedom while he awaits torture—eh?"

A hiss keened around Johan's feet. Even the emperor jumped, for the sound was of a thousand adders rustling. What he saw was sand swirling around his bare feet as if stirred by tiny dust devils. The guards jittered, always frightened by Johan's magic. Yet Johan glared at the druid. "Stop that! Desist! I command!"

The mage had to shout as the seething whispers rose to a volcano's roar. Sand sifted in through the open windows like a yellow curtain that obscured the sky. Swirling ankle-deep it pattered against Johan's robe, skittered over his books and oddments, and rattled against the iron-strapped door. Within a few heartbeats a ton of sand was sucked into the room. It spun like sea fog and dappled men like dry rain. Men of Tirras blinked as sand grated in their eyes, stuck to their lips, infested their ears and hair and clothes, chafed on cheeks, bogged their feet. All vision extinguished as the sandstorm threatened to blind or smother them.

"Kill him! Kill—ulk!" Johan yowled but choked on sand. Flailing his arms, squinting against the storm, he kicked through a small dune to smite the druid himself. He would tear out the shaman's eyes. Two guards retained a firm grip on the druid's arms as they stabbed blades through his body.

Steel shoved through sand. Flesh and cloth dissolved into more sand. The figure that had been the druid slumped into a gritty heap.

The eldritch breeze ceased. Sand suspended in the air rained with a tiny chittering noise. Winnows and furrows of sand marked the room, knee deep in some places, shallow elsewhere. A miniature desert had been transported to his chamber by magic. Sand was as thick on the tables and bookshelves as icing on a cake.

Emperor and guards searched about, but there was nothing to see. Certainly no druid. Just sand and silence. Realizing they'd lost their prisoner, the guards began to tremble.

Johan spat sand off his lips and tongue. He hissed like a poison adder, "I'd slay you all except that I need all the men I can scrape up, even useless drones like you. Go."

Not wasting a second, the four kicked loose of the sand and chugged for the door.

Johan called after, "And send a slave to clean up this mess!"

Chapter 3

Hazezon Tamar watched in terror and fascination as three soldiers died in three seconds.

The tiger man had shed his bark-cloth rags, so wore only the goat hide harness and long bronze dagger. His fur was still wet and clumped with sand. Moving as fast as the wind in great long leaps on all fours, he looked all tiger with no trace of man. Human cunning drove the cat to strike at the greatest danger first and to snarl a battle cry that curdled the blood of the victims and froze them in place.

Three crossbowmen had leveled their weapons to shoot the flaming Hazezon in the back. The arrival of the tiger man, like an apparition, something out of a dream, spooked them. They flinched and fired wildly. Two bolts sizzled past Hazezon's head. One spanked off the pine-board wall and shattered. The third quarrel—the mage swore his eyes tricked him—shot true for the tiger man's head, except the great beast flicked a paw backward and sent it zipping in another direction. Then claws like flaked chert struck, and people died.

Springing off his back legs, the tiger man swiped the air. He raked flesh from his attacker's head even as his neck snapped. The attacker cannoned into a comrade, a woman who gamely fumbled for her short sword, until black talons tore the skin and muscle from her arm. Howling, she saw the white of her arm bones for a second before they flushed red. Crumpling, she fell, and her forehead smacked stone. The last man dodged behind his companions, but a paw like a bundle of spears slammed straight into his chest, crushing ribs and lungs and splitting his heart.

All this, Hazezon noted dully as his protective sheath of fire sputtered out, all this in an eye blink.

With the missile weapons eliminated, the tiger man turned to the rest. Spinning backward, he batted a soldier's head so hard it crunched against a wall. The sergeant in the horned helmet shouted incoherent orders, sweeping his halberd to rein in his troop. A half-step, a blur of a paw descending, and the sergeant was silenced because his arm broke at the elbow and hung limp. A foot studded with claws kicked out and down, and the sergeant's leg was rent open in three long slices from crotch to ankle.

All the while, the giant tiger man gave off savage snarls and harsh coughs and queer mewlings like questions or cries of hunger.

Five dead or dying, thought Hazezon. Before he could crawl upright.

Two barbarians bellowed like bulls and raised their clubs so they tangled in the air, clunking together. By then the tiger was too close for clubs. Half diving, the striped creature slashed Johan's red star on the man's tunic. The barbarian's face went blank as he sank, disemboweled. A bushel's worth of purple and gray guts were ripped from under his ribcage and dumped steaming on the stone floor. Only ragged strings marked where his tunic had been shorn. Dying, the barbarian shook the ground when he crashed. A smell of blood and bowels made the air thick and rank, gagging the throat.

The remaining barbarian dropped his club and resorted to brute strength. He caught the spinning tiger man in both arms and dragged him close to his chest, intent on bear-hugging, crushing lungs or snapping the spine. He may as well have tried to catch fog. Soaked with water and now blood, the tiger man flexed and squirmed to drop from the clumsy embrace.

Watching the mammoth battle, Hazezon found the tiger's striped tail distracting, whipping and weaving in the air like a striking adder. Again Hazezon wondered if this creature was truly unique, or if some distant pride of tiger folk wondered where their wayward son had wandered.

Having slithered free, the tiger man rammed the barbarian's chin with his sloping head, then bit hard with white fangs. The barbarian gasped as his throat was torn out clear to the spine. Blood spurted from his mouth as he fell slack, but the tiger man was already gone.

Seven dead, counted Hazezon, in mere heartbeats and not a scratch on the man-killer, nor even a pause for breath.

Stunned by the savage attack, the other Tirrans bolted. None got far.

One of the orcs dropped his sword to run. The tiger brushed his back as if sweeping off a horsefly, but blood furrowed across dark-cast shoulder blades. The orc tumbled like a rag doll, spine severed.

On stumpy legs, two dwarves chugged down the corridor, the halfling in tow. With a blood-curdling screech, the tiger man scooted on legs like catapult beams and sprang. His incredible leap—Hazezon judged five yards or more—slammed down with both paws nailing the dwarves, bone crushing blows. Over seven feet tall, the tiger man must have weighed over eight hundred pounds, guessed Hazezon, enough weight to crumple a bronze door. Without pausing over the dying dwarves, the tiger man sank his feet into their backs and bounded again. The halfling was pounced upon like a mouse. The force tore the halfling apart at the middle. He died instantly in a gout of blood.

Ten, marveled Hazezon, who couldn't get his breath for holding it in shock.

Only one barbarian and human soldier were left, and they pelted for an exit at the rear. Amber-and-jet eyes targeted them. The tiger man's haunches quivered to spring after the fleeing enemy.

This next assault was arrested by Hazezon's voice. "Stop! Let them go! Please!"

The massive striped head turned so the glowing eyes pinned Hazezon like a butterfly. The mage shivered to see the blood lust and near madness reflected there. Then the baleful stare faded and was replaced by a keen human intelligence.

"Th-they'll run to—the Tirrans, and tell their story," Hazezon stammered. "How—? You killed ten quicker than a man can draw a sword!"

"So their fear will spread? Good. An affrighted enemy is half-beaten." Again Hazezon was amazed by the half-growling tortured accent, the words old-fashioned and quaint. It made the tiger man seem an elder. In fact . . .

With his first good look in the dust-speckled light of the main hall, Hazezon studied the creature's face. It was clearly a tiger's, with very little human about it, except the muzzle was perhaps shorter and the tufted ears small. The only tigers Hazezon knew were rugs hung on walls or laid on floors. White muttonchops laid flat against the tiger's cheeks, and a shock of mane stuck back stiffly as if pomaded. Altogether the face was a riot of orange, white, and black stripes, but Hazezon thought the bristles were frosted too white. The teeth too, though sharp and formidable, were worn thin, and whiskers were as thick as sea grass on the hills. Too, the massive white chest, as big as a hogshead barrel, heaved in and out so the tiger man's breath whistled though his black nostrils.

Impulsively, Hazezon asked, "You're—like me, aren't you?"

The furred muzzled curled over the fangs, but the mage

knew it was a smile. "Do you mean, past my prime? Yes. In my youth I would have killed them all in seconds, with none of this foolish jumping about. But I grow slow and feeble in my advanced years."

Tower of the Tabernacle, thought Hazezon, pray I never meet a tiger man at the peak of his prowess! Nine devils couldn't stand against such a warrior! Yet Hazezon felt a warm peculiar glow as the tiger man added, "In that way, yes, I am like you. Venerable, youngsters call us, when too polite to say ancient."

"Regardless of how we exhibit our strengths," Hazezon got back to the subject. "I thank you for saving my life."

"As you saved mine," rumbled the beast. "Water restored me to life."

"How did you find the way here?" Hazezon looked at the open double doors. "You can't know the city and have no guide."

In answer the tiger man sniffed.

Hazezon blinked, then chuckled. "You tracked my scent across the city? Eye of Orms-By-Gore! I said we could mutually learn —Oh."

Hazezon gulped as the tiger man licked blood off its fur with a rasping pink tongue. The beast straightened its scant goat-hide loincloth and belt, hitching the long bronze dagger to hang at its back. A slim strap ran over one shoulder, fastened by a queer buckle. Cast in bronze, the round talisman was curled like a ram's horns.

Seeing Hazezon's stare, the tiger man touched the worn talisman and said, "A keepsake," but no more.

The human got a crick in his neck from craning at the tiger's face, it towered so high. Up close, the tiger man radiated heat like a sheet-iron stove, and smelled not like a wet cat, but spicy-salty like desert sage at sunset, a wild and free smell. Were there other tiger folk, he wondered, and if so, where? Hazezon marveled that such a queer specimen was unknown to him, a learned man, until this morning, which seemed years ago.

Before the attack . . .

"Oh! Come! We must—" Rattled by the return of responsibilities, Hazezon gasped like a fish. "Defend the city, somehow."

The ruler of Bryce glanced about his makeshift palace, now a charnel house. Dead Tirrans littered the floor until Hazezon couldn't step without his boot sticking in blood, as if he'd been transported to the fierce sea battles of his youth. Yet the building echoed, empty.

He asked, "Where is everyone? I need runners to carry orders, scribes to scribble them, military experts to advise—"

As if by magic, faces peeked in the door. Eyes went wide and mouths fell open at the devastation and the looming giant tiger calmly talking to the city ruler. No one ventured inside.

"There you are!" Hazezon took heart from familiar faces. "Get in here! Speak of the raid! How many enemies attack and where is the fighting worst?"

Administrators balked to approach the tiger man until Hazezon resorted to threats and direct orders. "I tell you, this man, not a tiger, is a friend of our city! He saved my life! He won't bite! His name is—What is your name, my friend?"

"Jaeger." The foreign name rolled off the brute's tongue, sounding like "Yeaaa-grrrr."

To encourage the city workers, Jaeger hauled the bodies out of the door, though the way he toted a dead man under one arm, then broke the neck of a squirming dwarf, made the scribes shy away. Maids and boys fetched water to wash away the blood. Hazezon sent a runner to his house, if not ransacked, with orders for his manservant to fetch clean clothes, and mint tea and some cakes. The city's clerks and minor authorities all wore short capes of pale blue clasped at one shoulder with a pin in the shape of an albatross. On their heads were gold fezzes or skullcaps of yellow felt. Parchments were picked up, scrolls rolled, and palace guards barricaded the doorways. As more administrators arrived and the tiger man left the hall for some unknown purpose, by midafternoon the city managers were ready to grapple with this Tirran raid grown into war.

Hazezon limped on one stiff leg to unroll a crackling map of the city. Shutting off the stream of half-panicked information, he stabbed brown, callused fingers on the map.

"Hush, my children! Let us paint the menace we face, not the fears we imagine. You, Magda, what have you seen?"

Quickly people jabbered what they knew and what they guessed from the sounds of fighting, palls of smoke, and the babble of refugees. Hazezon sent staffers running to learn more. Rapidly he sketched a picture on the map, then grunted.

"No surprise. Lucky our city hall lies not at the center. It's the same old pattern but on a larger scale. Damn Johan and his stalwarts! Why can't they put their muscle to good use?"

One of Bryce's militia generals had been dragged from the fighting to report. Bloodied but unbent, General Seanchan had lost a sleeve of his townsman's bright yellow tunic, and his turban had been tugged over one shorn ear. Puffing and paunchy in middle age, he was a cool-headed veteran of many pirate battles at sea, and not one to panic.

He reported, "It could be worse. Despite the mess, the Tirrans do not kill at random. They've barricaded bridges with shield walls so half the army can loot shop by shop. They sack the warehouses and crafts market, as expected. No point in robbing the farmers' market and stockyards unless you're hungry. And the ships' chandlers frame the bay, which is too far to sustain a shield wall. Besides, cordage and pitch and masts makes damned awkward loot. The fates smile in that few citizens reside in the center itself. Our militia holds them at bay, penned in, if we flatter ourselves. If they rushed, we'd get hurt. They boast ogres and barbarians in their line, and mages who hurl spells like summer lightning. We can only hope that the Tirrans, damn their mothers to nine levels of perdition, just take what they want, then shrink the shield wall, and run back to their barges. They're tied to the widest bridges here, here, and here. If we wait them out, like every other season —"

"A thousand pardons," interrupted Hazezon Tamar, "but plans of previous years don't apply today. A sergeant who died here said Tirras had declared outright war on Bryce, and by inference, all the southlands. Johan's raiders are more organized and militarized than ever before. Danger signs can't be ignored. Tirras might smash and grab and flee, but then again . . ."

Hazezon swept the map off the table. "Enough talk. You, you, you, fetch polearms or offensive wands. Someone get me a fresh horse! I'm lamed by a sore leg. Find any malingering militiamen and drag them along. Whatever Tirras plans, Bryce will give them a fight!"

A thought struck. "And invite our guest to join us. If I've never seen a talking tiger, likely Tirras hasn't either."

* * * * *

The crafts market was a shambles. Smoke roiled to the sky, pushed to sea by the north wind. Citizens ran hither and thither in the narrow streets, rescuing children and household goods. A bucket brigade had fizzled, so buckets rolled empty. Dogs barked, women shrilled, men shouted. As Hazezon trotted at the head of his pickup force, he saw cobblestones littered with clothing, ironware, small coins, boots, half a tapestry, a broken chair, a cage of squawking chickens, a ham. . . . Below a bridge clustered Bryce's militiamen, some facing the foe and some arguing with their captains. A clanging and crashing came from beyond, isolated battles of Tirrans whanging at Brycers, but also raiders stripping shops bare. Hazezon knew some Brycers caught in the crush would be impressed to load the Tirran barges with loot. Many would be ferried north to slavery.

As Hazezon dismounted, a shout went up. His horse shied and almost threw him. A fireball sizzled overhead to splash and burn on the rooftop. His pickup force of poorly armed scribes, personal servants, and a dozen militiamen uneasily watched the building ignite, but also edged away from the silent tiger man who watched everything with glowing amber eyes.

Over centuries, Bryce had grown from a tiny pirate refuge propped on sandbars into a higgledy-piggledy tangle that rambled for miles. Some quarters of the city still prone to flooding sported open ground where goats and sheep roamed, fishing shacks built of driftwood and jetsam, and the poorest families living in beached hulks. Other quarters were crammed with houses so close that neighbors could shake hands out their windows. Pirate families had masked their homes with high stone walls to create virtual castles. Fingers of the river trickled where they would and occasionally changed course and undermined homes that collapsed. Canals intersected at haphazard angles, so some streets ended above water. Added to the mix were offal and sewage discharged into the canals, slag heaps from shops and ash heaps from homes, roaming chickens and pigs and dogs, and the smell of breweries, vintners, tanneries, dyers, incense, rotted fruit, and more, so the city bore a heady but human perfume. Everywhere arched bridges of limestone that hardened under the sun, most overloaded with shops along both sides, a deleterious practice Bryce's rulers could not eradicate. Bridges, Hazezon knew, were lovely but unlucky bottlenecks, and the Tirrans had seized several.

A phalanx of Tirrans in gray and red formed a shield wall across the Bridge of Flowers, so called because potted plants decorated its columns. Hazezon had heard they'd also barricaded the Bridge of Sorrows, where forlorn girls went to weep, and the Bridge of Ancestors, the first bridge ever erected. Thus the marketplace was hemmed tight. Bryce militiamen shouted obscenities at the shield wall, and Tirrans chorused back. Clashes sparked when hothead Brycers jumped at Tirrans or were cornered. An outraged woman shrieked behind the shield wall, and Tirrans yelled abuse at archers atop a house that peppered the militia with long fletched arrows. Many shops burned, and Hazezon feared the fires might grow out of control to punish Tirrans and Brycers alike. Otherwise, the action suffered a temporary stalemate. Smoke-grimy militiamen fidgeted and gawked at the tiger man.

Runners came and went, blue capes fluttering, gasping out reports. The other phalanxes of Tirrans still blocked the bridges. Spears, shields, and spells kept the militia at bay. One of Johan's mages unleashed a stinging cloud of acid rain that seared the skin as it wafted downwind. Another made Brycers scream with madness and claw at their skulls. A marble priest as pale as polished granite and clad in purple waved his hands and made building facades slump like sandcastles. Still, Brycer crossbowmen and slingers sent their own missiles winging, and a number of Tirrans who had been separated from their parties were hacked apart. On one street, the Brycers had hauled a boat from the beach as a blockade. In another place, they'd sunk a Tirran barge with a toppled chimney. Yet Hazezon couldn't help thinking all these antics were mere prelude to disaster.

"Their boats are clustered in the northern canals, Governor." General Seanchan sketched in the air with a thick brown finger. "I could send sappers through the sewers to sink the boats, or even swimmers, but I doubt we want the bastards for permanent company. Best we leave their escape route open. It's painful to corner a tiger." Recalling their guest, he glanced at the silent Jaeger.

Hazezon looked at the sky. In the desert's winter, days ran short. Dusk was three hours off. The fuzzy glow of the Glimmer Moon would give light after dark, unless sprinkles of rain swept in off the ocean as the breeze shifted on shore.

He mused aloud, "They'll loot and withdraw only if they keep to their traditional pattern. Always before they've withdrawn as night creeps on, poled out of the canals, then rigged their sails to catch the night breeze. But this time . . . How many are they, do we know, General?"

Seanchan scrubbed his bald head where his turban and crusted blood itched. "A rough count, four or five hundred. But someone said more boats pole down the canals stuffed with yet more troops. If true, I'm stumped as to a plan."

"It's bad news, if true." Hazezon dispatched a level-headed scribe to zip around to the high-arching Bridge of Gargoyles and see if reinforcements really did arrive. "An ill wind brings a ship to shore too soon. . . ."

Another militia officer jogged up, Captain Rikki from the fisherman's quarter. Young and tall, she was burned dark as a boot, with the sausage fingers of a seafarer who pulled nets and battered sharks. She still wore a straw hat and canvas apron speckled with mackerel scales, and carried an old kite shield painted with an albatross, one of the city's symbols, and a curved scimitar with a broken tip.

After gawping at the upright tiger, she gasped over the clatter and babble and cries, "Milord Tamar, my troop can't push back that shield wall. It's locked tight, and spearmen thrust behind. Anyone who ventures within six feet gets his gullet split."

"It appears, gentle friends," Hazezon conceded, "the Tirrans get their way. We'll harass them here and wait for dusk until they withdraw—What happens?"

A lull fell behind the shield wall, which was twenty square-sided shields interlocked. A guttural Tirran accent barked, "Make way!" The wall rippled at the center and, amazingly, broke apart. Hazezon Tamar picked up his chin to see over the crowd and thought to mount his horse for a better view, except he'd make a perfect target for archers. Why would the invaders breach their main defense?

A volley of noise and a triplet of *whooshes!* like the breath of a dragon sounded. Then came screams from Brycers. Militiamen nearest the shield wall turned and bolted in panic. Flames flickered in the street, and Hazezon imagined heat on his face. As the stampede rolled past him, he pressed against his horse to avoid being trampled. Screams and shouts were deafening.

General Seanchan bellowed, "Khabal's ghoul! They charge!"

Swinging into the saddle, chanting quickly, Hazezon expended mana to sketch a magical bubble to deflect any arrows. From high up he saw what transpired. Protected by four shields abreast, a female mage in gray with red sleeves blew fireballs from a curled ram's horn decorated with jewels and stones. The bell of the horn was charred and still smoking. Fireballs had smashed into Bryce militiamen who writhed and burned and died in the street. The Tirran shield wall advanced, stamping and grunting in time, while the second phalanx of spearmen jabbed with ten-foot lances.

Hazezon swore even as citizens surged like storm surf around his capering horse. So much, he thought cynically, for previous patterns and raids. This was full-fledged war. He shouted, "Stand fast, citizens! We can stop —" No one heard in the panic.

Hopping off his mount, Bryce's ruler fell to his own devices. He drew from an inside pocket a short stick topped by a two-faced head, a pop-eyed bearded fetish he'd acquired in his younger adventures. The stick was worn smooth and dark. Squatting on crackling knees, the elder mage stuck the wand in a crack of sand between cobblestones, then twirled it between his palms until they grew warm.

Hissing, Hazezon commanded, "Stand, sons of the sand!"

All of Bryce rested on sand. Now, tickled by a magical incantation, cobbles shifted and squirmed in a hundred spots under the feet of invaders and citizens alike. New screams welled up as people feared a quake on this day of punishment. Some folk fell and were trampled; others tripped over rising cobbles. The flat stones tilted, pushed from underneath, then slithered and clattered and ground together, an eerie tooth-grating spectacle. At each break humps of sand arose, until forty or more columns had swelled waist high.

"Come, come, arise!" urged Hazezon as he twirled his wand frantically. The magic coalesced slowly, for Tamar was a desert mage, and Bryce was not proper desert. The ruler feared the Tirrans would advance before his magic could block them. Some invaders balked at the strange upwelling sand. Some dashed past the columns, fearful of their touch. A few bolted back onto the Bridge of Flowers, but shouting sergeants spun them around. Protected by four shield bearers, Johan's northern mage—Hazezon recognized the woman now, called Xira Arien, or the Glass Mountain—whipped her arms in a circle and caroled some incantation at the rising humps. Hazezon hoped that she chose the wrong counterspell. He didn't have the mana to continue fighting her. Sweating, arms and hands aching, he kept twirling.

As the mounds of sand flowed chin high, they took on form. Heads wearing keffiyehs similar to Hazezon's met sandy shoulders that draped with multilayered capes, for the sand warriors were modeled after Hazezon himself. Arms cleaved from yellow-gray bodies of sand. Scimitars grew pointed and slim from curling fists. Finally, to the mage's relief, the sand men gave a lurch and tug of earthen legs and pulled free from the soil.

"Onward!" commanded Hazezon. "Attack!"

Raising his right hand as if clutching a scimitar, Hazezon laughed with glee to see fifty or sixty sand men do the same. When he thrust his arm forward, scores of sandy arms imitated him. At the rear of the substitute army, Brycers cheered their governor as he stamped forward and slashed, making the army sweep sandy scimitars through the air.

The living sand men stalled the Tirrans cold. Men and women in gray and red balked as the sand men trudged toward them. A sergeant strove to put heart in his troops by leaping forward with a polearm. Thrusting the halberd's top spike with brawny arms, the sergeant was astonished when the spike glanced off a sandy midriff as hard as a diamond. With a quick sweep, the sand man slashed and severed the pole, so the iron head clanged on uprooted cobblestones. Seeing that, Johan's army stepped back as the sand men advanced, despite the commands of officers who blocked their retreat across the bridge.

Hazezon's own militia captains had their hands full. Some Brycers edged away from the monstrosities while others shouted encouragement as if watching a horse race. As the sand men closed with the Tirrans, diamond-hard scimitars clashed on wooden shields to chip paint and iron. The sand men were slow, and could be dodged, but were so many—the magical army packed the street like puffins in a rookery—that Tirrans were pushed back by sheer numbers. Hazezon chortled as his sandy scimitars beat on shields, spear hafts, and the occasional helmet.

From the rear, watched by citizens and the impassive tiger man, Jaeger, Hazezon Tamar conducted his army into the breach. Brycer militia officers pushed the troops into rough ranks. Several hundred militiamen and women had gathered from all over the city. Watching the Tirrans bashed by the magical sand men, the milling throng cheered and hissed until the roar gave Hazezon a headache.

With one eye on his sandy warriors, he shouted to the citizens, "Hush! Attend your captains and stand fast! We must brace our own shield wall to advance when the sand men collapse! This ensorcellment won't last forever! We can rout them if—"

"What are *those* monsters?" A woman pointed at one rooftop, then others. Citizens gawked. Hazezon peered, his eyes not as sharp as they'd once been.

Of a sudden, every house in the neighborhood was topped by capering red orangutans that had seemingly dropped from the sky like seagulls. Still with one hand pumping to make slashing actions, Hazezon hopped in place to see over bobbing heads. Behind the throng of Tirrans, now shoved by sand men onto the bridge, the Glass Mountain waved her hands at the rooftops.

Kish! Tash! Sounds like breaking glass echoed. Hazezon saw one of his sand men struck by a stone hurled from above. The missile shattered the simulacrum into shards that slumped to the dust. Another sand man lost his head to a black lumpy stone. With the magic broken, the body reverted to soft sand that flowed like butter over the upset cobblestones.

"Scarzam's dragon!" Hazezon's sand men had never been undone before. Now, in twos and threes, they crumpled like sandcastles against the tide. Gaping at the nearest rooftop, Hazezon saw the stone throwers weren't monkeys but some hideous cousins to imps, furred red with ruffs around their ugly pointed faces. They snatched up black lumpy rocks by their bare feet and pitched them hard. The Glass Mountain had summoned them from some nether plane, Hazezon knew. They even brought stones with them. The governor wanted to wail aloud in anguish. His hard-wrought sand men were vulnerable to ordinary rocks! Soon heaps of sand and uprooted cobbles would be the only signs of his sorcery. Hazezon bleated to the sky, "Love of a lich! Schemes of a witch! Is this fair?"

Devils capered and danced and chucked black stones, and sand men were bowled over like ninepins. Crashing sounds like broken glass filled the air. With a hundred infernal devils lobbing rocks, soon only a dozen sand men hacked at the Tirrans cowering behind their shield wall. The Tirrans laughed as the devils scrabbled atop the roofs for more stones, but they'd run out. Some swarmed down the house sides into the street to retrieve more stones, only to be whacked and chopped by Bryce militiamen. Most devils scuttled back and forth along the rooftops, hissing and spitting and shrieking their complaints.

Six sand men fought on, steered from afar by Hazezon, but Tirran officers ordered the army to slip around them. With much cheering and clatter the shield wall bulged to avoid the mindless simulacrums and regrouped across the street. Seizing spent stones, soldiers threw them at the last sand men, who crumbled into dust. A lusty cheer of triumph and joy rang out.

Watching her troops warily lest they bolt, Captain Rikki called to Hazezon Tamar and General Seanchan, "What do we do, milords?"

With arthritic hands hanging limp by his sides, Hazezon suddenly felt old. "Precious little, child. That was my best spell—"

A war cry drowned out his words. In lock step, Tirrans in red and gray tramped double time, spears bobbing above the rims of the interlocked shields. Grim-faced, eager to retrieve their honor, the men and women of Tirras stomped to even the score with slaughter.

In ones and twos, then in dozens, the ranks of the Bryce militia melted away. Men stepped back, and that first step was infectious. Seanchan and Rikki and other officers bellowed to no avail as Bryce retreated. Even Rikki's and the general's catching militiamen by the tunic didn't slow them, so the officers had to step back slowly with scimitars and swords leveled. Hazezon went along. The war council, such as it was, quickly retreated to the first crooked intersection as the Tirran shield wall tramped on like a juggernaut.

"Bad, very bad," Hazezon muttered as he dragged his balky horse. If Tirras swept the city, every Brycer would be a slave to Johan's army, and the city would become its colony. Hazezon Tamar would be executed by strangling or decapitation or worse, but that seemed unimportant if Bryce itself died. Mind reeling, the ruler startled as a huge hand wrapped his elbow. Not a hand, but a striped paw.

"Why do your people not fight?" Excited, the tiger man's voice warbled between a gargle and purr. Hazezon's horse whinnied, whites glaring in the beast's bulging eyes.

"What?" Hazezon was flustered by the amber eyes boring into his. "Oh, we can't stop an engine like that. There's no way to break the wall. We can't fight—"

"There is always a way to fight," stated Jaeger. Hazezon shivered at the inhuman tone. "Watch."

Great clawed paws rose in the air, flexed, and drove straight at the astounded wizard's throat.

* * * * *

Alone in his mountain refuge, Johan's ruddy hands cradled an antique skull, as light and brittle as a wasp's nest. Alone, he spoke to the relic.

"You were old before the age of ice," said Johan. "Thus I command, speak to me the ancient prophecy."

Yellow-brown fragile bones and a few rotten teeth were bound with threads of silver wire drilled through a hundred tiny holes, so the orb glistened as if wrapped in dewy cobwebs.

Gently, Johan placed the brow of the skull against his own, resting between his down-curved horns. Touching mind to mind, Johan ordered, "Speak."

None, husked a voice in his mind, as dry as old leaves skittering in a bitter wind. *None, One, and Two. None comes, One comes, Two clash. None falls, One rises, One falls, Two become One. One is lost. None triumphs.*

"Gibberish!" Johan shook the skull savagely. "I want facts! Details! How shall I plan a strategy to thwart an entire populace if no one will advise me?"

From between rotten wired teeth came a stuttering like frost cracking. It took Johan a second to recognize that the skull's former owner laughed at him.

"Mock me." The emperor's voice was as cold as the walls of his chamber. "I'll erase your soul from the firmament, you vagabond!"

Johan coiled his arm and hurled the relic against the stone wall. More fragile than glass, the skull burst into a thousand splinters and a tangled skein of silver wire.

Snorting, Johan then grunted in surprise.

Astride the splinters of bone hunched a wizened man, as ethereal as mist. The emperor clearly saw the iron rivets of his door through the ghost's body. The ancient stood no taller than a boy. The brow was beetled, the nose pug, the hair scant and curly. He wore only a shriveled loincloth and finger-bone necklace. More pixie than man, thought Johan. Shockingly, he'd invoked one of Jamuraa's original inhabitants, a pictish aboriginal from the time when the desert was ocean and the forest a jungle, home to great lazy lizards and claw-fingered birds.

With a merry twinkling laugh, the ghost crooked a finger at Johan. "Temper, temper, child. Believe it or don't, but better to learn what folk want and give it to them, rather than force them against their will to satisfy thine own. I'd have told of the prophecy to win my freedom, but thy rage gives it to me unasked. Trapped I was until my cursed skull rotted away, but thou hast set me free, a bird from its cage."

Giggling, fading before Johan's eyes, the long-dead shaman gloated, "Prophecy dooms thee, Johan. Knowing't will make thy final defeat more the bitter and keep thee awake many a night till then."

Like a candle winking out, the aborigine vanished.

Johan stood still a long while, wondering if the dead always spoke true, or if they loved to deceive the living. As he pondered, his anger grew.

Seizing a heavy iron candlestick, Johan stepped to his table of magical toys and gimcracks and relics, and smashed and smashed and smashed.

Chapter 4

"Friend! Desist! I would—*Gahh!*"

Hazezon's heart skipped a beat as black claws swiped at him, but the tiger man only gripped the reins of the mage's horse.

The frightened animal had balked before, but now the overpowering cat scent drove it berserk. Hazezon dodged as the horse jumped, kicked, and crabbed sideways, the silver bells on its bridle jingling. At least his favorite horse, Belladonna, was safe in the stables.

In the clear, Hazezon saw the Tirran invaders had swept the street clean. Sergeants bellowed, and whistles shrilled as the shield wall was reformed wider and angled to overtake the intersection. A few Brycers stood their ground, swords ready, but they'd have to step back when the wall overcame them. City archers skulked on rooftops or shot over the shield wall, but they had to retreat or be surrounded on the ground. The stone-hurling imps, Hazezon noted, had vanished from the roofs, banished to whatever nether plane by the Glass Mountain.

Hazezon jumped as Jaeger roared, "Captains! Pick your bravest warriors and follow me!" The tiger man dragged the screaming horse toward him like a dog on a leash.

"What did he say?" bellowed General Seanchan. Captain Rikki, quicker and more eager to fight, immediately called names of men and women she could trust.

Dazed, Hazezon watched Jaeger jerk the reins high to drag up the horse's chin. One flint-clawed paw slashed the brown throat. Blood sprayed in a crimson fountain to douse Jaeger, Hazezon, and adobe walls and cobblestones. Jaeger's orange-black fur stuck up in red clumps. The horse's black eyes glazed over as Jaeger caught it by the mane and back, his claws sinking into brown hide. Hazezon staggered back, stunned, as the tiger hoisted the dying horse over his head, gave a tremendous grunt, and pitched a half-ton of horse-flesh onto the enemy.

Given the tremendous strain, Jaeger's aim was uncanny. The horse, four legs flopping, smashed atop ten soldiers who formed one edge of the shield wall. They shouted and ducked as the dead weight struck like a meteor. Men were crushed and spears knocked flying. Shields crumpled or slammed the ground. Other soldiers crabbed back from the appalling spectacle, for they'd been milling and reforming and hoping to kill when this attack smashed down from nowhere. For a moment the shield wall was breached six feet wide where the phalanx met the wall. Such a small break would have done the Bryce militia little good—except Jaeger the tiger man took the lead.

"Heroes of Bryce," came a raspy yowl, "*forward!*"

With that war cry, Jaeger bounded onto the dead horse, then dived straight as a ballista arrow into the Tirran ranks, his long striped tail whipping behind like a war banner. Caught in the madness, Captain Rikki and a dozen fisherfolk surged after the bloody foreigner in what should have been a suicide pact.

Mopping blood from his eyes, Hazezon grabbed his conjuring wand and tried to think of a helpful spell. More Brycers rushed along, hot to exact revenge on the invaders. Agitated,

Seanchan shouted in his lord's face, "What in Phanal's name does he do?"

"He killed ten Tirrans in two minutes in my palace!" Hazezon yelled back, just as excited. "He's worth a regiment of veterans! Follow him!"

What had been an implacable wave of victory-sure soldiers became a charnel house. Drenched in blood, a terrifying vision with man-killing black claws, Jaeger carved through ten more Tirrans before they could draw breath. He batted and crushed a skull, kicked and disemboweled, hammered and broke a collarbone, wrenched and snapped a neck. Dying troops bled and writhed in a circle around the tiger man, who rushed on like an engine of destruction.

Into the breach jumped the defenders of Bryce, striking hard and fast because they would not get a second chance. Captain Rikki lost her battered straw hat as she bashed a solder with her shield before driving a sword into her belly. Another fisherman rammed a trident into a soldier's gut and lobbed the man into his comrades as if pitching a bale of hay. A fishwife slammed a cleaver on a barbarian's head as he fell, then smacked him again, and severed his neck. More Brycers dashed up, barely aware of their companions' wild backswings with axe and sword, and bashed the Tirran army until the line broke and scattered halfway down the street.

Hazezon watched the battle unfold in slow motion, as if in a dream. Under a winter sky growing overcast and dull at dusk, a quiet street before the Bridge of Flowers had become a killing ground. Adobe walls were splashed with gore. Bryce fisherfolk used to walloping sharks and whales hacked and chopped at a recoiling enemy while officers on both sides shouted uselessly. Behind the melee the Glass Mountain used to her bejeweled ram's horn to trace patterns in the air. Across the famous bridge trotted more Tirran solders in red and gray, some human, some orc, and some dwarf, their tackle flopping and jingling behind a panting sergeant. A few women and children who'd stupidly crept from their homes to see the excitement were almost trampled.

Centermost to the action, wherever the Tirran shield wall threatened to reform, a red blur of half-man and half-cat waged war for a foreign land he'd never before visited. Never still, the tiger warrior jumped from victim to victim, spinning and spitting death like a giant cobra. As a sergeant lunged with a halberd, Jaeger snagged the polearm, yanked it close, then swatted, tearing the Tirran's throat and smashing his jaw. Jaeger booted the victim into another, dodged an out-thrust spear, then stabbed with his own pointed paw to bloody a woman's eyes. Squatting low, leaping high, he sailed over the dying pair and landed at the feet of three soldiers reforming with spearmen. Taken by surprise, the first rank died and crumpled or dropped flat, exposing their unshielded spearmen. One man's wrist was severed by what felt like a blast of wind, but were actually claws. The second spearman was hurled against his partner. Jaeger ripped away one spear, reversed it, and rammed so hard he pierced both men and drove the iron head two feet into the sand between cobbles.

Letting warriors make war, Hazezon Tamar jumped in place to locate the sorceress. Momentarily alone and unprotected, the Glass Mountain gamely conjured. She thumbed a dark sapphire on her ram's horn, for the jewels, bits of corals, and precious stones formed her grimoire: a memory trick that recalled her list of spells. The mnemonic device marked an amateur, Hazezon knew, for elder mages such as he had long ago memorized their mighty spells. From the blackened bell of the Glass Mountain's horn blew forth a black ooze like solid fog such as Hazezon had never seen. The ooze detached from the horn and hung in the air like smoke. Another toot sent the ooze spinning through the air so it elongated like a black octopus. It flew toward Jaeger, but brushed an intervening Tirran. Touched by the pinwheeling ooze, the man felt his neck, then screamed as if scalded. Other soldiers, seeing the black ooze flying their way, flopped flat rather than be nicked. Jaeger never seemed to notice as he battered soldiers away from Captain Rikki's hard-fighting fisherfolk. Xira grew red in the face as she puffed up more black ooze and sent it sailing, oblivious to whom it hurt as long as Jaeger suffered.

Hazezon could match any mage. Braced by three timid scribes, he jigged and jogged for a clear shot, then blew across his hand.

Wafting over the Tirrans' boiled helmets, a cloud of frosty breath enveloped the oncoming ooze and froze it in midair. Thwarted, the young Xira Arien, shook her fist at Hazezon, red sleeves flapping about her elbows. Grinning, Hazezon blew her a frosty kiss.

The Tirrans had backed to the wall and raised their shield wall in part, though they teetered on dead bodies, churned sand, and tilted cobblestones. A curious lull fell over the battle. Bryce fisherfolk, spattered in blood, stood heaving for breath and glaring at the foe. Jaeger, looking like some red demon ripped from the hottest hell, crouched as if ready to spring.

The only Tirran officer left had lost his helm, showing damp blond curls. His sash hung in tatters with his tunic, revealing a leather coat with steel scales on a skinny frame. While the officer looked discouraged and angry, his troop looked frightened. Oddly, Hazezon noticed the officer was just a boy. He had sons older than this Tirran.

Ready for more slaughter, Jaeger gurgled deep in his throat and licked blood off his muzzle and paws. Bryce fishermen hefted slick weapons. A few citizens were down and dying, but a woman began to sing. A silly pirate ditty for hoisting sails, the chorus ran "Yum-tum tiddy-tiddy," but in this theater of death it made the Brycers pick up their chins while the Tirrans trembled.

In the lull, Hazezon craned his head toward the distant marketplace, and heard more fighting. Best, he reflected, to decimate this knot of Tirrans, kill the rat pack before they escapcd. A quick count showed fifty or sixty bloodied soldiers faced by hundreds of Brycers. The coppery stink of blood and bowels and raw fear sickened the city's ruler, who'd always sought to spare lives where possible. Too, to spare a few survivors would spread terror among the Tirrans.

Before anyone could leap into a fray, Hazezon Tamar, Governor of Bryce, pointed to the Bridge of Flowers and commanded, "Go."

More than any war cry, that life-giving command sent the Tirrans flying for sanctuary. Officers and sergeants shouted in vain after the stampede, then raced themselves as archers sent arrows winging and Brycer hotheads ran after whooping. The Glass Mountain had already hiked her skirts and flown, white legs flashing.

Hazezon Tamar didn't want to celebrate with the street decorated with dead, but neither did he brood. Automatically he counted resources. Two hundred militiamen, so packed by the narrow street they couldn't all engage at once. Three captains pushing people into ranks. General Seanchan. A handful of raggle-taggle citizens underfoot. A dead horse. And a blood-soaked tiger man who again stood immobile, perhaps even napping like a real cat. The light failed as the sun set.

General Seanchan frowned, disapproving of Hazezon's laxity, but said only, "Shall I send runners to the other militias, Governor? We could box the Tirrans in the marketplace. A stout shield wall of our own would prevent their breaking out again."

"Yes, see to it. Make sure the runners explain our object is to contain and drive them to their boats, not fight —"

"Here they come again!" A militiaman pointed a bloody hatchet.

"Unbelievable!" gasped Hazezon. Some higher officer had whipped the fleeing Tirrans back over the Bridge of Flowers. Hazezon saw again the young lieutenant in tattered tunic and missing helmet.

"There's nothing for it, milord," said General Seanchan. "We must kill them all."

Sadly, Hazezon nodded. Without realizing it, he called on the fierce tiger man. "Jaeger, you stopped them once. Can you do it again?"

The great tiger man snuffed in contempt, though his breath came short. He rumbled to the militiamen, "Come, my brave warriors. Let's rid the house of rats."

With a roar, the motley citizen army of Bryce raced to battle. Hazezon watched the younger folk run and wondered what he, as ruler of this fair and assailed city, should do.

"Come, Governor." Pushing his bloody turban aright, General Seanchan nodded away from the carnage. "Let's circle and see how other factions fare."

The unsullied street was strangely deserted as they wended onto the Bridge of Gargoyles. Hazezon's manservant Conal kept a firm grip on his spear as he marched alongside his master, and some scribes and members of Seanchan's family tagged along. Pausing on the bridge, in fading light the two leaders looked north up the river's finger and saw the backside of the Tirran invasion fleet. The boats were mostly gundalows, long and flat-bottomed for navigating rivers, with stepped lateen masts easily raised and lowered. Fed by winter rains, the River Toloron was swollen but lazy and shallow here at the delta, and even a heavily laden boat could ease upstream under sail and oars or a long tow line. Tirran boats were clustered thick as autumn leaves, bumping together on the water, yet Hazezon knew he saw only part of the fleet, for the rest lay hidden behind buildings in canals. The boats were guarded by older soldiers with ready crossbows and axes to cut the anchor cables if needed. Some boats were already laden, heaped full of booty neatly lashed down under tarpaulins. Brycer prisoners labored under whips to ferry bundles and bales onto other boats. Hazezon toyed with the idea of sinking the boats, if possible at this distance. To suck a ton of sand from the desert on an eldritch wind to swamp the boats would consternate the Tirrans mightily. But General Seanchan noted, Bryce needed to be rid of the Tirrans, else every invader would have to be killed at horrid cost in lives and property.

As the scouting party plodded on, Hazezon wanted to sigh. In his younger pirating days, he'd swooped down like a hawk to strike fat merchants, then flew laughing into a rainstorm or fogbank, rich with loot. Now, come full circle, Hazezon was the crippled duck sitting on golden eggs while eager young wolves preyed from the hinterlands. Being a prosperous merchant brought pleasures and woes, and as age advanced, woes increased.

Turning a corner to circle back, Hazezon dismissed his city workers.

"Get to the palace. The fighting should end shortly, and there are lists and rolls to be processed. Death rolls, especially. Everyone and his mother will make claims against the city. Best start now."

"Are you sure, milord?" asked the head scribe named Echo. "We're members of the militia, too, and the city needs our might."

"A brave sentiment, my daughter," said Hazezon, "but the city can better use your talents to clean the palace and set things aright. The council will meet before night's out. Send word to the houses. Don't fret. Be off."

Not very reluctantly, the caped clerks shuffled away. General Seanchan dispersed his family, keeping only his youngest daughter as bodyguard. Hazezon looked at his sole attendant, Conal, who'd pirated with him in days past. Older than Hazezon, Conal was as bony as a cod, with knots in his brown arms, and bad eyes, for he'd once been stung viciously by giant bees when Hazezon's blunder led his crew into a benighted jungle.

After years of servitude, he still refused to wear a livery uniform, but simply a blue jacket with white frog clasps and blooming trousers like any pirate, topped by a white turban. The servant carried a long-bladed spear for jabbing at vague shapes looming before him. Hazezon asked, "Conal, can you adjourn home? Likely the raiders ransacked my chambers, and I'll need fresh clothes again to attend the emergency council."

Conal only grinned, the skin around his cloudy eyes crinkling in his brown face. "I'll stick, Haz. As long as you don't get us lost." Both chuckled at the old joke, then followed General Seanchan and his daughter.

Twisting through the streets, the leaders picked up an entourage of timid folk seeking protection, idlers and women and children, but didn't object. Soon they discovered a fight on the Bridge of Sorrows. This time a phalanx of a hundred Brycers formed a haphazard shield wall, for their mismatched shields did not possess the steel channels to interlock, yet they kept a company of eighty-odd Tirrans from leaving the city center. The Brycers had learned from their foe. Spear throwers now crouched behind shields to thrust at soldiers in gray and red. The Tirrans could only chop at spear hafts and whack the odd shield.

"Why should Tirras advance here, General?" asked Hazezon.

General Seanchan rubbed his black beard. "More lootin', milord. If they've cleaned out the marketplace, the bastards might prosper knocking in leather-workers' doors."

Consulting, the ruler of the city and the leader of the city militia decided the fighting was in hand, and likely to end soon with darkness. They continued circling the marketplace as far as possible.

Striding across the desolate Poor Quarter with its weedy sand and scrawny goats and decrepit shacks and shipwrecks, shooing seagulls who rested on the warm sand, Hazezon again thought of how many times he'd tried to uplift the poor with tax money and education, and how their numbers had only grown for no reason he could discern. Ragamuffins begged coins and anxious mothers begged news. Dispensing pennies and platitudes, they moved on, boots sinking in sand. Passing over the Bridge of the Immaculate Wind, they tramped toward the marketplace from the west as darkness settled between buildings.

Clashes raged in this quarter, some big, some small. Smoke told of burning shops and houses. Amid a jumble of old buildings being razed for new ones, by the light of a burning tree, Hazezon saw ten Brycers herded into a corner by twice their number of Tirrans. Hurrying that way, General Seanchan roared defiance to get the invaders' attention. The ploy worked, for a corporal snapped orders that split off eight brawny Tirrans to kill the general and governor.

Seanchan and his daughter jarred to a halt and stood hip to hip with shields and scimitars braced for attack. Behind them Hazezon puffed, "Allow me, General! You citizens, step back!"

Stooping, the mage drilled his fetish-headed wand into the sand of the unpaved street. "Watch your feet, Seanchan!"

From the tiny dimple made by the stick, a crack suddenly split the sand to the depth of a hand, then an arm. General Seanchan had to push his daughter aside as the magical cleft spurted away like a running horse, yawning wider than a man's arm span. Still squatting, Hazezon steered the stick so the crevasse zigged and zagged directly at the onrushing Tirrans. The splitting soil grumbled and shuddered, booming like thunder. Soldiers dived every which way in bad light to escape the gully that now dropped a dozen feet deep and swallowed walls and floors of crumbling buildings. Two Tirrans were too slow. As the man and woman panicked and jumped, a tilting wall bumped them into the crevasse. Both screamed as they sank out of sight into an avalanche of dirt and debris. Buildings creaked and cracked. Roofs fell in. Hazezon twisted the wand to drive the crevasse at the clutch of Tirrans, but this spell sucked up mana, and the magic was nearly spent. Still, the Tirrans had left off hectoring the

Brycers and pelted up the street. The crevasse petered out, the sandy sides slumping, the danger over. Yet two unlucky Tirrans had been buried alive.

Hazezon pulled up his wand and brushed off sand. The party of Brycers stood stunned by their strange rescue, having counted themselves dead.

General Seanchan barked, "You lot! Hoy, wake up! Get after them! Bark at their heels and push them back to the boats!"

The militiamen scampered after their foes.

Moving on, Hazezon and Seanchan aided where they could in the running battle of Bryce. Fights and fires sparked atop roofs, inside houses, beneath bridges. Tirrans and Brycers died or dragged themselves to safety. Hazezon had no idea what the final count might be, but he stepped over dozens of dead as the night wore on. To the ruler's mind, fire almost seemed a worse danger, for no one could form a bucket brigade or pull the flaming infernos flat. A high wind might immolate the city. Hazezon begged that the south winds blew gently. As the night dragged and his shoulders drooped, his tolerance was squelched, and his anger grew.

Once he said, "Damn the Tirrans and their greedy needless destruction! This city has the grace and charm of the loveliest of women, and Johan's troops commit rape! What matter if a thousand Tirrans die if that cruel cad Johan does not lie among them!"

No one answered.

Many times Hazezon glimpsed the tiger man Jaeger tearing into Tirrans like sheep. Once Jaeger dived headlong from a pack of howling Brycers, bowled into a squad of Tirrans, and rose up clutching three screaming men as his black claws shredded their thighs and backsides. Flexing mighty sinews, Jaeger hurled the bleeding Tirrans at their fellows, then growled and jumped so they ran away weaponless. Once Hazezon saw Jaeger leap in the air, spank off an adobe wall, and land between shield men and spearmen, too close to be stabbed before his claws tore windpipes. In another hellish scene lit by burning homes, Jaeger ripped a door from its hinges, banged it atop five Tirrans, then hammered until the door splintered and bones broke. On and on the tiger man fought, always in the thickest action, until Hazezon wondered if four or five talking tigers had also invaded Bryce.

Eventually, long after Hazezon missed his supper, shrill cries and trumpets announced the Tirrans retreated. "Look! They run! They make for the barges! Head them off! No, that way! Don't let them get away! No, let them go!"

Slowly the Tirrans retreated behind a ragged and bruised rearguard. Exhausted Brycers hurled rocks and debris and insults, but otherwise let the invaders step back through the ravaged streets. Citizens glowered and hollered as, by the light of torches on poles, Tirrans tossed in their weapons, cut their painters, and pushed the gundalows into the ash-speckled canals. Poled, bumping and banging, the boats crabbed up the canals into the river proper, then were lost to sight beyond docks and coasters and lighters. As the last boats pushed off, as a final insult, the Tirrans slaughtered many Brycer prisoners. Helpless, citizens watched friends and family knocked down and stabbed, or else shoved into the water with bound hands to drown. Only a few escaped by kicking free, swimming, or running. Shouts of abuse taunted the Tirrans as the remaining bobbing torches disappeared into the dark.

Yet clear above the boos and jeers of citizens roared a Tirran voice raspy from fighting and eating smoke. "We shall return, you bastard sons and daughters of pigs! Johan will burn this trash heap to the ground, and we'll dance on your bones!"

No one was more outraged than Hazezon. Angrier than he'd ever been, the archmage and ruler of the city flexed his empty hands and growled at the night. "No, you shall not. Not so long as I live. For I vow by the blood of my ancestors, Hazezon Tamar will find a way to stop you, Johan, and all your unleashed dogs of war."

* * * * *

"But what shall we do?" wheezed Councilor Ander. "Sit here on our fat hams and suffer wave after wave of attacks? Not I, my friend! I intend to fight!"

Outside the deep windows, the city was busy despite late hours. Some citizens celebrated, some mourned, some hunted lost relatives, and a few danced around lynched corpses of some Tirrans caught drunk in a cellar. Hazezon's idea of joyful release would be a long nap, but he had to sit with the city council. Listening to the loudmouthed Councilor Ander, he stifled a sigh. Ander was unlikely to attack anyone with his decrepit lungs. The old man was as skinny as a pike, too, and Hazezon wondered if "fat hams" was a personal slur. Ander's clothes were richer than Hazezon's, too, a turban of cloth-of-gold and a silk jacket trimmed with otter fur. Ander represented the Hanging Gardens, as the richest quarter of Bryce was called. His shopkeepers and ship owners had the most to lose in any raid.

The city council met in the palace's main hall. Blood had been scrubbed from the flagstones, red-edged papers stacked on the tables. Servants spruced up, stifling yawns. Iron braziers at four corners of the room burned brightly to stave off the nighttime chill.

"We need to know," drawled Councilor Pia, a large woman who represented the dockworkers, "what Johan intends for Bryce. I saw some fighting. This was no shopping spree."

"True." Hazezon sat in his ornate carved chair, for his feet hurt and back ached. A servant set down a flagon of wine mulled with cinnamon and oranges, and the master sipped the spicy steaming brew gratefully. "Johan has taken his first step. He doesn't plan to raid, but to conquer, us, and all of the rest of Jamuraa. So I guess."

Councilors closed their eyes, mopped tired faces, and thumped angry fists. No one was surprised. Councilor

Meraud, a quiet thoughtful woman, asked, "Have you alerted our neighbors?"

"Yes. I dispatched packet boats on the night tide to Shaibara, Yerkoy, Enez, and Kalan. They'll stop at the Red Agates, too. I requested any troops and materials they can spare. They might send some, or not." Hazezon swallowed another sigh. The largest city-states along the Craggy Coast were trading rivals and partners, a ticklish business. They might vote to send help or to let Bryce sink.

"We should have forged a strategic alliance years ago," gasped Councilor Ander. "We could be attacked from any arm of the Sea of Serenity, or even farther. A mighty-enough mage might shift an entire army without warning. We should have planned better."

"We were too busy counting coins," sniped Hazezon.

Silence fell as Jaeger padded into the room. Councilors who hadn't seen him gawked with open mouths. Striving to maintain etiquette, Hazezon said, "Uh, Councilors of Bryce, may I present the hero of the day, Jaeger of, uh, never mind. I'd like to publicly thank our, uh, friend for his aid. . . ."

Hazezon's words ran out as the tiger slid past, as silent as a ghost, then curled up on the flagstone floor between two braziers, and fell fast asleep. Jaeger had washed off the blood and ashes and soot and groomed his fur, Hazezon noted. Oddly, he wondered how the kitchens would feed the new houseguest.

"Is that him?" asked Councilor Tavis, as dull-witted as a trout. He never said anything useful. Why the eastern families chose him for their spokesperson Hazezon never understood. "That's the tiger man who fought like a, uh, lion?"

Hazezon wanted to snap, Who else? but refrained. "I found him near death in the desert. After a quick dip in a fountain, he ripped through Johan's army as through a flock of chickens. I know not where he hails from, nor if he's unique or one of a tribe. We haven't had time to chat."

"I'm glad he chose our side," said Councilor Pia, to which everyone agreed. Then he spoiled it by adding, "He'll want to be paid?"

Councilor Meraud returned to their problem. "Johan, ruler of Tirras. One hears his name over and over, but who knows him? Has anyone ever seen him?"

"I have." Hazezon sipped his wine before it grew cold. "At least, I met one of his forms. He wears disguises, they say, like the chameleons of the south seas. No one knows his true visage, or so it is claimed. I met a long face, prissy manner, and blue eyes that glow like sapphires. Johan's powerful, make no mistake. He's lived longer than all of us combined. Volumes speak of his wreaking mischief ten score years ago. He's always ruled Tirras. Any opposition dies horribly. One assassin was turned inside-out, I know, then hung on a meathook outside the palace until the birds picked his bones clean. They say Johan forged a dark pact with trolls or goblins. Howsoever, his powers increase with the people's prosperity, for his lands are fertile, and his population explodes. He channels mana like eating fire. And those hardy young men and women penned in those rocky valleys champ at the bit for adventure and lust for new lands—ours."

In the silence, Councilor Meraud sighed, "Why must prosperity always beget war? You'd think it would engender peace."

"If they kill or enslave every man, woman, and child in Jamuraa," huffed Councilor Ander, "things will be as peaceful as you please."

"If only we weren't the first stop along the river," lamented the useless Tavis.

"Do you propose to shift our city elsewhere?" sneered Ander.

"We're not the first stop along the river," corrected Councilor Meraud. "That's Palmyra."

"Palmyra!" snorted Ander. "South Tirras, you may as well call it."

"No, not true." To ease his aching back, Hazezon stood and paced behind his chair. "Palmyra has no love for Tirras. They're just canny. They tax the bastards and let them pass. Like mice living at the mouth of a bear's den, they keep from underfoot and pick up crumbs."

Councilors shook their heads. Palmyra was a pest. The River Toloron flowed from far-northern Tirras some two hundred leagues, or six hundred miles, across the desert of Sukurvia, to end at Bryce and the Sea of Serenity. Only one village thrived along the river's length, seventy leagues above Bryce, for the forbidding desert would barely support nomads and goats.

That village was Palmyra, nearly as inhospitable as the sands, a town of misfits, wayfarers, mercenaries, and criminals who only agreed never to meddle in neighbors' affairs. Palmyra stayed strictly neutral, hung between Tirras and Bryce, and levied a tax against anyone passing by on river or dunes. Palmyra also served as a safety valve for both cities. Troublemakers turned out of the gates usually gravitated to Palmyra, where no one pried into secrets.

"It's just possible," mused Councilor Meraud, "now that Johan clearly intends to conquer, Palmyra might join our side."

"It's impossible!" snapped Ander. "What would you ask? 'Please, peace-loving Palmyrans, may we occupy your village and fortify it against Johan's invasion? You won't mind a few thousand soldiers, would you?' Preposterous! If we even hinted a plan like that, Palmyra would become a ghost town by dawn! Those wastrels and criminals would never knuckle under to us!"

"That's right," said Councilor Pia. "Why let your village become a war zone? Johan's army could crush them before noon."

"Then again . . ." Councilor Ander was brash and disagreeable, but also honest and sharing of his shrewd thoughts. "If we did chase everyone from Palmyra, we gain a stronghold. Better we entrench there than along Bryce's north wall."

"Palmyra is the first rung in the ladder, so we must mount it," declared Councilor Pia.

"We've convinced ourselves," summed up Councilor Meraud. "Howsoever Palmyra desires to live, Johan's plans will discommode them, so they must accept change. Better to bargain with us. Talking to Johan is sticking your head in the lion's mouth. If we must approach them diplomatically, our only question is —"

"Who shall go?" asked Councilor Ander smugly.

All eyes turned to Hazezon Tamar.

Sighing, the ruler conceded, "I knew it. I must go. Lady Evangela, lend me strength! I'd rather face a phalanx of Johan's warriors barehanded. . . ."

Chapter 5

In the northern city of Tirras . . .

"For what do we wait, Captain?"

"Bide your tongue, son, and tend your horse."

Soldiers in gray and red sat on their horses or climbed down to stretch their legs. Their tunics bore Johan's red star, but painted upon them were horseshoes denoting cavalry. The rocky defile lay west of Tirras, a tall cleft in rocks masked by birches and buttonbrush. The captain was a stocky blonde woman, and loyal to Johan's cause, though in a small way the veteran resented this mission, whose purpose was kept secret even from her. The troop had been ordered to pack for thirty days and hide in this defile until contacted. Easy to guess, they were either scouting or spying.

A picket rider tripped to the end of the canyon and called, "A man comes. Alone, in uniform."

The captain straightened her leather harness and yellow officer's sash. The lone rider turned out to be a man younger than she, bony and oddly bald, with a wicked pointed chin. He wore a metal helmet and soldier's tunic with red four-armed star, but painted in the star's center was a flaring yellow torch.

"Welcome, Provost," said the captain. Inwardly she frowned. Provosts were something new in Johan's swelling army. Their torch badge announced their occupation as a day-and-night police force to keep order among soldiers. Handpicked by Johan himself and given broad powers, provosts could arrest and imprison anyone in the empire from the poorest lamplighter to a general or senator. That bothered the captain. Why should a provost need a tiny troop of cavalry far outside the city walls?

"Captain." The provost had black piercing eyes over an eagle's nose, reminding the captain of Emperor Johan, whom she'd once seen at a distance. "I have orders to join your company, which is all I can say. I outrank you but leave procedural command to you. Just ignore me, and follow the river for Palmyra."

A spy, thought the captain, or an assassin. Face blank, she said, "Very well, sir. It will be our pleasure to escort you—Uh, may I ask your name, sir?"

For the first time, the young man smiled, a ghastly sight like a crocodile's leer. "Call me Lieutenant Johan."

"Thank you, Lieutenant." Noting how young he was, she ventured, "Named after our esteemed emperor, were you?"

"Something like that." The chilling smile vanished. "Saddle and ride, Captain. The day wanes, and I have much to accomplish."

* * * * *

On the road to Palmyra . . .

"So, my friend, from where do you hail?"

"The east."

Hazezon Tamar chewed over the tiger man's curt and unhelpful answer. He and Jaeger rode at the head of a small party bound for their diplomatic mission. Four palace guards rode at four points of the compass. Palace guards wore tunics and turbaned helmets of gold and blue that represented Bryce's wealth come from the sea. Lieutenant Peregrine rode at the rear where she could see everything, while the foremost guard carried a tall lance with a streaming pennant painted with an albatross. Hazezon was attended by his servant Conal in his blue sailor's jacket and white turban. Four other servants, a cook and water boy, two scribes, and a clerk with a key to a strongbox. Horses were gaily draped with tasseled mantles, as was a string of camels bearing the party's effects. Most important to Hazezon was an elaborate scroll proclaiming eternal friendship and alliance between Bryce and Palmyra, signed by all the councilors; of course, the Palmyrans were as likely to blow their noses on such a proclamation as accept it.

Behind Hazezon's party straggled a handful of merchants, one bringing his entire family. The merchants joined for the protection of the palace guards, though Hazezon had said they were likelier to be robbed in Palmyra than outside it. The party plodded slowly to match the camels and because Jaeger rode a monox. This queer and pokey beast looked like a cross between a camel and a horse. Monoxes were rare because they were difficult to breed, slow and balky, and required brute strength to guide. The beast was half as big as an elephant, so tall that Jaeger's clawed feet hung level with Hazezon's head even on horseback. It stank too, like moldy, burning hay. Still, the monox could bear the tiger man's great weight easily and didn't shy from his cat smell as did horses and camels. Slow was good, too, for it meant the land party wouldn't see any of Johan's raiders along the river—and the other way around. The travelers wore sand-colored robes over their street clothes to keep off dust and sun. Only the tiger man's orange-black hands and feet were seen, and his tiger snout where his keffiyeh hung loose. The tiger man scanned the horizon often, as if expecting trouble. Yet even Hazezon, born to the desert, saw little of interest. The land was yellow-gray sand and pebbles that undulated like frozen waves in all directions, speckled by runs of coarse grass and cactus and the odd clump of stunted cedars. The lazy River Toloron had carved a bed of its own, but was just as likely to shift as sandbars built up and sandstorms smothered the countryside. The trail to Palmyra was marked only by patches of hard-pack and dried manure. For all the drab drear, Hazezon loved the desert's clean air and wide freedom and big bright sky that made a man turn inward to peaceful contemplation.

"The east." Hazezon rocked in time to his horse's pace, testing his guest's temperament. Privacy was jealously guarded in Jamuraa. "I could not tell by your trail, for it wandered where I found you. Legends tell us the east is nothing but infernal desert, the most desolate part of Sukurvia, where giant worms gobble up anyone who steps foot on sand."

"As with all legends, partly true." The tiger man stared straight forward as he bobbed atop the lumbering monox. "I come from beyond the desert, from a jungle land, where a tiger man can walk as a morning breeze without disturbing the sand and warning the worms."

Hazezon pondered, but still had learned nothing. Everyone knew jungles lay east. Sailing along the Craggy Coast as a pirate he had passed hundreds of leagues of lush green coast.

"You speak of *a* tiger man," idled Hazezon. "Are there more than one? A tribe, a race?"

"No, I stand alone under the moons." Jaeger's gaze turned east. In winter sunlight, his pupils had contracted into black vertical slits, just like a house cat's, so his eyes were lamps of glowing amber. Hazezon shivered to see those jet slits. "A sorcerer who should have known better wanted to tempt the elements, and bring new races into being. I am the spawn of one such experiment, turned loose to explore the world."

"You've done more than explore it," said Hazezon. "You threw yourself into the battle to save Bryce more heartily than any of my homegrown troops. What drives you to be a war juggernaut?"

A shrug of striped shoulders. "This land is my home now, for I am shut off from the east. I could never cross the desert again. You saved my life, and I sought to repay you by aiding your city, or my city now, when it suffered strife. Loyalty is a trait —" The tiger interrupted himself, leaving the thought unfinished.

Hazezon glanced sideways but said nothing. As with all legends, he believed only part of the tiger's words. He mulled Jaeger's words and tasted a hint of other tiger men. He'd arrived in a goatskin breechcloth painted with a crude but artistic pattern that smacked of tradition, as had his bark-cloth rags. Too, his bronze talisman, the ram's horn keepsake, had been crafted by some jeweler or mage. Jaeger's accent was barbarous and antique, but his words common enough. Hazezon let the subject drop, but made a mental note to listen for more clues and sometime explore to the east. A score of tiger men would equal a ten-score of Johan's. Especially if loyalty were drilled into them, as Jaeger seemed to hint.

With that topic dead, Hazezon returned to one of his favorites.

"If magic made you, it must be powerful stuff. I wish I had such magic."

"I saw many examples in the raid on Bryce," returned Jaeger from his high perch. "You summoned sand men and split the land and ensorcelled other miracles."

"Tricks," dismissed the mage. "Anyone can conjure with practice. The desert gathers magic slow and thin, grudgingly. In the old days, when magic was new and thick on the ground, mages improved their craft until they mounted to the stars, or so it's told in tales. I've labored my whole long life and can tap only the tiniest resources. Far-reaching enchantments are beyond my powers, and now that I dodder into my golden years, will always be."

"It is no sorrow to grow old," said the white-whiskered tiger man. "The sorrow is to squander what the fates allot us day by day."

Comforted somewhat, Hazezon only nodded and dreamily watched the colors of the sky. As if old friends, the pair rode in companionable silence. The land inclined gradually from the coast, folding in rills, and the party alternately topped the crests and navigated the troughs as if sailing a dirt-brown sea. Finally a pointed minaret showed above a long ridge. The point guard spurred his horse, spun atop the ridge, then returned to announce Palmyra lay ahead, not that any other structures existed in the wasteland called Sukurvia. Breasting the ridge, Hazezon gazed down at the sleepy town, some fifty tiny dwellings atop a bedrock knoll, as permanent a place as one could find in the ever-shifting desert. The River Toloron bent around the town, forming a tight oxbow barely a bowshot wide. Thus Palmyra, Hazezon noted, would be the perfect place to entrench and blockade the river. A dam with locks would mean no boat could sail north or south without Palmyra's permission. Bryce's ruler ground his teeth to see that amid Palmyra's small fleet, twelve days after the attack on Bryce, several of Johan's barges were moored to docks. No doubt the loose-living Palmyrans snatched up bargains in distressed goods ripped from the houses of Bryce's good citizens.

As the party started the slow winding descent, Jaeger posed a question, and again Hazezon was reminded that while the tiger man might look more animal than human, he possessed a keen and canny mind.

"Friend Hazezon, why so much reluctance to pursue this mission? What in Palmyra distresses you?"

"Not what, who," sighed the leader. "Palmyra is a rat hole populated by criminals, wastrels, cutthroats, outcasts, crackpots; the worst trash and gutter-sweepings you can imagine. Unfortunately, their esteemed leader is my ex-wife."

"Ex-wife?" The tiger man gurgled deep in his massive chest, and Hazezon wondered if he chuckled.

"Such was not my wish," sighed Hazezon. "Adira and I pirated together and fell madly in love, but the fates vied against us, or the decades. I entered my middle years while she was still young. We reaped a fortune on the high seas, seizing an entire fleet bound for a prince's mansion in Corondor. Not treasure, but chattel. Hard-carved inlaid couches and tables, rich rugs, honeywood paneling, statues, chandeliers hung with beryl pendants, tapestries, tea services, and lesser stuff such as alum and coriander and pigment. Awkward stuff, but real riches if a man knew where to auction them. I went ashore to Bryce to market them. Adira returned to freebooting as leader of the Robars. Hunding Gjornersen had moved on. That was ten years ago. . . ."

Hazezon's voice trailed off, until the tiger man cleared his throat. The ruler blinked. "Oh. Anyway, strange indeed are the turns a man's life takes. I found buying and selling a challenge, even fun, and no longer wished to jump aboard burning ships swinging a cutlass in either hand. I actually had experience in bargaining. You may not know, but unlike your typical hired crew of sailors, pirates tip their hats to no one. I had to haggle with my crews every day at sea, and I had to produce fat prey and profits, or I'd be deposed—or pitched overside. Having made so many contacts in Bryce, a friend suggested I vie for the governorship. He hoped I could loot the city treasury, for such was custom. But, queerest thing, I found a simple joy in being needed, and in administering, and watching the city grow and prosper like a brood of children. And since things ran peaceably, the city let me reign. After fourteen months Adira returned. She was, uh, displeased. She called me—well, many unkind and undeserved names—then stormed out. Needing a base of operations, she shifted her small fleet to Palmyra. It's far from the sea but accessible, and she'd accumulated enemies in her voyages. Adira Strongheart is not one for half-measures, and rumors circulate that she burned a city flat after the citizens insulted her. Yet there's irony in her choice, too—and how the elements must laugh to watch our tiny scramblings here below, such as a child watches an anthill. To get the ship fitters and supplies and dockage she needed, and board for her crews, Adira had to take command of Palmyra, which previously had had no particular government. Thus Adira's become the in-small governor of her own tiny town!"

"Amusing," rumbled Jaeger. "I see why you'd rather fight a phalanx of Johan's warriors than face this fiery vixen."

Hazezon startled, for he'd thought the tiger man slept on the floor of the council chamber while he'd made that statement. Evidently tigers were like house cats in that their ears never slept. Taking advantage of the camaraderie, Hazezon ventured, "Have you ever been married, Jaeger?"

The only reply was a gurgling chuckle.

* * * * *

Bryce's diplomatic entourage arrived in Palmyra, a colorful troupe of thirty or more on gay horses and camels and a mammoth monox accompanied by dashing guards flying a palace pennant—and met no reception at all.

The party clopped past decrepit houses and shacks built of adobe and driftwood and thatch, entering the town easily because there was no city gate or wall, and barely any streets. Huts faced whichever direction the owners desired either to catch the morning or evening sun, dotted about with no more planning than children's blocks. Goats picked at garbage, women carried water from crumbling wells, children shrieked and played and dodged among ramshackle houses, for half were abandoned. Soon Hazezon's entourage reached the central square, a dusty plaza framed by three long buildings, with the fourth facade missing because it had burned. Adobe flaked in patches. Rain had leaked inside the walls. Some tilted and bulged so badly a strong shove might tumble them. As Hazezon's party scuffed to a halt, only chickens, a naked child, and two men were there to greet them. The chickens pecked at bugs, the child ran off, and the men slept, wrapped in robes on a bench in the wan winter sun.

As the Brycers slid from their saddles and stretched their stiff legs, Hazezon passed under the arched doorway of the biggest building, the purported town hall, looking for any signs of life. The first floor was one room with rickety benches and dust and someone's forgotten keffiyeh hanging on a peg. The back door hung open, no one having bothered to close it. Hazezon swore at the lack of clerks or guards or guides, and remembered again why he hated this pesthole.

Stepping outside, he saw the two citizens still slept, oblivious to the visitors. Bryce's ruler toed the bench and said, "Gentlemen." Getting no reaction, he drew a silver coin from an inside purse and dropped it on the bench. "Gentlemen." Only snores.

Disgusted, hungry, and angry, Hazezon nodded to Lieutenant Peregrine. Peregrine nodded to a guard. She levered a lance behind the bench and abruptly tipped it forward. The sleepers hadn't been faking, for they tumbled like the dead into dust.

"Wake them up." Hazezon ordered.

Three Brycer guards, just as insulted as their leader, kicked the sleepers in the ribs, rumps, thighs, and backs, but not the heads. The Palmyrans yelped and cursed and pleaded until Hazezon called off the assault.

"Gentlemen," said the ruler of Bryce, "a small request, please. If not too troublesome, and you've no pressing chores, could you please notify Adira Strongheart, wherever and with whomever she might be abed these days, that diplomats from Bryce await her presence. That is, if Adira still resides in this dung heap and no one's slit her throat for cheating at dice."

Climbing to their feet, the two Palmyrans sullenly jerked their robes aright.

"You needn't boot us bloody," one complained.

"I need not impale you either," said Hazezon pleasantly, "say, by ramming a spear up your backsides and planting you like scarecrows here in the plaza to die slowly over four or five days. But I shall if you don't go find your leader, please."

The Palmyrans scurried away. Jaeger, still swaddled in traveling robes, slid off his tall monox and joined Hazezon.

Watching the men limp away, Jaeger rumbled, "Your diplomacy looks akin to your warfare."

" 'Speak to natives in their honest tongue,' say the sages. To get attention in this hellhole, I might publicly disembowel a few layabouts."

Lieutenant Peregrine groused, "Likely those two'll just hide in some cellar or grogshop, milord, and tell no one we've arrived."

"Word will get out," said Hazezon. "Adira will entertain us in her own sweet time. Meanwhile, break up some benches in the town hall and build a fire. We shall take tea. Nothing's too good for visitors as welcome as we."

* * * * *

Leaving two guards to watch the livestock lest they be stolen, Hazezon's party took over the town hall. They dumped their bags and robes then smashed furniture for a smoky fire and took their midday meal. They had just wrapped in robes for a nap when Adira Strongheart boomed in.

"What's the idea of kicking two of my townsmen half to death, you bloated hagfish?" The erstwhile governor of Palmyra shrilled like a fishwife. "If you want to abuse innocent people, sheer away home where you can kick dogs and flog orphans and throw maids down the stairs! You always did have a cruel streak, you gut-twisted grouper, and now that you're older than dirt you've only gotten nastier!"

"Do not seek to flatter me with sweet talk, Adira." Hazezon's voice dripped acid. "You knew we were coming. I sent a messenger. And your carefree citizens were rude. Even the poorest nomad offers water and a crust to a traveler. As it was, we had to hold our noses while we kicked your citizens and then had to wipe our boots clean. They're likely your trusted advisors? And how great can your outrage be, when we bespoke them three hours hence?"

"No one asked you to drop anchor, High Lord Tamar," spat the leader of Palmyra. "I could demand you leave—"

"But no one gives orders in Palmyra," finished Hazezon. "Some things don't change willy-nilly. That shirt you wear, for instance, looks to be mine, ten years old if a day. Fashion news trickles slowly upriver, does it?"

Huffing, pouting with her lower lip, Adira Strongheart glared. A stunning woman decades younger than Hazezon, she boasted a lovely lean face and chestnut hair that seldom saw a comb. As a freebooter and pirate, she dressed like a man in a headband, baggy shirt, and tight trousers that met knee boots, yet the shirt hung open to reveal a tight halter that emphasized her bosom even as the kerchief dangled to conceal it, a peekaboo effect that Hazezon guessed was calculated to distract. Though he noted her bronzed neck and breast were laced by new scars. Flamboyant and proud, Adira wore gold bangles in her ears, her hair, around her wrists, and even over the ankles of her boots, so she jangled at every step. Behind her came a bodyguard of two women cowled in blue carrying curved bows of horn and wood and long quivers jutting at their hips. Archer acolytes of Lady Caleria and members of Adira's infamous and fallacious Robaran Mercenaries, Hazezon was sure.

Members of Hazezon's entourage had stood up behind their leader when Adira arrived. Now they squirmed in embarrassment as if they'd intruded on a family squabble. Tallest but unrecognizable in his bundling robes was Jaeger, who peered above a keffiyeh.

Sighing, Hazezon started over. "Adira, I didn't come to fight—"

"Then you picked the wrong town! *T'ala-farook!*"

The woman's hand, hanging by her side, suddenly whipped upward like a cobra. A spinning sphere of pure energy sizzled straight for Hazezon. Fortunately for him, Hazezon had seen it a hundred times when they were married. Unfortunately for those beside him, his instinctive defense was to fork his fingers and erect an indestructible aura. As everyone else flinched, the crackling mana sphere, as wicked as a ball of lightning, spanked off his invisible shield and smacked square into Jaeger's robed brisket. The towering tiger man caromed off a wall and crashed atop a leaning table, which shattered. Jaeger spilled in a tangle of robes and smashed pine.

Adira Strongheart blinked and stared at paws, claws, and a striped tail trailing from the rumpled robes. "Heart of a hart, what's that thing?"

Conal and a scribe helped Jaeger to his feet. His robes were burned away so his white belly showed charred hair.

Irked, Hazezon Tamar explained, "He's a guest to our fair nation. A thinking, talking tiger. One you'll do well not to slay out of petty spite."

Adira sniffed, pointed nose in the air. "Diplomacy is a rough business. Why did you bring him? Will you exhibit him in a cage for pennies? That's what I'd expect of a gull-headed fat-bottomed peddler!"

"Who calls names but a tart-tongued throat-slitting shrew!" Despite his resolve to stay calm, Hazezon found old anger roiling in his breast. "If you can't control your childish tantrums, you shouldn't speak for this village! It is threatened from without like never before, yet you hurl magic at the only people who can save you and yours!"

"Save us! Ha!" Adira trilled a laugh she knew stoked her ex-husband's anger. "Palmyra has always stayed neutral, and for good reason. Now Bryce would rescue us from Johan's imaginary invasion? Better we're plowed under by an iron keel than smothered by perfume. And why should anyone seize

Palmyra? Even the people who were born here would abandon it in a trice! It's a rat hole! You'll need a bigger threat than the Tirrans! If Palmyra climbs into a bunk with Bryce, they'll be as disappointed as I was crawling into yours!"

As insults piled up, guards and palace staff studied ceilings and floors. Hazezon growled through his teeth, "You were never fussy about whose bed you crawled into, you slat-sided doxie! But I didn't come for hospitality! I want to warn your people about Johan's threat and Bryce's counterproposal to trounce him! I hope by the beard of Boris that your citizens listen to sense, because if they depend on an empty-headed trollop to lead, they might as well bow their necks to slavery's yoke!"

Irritatingly, Adira flipped her hand to break off the argument. She simpered, "Very well. Beat to windward. We'll call a drumhead for midnight. Unlike you hard-working hermit crabs of Bryce, Palmyra doesn't rise until the sun sets. State your position to the village and take the consequences. Who knows? They may embrace your plan. Or whip you back down the road with thorn branches!"

Cocking a saucy hip, Adira Strongheart flounced out, leaving her ex-husband to stew.

An uneasy silence hung in the air. Jaeger rubbed his scorched stomach and said, "That went well."

Lieutenant Peregrine asked, "How long were you married to her, milord?"

"Four years," said Hazezon.

The lieutenant whistled.

"You must be made of iron."

"What of the proclamation of alliance and mutual devotion?" asked a clerk.

"Save it to light candles. Bickering aside, we made progress. We're granted an audience with the townspeople." Hazezon blew out his breath. "Adira has calmed down appreciably. She must mellow with age. But damn the bitch! I could strangle her with both hands and laugh all the way to the gallows!"

No one dared reply except the elder Conal, the ex-pirate and servant since forever.

Sliding up his turban, he scratched a hairy ear and said idly, "Aye, love's a funny thing."

* * * * *

". . . Take heed of my warning! Johan is a threat to all! You've seen his flotilla and army! You know he prepares not for simple raids but total war! This storm cloud has been brewing for years! Can you believe Johan plans anything but the conquest of Jamuraa! Will you be reduced to vassals of Johan's ambition, forced into slave labor, whipped in the fields or else conscripted into his army? Palmyra is the first obstacle blocking Johan's way! Common sense dictates we collaborate to stop him *here*—"

A roar drowned Hazezon out, and bitterly the governor of Bryce reflected that common sense was not common. Especially to this motley lot.

Palmyra's town hall, abandoned to spiders this afternoon, was packed wall to wall with angry Palmyrans. Hazezon couldn't believe how many people had crawled out of their desolate huts and shanties. His scribes counted over three hundred adults, and more clustered at the door but couldn't squeeze in. As they'd filed in earlier, gossiping and greeting and pushing and laughing, Hazezon Tamar had studied them. The populace was uneven, two-thirds were men, most of fighting age. Palmyra was not so much a true village as a hangout and hideout for the falsely named Robaran Mercenaries. The Robars had first banded as thieves led by the dwarf Hunding Gjornersen. After Hundling quit for reasons unknown, his lieutenant, Adira Strongheart, had taken command. Since thieves usually ended their lives "dancing on air," Adira remolded the Robars into a motley mercenary army, then hired them out to the highest bidder. Skirmishes flared into war around the rim of the ironically named

Sea of Serenity as frequently as storms, and the Robars seldom lacked for work. The men and women facing Hazezon were able-bodied and scarred veterans who feared nothing, neither tyrant nor trouble, ghost nor devil. If Hazezon could only win these mercenaries over to Bryce's side in the coming war with Tirras, they'd be a potent fighting force.

Unfortunately, being freebooters and pirates meant they were scrappy, independent, and resentful of authority. Everything he said was contradicted, twisted, rejected, or shouted down. Hazezon wondered how Adira controlled them at all. Now they bickered among themselves just as fervently as they'd opposed Hazezon. The only one who abstained was Adira Strongheart, who leaned in a far corner surrounded by her bodyguards and watched the proceedings with a mockingly tilted eyebrow.

Standing at one end of the room behind a rickety table, Hazezon was flanked by his palace guards, scribes, and manservant, Conal. In the corner, ignored, lounged the big tiger man Jaeger. Haranguing had railed for hours until Hazezon grew hoarse and the packed torchlit room sweltered hotter than an oven and reeked of soot and sweat. The diplomat sipped watered wine and harbored his strength, for his only hope was to wear the town down by sheer persistence. Filling his lungs, Hazezon launched back into the brawl.

"Attend! Listen, please, my friends!"

"We're not your friends!" someone jeered to coarse laughter.

"I hope that can change!" returned the politician. "You know in your hearts my words make sense. Yes, Bryce wants to defend Palmyra to stop Johan. And yes, that means Palmyra would brave the first wave of fighting. But Bryce would back you to the hilt!"

"The hilt of a sword shoved in our backs!" called someone.

"Listen! My proposal benefits us all. If we construct a dam below the town, the river will back up immediately. Before long you shall have a large and pristine lake that will ensure a fresh and steady water supply, will teem with fish, help you irrigate crops and gardens, even make your village cooler in the summer! By ditching across the village neck, you gain a moat that could stop any army! And as allies of Bryce, you would prosper from trade connections, eschew tariffs, create greater opportunities for your children—"

"Bryce will benefit, not us!" shouted a woman.

"A lot of work for nothing!" shouted a man. "Who'll haul rocks and dig ditches? Not me!"

A third bellowed, "We've always been neutral, and we'll stay that way! Johan's nothing to us, nor is Bryce! I say, let the army pass by and tax the bastards!"

"It's taxes Bryce means to get from us!" piped a woman.

"Where will we get food if we shut out Tirras?" wheezed an older man. "We buy good grain and fat cattle from Tirras, and cheap! What can Bryce offer? Fish and rice at a pretty profit?"

"Let's vote!" called a voice, and everyone shouted assent. "All in favor of keeping Palmyra free and things as they are, raise your hand!"

"Aye!" roared two hundred or more as hands shot in the air. Laughter welled up with cheers. When the chuckles and guffaws had run their course, a buzzing silence fell. The Palmyrans watched Hazezon, expecting he'd be angry or frustrated, but instead the dignified elder in fine clothes and a white beard looked genuinely sad, like a father heartbroken over his children's misfortunes.

Flicking his keffiyeh away from his sweating face, shaking his head, Hazezon turned to his staff and said quietly, "Let us go."

Jeers, hoots, and catcalls followed him out the door and into the plaza, but the governor was glad to taste cool night air. The desert sky was a canopy of brilliant winking stars, millions upon millions.

He sighed. "Maybe I'm too old to command. Maybe I should retire to a vintry in the hills and grow grapes."

"They'll see the light, Haz." Only Conal used the familiar term with his old captain. "They'll learn you were right."

"Small comfort to learn too late. You cannot dig a moat or erect a dam as soldiers break down your door, enslave your family, kill your feeble elders, and drag your sons and daughters off to a foreign war—"

"Satisfied?" Adira Strongheart pushed free of the throng by the door and joined the governor. Yellow light spilled from the hall into the plaza, but otherwise the village was black, with only ghostly silhouettes of adobe walls illuminated by stars. She mocked, "Palmyra heard your honeyed words and silver promises but decided to keep her virginity. Give our regards to the lizards on the south road."

"This is your fault!" Hazezon's pent-up frustration flared. "You lead these scurrilous cutthroats! We never needed a town meeting! Under threat of war, you could simply order them as governor to fortify!"

"My, how loud the shag squawks, but all nonsense." Adira's tone cut like a razor. "Did you forget everything about pirating? I'm not elected to captaincy because I best barter rugs! I rule at the behest of my killers because I sniff out the biggest treasure with the least fighting! You've grown accustomed to herding southern sheep, but my crew are free men and women who act on their own sufferance! Even then it's tooth and nail most days! Where do you think I got this gilding?"

Standing in the light, Adira Strongheart yanked her kerchief aside to reveal the scars on her neck and breast. "Half came from beating down foreigners and half from gutting my own crew! Remember those days, when Hundling ruled with his fists? Anyone can challenge the leader at any time! I've defended my post by killing four jackasses in knife fights in the last six years, and one was from my own circle!"

Swallowing bitter retorts, Hazezon reflected when arguments broke out in his city council, a meeting was simply adjourned until heads cooled. Shore life had indeed softened him.

Sniffing, bangles jangling, Adira stuffed her kerchief in her bosom and stamped across the plaza for a stable where Hazezon's livestock waited. Yanking open the big wooden doors to warm scents of hay and manure, Adira snarled.

"Up oars and row. If my misfits get into liquor, they might vote to send your head to Johan on a pike—*Ulk!*"

Adira's last words were cut off by a slim chain whickering from the blackness and cinching around her neck. A savage tug yanked her into the dark stable.

"Adira!" shouted Hazezon.

The practical Conal shouted louder. "Turn out! Turn out! Assassins!"

Chapter 6

"Adira!"

Despite his diplomatic defeat and Adira's tart taunts, Hazezon Tamar followed instinct and grabbed at the darkness for his ex-wife. Immediately he felt a thin chain whisper and sing around his arm. He was jerked to his knees like a balky horse.

Reflexively Hazezon chirped, "*Lan-lay tye!*" to erect a magical aura that could protect him from most assaults, but he was slow. Sharpened steel whisked for his throat, and Hazezon felt the tip jab his chin before the sheath of magic closed about him. The knife squirted out of the field like a watermelon seed, and someone before him in the blackness cursed.

Chaos split the night. At the gaping barn door, two of his scribes yelled uselessly, given the temper of the town toward Brycers, but some Palmyrans ran shouting, "Assassins are after Adira!" Men shouted in the plaza even as a raucous snorting of horses and howling of men erupted behind the stable. Then came a hideous roar like a bonfire exploding—the battle cry of a giant cat.

Yet in seconds Hazezon might be dragged into the jaws of death. The elder mage grimaced as the thin chain tore his shirt, ripped skin down his forearm, then snagged on his arm bracer. He was hauled to the left, away from Adira, and briefly he wondered if these were assassins or kidnappers. A stable door clipped his knee as one killer tried to swing it shut. Gritting his teeth against the pain Hazezon dug his knees in straw and dirt but skidded sideways and fell on one hand. All during the silent ordeal, he dreaded the cold kiss of a knife.

Conal, ex-pirate and friend, called for a torch. Not waiting, he drew a long knife from under his sailor's jacket and charged, yelling, "Boarders away!" as if leaping onto the pitching deck of a caravel on the high seas. Knowing his master had been yanked low, the old pirate sliced high, knife backward in his right hand for the longest and most powerful swipe. Hazezon heard the assassin in front of him grunt and lunge. Conal gave a heart-stopping gasp that turned Hazezon's guts to water. Then the old retainer collapsed across his master like a sack of oats. Warm rain splashed on Hazezon's free hand.

Furious, not thinking, just surviving, the ruler of Bryce caught Conal's ankle, hoping to prop the man or ease his fall. With more weight, Hazezon skidded to a halt, though he felt his right hand would be torn off as if by an eagle's beak. Conal again crumpled atop Hazezon, who struggled to keep him off the ground. As superstitious as ever, he feared that his old friend would die if he touched soil that fed a grave. His aging muscles quivered from agony blazing white-hot along his mangled skin and wrist.

"*Ah-shisht!*" Light flared, so bright that Hazezon squinted, blind. A nimbus of cold white fire marked Adira's face and hands, as if her ghost had returned to wreak vengeance. The queerest spell, thought Hazezon wildly, one that lit her skin like a waxed-paper lantern. Adira's few tricks mostly sprang from altering light.

By the spooky glow of skin as pale as death, Hazezon saw Adira jam her thumbs under the choke chain. Hazezon then saw the startled attackers. Two men, one pale, one dark, and a pale woman brought immediately to Hazezon's mind the hill folk of northern Tirras—and its dictator Johan. All three wore keffiyehs tucked around their faces. They'd retied long sashes around their waists and then diagonally across their chests to still the rustling of their robes. That alone marked them as troublemakers, thought Hazezon. The darker man leaned far forward to haul in Adira like a wounded shark. The female assassin hunched with another chain and a lead-filled cudgel in one fist. Kidnappers, noted Hazezon, with tools to tangle and club rather than cut and kill.

With a double thump, the attackers slammed the doors shut against Hazezon's retainers. The back door between the horse stalls hung open for a quick getaway, and Hazezon saw sparks of action out there too. Bales of straw and hay tumbled as people bumped. Panicky horses kicked their stall walls, snorting and whinnying.

All in all, Hazezon thought this a clumsy and amateurish ambush. Did they really hope to get away with hundreds of Adira's faithful just across the plaza? What fool planned this attack?

The pale man who dragged Hazezon by one bloody wrist wore a glove to keep the chain from ripping his palm. From his sash bobbed the curved wooden pommel of a scimitar polished by frequent use. From his free hand jutted a northern straight-shanked knife wet with Conal's blood. The night stalker cursed through his kerchief at Adira's magic light and hissed something to his companions.

Too late. Now able to see, Adira Strongheart lived up to her name. With her right hand jammed between the constricting chain and her throat, she plucked from her waistband one of the two matched daggers she always wore. Then she pounced like a lioness upon an antelope, the bangles at her boots and wrists jangling.

Spinning backward against the rigid chain, Adira kicked high with her boot heel to smash the assassin's nose. He saw it coming and ducked, still hanging on to the chain. Adira had planned for that. She was, in fact, using the chain against its owner. Braced as if by a bar of steel, Adira kicked past the man's head, making him duck back, but she deliberately missed. As her foot completed the whirl, the chain lodged in her crotch. The weight of her body jerked the assassin forward—right into Adira's dagger thrust backward. Pointed steel slammed into the man's eye socket. With a short howl he released the chain and collapsed, stabbed in the brain.

Her face glowing like a full moon, Adira didn't even bother to loose the chain, but scooted, shifted her weight, and lashed out with a long leg for the female assassin. Hunkered, frozen by her companion's swift and grisly death, the woman swiped sideways to bat the boot away, but she was pinned against the stalls. Adira's boot pronged her fingers, thumped her chest, and bashed her against the door. A second kick smacked her face soundly. Stunned, the woman tried to shake off the blow while pointing her cudgel like a sword. Hopping upright, Adira snapped her leg like a cobra and kicked so hard bones broke in the woman's face as her head caromed off the stable door. She slumped into a heap.

Hazezon's assassin was just as hapless, or unlucky. The swooning Conal slid from Hazezon's weakened grip and pitched forward. As with Adira's ploy, the dead weight drove the thin chain to the stable floor. Connecting, Hazezon and the assassin almost banged heads. Hazezon had felt his lifeless friend slip, and was prepared. As the Tirran buckled, Hazezon's free right hand snagged the man's knife hand. Grunting with the effort, the ex-pirate and ruler of Bryce twitched the man's own knife to tickle his throat. The steel was sharp. The Tirran's eyes flew wide in the eerie luminous light as steel pricked his throat. Blood geysered over Hazezon.

Exhausted by mere seconds of furious action, Hazezon stayed crouched and pinned until the Tirran's strength failed and he sagged over Conal. He watched Adira sink to her knees and unknot the chain from her throat as the magic glow faded from her face and hands. Blood stained both of them, and the coppery stink made Hazezon want to gag. He clamped down on his stomach not to appear weak before his followers.

Speaking of whom, the shaking ruler thought sourly, Why did it take those useless clots so long to batter open the doors?

The barred doors splintered and burst open. Hazezon was surrounded by scribes, servants, and strangers who cooed and fussed. Torches threw wild shadowed light. Shaking and angry, Hazezon cursed as helpers pried him from the chained grip of the dead Tirran and limp Conal. Hazezon gasped as the blood-crusted chain was pulled from the folds of his raddled skin. Helped the same way, Adira used the same curses, her mildest, ". . . you dung-eating beetle-headed bastard sons of blanket scorpions . . ."

The towering tiger man entered through the open back door, his desert robes pulled awry to reveal orange-black stripes and a white belly. Palmyrans shied away from the apparition. Jaeger breathed hard, and blood smeared his muzzle and black claws.

"Master, I'm sorry," one of Hazezon's scribes told him gently, "but Conal is dead."

"He can't—" Hazezon Tamar halted. In his former bloody trade, he'd seen dead men, and he'd felt Conal fall. Lifted to his feet, shedding straw and manure dust, he sighed, "Oh, Conal, my friend, I shall miss you."

"Wake her up! Toss that bucket!" Furious, Adira swung a bony fist to get elbow room.

The stable was crowded as seemingly all Palmyra clustered inside and outside. Faces shiny in torchlight gawked and elbowed and asked inane questions.

She shrilled, "Get her up!"

Two Palmyrans had hurled a bucket of water in the Tirran's face. The sole survivor of the kidnapping attempt, she was a wreck, her face hammered and puffy, nose and lips leaking crimson, blonde hair stippled with straw and blood. Palmyrans twisted her arms and backed her against a stable door. Groggy, the woman tried to keep her head up, but her chin kept drooping.

A scowl creasing her face, Adira Strongheart revived the Tirran by gouging a thumb into the woman's shattered cheekbone. The kidnapper yelped as her swimmy eyes snapped open. Adira studied her garb a moment, then plied a dagger to slit the woman's tunic down the front. Ripping cloth, Adira exposed a red four-pointed star marked with a horseshoe painted on the inside. The skulkers had turned their tunics inside-out.

She spat, "The concealment is enough for me to hang you as a spy, so sing, Tirran! Did Johan send you? Were you to waylay one of us, or both?"

Focused by pain, the woman only glared. She mushed her words pronouncing, "A soldier of Tirras doesn't reveal her mission." Her lower lip trembled in betrayal.

"This one will." Snatching a torch from a villager's hand, Adira ground the blazing wood against the Tirran's ear. She screamed as her flesh scorched and her hair sizzled and caught fire. The two villagers pinning her arms grunted to hold her still while leaning far back, for Adira was as likely to sear them. Some Palmyrans and Hazezon's Brycers hissed to see the vicious and vigorous torture, and wrinkled their noses at the stink of burning hair.

"Adira!" yelled Hazezon over the woman's screams. "Is this necessary?"

"Belt up, Haz! You were never this soft when you walked the quarterdeck of *Stangg's Talon!*" Drawing the torch back, Adira said only, "Wet her down."

Someone used a rag to slop water on the Tirran's burn. The woman wept for pain and writhed hard enough to twist her arms from their sockets. Adira stood implacable, dark eyes as cold as a shark's. "You'll tell us—"

"I—can't," gasped the woman.

"Be brave." Adira mashed the flaming torch against the woman's other ear. Flesh and hair sizzled—

— and the soldier broke. "*Aggh!* Please! No more! We came to kidnap you! To throw the blame on Bryce! Tamar—we didn't care about, but we hoped to grab him as a—Uh!—bonus!"

"What else?" Adira flicked the torch, and the soldier flinched. "Where were you to bring me?"

"Please! I don't know!"

"Where?"

"*Ahhh!* Oh! L-likely to the emperor!"

"Emperor?" Adira wrinkled her nose. "You mean Johan?"

"Yes! Some had horses—"

"Had horses," interjected Jaeger, and licked blood off his paws. Hazezon realized the cacophony behind the stable had been Jaeger ambushing the getaway party.

The tortured Tirran rattled on. "We attended the meeting to—Oh!—gain the temper of the village and—Uh!—agitate! Oh, Johan save me, it hurts!"

Pushing the torch into a man's hand, Adira flicked a finger at the crowd. "Mykler, Roanna, drag this trash to the midden and slit her throat. Let her feed the vultures. And don't get soft and release her, or I'll have to clip your ears! Take these dead ones with you, but search their garments for a map or orders."

Raising her voice to the crowd, Adira bawled, "The rest of you troll for strange faces! See if other Tirrans lurk about! Then I suggest we reconvene the drumhead and reconsider Hazezon's offer, for Palmyra is hot at war with *Emperor* Johan whether we like it or not!"

People buzzed, shuffled, argued, and questioned. No one was silent as they filed into the town hall.

Feeling old and wrung out, Hazezon gritted his teeth against the pain in his skinned arm and wrist as he told his ex-wife, "Thank you, Adira, for reconsidering—"

"Swallow your tongue, you crosspatch codfish!" Adira's neck wound wept red rivulets down her neck and bosom. "For all I know, *you* staged this assault to seduce us to your side! That's a politician's trick! You might even be in league with Johan, and you'll get Palmyra as your fief and rule as the emperor's puppet! Know this, merchant! I'll dredge up the truth behind this conniving if I have to lash you to the gratings and roast you like a pig at a harvest feast!"

She stomped away into the flickering darkness, leaving Hazezon Tamar to stare.

A scribe asked, "Milord, may we tend your wound?"

"Eh?" Hazezon fixed on the youth. "Oh, yes. Please do. It stings fierce. But Conal can—"

Then he recalled Conal was dead, and his wounds felt like nothing compared to the stab to his heart.

He mused, "Conal the first. How many more . . . ?"

* * * * *

"You got your way," sniped Adira. "I hope you choke on it."

"It's not what I wish," replied Hazezon wearily. "It's what's best for both Bryce and Palmyra, and every other kingdom in the southlands."

Adira Strongheart snorted. Dawn was not far off, for the town meeting had dragged while everyone had their say. Wroth by Johan's duplicity at sending agitators to spread dissension and kidnap their leader, the village had voted to adopt Hazezon's proposal to fortify Palmyra. Provided that Bryce and the other city-states of the Craggy Coast sent provisions, materials, workers, and most importantly, money. Hazezon had orated until his throat was raw, not promising anything from neighbors, but citing hope and the better nature of people facing a common threat. "Better nature" was not a popular topic with pirates and mercenaries, and finally Hazezon had agreed to whatever they demanded just to end the debate, banking that later neither he nor they would remember. As details bogged and arguments tangled tighter, Adira adjourned the meeting and cleared the room, in some cases pitching people into the street to argue elsewhere.

Now the rulers of Palmyra and Bryce slumped at a table and slugged red wine to dull the pain of peeled skin, sprained fingers, and more. Yellow torchlight etched their strained features, for even wine could not promote harmony. Adira's Circle of Seven sat on benches and tables around them dozing or listening. Some were wrapped in sheepskin jackets or wool cloaks against the night chill. At their feet, like an enormous rug, lay the tiger man Jaeger, purring slightly as he pursued feral dreams.

"Draping your demands in altruism and fancy platitudes doesn't change them," persisted Adira. "Seal of the Syphon, I can't believe what a mealy-mouthed backsliding double-talker you've become since they made you prince of that poxy pesthole."

"You can't understand my capacity to view both sides of an argument." Hazezon gritted his teeth. "Maturity has brought me wisdom, better late than never. You still smack your head against walls like some balky daughter denied a new dress for the ball."

"If maturity means staying within eyeshot of graveyards in case you drop dead in the next hour, I'll take brash youth." Adira glugged wine and finger-combed her tousled chestnut hair. Her neck and both hands were bandaged and smeared with foul-smelling salve concocted by a witch woman. Dark blood stained the bosom of her shirt, which had indeed been Hazezon's.

The room was quiet as the sun split the eastern horizon and leaked into the room. Cole, a tall bald man with a neat black beard, snuffed torches and candles. Jaeger gave a jerk and chirp like a kitten, and Adira resisted the urge to rub his tummy.

"So," Hazezon chose his words lest he spark another flare-up, "what's your first venture?"

"What else? I'll kick my worthy citizens off their scrawny rumps and sail south to scrounge some money. A carrack full. There's always a war simmering somewhere. Fysmatan and Lucrezia are grappling like lovesick octopuses, they say. I'll leave Palmyra's defenses—Ha!—to old Declan. He's blind now, but when he was young he planned the fortifications of Fear Island, where King Gaynor's navy split on the rocks. He'll lay on with your city engineers to see Palmyra sewn up tighter than a priest's purse. I'll leave half my mercenaries here to grub rocks. That's task enough for most of the dullards. These clubfooted clownfish will go with me. They're not worth more than ballast, but they'll stop arrows if they don't fall flat first."

Hazezon Tamar listened to chuckles and titters roll around the room. Adira Strongheart's Circle of Seven was a ring of steel with no weak links. The number and faces varied, for occasionally one drew an unlucky card, but freebooters from all over the south seas flocked to Adira Strongheart's standard, and from the best of the best she selected her personal bodyguard of seven, more or less.

This time there were eight, which Hazezon thought a nice piece of misdirection, like hiding an extra knife in your boot. Some he knew. Most familiar was Cole, Adira's dependable lieutenant, a bald, bearded man who watched everywhere with dark eyes and missed little. Famous was Heath, a pale and melancholy man who was either an elf or else a forest spirit, for he'd sailed with Hazezon more than thirty years ago but never aged a day. Simone the Siren was a buxom black woman with a big smile and frighteningly fast cutlass. Treetop stood thigh-high, a wizened and squinty dwarf who had some magic and a rapier like a wasp's sting. Badger was an old sailor named for the gray streaks marking his scalp and beard. New were a skinny man who dozed in a chair against the wall, and the archers of Lady Caleria, sisters in name and faith but not blood, for one was slim and flaxen and the other stocky and dark. As a badge of their mysterious order, they carried ornate bows of horn and ivory everywhere. All of them, Hazezon thought, looked capable of kissing a virgin or killing a clergyman on a bet or a whim.

Adira's Circle of Seven dressed like their leader, in vagabond clothes suited for sea or desert: baggy shirts and trousers in faded colors, dusty boots or sturdy sandals, vests for pockets and sashes to bind them close. Heath wore a deerhide jerkin, so old it was scuffed white, laced across his chest. The Calerian archers dressed in dark blue with tan cowls and wore leather bracers anchored between their fingers.

"This ill wind fits our sails, I suppose." Adira tossed off her wine and rose, though she swayed for a second from a long night of fighting and politicking. "Our hulls go rotten in this soft berth. There's only so much wrestling and cockfighting and horse racing. We'll spread terror across the Sea of Serenity and set fat merchants a-tremble in their beds."

Ignoring the dig about fat merchants, Hazezon asked dryly, "Try not to sack any ships flying flags of Bryce or our allies, will you? It's embarrassing to pay people in their own coin."

"Not for me. I don't give a damn who I offend." So saying, Adira turned to the new crewman who dozed against the wall, hooked her foot under his chair, and snapped her leg up. The chair crashed, yet the pirate sprang into a crouch, a dagger in one hand as if by magic. Adira skipped and kicked, and the dagger spanked the far wall. When the pirate made the mistake of looking, Adira's next kick clouted his jaw and laid him out flat.

"Fast, Virgil, very fast," cooed Adira. "If all we face are blind old woman crippled by rheumatics, you might survive to waste your pay in the stews of Kalan."

Hazezon frowned at the callous abuse, but Cole chortled. "New ones expect some breaking-in. Like wild horses. Virgil wouldn't be invited to the Circle unless he were capable. And if he don't trust even his mistress, he'll stay alert."

"Pack your duffels," Adira told her circle. "No point in lying idle while Hazezon turns Palmyra into a temple garden. Heath, pack your good luck weather magic. We'll need it."

"I wish to go too."

Everyone startled at the rumble rolling from Jaeger as he unfolded from the floor. Draped in desert robes, the creature looked as big as a canopied elephant. Yawning and stretching, the tiger man had to crook his elbows below the ceiling beams. His black claws flickered in the dawn light like shards of jagged glass.

"You'd go a-pirating?" asked Adira. "You might make a nice rug for the captain's cabin, but those claws will scar my holy-stoned decks. And though I've heard of dogfish and catfish, never have I seen a tigerfish."

Shoulders as wide as a church door shrugged. Jaeger might have smiled. "Then it's time. We witness an era of legends. Let's write a new chapter in the epic of Adira Strongheart. I wish to see all of the human's world. Such an opportunity I cannot let slip."

Despite her imperious manner, Adira gauged the opinions of her circle. Most squinted, unsure.

Hazezon put in a good word. "Jaeger led Bryce's militia to victory in the Tirran raid. He saved lives and put heart in my people. Recall too he dispatched four riders and their horses last night while you and I were being strangled in the stable."

"Aye," conceded Adira, but chided, "You might have kept one alive for questioning."

"Man or horse?" asked Jaeger, almost smiling.

Shedding his desert robes in a pile, Jaeger revealed his glowing hide and scant breechcloth and buckled harness and bronze dagger. "If you wish, test me. Here, I'll make it easy."

Hands empty, Jaeger turned his broad back to reveal a swath of orange and black stripes. "Strike—"

Adira Strongheart whisked a hand behind her back, plucked one of her matched daggers, and slung it underhand. Cole dipped to one foot and aimed a savage kick at Jaeger's knee. Simone the Siren leaped off her table, cutlass in hand, and sliced high as if to skim off the tiger's ears. Salt-and-pepper Badger laughed as he hooked his foot under a stool and lobbed it at Jaeger's head.

Afterward, Hazezon Tamar thanked the fates for giving him sight, for he never saw anything move so fast or with such grace.

In an eye blink, Jaeger hopped in the air above Cole's kick and raked Simone. He slammed her atop Cole even as his free hand snagged the flying stool into the path of Adira's dagger so it chunked in wood. While landing, Jaeger upended a table as a shield in case an archer shot. Then he dumped Simone and Cole halfway across the room.

For a second, no one could speak. Then, as Jaeger righted the table and plucked Cole from the floor like a child, Adira's Circle laughed and hooted and cheered to welcome a new crewman.

Adira Strongheart plucked her dagger from the stool and examined the tip. Tapping steel on her callused palm, she asked Hazezon almost civilly, "Can you glean any more striped ones from the desert?"

Hazezon shook his head. "Only one I know of."

"Pity," said Adira. "So. Our Circle of Seven encompasses nine. Sounds like an omen."

"Or a prophecy . . ." mused Hazezon.

* * * * *

"Jaeger, my friend." Hazezon smiled, and the huge tiger man smiled back. "Know you the prophecy, the omen, of None, One, and Two?"

The tiger's amber eyes were slitted against morning sun. "Yes. I have heard of it."

Man and tiger man stood in quiet communion, unsure how to say good bye. Before the stable, Adira and her bodyguards readied their horses, checking hooves, tugging cinches, tying on saddlebags and blanket rolls, winding head scarves, draping traveling robes. Cole kissed his wife and children and Simone kissed her husband.

Steadying his mule, the dwarf Treetop climbed a rope ladder to a basket strapped atop a pack frame like a howdah on a war elephant.

Hung in desert robes like some primitive elemental, Jaeger murmured, "Here I journey southward, my debt unpaid for your saving my life—"

"You helped save Bryce," cut off Hazezon, "so repaid us a hundredfold."

Still, tension lingered, for the mage had a hundred questions to ask, but no time. Jaeger prompted, "This prophecy?"

"Yes." Urged, Hazezon gushed, "I first heard it from a desert druid, Stone-Bringer. She touched you and recited prophecy. That when None and One meet, only Two shall remain. I think you're the key to the southlands' future. Else why would the fates send you here?"

Jaeger's amber eyes were dreamy. "I knew a seer once spoke of the prophecy. It's written on the desert wind. Time was . . . never mind."

"But who's none, or what? Who's the one?" Curiosity overcame manners, and Hazezon asked, "Is it you? If there are no more tiger folk in the east—"

"Mount and ride!" called Adira. The Circle kicked stirrups and swung into saddles. Jaeger glanced at his lumbering monox, whose huge stupid head hung slack as it dozed. The party waited on their last member. Jaeger raised a paw.

"My friend." The paw, as big as a barrel top, came to rest on Hazezon's shoulder. Jaeger hesitated, and Hazezon sensed he didn't want to tell a lie. The tiger rumbled, "I regret we part so soon, with so much unsaid. But I must see man's world, and destiny leads me south. Perhaps when I return some secrets can be spilled."

Frustrated by superstition and ignorance, Hazezon walked with Jaeger to the waiting monox. Nimble as a monkey, the tiger man climbed the long stirrup and plunked in the saddle, bringing the monox's dull head up.

Chagrined, Hazezon said, "Good luck, Jaeger, and be careful. With their thick heads, this crew sails into the thickest fog. Not all of them crawl out."

Jaeger rubbed his muzzle. "I fear not to return. Prophecy must be fulfilled, so there's my protection. Farewell!"

* * * * *

From the shadows of an alley, a tall nomad cloaked in moldy robes watched Adira's party depart, then nodded to himself, a wickedly pointed chin bobbing.

Johan had left his cavalry escort on the outskirts of Palmyra, donned a disguise as a nomad, and had infiltrated the city to gauge its temper. The town meeting had gone much as he had guessed. No matter. Palmyra's plans could scarcely undo his. Johan's vast army was growing daily. One regiment of his dwarf sappers boasted more recruits than all of Palmyra's populace. His soldiers would tramp this bump in the road flat. Still . . .

As the meeting had wrangled on, Johan had trekked from the village and ordered his cavalry escort to lie in ambush for Adira Strongheart and Hazezon Tamar. The captain's soldierly pride would be tarnished, she'd argued, if they must skulk around like spies, but she'd followed Johan's orders, unsure of his mysterious capacity.

Untrained in stealth and with their getaway shredded, the loyal Tirrans had muffed the kidnapping and suffered for it.

Johan didn't really care. Had the two leaders, Hazezon Tamar and Adira Strongheart, been seized or killed, well and good. If not, they'd die later. Johan had lost only a handful of loyal soldiers, and he'd learned much from the miscarriage. The tiger man was certainly a surprise, and a formidable one, for he'd raked to ribbons four riders and their mounts without earning a scratch.

Watching the monox and its striped rider disappear below the ridge, Johan asked himself, "How best to exploit what I've learned . . . ?"

Chapter 7

"She'll make a pretty prize! Bear down, Cole, and bring us alongside! What the hell does Mabyn wait for? Does she fight or fish? Signal her to get the lead out!"

On a green rolling sea, three ships ran before the wind and converged on a collision course. One was a beamy caravel like an upturned shoe named the *Pride of Perth*, wherever that was.

Shadowing it was Adira Strongheart's pirate ship *Robar's Crush*, a big cog with castles fore and aft, able to stow five tons or more, but slow. Skittering alongside the big ships zipped *Robar's Arrow*, a sassy two-masted sloop with lateen sails, swift as a barracuda.

Adira cursed from the quarterdeck of *Crush* for *Arrow* to do her job, as did a hundred greedy pirates who hung from the rigging or perched atop the yardarms. *Crush* and the merchant ship *Pride* were almost matched in speed. The merchant ship was heavier and carried more sail, while Adira's *Crush* was lighter but old and slower to respond. Thus *Crush* needed the tiny *Arrow* to slow the merchant ship. Across the water, *Arrow's* captain, a stocky redhead named Mabyn, cursed and shrieked orders in imitation of Adira.

Aboard the merchant ship caught between, a worried captain bit his nails and shouted at a marine lieutenant to act. A veteran, the marine ignored him and calmly waited. The marines were Lucrezians assigned to protect merchant vessels in time of war. The lieutenant had twenty-seven marines under his command, all in sturdy coarse shirts and trousers overhung with white tunics painted with two blue cranes entwined. In addition, the marines wore metal helmets embossed with curls like a nautilus shell, a custom along the Sea of Serenity. The marines waited behind with small oblong shields and short swords with leaf blades, grim grins on their faces. By any count, they were outnumbered five to one. The merchant ship's crew, another sixteen men and women, had been issued cutlasses painted black to resist rust, but none of these civilian sailors looked happy to die for their cargo or country.

Aboard *Arrow*, Captain Mabyn ran back and forth on the short flush deck, making sure her crew had prepared. Three catapults had been pulled from the hold, assembled, and bolted to the deck with hard hawthorn pegs. The siege weapons looked like toys, no bigger than a pine table. Cupped in the leather sling of each catapult was an iron ball as big as a man's head. Chains trailed from the balls were laid precisely along the decks. Iron hooks like shark hooks studded every tenth link on the curious chains.

Mabyn watched everywhere at once. She checked the set of the sails, glanced at the merchant prey hissing through the water fifty yards off, noted *Crush's* position on the opposite beam, double-checked the lashings and chains on the catapults, then spat to leeward for good luck and gave the orders.

"Helm, bring her ten points abaft the wind! Sailmaster, tail onto the sheets! Shotmaster, ready your slings! Mind the booms! Here we go! *Hard a-port!*"

As the rudder cut the water and canted the sloop's bow thirty degrees away from the wind, the sailmaster hollered to let go the sheets and mind the booms. Snatched by the breeze, twin slanted sails like seagull wings swept the width of the ship. Every sailor ducked as wooden booms whipped over their heads like tree branches hurled by a hurricane. Kicked in the stern and pitched by the wind, *Arrow* leaped in the water and charged at the merchant vessel like a bulldog. Pirates craned on tiptoes and wiped sweaty hands by the catapult levers.

Seconds before *Arrow's* sharp prow rammed the merchant ship, Captain Mabyn hollered, "*Away the grapnels!*"

When the huge sails whisked out of the way over the side, the blue tropical sky yawned clear. Poked by the shotmaster, pirates yanked catapult levers. Three greenwood springs released pent-up energy and hurled the iron balls at the crow's nest of the merchant ship. After the balls flitted the stout chains with their vicious iron hooks. The far ends of the chains were bolted to the sloop's gunwale, and almost immediately the ends clanked to a halt.

The long grapnel chains did their job. Hauled skyward by the heavy iron balls, chains and hooks whickered around, over, and through the merchant ship's sails and rigging. Linen sails tore as hooks caught hold. Slashed rigging parted with a *pung!* so masts and sails abruptly tilted. Tangled tarred lines jerked loose, spars and yardarms cracked, sails flopped. More damage ensued as Captain Mabyn ordered the sloop's helm slammed hard to starboard. Chains anchored at the gunwales again snapped taut and again hashed the merchant ship's rigging. Sailors and marines aboard the *Pride of Perth* ducked as ropes, blocks, and shreds of linen tumbled on their heads.

Yet *Pride's* troubles were only beginning. Tangled with tiny *Arrow* by the grapnel chains, the merchant ship immediately lost headway. Just as the crew caught their breath and gaped at the damage overhead, *Robar's Crush* smashed alongside. Canny pirates flicked grapnel chains to lash the two big vessels tight. Then the ships bashed again, rocking everyone on board.

Adira Strongheart had waited hours for this moment, and screamed at the top of her lungs, "*Robars! Board the bastards and feed 'em cold steel!*"

Howling "*Robars!*" Adira's pirates leaped the gap of churning water between vessels and plunked on the merchant's deck with cutlasses and boarding axes. Lucrezian marines met them with short swords and shields and the battle cry, "*Glory to the Princess!*"

The two crews clashed like iron-scaled dragons, and before long blood spattered the sails. The marine lieutenant had bunched his men and women in knots of five so they could circle back to back. Adira's mercenaries were not so fussy with superior numbers and hot blood, and attacked however they might. One marine squad was immediately surrounded by a score of pirates. A cutlass blade skinned the top of an iron-bound shield with a hair-raising *screek!* and jabbed a marine in the jaw. A pirate used her steel handgrip to bash a short sword aside, then drove her blade straight between shields to spear a belly. One big pirate simply locked two hands on the haft of his boarding axe and walloped a shield. Hit hard, the marine tripped over a spar dangling from the rigging. As he fell, the big pirate slammed the boarding axe down so hard it lopped off the marine's foot and sank five inches in the oak deck. With the squad's formation broken, the other four marines were quickly knocked down and dispatched with red blades.

On the high castle quarterdeck where the two ships ground together at the stern, Adira Strongheart surveyed the fight. The ship had to be manned and sailed on an even keel or *Crush* might lose its own sails and riggings to an errant squall. *Robar's Arrow* also had to beware lest, chained to the bigger vessel, she were crushed or plowed under. Thus even while the boarding raged, some pirates cleared decks, or guarded with axes, or were stationed on yardarms to make sail. Lookouts in crows' nests watched for oncoming storms or enemy ships, either someone's interfering navy or else rival pirates.

Of her Circle of Seven, Cole manned the helm and served as sailmaster, and Badger, worn cutlass in hand, directed the boarding on the forecastle with Treetop while Heath shot arrows from a crow's nest. So Adira had for bodyguards the archers Wilemina and Marigold and the new member Virgil with his long-beaked boarding axe. Jaeger had declined to partake in the battle, wishing instead to observe, so Adira had posted him in the forward crow's nest to keep watch with his keen amber eyes.

"Wil, Marigold!" Adira pointed to the merchant ship's waist where the marine lieutenant directed his squads with precision and sound judgment. "He's too good! Kill him!"

Together, the archers raised ornate bows of horn and ivory drew nocks to chapped cheeks with callused fingers and let their arrows fly. But the marine lieutenant, alert or lucky, hoisted his small wooden shield painted with the crossed cranes. Arrows slammed into the shield with iron heads piercing the stout rowan wood, but the marine captain shifted behind a mast and continued to exhort his troops.

"So much for the value of virginity! Never mind! I'll do it myself! *In-sin-yon!*" As the archers chirped in protest, the pirate leader seemed to blink out and reappear a yard to one side. Slinging her baldric behind her hip, Adira grabbed a trailing rope and kicked off the gunwale.

Left gawking when he should have been guarding, Virgil yelled, "Hoy, wait up!"

Swinging through the air for two dizzying seconds, Adira let go and plunked on the merchant ship's quarterdeck almost atop the fretful master. Surrounded by six sailors with black-painted cutlasses, he bleated, "Her! Kill her, and I'll reward you handsomely!"

Heartened by bounty and high odds, the six converged to kill Adira Strongheart before any of her crewmembers could come to the rescue. The pirate leader only sneered as she drew her cutlass and dagger.

Sailors swung cutlasses to slash high or jab low, but something foiled their attack. Black blades whanged the taffrail, chipped the varnished wood, and chopped the tarred rigging. Their stabbing blades pierced only air. Meanwhile Adira Strongheart struck from three feet to one side, teaching the sailors not to trust their eyes in a world where magic was common, for she was masked by yet another light spell. Her whistling cutlass whacked a man's wrist, crushing bones and severing an artery. Frothy red blood gouted across the deck. Adira's dagger raked a woman's shoulder so she screamed and cannoned into a companion, and both went down in a tangle. Her backslashing cutlass beat a man's face from beneath, the blunt edge breaking his nose and skinning his forehead. Hooking her dagger through a short arc under her arm, Adira punctured a man's ribs and ripped him open so he died writhing in crimson. The sixth sailor Adira tripped, and he sprawled on the red-stained deck, where she kicked in his temple.

She'd dropped six hardy sailors in seconds. Faced by this savage steel-toothed tigress, the merchant captain flopped on his knees and begged for his life. Flinging auburn curls from her sweating face, Adira told him, "Order your crew to lay down their arms! It's stupid to resist!"

"I can't! I can't!" blubbered the captain. On his knees in blood, he looked like a misplaced marketplace beggar. "I told Lieutenant Orville to surrender and not fight, but he refused!"

"Glory hounds!" spat Adira. Abruptly, the light-diversion spell expired, so she winked out and reappeared three feet to her right. Whirling, she tracked the battle raging in the waist.

The marine officer Lieutenant Orville was bound for glory or death. Crouching amid his troops, with broken arrows jutting from his shield and one of Heath's long arrows protruding from his shoulder, the officer exhorted his marines to keep their ranks tight and work in tandem. The pirate attack had temporarily stalled, though arrows and lead sling balls continued to rain down on the ship.

"Heart of a hart, must I do everything myself? Hoy, Orville!"

Called by his name, the marine lieutenant turned just in time to jerk up his shield. A dagger, perfectly balanced, was hurled pommel-first to brain the man. The dagger bounced off his shield, but Adira had only thrown it as a distraction. As Lieutenant Orville peeked again, a wooden bucket clonked his forehead and laid him out cold.

"Cease fighting!" bawled Adira. "Desist, both sides, and we'll let you live!"

With their officer down, the marines saw no point in dying. Short swords clanged on the deck. Adira screamed at a pair of pirate hotheads who would strike the unarmed marines, warning they'd hang if they harmed prisoners. Threatened by her steely stare and ready blade, the pirates' passion and battle lust cooled. Virgil puffed up, blood spattered across his face and axe blade.

Adira told him, "You're late."

In the loud silence after battle, Adira barked orders.

"Swab that blood out the scuppers! Reef that damned sprits'l before it rips loose! You, coil the grapnel chains! And shut that yowling maniac up, or we'll heave him to the sharks!"

Striding the deck, ordering everyone to work, for a busy crew was a happy crew, Adira stopped beside Lieutenant Orville lying stunned on the deck. Toeing the arrow jutting from his shoulder, she asked, "Did you ever think of becoming a pirate?"

* * * * *

In three weeks at sea, *Robar's Crush* and *Robar's Arrow* had bagged four Lucrezian merchant ships and sunk a score of fishing smacks and small craft. The Robaran Mercenaries sailed under the flag of the shah of Fysmatan as privateers in the latest war with the Princess Lucrezia. The shah had promised a larger share of booty.

Adira supervised the long hard part, which was cleaning up wreckage, discovering and divvying up the booty, guarding prisoners, and gauging how to send the captured vessel back to Fysmatan through pirate- and navy-infested waters without it being captured back.

Standing by the black square of a hatchway, she called, "What for cargo?"

"Not much." Cole's bald head, wrapped in a kerchief against tropical sun, appeared in the hatchway. Two-handed, he pitched up a dark rusty block that scarred the caravel's holystoned deck.

Adira nudged the bar with her foot, but it didn't budge. A fearsome stink of dead things welled up from the hatch, which had been sealed and stifling hot.

Eyes watering, Cole cast about in the dark by his feet. "Pig iron, mostly. Two tons'r more. Some raw steel in bars, greased and tied, bales of dull cloth, and green cowhide. Rats so fat they can barely waddle."

"I smell the hides. Is that all? Blast it, come on up." Adira Strongheart leaned away from the stench and looked about the ship. Her pirates had tidied the deck, chucking most debris overboard. The captured crew and marines huddled in the prow, guarded by swords, and clamped their teeth against wounds lest they be, as Adira had warned, pitched overboard for making noise. Meanwhile, every pirate listened with half an ear for Cole's appraisal of the booty. Pig iron and cowhide was unwelcome news. Badger was so disgusted he pitched a perfectly good cutlass over the side along with the litter.

"This trash is it?" Adira asked her first lieutenant.

Cole peered from under bushy black eyebrows.

"Trash to you. War material to Princess Lucrezia. Pig iron and steel bars for swords and pikes. Cloth for uniforms and blankets. Leather for shoes and hauberks and harness. But nothing we can hawk at the docks in an hour, no."

Adira spat on the deck. "Pox and privation, we must live with it. Badger, toll off a skeleton crew to make for Fysmatan.

Shift some of this booty into our hold in case we get separated. Yes, raw hides too! Jaeger! Hail *Arrow* to stay alert to eastward. Cole, let's read the manifests. Treetop, come with me."

The master's cabin reeked of cabbage and beer. Adira slid aside a shutter and ordered Treetop to chuck anything unsellable. The dwarf climbed on the master's filthy bunk and sorted things two ways: into a pile or out the porthole. Cole and Adira broke the lock on a built-in desk and perched on the bunk to decipher letters, manifests, customs clearances, rolls, and other papers. Most fell to the deck until Adira unrolled a crackling parchment.

"What's this? Boat plans."

"More cogs. Troop transports." Cole, long a pirate, squinted at the fine blue lines in the sun slanting through the hatch. "See the partitions in the hold? Eight soldiers to a berth, or four horses. Three shifts sleeping turn about. That's, uh, four hundred-some men in a single ship. Ten of those and you could capture any port on the Sea of Serenity."

"Lookee." Treetop unwrapped a roll of gauze wedged above the master's bunk. Revealed was a half-hull model of the same ship as on the plan.

Intrigued, Adira studied the desk where it curved to meet the hull. Some boatwright had worked long hours crafting the desk, even inlaying someone's initials into the sides and the drop-down leaf.

"Tree, take a peek."

"Clever." The dwarf ran his hands down the sides of the desk, then pressed on the inlaid initials. A catch clicked, and the whole side flopped open on a hidden hinge. Plucking a gray-wrapped package from a cubbyhole cleverly masked behind. Adira snorted.

"Aha! Weighted with lead. Our bold merchant captain was both foolhardy and sloppy. He should have sunk this."

Prying up the wax seal Adira unfolded more crackling papers. More boat plans with refinements; chandlers' lists of supplies needed to outfit the boats, appointments for three captains from Lucrezia, and other details. A map pinpointed in red one island amid a dimpled sea.

Adira frowned at the latitude and longitude.

"The chart position's nonsense. The numbers are too high. It must be code."

Cole squinted awhile, pushing back his kerchief to rub his bald pate. He called Badger down into the cabin, which was getting crowded. Together the veteran sailors turned the map every which way. Badger scratched his salt-and-pepper temple, muttering.

"That's a volcano island, or I'm a centaur's stern. Those are atolls in a ring of fire. And volcanoes happen only south of Albatross Alley."

Adira contributed, "This ship is leased to Princess Lucrezia. The island mustn't be too far from their sea lanes."

"If older atolls lie to the south, the map goes this way." Cole turned the map right. "Better. . . ."

Badger fingered the chart plots and juggled numbers in his head.

"Then these figures are too high by . . . eighty. Subtract eighty and you get—"

"The Isles of the Scarabs!" burst all three navigators.

Cole asked, "But what lies at this red mark?"

Adira Strongheart chuckled, a twinkle in her eye. "Let's find out!"

* * * * *

"Heave to! Drop the anchor but stand by the capstan! Jaeger, what do you see?"

"Green!" High in the crow's nest, the tiger man shielded his eyes with crooked paws as he studied the island, which rose from the sapphire sea into a smooth peak several hundred feet high. "Precious little else! No one moves on this side of the island, but there are some huts!"

"Damn. He really does have the eyes of an eagle."

From the deck of the small sloop *Robar's Arrow*, Adira and others saw only uninterrupted foliage cladding the ancient volcano. Lush vegetation in a million hues of bright green rose in tiers almost to the weathered gray peak that trickled smoke in a long plume streaming eastward. Jaeger pointed above a tiny white beach, but the humans saw only shadows amid green. The pirate chief said, "Let's take his word a village lies there. Break out the jolly boat."

Besides her Circle of Seven, which had eight members at the moment, Adira had nineteen other crewmen she'd handpicked from her two-vessel fleet. *Robar's Crush* and the prize *Pride of Perth* had been sent to Fysmatan. Leaving Badger to man *Arrow*, and arming themselves with cutlasses and some longbows, Adira chose to go ashore with Sister Wilemina, the flaxen-haired Calerian archer; Treetop the dwarf; the gloomy Virgil with his long-beaked axe; Simone the Siren, so-called because of her glorious singing; and her lieutenant Cole, who wore a straw hat to protect his bald head from the fierce sun. At the last moment Jaeger slid down the ratlines and thumped on the deck, insisting to go because the island "reminded him of home."

Crammed so a few rumps jutted over the water, the boat plugged through the sapphire waves under a tiny sail. Cole manned the tiller while Simone hauled the sheets. Wilemina, with her sharp eyes, hung over the bow and stared at the sparkling waters.

The lieutenant objected in a gentle way.

"We should heave to and wait for dark, then circle the island and look for campfires."

"That's one way," said Adira, "but I'd post lookouts atop that mountain if I were up to mischief. If so, they know we're here. If not, they're as numb as hakes, and we'll surprise 'em."

"Coral head!" In the prow Wilemina pointed, and Cole sheered away. Most tropical islands boasted a reef, but even more dangerous and erratic were the bulging rock-hard columns that hid just below the waves. The archer pointed out another, then another, so the crew was silent concentrating to thread the tricky passage.

Virgil hopped out and skidded the boat's keel high so Adira could land dry-shod. No one spoke, and all listened. The narrow beach climbed to a muddy clearing, then rose steadily uphill. Palm trees lined the shore, but magnificent tall straight teak trees soon displaced them. The forest marched steadily up out of sight. Adira and Cole whistled. The crew was puzzled until Treetop rubbed his fingers together: the durable and exotic teak made the forest worth a king's ransom. Sun slanted through the trees in green and yellow bands, and birds whirled in the golden shafts like dust motes. A herd of tiki deer barely larger than rabbits skipped away. Adira measured the signs of humanity. Houses with stout frames stippled the mountainside. The natives used fronds for easy yearly thatching, but all the thatch had collapsed. As their eyes adjusted from the searing glare to the green aquatic dimness under the trees, they counted enough big houses to hold hundreds of families. Dugout canoes lined the beach like sleeping whales, newly made but neglected, full of rainwater and dead bugs. No smell of humans or dogs or garbage floated from the village. No voices. Just an eerie silence pierced by birdsong.

Jaeger raised a white eyebrow to Adira, who nodded. Silently the tiger man cut left to circle the village, his golden stripes fading into the dim creased shadows. Adira sent Treetop circling left. The rest investigated the houses.

Cole whispered, "These fronds were cut last summer, when they were thickest. Seven months or more."

"They collapsed not long ago." Adira pried up a fallen frond, still green underneath. "So where went the natives?"

"They're still here." The rumbling voice of Jaeger startled them. "On the southern face. Hunters came seeking deer and boar and returned over the shoulder of the volcano. Too many hunters. The animals are all but wiped out."

"Of a sudden," puzzled Cole, "people abandon their houses and canoes and move to the south face, into the teeth of the tropic sun, and only come here to hunt? That makes no sense."

"Unless they're forced to stay there. . . ." One eye squinted in thought, Adira gazed up at the fabulous teak trees like pillars of black marble. "Recall what lured us to the island in the first place. . . . The day's young. Signal the ship to wait, and let's take a walk."

With Jaeger in the lead, the pirate party climbed the steady slope up a worn trail. Green leaves as big as elephant ears tickled their elbows and occasionally dumped water onto their trousers. Red and blue birds kited overhead or heckled from banana treetops.

A northerner, Wilemina asked, "This volcano is smoking. Might it erupt anytime soon?"

"Could," Treetop told her. "Smoke means it's fixing to blow, so put your feet down lightlike."

Everyone kept a straight face as the archer worried. Most knew full well a smoking volcano safely vented steam. Inert volcanoes were more in danger of blowing their tops. But for now they let the joke stand as Wilemina minced on tiptoe.

On point, Jaeger would venture ahead a hundred feet, within eyeshot, wait, then move on. As they skirted a black basalt outcrop capped with grass and tiny pink flowers, they met the full fury of the southern sun streaking toward noon. The leaf-enclosed trail baked them like an oven. Sweat ran from everyone. More than once, Virgil and Cole and Treetop missed their footing. Sister Wilemina's fair northern complexion began to glow with sunburn. Treetop plucked two elephant-ear leaves and wove them to make a green hat to shade her face.

Where the basalt outcrop fell away, they saw sea stretch to the southern horizon. Jaeger hunkered in the trail like an orange-and-black ball. The mercenaries dropped and crawled to peer over his furry shoulder.

"Now we know why they moved to this side," said Cole.

"And why they need ship plans," added Simone.

"And have scoured the island clean of food," said Treetop.

"Bad news for Fysmatan, ain't it?" asked Virgil.

"The shah won't like it, that's for certain," said Adira.

Jaeger squinted against the harsh noon light until his eyes were amber lamps split by a black crescent. He mused, "Those soldiers of Lucrezia enslave the islanders to build ships?"

"Those are Lucrezian marines like the ones we fought. Sea-soldiers, really, enlisted in the navy. But, yes," Cole said.

Along a wide beach, above the tide line marked by black kelp, eleven beamy ships were propped by crooked buttresses. They were troop transports, the same as the plans, built for mass invasion. Cole explained that the ships were almost finished, because the decks were almost laid and alongside each waited twin masts. Lucrezian shipwrights and carpenters rounded dozens of long oars with spokeshaves. Stepping the mast was traditionally the last step before launching. Once afloat, a hundred tasks remained such as ballasting with stones, running the rigging, furling the sails, and hanging the rudder, but eight or nine days would see them seaworthy. The guards wore crossed cranes painted in blue on sleeveless white tunics and nautilus-curled helmets of marines.

Cole pointed to dark-skinned humans who lugged logs and rocks to the shore, staggering, chained in pairs, whipped by guards when they blundered. "Slaves," said Cole, "because no one works in noonday sun unless goaded." Native fishermen in these latitudes would nap in grass huts and work in the evening when the fish neared the shore. Jaeger nodded but puzzled at the strange ways of humans. Cole counted the enemy and studied their work habits.

"What shall we do?" asked Treetop, his nose dripping sweat. Simone's black face shone like glass. The explorers sat in the trail to keep low. Adira sent Sister Wilemina down their backtrail to keep watch for stray hunters. The dwarf essayed, "We could sail into the offing and swoop onto the beach by night and fire those ships. There must be barrels of pitch or oil about. If not, we can improvise something that will burn like hellfire."

"What if they work by night under torches?" said Virgil.

"We must watch out to sea too," added Simone. "Those marines and carpenters must be provisioned regularly. If we get too close we could be blocked by Lucrezian reinforcements."

The crew kicked around methods to approach and burn the ships. Only Jaeger and Adira contributed nothing, the pirate leader resting, seemingly asleep, sweat coursing down into the valley of her bosom. When the Seven ran out of ideas, Adira opened one eye.

"Times like this, I know why I'm captain and you're crew."

"Eh?" asked four puzzled faces.

"Haven't I taught you," Adira chided them like children, "when you're at sea with nothing but a ship and your wits, you have to use what lies at hand to grab all you can get? You fire-bugs want to dash down there and burn the ships and tools and lumber and your own trousers, most like. Can't you think bigger? What do you see?"

"Uh, ships," said Treetop.

"Good." Adira's green eyes mocked under her green head scarf. "And ships can be sold for what?"

"Money," said everyone. "But—"

"Think, you codfish! You won't find gold floating on the waves, so make do! We're pirates, ain't we? If we stole those ships and jury-rigged them and sailed to Fysmatan, what would we be?"

"Rich!" chorused everyone.

"Fair winds, we would! Especially in wartime when ships are dear for being sunk port and starboard. We'll get hernias hauling the money home!"

"But . . ." Unused to deep thinking, Virgil was nonetheless learning. "There's three hundred marines and shipwrights, and only twenty-eight of us Robars."

"And what else?" urged Adira. "Look again."

Black brows wiggling like beetles, Virgil peeked through the green bushes. "Well, there's the slaves."

"Bonny, Virgil!" Adira biffed his arm with her fist. "*Hundreds* of slaves seething with anger, every one just waiting for the tiniest chance to snatch up a rock and smash a marine's skull!"

"So," Virgil labored on, "we . . ."

Adira laughed. "Give 'em a chance!"

Chapter 8

"Clasp hands. No talking. You can't see your feet, so don't look down. Just walk as if it's pitch dark. *Enet-seet la-tye!*"

Adira held hands with Cole, Simone, and Jaeger, whose great paw engulfed Simone's lower arm. The four crouched on the trail they'd scouted earlier. They had rested in the afternoon. Midnight with the Glimmer Moon sinking prompted their next move. The tropic night was bright with stars and the glow of white sand, so the world seem reversed, dark above and light below. Adira invoked a spell to trick light itself.

As the magic sparkled, Adira's free hand lost fingers, then palm. Her whole arm disappeared. The invisible wave swiftly seeped across her body, as cold and slimy as the caress of a mermaid. For a moment Adira felt cut in half. Then her torso vanished. She squeezed her eyes shut as they tingled. Blinking, she saw the world distorted as if underwater. The spell crackled on, eating down her left arm until only her brown hand showed.

"Remember," warned Adira. She clutched tightly to Cole's callused hand. "Don't let go, or the spell's for naught. You might feel sick in the belly. Pay it no mind."

Beside her, Cole hissed as cold fire coursed through him. She hoped he wouldn't vomit. As the grinning Simone vanished Adira cautioned, "Jaeger, are you braced up?"

The tiger man gurgled, "Do all men have this magic? And I still contend I could cross that beach without magic. What do we need with it?"

"You might slip through shadows like a shadow, but nothing could disguise Cole's ugly face or Simone's fat backside. Let me look at you." Adira curled the line in a circle, saw nothing but felt Jaeger's warm furry chest, and chuckled. "Easy as brewing slumgullion. We're off!"

Hands joined like those of children in a game, Adira led them onto the white beach. The camp and shipyard were quiet. The Lucrezians didn't work the slaves by night. The few marine pickets watched the sea and the log palisade around the slave pen. Adira almost tisked aloud at their sloppiness, for why shouldn't an enemy come overland? Stepping in sandy hollows to mask their footprints, Adira led her crew within ten paces of a marine who probably slept on his feet. The camp was a mess. Saw pits shored with boards gaped everywhere. Logs, sawn timber, wood chips, bark, broken tools, slag heaps from blacksmithing, barrels empty of pitch, and ashes from fires were scattered higgledy-piggledy amid kitchen slops, fish heads, garbage, shallow latrines, seaweed, and other trash.

Houses with sturdy frames but renewable thatch had been constructed against a cliff wall. Some Lucrezians slept there, but many marines and shipwrights slept on the hard decks of the unfinished ships to avoid sand fleas. Cooks and helpers labored at the near end of the beach to make hardtack, and fish stew, and gruel. One house was lit with braziers as officers or boatbuilders conferred, and a few on-duty marines dozed in blankets around a fire. Otherwise the island was silent except for the hush and rush of surf, a croak from a sleeping pelican, and a persistent moaning behind the palisade. As the infiltrators approached the barricade, they wrinkled their noses at an evil, eye-smarting stench. The moaning, a ghostly babble of pain and suffering, made their hair prickle.

The palisade ran from the cliff to a tall pile of rocks at the ocean, completely walling off one end of the beach. Two guards slumped against a section of wall, and Adira tugged her comrades close to see why. Gradually, in wan starlight, she noticed one entrance, the gap barely a foot wide. Only one slave could pass at a time, wriggling sideways. A log was braced in the gap as a door.

Rubbing her tingling nose with her invisible hand, Adira crept along the wall and peeked inside in vain. This was the tricky bit. Clutching Cole's sweaty hand, the pirate leader groped down the line to Jaeger.

As low as an insect's buzz, she whispered, "Where to go? We want to climb in but not step on any native who'll shout and spoil the game."

Without a word Jaeger towed the others like fish on a line, toward the ocean and up the piled rocks. Hampered by hand-holding, they slithered over the rocks, steep on the inner side. Hemmed by the palisade and cliff, the slave compound enclosed a bare few acres. Into this tiny plot were packed several hundred islanders, crowded too close for proper sanitation, hence the sickening stench. Someone wailed in pain and was hushed. Others whimpered in uneasy sleep. Children cried. From a mossy patch on the cliff trickled a thin stream of freshwater, so at least the prisoners could drink. A dark-skinned woman wearing a ratty skirt caught water in a cracked gourd. Her hair was tufted and shorn short, her breasts small and flat. Despite weariness her mind was keen. Alerted, she looked up directly where the invisible four crouched on soiled sand. She lingered awhile, watching and listening, then cradled her calabash and scurried off.

With the woman's back turned Adira abruptly let go of Cole's hand. All four pirates winked into being in their empty footprints. While Simone and Cole looked at their hands, Adira flicked Jaeger's wrist and pointed. In three silent bounds, Jaeger caught the island woman, a giant paw obstructing her face.

Adira hurried up. The woman squirmed, but Jaeger enfolded her like a rolled rug. Her dark eyes flew wide beholding Adira, but she quieted.

"Our apologies," whispered the pirate. "We've come to help, but you can't make noise. Will you be silent? Nod if so. Good. Can you take us to your headman? Good. Jaeger, release her."

The woman whipped around and recoiled at the sight of Jaeger looming above. So frightened she pressed her hand to still her fluttering heart, she signaled the four intruders to follow.

People slept coiled in the sand without coverings. Here and there a family eased the suffering of someone sick or hurt, bathing a brow with water or cooing. Many natives, the pirates guessed, had suffered lashings and beatings. Crowded together in such filth and malnourished, it was no wonder many raged with fever. Some sleepy helpers gaped at the four strangers, especially the hulking tiger man, but their guide beckoned silence. Clear across camp she led a meandering line, and finally reached a crack in the cliff wall. Faded blankets were propped on poles to give the headman and his court a semblance of privacy. By now many natives had followed, as quiet as cats, to hear the news.

The guide prodded a girl awake, clapped a hand over her mouth, and pointed within the crude tent. Soon an old woman crawled out. Her ebony skin was as wrinkled as alligator hide, her hair shone as gray as ashes, and her breasts sagged to her ragged skirt, but she sat back on her knees with the calm severity of a queen. Behind her knelt two young men bearing a family resemblance. The girl, probably a granddaughter, signed the visitors should also kneel, in a precise circle with knees touching just so. The queen was given a cracked vessel to sip from, which was passed to Adira as the leader, then each guest.

"I am Pulli, sitting as headwoman of the Unawanna. These are my grandsons, Yanni and Filla." The queen's accent gurgled like rainwater, an older dialect from far south of the Sea of Serenity, but the foreigners tuned their ears by listening closely.

"I am Adira Strongheart, captain of the Robaran Mercenaries. We've come to help you."

"Who is Robar? Your king?" asked the woman. "Why would he help us?"

Direct, thought Adira, just like herself. A small grin slipped. "Robar is—dead. I lead in his stead. We are enemies of these slavers and would steal their ships from under their noses, Your Majesty."

"You may call me Queen Pulli." The woman's eyes flickered as she calculated. "My husband and all my sons were killed by the evil ones for rebelling. I stand in until my grandson Yanni comes of age. How many are you?"

"Thirty," said Adira. When the woman didn't nod, she tried, "Three tens?"

"Not many," said the queen. "There are nine tens and four of the soldiers, all with long knives and shells like the sea turtle. And six tens and three of the woodcarvers. You have a big canoe? How many will it carry?"

Back and forth went details, both sides learning. The natives had migrated to this island sixty years ago. Since resources were limited, they had planned to split the tribe soon and move on. Then came the invaders during the rainy season. Killing anyone who disobeyed, whipping and beating the rest, they herded the natives to the bigger beach on the north, penned and chained them, and forced them to fell the teak trees and slice them into lumber in hellish saw pits.

Queen Pulli finished, "Near eight tens of my people have they butchered, and thrown their corpses into the tide for Hellab the Crab and Tuttuamo the Barracuda. Our copper weapons are not as strong as their iron. They threatened to murder all the children if we resisted more. So many soldiers can kill us all in one, two hours. So we endure until they leave."

"Likely they'll take you along." Cole spoke for the first time. "They've cut small ports in the upper decks. Their carpenters shave sweeps, very long oars, eight or nine to a side. That makes the ships row galleys, and they'll need many slaves to drive them."

The queen's mouth clamped tight. "I feared such. Then we must kill the evil ones soon."

"We'll help." Adira grinned at wicked mischief to come. "We've some pig iron in our hold. It'll make fine swords."

"We must act quickly." Queen Pulli's fat fingers, crooked from arthritis, fiddled with the waist of her skirt eager to get started. "Many of my people will fight, but some are faint of heart. And some are traitors with the black heart of Zuniwa, the Cruel Shark of the Deeps. They sleep with the enemy to gain riches."

"Can you bottle up the traitors for one day?" asked Adira. "We can fetch weapons here tomorrow night and bring our ship into the harbor to distract the foe."

"Yes." The queen's voice was firm with new hope and defiance. "We can pen the timid and the talkers and claim they are sick. So many have the wasting or the coughing sickness. If we take care, the villains will not know. They think we are mindless."

Behind, silent, Queen Pulli's two grandsons lifted their chins as if ready to fight. Adira Strongheart nodded to herself. Maybe they would at that. . . .

* * * * *

Wending the trail down the back side of the mountain, Adira Strongheart's only warning was a sandal scuffing in leaves, but it made her instinctively drop. She jerked one of her matched daggers from behind her hip and stuck it high and crosswise—just in time to deflect a sword blade slashing at her face.

The sun was barely up. Dawn had driven the adventurers back over the mountain before they were discovered: Adira's invisible mask would shine watery and pale in a tropical sunrise. Sunlight had yet to broach the volcano and penetrate the forest canopy, but the dim green light, seen as if underwater, revealed four soldiers with swords bursting from behind teak trees.

Surprise was on the Lucrezians' side, and the pirates were tired from a long night, but the numbers were even, and Jaeger was equal to ten.

Still on her rump, Adira snapped her other hand, barking, "*T'ala-farook!*"

The sphere of invisible force smacked the marine's knee. Arching for an overhead slash, he teetered and crashed. Adira would have slit his throat backhanded but three more marines charged.

The four didn't wear their seashell helmets or even white tunics painted with two blue cranes intertwined. Even as she fought Adira wondered about their mission on the abandoned side of the island, and whether reinforcements might come running. They must be either hunters sent overnight to ambush game along the trails at dawn, or soldiers larking against orders. They fought silently, so Adira favored the latter notion.

The second man to charge ran his liver onto Simone's cutlass. The black woman hopped forward to protect her chief, feet planted wide and solid for balance, then thrust from deep behind her shoulder. Though the marine was doomed, his flailing sword was a danger, and Simone instantly whipped her blade from his gut and flashed backhand to spank his sword, which cartwheeled into the elephant-ear bushes. Stricken, the man grabbed his bleeding brisket. Simone ended his agony by popping steel beneath his ear. Blood sprayed, and he dropped.

The third man balked as his two companions ran into trouble. His hesitation cost him dearly. Cole hacked overhead and walloped his sword arm just at the elbow. Tendons cut, the arm went limp as blood pulsed. Cole stiff-armed his face so he crashed on his back, then shoved his point under the man's chin and held until he stopped kicking.

The fourth man whirled to run, but an orange-black meteor hurtled over Adira's head and crashed into the man's back, crushing his ribs like twigs.

Free to act, Adira nicked the man she'd kicked across the throat. Windpipe bubbling red froth, he thrashed like a beached fish. Rising, Adira cursed.

"Where's that keg-head Marigold? She was supposed to guard the trail! If she dozed off—"

"She sleeps forever, sad to say." Having scouted under the trees, Jaeger returned with Sister Marigold limp in his arms. Her belly bore a neat slot barely three fingers wide, but all her blood had coursed down her skirt and legs and boots.

"Bastards! They must have spotted her first, and she walked right into a sword. And I accused her of sloughing off." Ashamed and angry, Adira tore some leaves down to scrub blood off her hands and snapped at Jaeger, "Don't just stand there! Take her down to shore! We'll sink her in the blue. No, wait. First dispose of this trash."

They couldn't drag the bodies into the elephant-ear bushes lest they break stalks and leave a trail. Jaeger solved the problem by hooking a corpse with black talons, hoisting it overhead, and chucking it deep into the greenery as if lobbing a ball. When all four had gone the same way, no trace remained but blood on the trail, over which the pirates sprinkled dirt and fallen leaves. Silent, they stumbled down the trail, weary from a night's escapading.

Discontent to leave a single pirate on guard to be killed, Adira picketed Jaeger and Simone to watch this side of the island, for any enemy could see *Robar's Arrow* bobbing at anchor beyond the coral heads.

She told the two, "Take turns to watch. Sleep if you can. Kill any wandering Lucrezians. We're still unknown, I hope, but we'll be old chums before another dawn. Have you got rations? We'll row some ashore. Get under cover."

Weary and heartsick, Adira ordered herself rowed to the ship. Marigold was laid in the bottom of the jolly boat, looking as small and helpless as a sleeping child. If Adira's eyes leaked tears, she claimed it came from a long fretful night. As they bumped alongside, Sister Wilemina broke down sobbing.

* * * * *

"I want you four to strap eight boarding axes on your backs, scale that volcano, and skirt the peak."

Adira addressed Heath, Sister Wilemina, Treetop, and Jaeger, who gazed in astonishment through the tropical forest up at the gray peak soaring to the heavens.

"Lower on ropes into the slave compound and stay there. The islanders will hide you until tonight. When the Glimmer Moon arcs over the Dryad Sisters constellation, share out the axes and chop through the log palisade. We don't want the slaves trapped like chickens in a coop once we start the attack."

"How will you attack the camp?" asked Treetop.

"Don't frazzle your brain, sailor," said Adira. "Trust your captain."

"What if we can't descend the slope into the compound?" asked the pale Heath.

Treetop added, "What if the Lucrezians see us climb down? They've got crossbows. We'd be picked off like dodos!"

Adira fixed the four with a steely gaze. "If you clownfish get shot full of arrows and give away our plan, you better die when you hit the ground, because I'll throttle you otherwise. Am I the only one aboard who's not blind or stupid? The cliff wall above the slave pen was gouged full of holes and wreathed in seagrapes and fronds, or didn't you notice? If you hog-footed sea cows can't climb that as easy as a caravel's ratlines then you're not pirates. Stop whining and hoist anchor!"

Humbled, the party departed.

The four followed Jaeger's twitching tail up the volcano's side. The appendage curled with Jaeger's efforts, seeming to beckon them upward like a finger. There was no trail, just a steep slope that made ankles and backs ache. In some places they climbed on all fours, tugging on roots and stiff green plants that wept white milk when bruised. At times they wanted to use the coils of rope that each carried over one shoulder, but then Jaeger would extend a paw from above and hoist them to the next root or knob, and they'd keep climbing. The axes slung on their backs were bothersome, for despite leather wrapped around the bits, they thumped and chafed the climbers' backs. Their own bows and blades weighed like anvils.

"This is worse than a mountain," said Wilemina. "A volcano can erupt any moment, can't it? You said so."

Behind the archer climbed another, the pale Heath with his pale hair streaming. "Don't believe everything Treetop tells you. I watched him sell a saddle ring to a drunken sailor and swear it was a love charm to slide on your manhood."

"On your what?" asked the virgin.

"Never mind," interrupted Treetop from above. "Just tread light there, girly, lest you break through the volcano's crust and sink in molten lava."

"We're at the peak!" announced Jaeger. "Come up and rest!"

"All praise Lady Caleria!" puffed Sister Wilemina, and her two companions chimed in.

The adventurers flopped atop soft greenery where emerald-green dragonflies buzzed by their noses. All four were fatigued from the vertical climb, and gladly shed the ropes and leather-wrapped axes. Sitting quietly, they huffed and gulped water from canteens, and gradually regained their breath. Only then did they study their surroundings.

The first thing they beheld was the sea. Seated on the verdant lip of the volcano, which was wider than they'd imagined, the sheer slope seemed only a ridge of curved green that fell to a thousand square miles of sparkling sapphire water jotted with emerald islands, a few of which trickled gray smoke blown eastward in straight plumes.

For a while no one spoke, mesmerized by the view. Just past their toes, where *Robar's Arrow* bobbed like a toy, the ocean seemed as clear as glass with a rainbow-colored sea bottom. Farther out the water was a heartbreaking blue and in the vast distance, water and sky melded in a gentle white haze.

Wilemina said, "I could stay here forever and just live on the view!"

"Come see this." Jaeger's voice startled the humans, who reluctantly picked up their burdens. Standing made them dizzy, and Wilemina caught Heath's arm lest she topple off the lip like an angel off a cloud.

The tiger led them into a miniature forest of odd trees, all identical with smooth gray bark, all the same size, like wooden columns in a cathedral. The forest floor was devoid of vegetation, for the trees interlaced roots underfoot and branches overhead so no light penetrated. Through the eerie woods Jaeger led them thirty paces. Then the tropical sun struck again, blinding in midafternoon. Standing at yet another verdant lip, Jaeger pointed down with a black claw.

The humans gasped. Far, far below, as if down a well, bubbled angry red-orange lava, pulsing like the beating heart of a giant. A gray ash or scum constantly formed and broke on the surface as flaming red gouts bulged upward and burst. Misty smoke trickled upward not far from their faces. Watching it rise and sheer east on the wind made them dizzy again.

"I was never an eagle in any past life," Treetop said.

"Fascinating," said Heath, "but I'm more interested in these queer trees. I've never seen any like them."

Without answering, the pale man stepped into the eerie forest of columns. Jaeger joined him, and said, "Banyans."

"What?" Heath peered upward, studying the crowns of the trees. "These aren't single trees, they're—"

"One tree," supplied Jaeger. "I've seen such in my homeland. Somewhere up here lives the mother tree with long outsweeping branches that touch soil and take root. Thus one tree becomes a grove, lord of all it encompasses."

"And kills," said Heath. He knelt, ebony bow upright in his hand, and examined the soil. "The tree leeches the vitality from the land. There's nothing here but thin soil, rocks, and banyan roots."

"Johan must have been such a tree in a former life," opined Jaeger, and Heath looked at him curiously.

Once the four got over the wonder of their new world, they returned to business at hand: getting down the far side of the volcano to the slave pen. The banyan grove encircled the rim like a woven wooden bracelet, so their only choice was to thread the multitudinous trunks to the southern side.

Without a word Jaeger increased his pace and flitted off until he was lost to view behind trunks. Sister Wilemina, Heath, and Treetop found themselves walking warily, spread out, stepping light, watching at all points of the compass. In part they felt silly, for what could threaten them up here? Yet the silent unending grove was as sinister as a graveyard, even though they could see sunlight winking thirty yards off at either hand.

As they crept along, feeling somewhat foolish, Treetop said, "Maybe we should find this mother tree, just to see it. It's our only chance, because I'm sure as hell not climbing anymore volcanoes in this life.

"Perhaps we should," said Heath. "I wonder if that's where—where, uh, Jaeger went."

"Then again, it sounds a lot of work." Treetop yawned. "I'd rather take a nap."

"D-don't." Caught by contagion, Wilemina yawned too, covering her mouth with a callused hand. "We've plenty more work to do. We—we can sleep in the slave pens, I hope—hope."

"If we make it." Heath's head drooped, and he stumbled on a root. "Oh! Clumsy of me. Hey, what's this?"

Peering in the gloom, Heath made out that ten, no fifty, no, a hundred tiny skeletons littered the carpet of tight-woven roots. Kneeling, Heath picked one up. His eyes wouldn't focus well, but he realized it was a bird skeleton with a needle bill, totally desiccated.

"That's strange. A flock of hum-hummingbirds must have landed—in the trees. Tree. But why did they die?" He yawned. "Oh, I really am sleepy!"

"Me too." Treetop halted and squinted past his big nose at the gloomy grove ahead, identical as everywhere. "How much farther? And where's Jaeger?"

"Dunno." Sister Wilemina sank to one knee, propped up only by her bow. "Maybe—maybe we should wait—for 'im."

"Good idea." Treetop lay down, still with axes and rope on his back, then pillowed his head on his craggy hands and snored.

"Wait." Heath leaned on a trunk and shook his head. "Something's—wrong. Dead birds . . ."

Wilemina's bow clattered on the roots below as she slumped on her knees.

"It's—it's—" Heath's iron will crumbled to rust. He sprawled down the trunk and slept.

* * * * *

Halfway around the island, Jaeger found what he sought. The tree was huge, immense, a small mountain of wood.

It sat in a depression long ago chipped into the lip of the volcano. Or perhaps the massive weight of the tree had dug the soil away, or even ground stone like flour with countless ages of countless roots drilling for nourishment. Howsoever, the tree ruled the island's rim. It would take fifty men at least, Jaeger thought, to clasp hands around that tree. The bark was dark gray and split by crevices so deep Jaeger could have slid inside them. Knobs hung on the bark as big as wagons, and patches of bark that scaled off could overlay a house. Roots were stacked on roots until wood became a maze, and Jaeger wondered how far down they reached, and if the most distant tips touched volcanic lava. The tree dominated the sky, for the lowermost branches began ninety feet from the ground. Too many branches to count, as many as stars in the sky. Some curled back to the ground within a hundred feet of the trunk. Others stretched a hundred yards to touch down. And all around the rim, which was visible beside the tree, reached the sinister dead forest of identical and grim gray trunks.

Jaeger breathed deeply to see this phenomenon, breath whistling through his black nostrils. The still air and silent hush recalled to mind stories of the legendary forest called Pendelhaven, where all the trees were white. A place of hushed beauty and infinite peace, t'was said, where no strife ever intruded.

Except this volcano-loving tree was stained dark with a sooty substance. From the volcano? Again Jaeger breathed deeply, and stifled a yawn. All this heady high-blown air, he thought, is making me sleepy. Best I find my friends and move on.

The tiger turned to go, and stumbled on a root. Righting himself, he almost pitched backward. He felt drunk, or stunned from a head blow. Perhaps I should rest. Just a little while.

Sinking to one knee, then hands, he lay down until his muzzle pressed on wood. One fang ground stingingly on the hard surface, yet he didn't try to move or shift. *Why not?*

With an effort, Jaeger jerked up his head, but keeled over and banged his shoulder hard. A sharp pain got his attention enough to make him hunt the source.

His paw touched cold metal. The ram's horn talisman, a keepsake, he'd told Hazezon Tamar. Yet the simple medallion was so much more. All the history of his people, almost, was encapsulated in a few twists of bronze. The pin had jabbed his shoulder.

Thought of his people cleared Jaeger's head a little. Thoughts of deeds left undone.

Slowly, as if crushed by a great weight, Jaeger crawled. And crawling, realized who his foe must be.

The tree.

The tree must feed. Everything must feed. The massive tree occupied the entire rim of the volcano. Eventually it must have depleted the soil, in the same way that farmers who grew the same crops year after year suffered diminished harvests. The tree needed fresh food. And one way to get it was to send out—What? A scent like salt in ocean air? A seductive perfume or golden pollen such as attracted bees to flowers? Or unseen fumes such as blossomed from rotting corpses? Whatever, the unsmelt vapors felled anything that came near, so the victim slept – forever, and their corpse fed the tree.

Realizing this helped Jaeger crawl. To sleep was to die, and he had promises to keep. Promises implicit in the worn bronze talisman that adorned his shoulder.

Cautiously, lest he black out, Jaeger concentrated on inching over the tangled gray roots. He knew the rim of the volcano wasn't wide, a few dozen feet. Surely a tiger with his prowess could crawl like a newborn cub a few feet? Voices rang in his head, purring and coughing in an antique tongue, urging him on. He gasped for air, even knowing the unseen fumes must be poisonous. He had to live, if only to see his wife, his son—

Suddenly the gray roots ended in a sort of shelf, and Jaeger was peering down at greenery, though his vision waxed black and sun bright. He'd reached the edge of the volcanic lip, where the roots overhung, and some vague distance below began the lush jungle foliage. A killing drop, perhaps, but Jaeger had no choice. Too many people counted on him to survive.

Exerting the last of his strength, Jaeger rolled off the lip of the deadly all-consuming roots and fell.

* * * * *

"Where am I?" mumbled Heath.

Wilemina clutched her flaxen skull in two hands. "Oh, my head! It aches!"

"I'm so sleepy!" yawned Treetop.

"You came within a hair's breadth of sleeping forever," rumbled a voice.

The three humans again lay on rich greenery in sunshine that made them squint. Axes and ropes lay beside them. A stiff ocean breeze reeking of salt filled their nostrils and lungs.

Heath muttered, "Salty. This much salt, it'll encrust my bow—stain it. But a delicious smell, not like that dratted grove—"

Suddenly the archer and his companions jolted wide awake. They whirled upon Jaeger and stared past the great tiger at the forbidden forest rimming the volcano.

Together they said, "The trees!"

"Parasites. One great parasite." Jaeger explained his guesses about the tree's sinister diet while the rapt listeners cleared their heads. "I succumbed too, but luckily fell on this."

He indicated the shoulder buckle of bronze, the circlet with twin curls like ram's horns inside. "This talisman is ancient. It belonged to—someone dear, who passed it to me. The sigil represents a—mighty heritage."

"But how did that device help you escape the tree?" asked Wilemina.

"It goaded me, in a way, to crawl," said Jaeger. "I fell off the lip into the jungle below."

With their vision clearing, the two humans saw now that Jaeger was dinged and scratched and scraped. Neither asked how far he'd fallen. They simply shook their heads that the tiger seemed unkillable.

"I suggest we skirt the mouth of the volcano." Jaeger's muzzle curdled in a tiger's smile. "Now come, if you will. We're expected."

Chapter 9

"You are lucky people. Your gods send you favor even this far south."

In the dead of night, the headwoman Pulli of the Unawanna received them with her usual formality, even though they were crammed in a slave pen stinking of human manure. A wail warbled from an islander suffering whip scars, part of the never-ending music of misery that surged throughout the compound like the surge of surf. Sitting behind the queen, as grave as statues, attending and absorbing every word to learn the trade of politics, were the two grandsons, Yanni and Filla. Queen Pulli repeated, "You were very lucky. Not many enter the forest of the Monarch of All Trees and get to leave."

For all the anticipated problems, the descent down the volcanic slope had been easy. Roped together, with Jaeger highest acting as anchor, the humans bounded from knob to knob, helped by clasping vines. Oddly too, their brief and almost lethal sleep had refreshed them better than fine wine and a night's rest. In no time they had skidded to a shelf sheltered by greenery that overlooked the slave compound. Memorizing the slope's face, its protuberances and green patches, they waited until full dark and completed their descent into the malodorous prison. The islanders immediately met them and guided them to the queen in her tattered outdoor throne room.

"Many smoking islands in these seas wear a crown of Mummuir, the Monarch of All Trees," explained Pulli. "The seeds are blown by the wind from the south, or perhaps the birds carry them in their droppings. The Monarch drinks the blue air and soaks up the heat of the volcano, then banishes every living thing from its sight. A cruel ruler is Mummuir, and greedy. Too greedy. He eats all the nourishment in the soil and then demands more. Anyone who steps into his lair stays, forever. That is why we *never* climb volcanoes."

"Oh," said the four visitors. Jaeger sat awhile, remembering his encounter with the majestic tree. In its presence, he'd felt an almost-holy reverence, as if the tree were not only alive but a thinking being, brooding and plotting with infinite patience to increase its fortunes. This Monarch Mummuir might even be a wood elemental, thought the tiger, but said nothing.

"Had I known you would climb so high, I could have warned you." The queen shrugged round shoulders. "I am sorry you suffered, for you and 'Dira of the Strong Heart have been kind to our people, strangers though you be."

"We hope to be kinder, and useful, Your Majesty," intoned Jaeger, as formal as the queen. He laid a pair of axes before the queen's fat knees, and explained their plan.

Details were mapped out. Pulli sent her royal page running to fetch named islanders. Soon the pirates were introduced to two men and two women, scrawny but still knotty-armed despite near-starvation and abuse from the Lucrezian slavers. The four had been expert canoe carvers before "the evil ones" came. Sister Wilemina, Jaeger, Treetop and Heath all agreed to bear one axe to chop the palisade uprights.

As promised, Queen Pulli had ordered any islanders who were timid or potential collaborators to be trussed up and stashed away. So far, she said, the Lucrezians suspected nothing.

"Good," said Jaeger, glancing at the sky to find the Dryad Sisters. "Then we have a few hours to wait. Best we get some sleep."

"Don't say *sleep!*" chirped Wilemina.

* * * * *

All the previous day, Adira's pirate crew had frantically crafted weapons.

With much rowing back and forth, most of the pirates moved ashore. Cole assembled a tiny forge with a precious handful of coal to chop steel bars into quarters. Pirates whittled saplings, split the ends, and bound the points with rawhide that shrank in the sun. For a while they worked to Simone's siren singing, but even she ran out of breath and tunes. Crewmen sweated to turn the balky grindstone while Simone or Badger ground points sharp. With one breath they reluctantly praised Adira's foresight in having "worthless" booty shifted to *Robar's Arrow*. In the next grunt they cursed her for slave driving. Hours passed as raw steel, green hides, and harvested wood became near two hundred wicked stabbing spears.

The day waned, but despite the tropical heat, no one got any rest.

When someone grumbled, Adira snarled, "If you have strength to complain, you're not tired! I missed last night's sleep, and we won't get any tonight, but I'm not bitching, so belt up!"

By torchlight pirates fashioned torches, sharpened the ship's cutlasses, boarding pikes, fighting axes, and other weapons. Some they lashed into handy bundles and ferried ashore, while others were stacked and tied near at hand aboard *Arrow*. Munching jerked beef and hardtack while they labored, they stripped the ship's upperworks of anything unneeded in the coming fight. More preparations were laid, the workers fumbling like zombies, until Adira declared they could nap. Seemingly they'd just closed their eyes before the pirate leader booted their ribs and shushed their groans under a star-spattered sky. Banging and thumping in the dark, the pirates donned baldrics hung with cutlasses and axes and daggers, then heaved heavy bundles of greenwood spears and torches onto their shoulders. Prodded, sixteen pirates trekked the steep slope up the volcano's shoulder.

"I bloody well hope Jaeger and Treetop 'n the rest gain that slave pen without bustin' all their legs," groused Badger. "I don't look forward to fighting a hundred ugly marines with a bundle of sticks."

"Belay there, blabbermouth," hissed Adira from the front, "or I'll lop your wagging tongue!"

Swallowing complaints, the crew trudged uphill in the dark and hoped their captain had laid her plans well.

Soon enough, Adira hissed, "Halt! Where's the Glimmer Moon?"

Where the path opened onto the beach, they cast their eyes to the heavens to mark the Dryad Sisters. Less than an hour to go, Adira judged, before the smaller moon arced over the western arm of the constellation. Virgil shifted a bundle of spears to set them down, but Adira punched his chest.

Drawing the sixteen close, she hissed, "Same plan as before. The first four'll link hands, and I'll render you invisible. Walk on the softest sand and don't let your bundles rattle. Steer where the palisade joins the cliff. Watch the moon, but wait for Jaeger and Heath to hack at the logs. Half of you help pull down logs and half untie the bundles. Be ready to strike the torches alight and give spears to the natives as they rush out."

"What if they don't rush out," asked a pirate, "but leave the fighting to us?"

"Then we die with blood on our blades and a battlesong on our lips," growled Adira. "Any more cockeyed questions?

Right, join hands, you four. Cole, you lead. *Enet-seet la-tye!*"

One pirate gasped as the cold tingling rushed over her skin, but the rest stood it stoically. One after another, pirates faded away under the stars, then were gone. Only the faint chuff of sand gave any clue four people were sneaking off.

Adira waited a moment before enspelling the next quartet, lest they blunder into the first four. Soon she packed them off, Badger in the lead.

The third group was halfway cloaked, with one pirate split down the middle, when a cry shattered the night like thunder.

"Alarm! Alarm! Enemy in the camp! Rouse, all!"

"Heart of a hart!" Concentration broken, Adira's spell splintered, so two pirates who'd vanished winked into view. "Our surprise has gone to smash! Keep those bundles high and follow me! Stay together!"

Ripping a cutlass from its worn leather sheath, the pirate leader raced across the sand so fast her crew stumbled to keep up. A hundred feet in, her first four sneak-thieves had parted hands and their magic shell evaporated. They looked about dumbfounded as Lucrezian officers charged from the big houses framing the cliff. Most were half-asleep and rattled by the alarm, but some veterans had thrown on baldrics and shields and vaulted outside, some only in loincloths and some lacking even that. The unfinished ships lined on the shore buzzed with activity, as busy as broken anthills. Officers kicked marines awake and yelled for guards to kill the interlopers. A half-dozen pickets converged on Adira's crowd but slacked their pace as they counted twenty or more pirates.

"What do we do?" shouted Cole.

"Get to the palisade!" shrieked Adira, too busy to curse. She screeched across the beach, "Jaeger! Chop logs! The rest'a you, *run!*"

The pirates pelted headlong toward the palisade, but the sand sucked at their feet treacherously and slowed them.

The beach was more than half a mile long, and they'd barely traversed half when the marines swarmed off the unfinished boats. A hundred armed foes raced to intercept the pirates, clattering into a steel-edged wall lying between them and their goal.

"This way!" Adira swerved and almost sent Virgil sprawling.

The marines and shipwrights numbered nine hundred, Adira knew, so a pitched battle could only end with pirates' heads stuck on pikes. Thus she swiveled her force toward the central house of stout teak.

"Up the stairs and give 'em steel!"

Half-naked, but armed, the officers blocked the doorway. As cutlass-wielding thugs pounded up the stairs, the veterans dived off the porch or fled into the house to sail out of the windows. Adira's valiant seventeen stampeded into the house and clapped shut the doors, which were not solid, but layered with slats to admit a breeze but keep out tropical rain.

Pirates wrenched down the flimsy shutters.

Badger bellowed over the banging, "Now what?"

"Damned if I know!" Adira Strongheart shoved her crew over to bracket the windows. She snuffed candles with her hand. "Unbundle the spears! We can thrust through the windows—"

The front doors splintered as four doughty marines thundered inside. Hard behind them charged a dozen more. No one could see in the dark house, though polished seashell helmets and white tunics made glittering and glowing targets. Simone thrust a spear into someone's ribs. Virgil shot a crossbow and nailed a marine to a post. Badger swung a bench and bowled over a marine that Cole had already stabbed. More hard-handed veterans charged inside. For furious minutes there rang a frightful clanging, shouting, screaming, and thrashing. A marine smashed into a post so hard the roof beams creaked. A pair ganged up on Cole and crushed him into a corner. Simone swung her crossbow like a club and flattened a man. A female marine with looped braids bashed Simone's jaw with a knuckle-duster sword guard. Spears flew like surf spray. Virgil and Badger lugged a table like a battering ram and cleared the doorway. Pirates pitched the benches and tables into the gap, then sobbed for breath.

"Who's alive?" called Adira. "Answer!"

Names tolled in gasps. Badger, Simone mumbling, Virgil, others of Adira's pirate crew. Adira replied, "Where's Cole?"

"Dead," called a voice from the corner.

Adira bit her lip, picturing Cole as he kissed his wife and children goodbye.

Not daring to show weakness, she snarled, "Pick up the spears! We're not done yet! When the *Arrow* rounds the island she'll see something's wrong, maybe fire the ships—"

"Speaking of fire . . ." said Badger.

Light blossomed between cracks in the floor. This had a sturdy frame raised six feet off the ground to avoid storm swells. Lights flickered at all four corners, then flared as trash or rags ignited. Everyone trapped inside smelled the oily smoke.

"We'll burn!" whimpered a man.

"Belay that!" Adira's voice rose with the crackling of flames. A hiss like a tea kettle piped steadily as leaves and trash and driftwood burned, shoved under the house by Lucrezians. Flames licked through cracks like giant questing fingers. Sweat ran down their faces in oily drops that seemed to sizzle on the floor. Wallboards at corners charred and puffed flame. The pirates retreated to the center of the room, butting into posts and each other. The fire followed them hungrily. Smoke tickled and scorched their throats causing them to cough.

Adira sneezed and wheezed, "When we can't stand it, we'll rush the door. Yes, I *know* they'll be waiting—"

"Listen!" hissed a woman by a window.

Down the beach arose a roar like surf in storm. An eerie squawking, yowling, almost a fierce singing, jangled the listener's nerves. Badger blurted, "What the hell—"

"Unblock the door!" commanded Adira.

"The marines—" objected Badger.

"*Unblock the door!*" Adira almost cleared it with her command.

Furniture was lobbed outside. By the fitful fires burning underneath, the defenders saw no one awaited them on the gritty sand. From the double doorway Adira looked right.

"Catch up those spears! We've got customers who need 'em!" Bandana and ragged shirt tails flying, Adira Strongheart leaped into the night like a panther.

Pirates with their arms full of spears clattered down the wide stairs. Then they recognized the roaring. Past scrambling Lucrezian marines the pirates saw the slave pen lacked uprights as if rotten teeth had been plucked from a jaw. Through the gaps in the starlit night surged half-naked screaming islanders free and anxious for revenge. Eight carried boarding axes, and amid the bunch raced Heath, Treetop, and Sister Wilemina. Towering head and shoulders above all bounded Jaeger like some primal tiger-spirit from the clouds.

"*Robars!*" Adira Strongheart waved her cutlass onward. "*Robars!* Bring up those spears, you bottom-feeding goosefish!"

Never were orders more quickly undertaken. Lucrezian marines, sailors, and some shipwrights had formed a thin line that wavered in the face of screaming natives. Pirates juggling spears dashed up behind the thin wall almost onto the marines' heels. Before the Lucrezians knew what happened, spears were lobbed over their heads. Like cats pouncing, the Unawanna scooped up the stabbing spears, even tussling with one another to grab a weapon. More spears flew until a hundred or more were delivered. By then the Lucrezians had turned in the dimness to see the grinning pirates heaving the weapons. Conflicting orders from officers ripped up and down the line. The marines dithered a moment too long—the worst mistake in warfare.

With a bloodcurdling cry, the liberated Unawanna charged their tormentors. Howling with joy at their own rescue, Robar's Mercenaries rushed with blades swinging.

Blood spattered the sand in a long red line from the ocean to the cliffs. Caught in a pincer by twin enemies, the marines braced back to back, locked shields where they could, and slashed figure-eights and windmills with their swords. Nothing saved them. Natives with hate stoking their hearts almost ran into the blades to strike their foes. Spears outreached short swords, and quickly the natives drove jagged steel into faces, throats, armpits, bellies, groins, thighs. Any marine who fell was immediately swarmed by ten natives, some with spears, some with only sticks or rocks or bare fists. The enraged islanders hammered their enemies without mercy, paying back every lash with a hundred blows. An officer had his head grabbed by three strong men and women, his arms and legs grabbed by others who twisted as if braiding rope. The unlucky Lucrezian choked before his head was ripped off like a chicken's. A marine speared in the stomach killed her attacker with an overhead stroke, her last. More natives grabbed onto the spear and hoisted the woman overhead, then jostled the spear so the woman slid slowly down the shaft, impaled through the guts, shedding blood like rain. A marine who tried to burst free of his circle was pounced upon. His face was jammed into sand so he inhaled it and suffocated. Nine marines cut off from their comrades were herded at spearpoint into the surf. When it bubbled over their heads, some sank and were pinned by eager feet. Some were speared like crabs. One marine escaping through a red cloud banged headfirst into what he thought was coral, but turned out to be the yawning jaws of a shark attracted by blood. At the cliff end, two marines were knocked down, grabbed by the feet, and swung like children until their skulls bashed outthrust stone.

Revenge made a feast of slaughter. Dead marines and sailors were stabbed a hundred times to red pulp. Some natives hammered bare fists on corpses, breaking bones and mangling flesh. A hundred more atrocities were committed before the last Lucrezians was dragged by the heels and shoved into the surf to be eaten by sharks. A mocking victory song floated on the air, sung in a hundred different keys that melded into a single chaotic chorus of joy.

Weary to the marrow of her bones, Adira Strongheart sank to her knees in the sand for a moment's rest. Robaran Mercenaries joined her, just sitting or lying in red-speckled sand, happy to do nothing. To stay still felt divine.

Yet Adira had to tend politics when Pulli waddled up on arthritic feet, her white hair puffing like a cloud. With her, somber and quiet, came one young grandson. Adira could remember neither boy's name. The headwoman sat in the sand with her grandson behind. Adira forced herself to sit up and pay attention, though she craved sleep.

Cutting formalities short, Queen Pulli proclaimed, "Thank you. Our people are free through your efforts. Anything we possess is yours, from this day forward until the sun sinks into the ocean one last time and extinguishes."

"Your Majesty, we are flattered." Adira was taken aback by the woman's regal sincerity. "Our part was small compared to that of your valiant people. They rushed the Lucrezians with only bare hands or rocks to start. Lucky my crew could chop the walls as the Lucrezians sounded that alarm—which reminds me. How did our plan go awry? My pirates were invisible and quiet, so how—"

Queen Pulli raised a fat hand. "It brings my heart shame to know the answer, and more shame to tell. My own flesh and blood, my second grandson Filla, betrayed us."

Adira blinked as the traitor's brother set his face hard in embarrassment and anger.

With a bosom-heaving sigh, Queen Pulli went on. "I do not know his true desire. I only guess he wanted the ancestral throne, to supplant his brother Yanni, who has remained loyal through this trial. Knowing he would never ascend to reign while his brother lived, Filla crept to the enemy and uttered our secret. Perhaps he planned to rule when many were taken as slaves. No tongue can tell now, for Filla was seen among the enemy, run down, and torn to flinders. So his blood feeds Zuniwa the Cruel rather than fosters the heritage of our people."

No one spoke. A raucous hurrah from the last house announced the discovery of four Lucrezian carpenters hiding. They were dragged screaming and pleading from the house by a hundred hands, banged down the wooden stairs, danced and spat upon, kicked to roll over and over, and otherwise played with as a cat torments a mouse. Even Adira's tough pirates turned their heads rather than witness the Lucrezians chipped to pieces by crude spears. The invaders had earned their fate by seizing the island, killing protesters, and enslaving the populace. Still, it was horrid to see the hot vengeance they'd stirred in the hearts of innocent people.

"Cruelty brings its own punishment," murmured Adira. Oddly, she wondered how her ex-husband Hazezon Tamar fared in Palmyra's preparations for Johan' onslaught. She breathed, "Fyndhorn's Fish! When that dam breaks, these horrors will seem a midsummer's fair. . . ."

* * * * *

Flushed with victory, the Unawanna sang the days away as they helped the Robaran Mercenaries finish the waiting ships. Since Adira needn't outfit the boats for war, only seaworthiness, details quickly fell into place. Gaps in the decks were patched over. Masts were hoisted and stepped and jury-rigged with simple sails found in a shed on the shore. Pirates and islanders rove rigging like spiders spinning webs, then didn't bother to smear them with pitch for waterproofing. Anchors and cables were heaped on decks and dogged to the scuppers instead of being fed down hawseholes. Rudders were hung in their iron brackets, but steering ropes were just warped over the taffrails.

People were stunned as, late one balmy evening, Badger reported, "Captain, we'd be ready to sail once we topped off the water casks—if we had the crews."

Adira Strongheart stared at the looming cogs, seeming as eager and poised as a gam of whales launching their breasts into the salt waves. Adira had dreaded this moment many a sleepless night, for the pirates were shorthanded. Even a skeleton crew for one ship would require fifteen hands to haul the sails and man the tiller, and she had but twenty-seven pirates all told. Fashioned of green wood, the ships would leak like nets until they swelled, so pumps must be manned day and night. She'd juggled numbers until dizzy but always reached the same grudging conclusion: she could take only one ship along with *Robar's Arrow* for protection. One ship sold in Fysmatan would provide enough money for new crews, provided she could find any in wartime, to sail hither for the rest of the green fleet. New boats jury-rigged were notoriously slow, and the two voyages might take months, with every potential for disaster such as storms, rival pirates, random sinking, or even the war ending prematurely, causing boat prices to plummet. Meanwhile Palmyra and Bryce raced to butt heads like war mammoths.

"Captain," Badger interrupted Adira's churning thoughts. "It's not my place to advise, but we might hire some natives as a jury crew to make Fysmatan."

"Wh-what?" Adira shook her head as the idea bounced off.

Badger waved a horny hand. "While you've been supervising ashore, I've watched these natives work. Most are quick and strong and canny. They know the sea, like I know a beer, from years of fishing. I sounded out a few, asking if they'd like to sign on. A lot do. They come from the south, you see, and have never traveled north of here. If we spread our crew through the fleet as officers, barring storms and sea serpents, I don't see why we can't make Fysmatan in three weeks, the elements willing and knock on wood. You did lecture us to use what lay at hand to grab all we can."

For a moment Badger thought he'd erred, aping Adira's advice, for her stare bored into his skull like an auger. Then she smiled like a love-struck girl, clapped her hands to his scruffy face, and kissed his nose, laughing with delight. While the old sailor rubbed his tingling nose, Adira Strongheart skipped down the shore hollering.

"Queen Pulli! Where are you? We must talk! We're all going to be rich, rich, rich!"

* * * * *

Adira Strongheart dipped a quill pen in ink and scrawled her name in bold letters across the yellowed page, then drew a heart and hammer, her personal sigil. She grinned for joy as the shipyard owner pried open a brass lock and dropped six bulging sacks upon his scarred desk.

Outside the cramped office, seagulls wheeled and keened as fishing fleets entered harbor at dusk, each fleet escorted by a rakish cutter full of Fysmatan marines. The harbor was packed with ships, so many a person might hop from deck to deck to shore. Even at this late hour, the boatyard rang to mallets and caulking hammers and barking adzes, for the war with Princess Lucrezia waxed hot, and the city-state rushed to ferry soldiers and supplies to the fronts.

The shipyard owner rubbed his white brow and wheezed, "We can't thank you enough for those cogs. We'll get them shipshape in ten days' time. Our shah is hungry to strike those Lucrezian bastards where it hurts. Now we can teach the villains a lesson."

"Good luck and smooth sailing." Adira couldn't care less if Fysmatan and Lucrezia burned flat. She had her own troubles like getting back to Palmyra before it was sacked by a cruel and callous despot. Loading the bulging sacks into the arms of Badger and Jaeger and Virgil, she asked, "Can you direct me to the Mariners' Guild? I need to hire watermen for river barges back home."

"Ouch." The shipbuilder rubbed his white caterpillarlike brows. "There's a mighty chore. We can't find enough hands ourselves. The Serenity's been stripped clean of any man or woman can tell a halliard from a halibut. We hire farm lads and lasses as never trod wood, and glad to get 'em. Seasoned watermen are scarcer'n snow."

"Really?" Adira gazed at the harbor, where seeming hundreds of able-bodied sailors, boatmen, shipwrights, and more bustled. "Your war makes you that shorthanded? I didn't think—"

"Not our war," said the shipwright. "Up the Bay of Pearls, a wizard named Johan fancies himself an emperor. He's landlocked up the River Toloron, I'm told. He's paying the highest wages ever offered, and watermen flock to Bryce to sail upriver before the emperor changes his mind. He's assembling a whole barge fleet, they say."

Despite tropical sun slanting through windows, Adira Strongheart felt a chill. Her Circle of Seven shuffled their feet and shifted heavy sacks of coin. The pirate queen murmured, "Barges and watermen . . . That puts a fire under our feet. Stir your stumps, Robars! We sail with the tide!"

Chapter 10

"Love of ten thousand virgins!" exclaimed Adira. "Look at the place! I hardly know it!"

"You've sailed away a mayor and returned a governor," jibed Badger.

"Where do we tie up?" asked Simone, who'd taken Cole's place as navigator and sailmaster. "Our old mooring is drowned, and those new docks are as busy as a beaver den. Scarzam's Dragon, is there any room left for honest pirates in this town?"

Adira Strongheart and her crew gaped as their pinnace bobbed idly at anchor. They'd come home to the Bay of Pearls with two ships loaded with loot that they'd left to Treetop to cash and distribute to over a hundred pirates. Adira had hurried on toward Palmyra, curious to see how her village fared. Jaeger, Simone, Badger, Heath, Virgil, and Wilemina accompanied her. Now, instead of a sleepy village, they found a near-fortified peninsular stronghold.

Unfloodable and unsinkable, Palmyra occupied a shelf of bedrock where the River Toloron carved a hairpin curve, just a sleepy village on a lazy river. Now a wide stone dam and narrow spillway blocked their path, a rock wall had arisen as if by magic in the desert. The dam was not tall, only rising a dozen feet, but it trapped an immense volume of water. By climbing the pinnace's slender mast, the returnees could see a new lake had drowned the hairpin, filling an entire basin of land. A glittering blue expanse, acres and acres of water cooled the eye and soothed the soul after months on salt waves.

"It's magnificent!" Even the irreverent Simone was moved by the brilliant sight as she dismounted the mast. "Who'd believe our dusty little rat's nest could sport such a beautiful lake?"

"I liked our old rat's nest." Adira Strongheart stood frowning with one boot on the gunwale. "This lake will prove a pox. It'll attract every beggar and vagabond and troublemaker from all Jamuraa."

"You mean," sniped the puckish Badger, "people like us?"

"It'll mean more money in our pockets in the long run," added Simone.

"There's not going to *be* a long run," snapped Adira. "When we were a pesthole, no one cared a fig. Now that Palmyra's the paradise of the Sukurvia, Johan has one more reason to snap it up. Only the rich get robbed, remember. I should have vetoed this cockeyed scheme. Let's get ashore. Moor us at that floating wharf, Simone, and ram anyone who crosses our course."

An hour later, Adira and her Seven toured the town with old Declan, Palmyra's official city engineer. A brawny daughter with flaxen hair and a stonemason's apron guided the blind man, his gnarled hand gripping her sleeve.

"We've endured more chaos than a fleet in a funnel," the elder chuckled dryly. "We're low on food, steel tools, horsepower, copper, wicker, wood—you name it. The only thing we're fat with is stone. And new folk looking for work. Too bad I have no way to pay 'em."

"Money we've got." Adira grew agitated as she stomped along behind Declan and his daughter. Everywhere bubbled changes that ensured Palmyra would never again be a sleepy little burg.

Previously she'd known most citizens by sight, but now strangers filled the streets, all of them busy. Black-skinned freighters led a placid elephant hauling a stoneboat heaped with rock. Two hawk-nosed desert elves with black hair and piercing eyes haggled with a shaggy woman selling pots. Mud-smeared dwarves slathered bricks with adobe, laying a wall even as more dwarves atop spindly ladders fitted red roof tiles. Northmen with flaming pink sunburns leveled a house with crowbars and sledgehammers. A caroling water seller sold her last gourd. Two white-robed faith keepers admonished a whore with hennaed hair while a Palmyran in a yellow smock looked on. An armored man waited while a blacksmith adjusted his visor. When Jaeger shucked his enveloping disguise of desert robes and walked naked in his striped hide and breechcloth, hardly anyone noticed. Goblins in rags pursued a panting dog.

Adira stared at that. "Goblins run loose? They're only good for bait! And who invited those Keepers of the Faith? And that joker in the yellow smock with the red crescent, isn't that Darshan, who used to crew with us?"

Declan chuckled. "The goblins were stealing and digging up garbage and generally making mischief, so we imposed a bounty on stray dogs, cats, and rats. They get a penny a tail and can keep the meat. We kicked the Keepers out, but they came right back, claiming Palmyra was their calling. They expect the archangel Anthius to alight any day and scourge this rat's nest of sinners."

"I'll lay odds on our rats," quipped Badger.

"And me. Makes me wish I had eyes to see that fight. And Darshan in the yellow smock is one of Palmyra's new deputies."

"*Deputies?*" burst the Seven.

"Aye," snorted Declan. "Someone's got to keep order. Cole's wife was voted sheriff. A first for this viper pit, eh?"

"Hell's bells." Bewildered, Adira asked, "How many folk camp here?"

"No idea," said Declan. "More than the two or three hundred you left behind. Couple thousand, maybe four thousand. And we can't house a third. Most sleep in the desert in tents."

"Four thousand." Adira gaped at the crowds. "Johan's got tens of thousands ready to scourge us like a locust plague."

"Pub talk," countered Declan. "He's not got nine thousand, say our spies."

"*Our* spies?" chirped Adira.

"You have been absent awhile, ain't ye?" Declan inclined his head as if he could see. "I meant scouts. Decent folk employ scouts while villains employ spies. Any road, Johan won't find Palmyra an easy nut to crack. Celeste, bear south."

As the Circle of Seven tagged along, Declan brought them to the tip of a wharf that overlooked the new dam. As wide and flat as a cart path, the barrier had been laboriously laid stone by stone by human, orc, and dwarven hands, a touch of magic, and the efforts of horses, oxen, camels, and elephants. The spillway was constructed of pegged posts and boards that let engineers control the level of the lake. As the river reached the bottleneck, an avalanche of seething water rushed into the lower river. A new oxbow lake spread westward from the dam for more than a mile. The lake water was murky and brown, swirling with newly churned silt, but Declan judged it would clarify in a few months. Already, he said, fish from upstream bred in great numbers. Fishing was a new hobby, and a boy and girl casting lines off the dam pulled out a whopping silver fish to prove it. Since Palmyra sat on a stone knoll, only a few ramshackle huts and wharves had been drowned.

"That's not all," announced Declan with pride. "Come see how Palmyra will soon be an island fortress!"

Nestled in the hairpin river, Palmyra had only one small neck of land connecting it to the desert. That too was about to change. Not far above the dam ditchdiggers sweated in morning sun to sink a moat. Palmyra's bedrock made it a tough job. Human men and women, dwarves, northern barbarians, and even three filthy ogres drilled and chipped and smashed rock with steel bars and sledgehammers.

Declan noted, "Some goblins hint they've got a magic black powder that'll fracture stone like lightning, but either they're lying or holding out for a better price. . . ."

The party walked beside the ditch, a tortured line that writhed to avoid the toughest bedrock. Stone quarried from the ditch was immediately packed tight into a new city wall.

Declan led them across the ditch down a twisty path into the desert so they could view the whole fortification from a distance.

"I hoped to raise the walls all around the city ten feet high. If we have time before Johan sweeps upon us."

Adira pushed her green headband onto her tangled chestnut curls to wipe her forehead. With spring warming the desert, the noon sun grew hot. Sweat trickled between her breasts, and she scratched indelicately. Gawking, she tried to make sense of the scene. Palmyra's neck, just under a mile wide, was being cut deep and piled high by hundreds of laborers, an unassailable defense of moat and wall. At the center skilled masons, human and dwarf, carefully erected twin towers of stone to brace a stout gate. They built slowly to be exact, chipping and fitting the foundation stones without gaps, for an attack would first strike this weak link in the chain. Cut off from Palmyra were only a few huts and tent sites and stone corrals for penning sheep. Whereas before wayfarers had simply trickled into town by rude paths, already a formal road was being beaten flat by elephants and mule teams steering for the yet-unbuilt gate. Adira turned to look at the desert, seeing it in a new light. Pebbly folds and rills were jotted by thornbrush, overgrazed grass, and pockets of wiry cedar. The rolling hills restricted eyeshot to a few miles.

Adira murmured, "I suppose a watcher posted in the new gate towers will see ten miles or more. We could even raise a derrick."

"We might erect towers on those two hills," added Heath. "With a clear run back to the gate."

"Put spears in a ring around the tower tops," said Simone. "Make them long enough to reach the ground. We could sink the shanks through holes in the floors. . . ."

Together, consulting with Declan, Adira and her circle debated suggestions. At one point the pirate leader noted Badger grinning, and asked why.

"Didn't take you long to find the spirit of the game," chuckled the old advisor.

"Oh." Adira was embarrassed at her swift change of heart from grumpiness to enthusiasm. "Building a solid defensive line is no harder than conning a fleet to storm a town or flank an armada."

"Ah," chortled Simone. "So you approve of a prettied-up Palmyra?"

"I didn't say that!" snapped Adira, and stormed toward town. Behind her back, her Seven shrugged and followed.

The strolling survey led to the northern waterfront where the river bent west. Another foundation for a city wall was being laid atop a line where huts and warehouses and wharves had been demolished. Adira noted the river had swollen to twice its width where it entered the lake.

She asked, "Will we just call it 'the lake'? That seems drab. Everything needs a name."

Declan chuckled, "Wags call it Johan's Joy, because we hope his army and navy founders in it."

Adira Strongheart watched the hustle-bustle and shook her untidy curls. "I can't fathom it. I know our town meeting voted to defend the city, but why does everyone now break their backs? People in this dump were too lazy to kick a dog out a door before!"

"It's queer, I'll grant you." Declan's frosted eyes seemed to gaze north toward Tirras, one hundred-thirty leagues distant. "Some wanted no truck with fortifying, and walked out. Some skipped to Bryce or beyond, some retreated to the desert. More'n a few went north to join Johan's crusade, the knot-headed fools. But that just means everyone who stays wants the town defended, either digging directly at it, or selling meat and beds and what-all to the workers. It's not just Palmyrans. Hazezon's sent near four hundred men from Bryce, and promises more. Enez and Kalan sent some too. More important, Tamar's scrounged up tons of food and shipped it by barge; a good thing since we can't buy from Tirras. It takes beef and bread and beer to keep this lot diggin'."

"We know. We just came from Bryce," said Adira. "Hazezon's up to his armpits in intrigue. Spies spy on other spies. Everyone's hunting able-bodied workers. Anyone who wants to sail upriver has to persuade Bryce's palace guards they're not a double-dyed liar. Meanwhile sailors are crimped off the docks and stuffed in holds; then whole fleets set sail for Buzzard's Bay so men can march overland to join Johan! Half the goods imported for Palmyra end up stolen and sold on the black market—Oh, it's a mess! The city's a sieve. If Hazezon weren't overseeing operations, we'd get nothing!"

"And everyone who joins Johan's army will pass this point to invade the southlands," finished Declan. "So we'd best prepare a hearty welcome. Too bad we can't toil by night."

Adira squinted at the noon sun, distracted by a million details. Once the rest of the Robars arrived, she must feed and house them—

"Wait," said Adira. "What? Why can't we work by night? It's better than frying in this flaming sun. Those crowbars and hammers must get so hot they sear calluses off your palm."

"That they do, but we've queer goings-on once the sun sets. A score of folk have disappeared."

"Disappeared?"

"Aye. Some working and some carousing, but plain gone. Vanished by the docks. Just puddles left where they were standing, like they melted. Folks say a monster lurks in the river and don't like our dam, and it snatches victims off the docks for sacrifice."

"Poppycock!" spat Adira. "What fool would believe that? Before that dam went up, the river was as clear as glass and so shallow in summer a child could wade across! Where would a monster live?"

Declan blew out his bristly cheeks. "It's no good talking. Come dark, people bar their doors or stay bunched up like sheep. We're falling behind schedule, and from what you say, we can't waste an idle day or night."

Clearly this problem topped Adira's infinite list, for her crew was most qualified to fix it.

"Don't fret, Declan. We'll beach your monster. Nothing can kill the Circle of Seven, at least not all at once. Am I right?"

Surprisingly, Simone, Badger, Jaeger, and the rest stayed quiet. Adira fixed them with an icy glare as workmen bumped her elbow lugging sacks.

"Are you pirates or pissants? What's wrong?"

Badger scratched a peeling nose. "Well, Captain . . . Killing men's one thing. Hunting watery beasties that we don't know jack-all about—"

"Shut your trap, you scurvy wharf rat!" Adira spat at their superstitious cowardice. "You'll scour the night streets and kill this thing, or I'll splice your spine with a cat-of-nine! Jewels of the jester, I hope it does eat you yellow rats and chokes on your miserable bones! Then I can enlist a crew worthy of the name and not a school of gutless guppies! Get back to the pinnace and sharpen your cutlasses! You'll patrol as soon as dusk drops!"

* * * * *

"I wish you'd make more noise, Stripes." Badger groused under his breath as four of Adira's Seven scouted black empty streets and alleys along the waterfront. "You padding beside as silent as the ghost of death gives me the creeps."

"My apologies." Jaeger's voice, coming from on high, was a purr in the velvet darkness. "Perhaps I should also half-turn my left heel and scuff it, as you do."

"I broke this leg in the Sultan of Shaibara's navy. Our main mast let go in a battle, and a falling spar smashed my leg like an egg. For thanks I got a handful of coins and a discharge from honest men. I've been pirating ever since."

"Why don't you two shut up," hissed Simone, "before the water monster seeks the source of squawking?"

"Life's been dull," quipped Badger, "but when the monster comes, matey, we'll give you first shot. Which way now?"

Jaeger, Badger, Simone, and Sister Wilemina had tramped seeming miles during their night shift along the docks. Back and forth and roundabout they searched, tripping over sleeping pigs and building rubble, bumping into walls down stinking alleys, surprising drunks and lovers and stray cats. By Adira's orders, they carried neither torch nor lantern. Talking hadn't been forbidden, and Badger babbled to keep his spirits up.

"I'm not afraid, mind you. It's just not my desire to be eaten by night stalkers when so many others deserve the honor. All still here? Good." Badger rapped his knee against a new stone foundation and cursed colorfully. Pausing, they heard water move under the wharf. Badger mused, "This street's blocked. Have we been down that one? Ach, who cares? One direction's as bad as another. If Adira wants us trolled as bait, why not smear us with bacon fat and sink us on an anchor chain?"

"We should patrol in a tavern," said Simone, all but invisible with her dark clothes and skin. The seekers tried to keep apart, for three carried naked blades.

"Adira vowed to purge our village of this mystery menace, and we are her arms, bound to duty," said Sister Wilemina, pledged to honor.

"Beside which," rumbled Jaeger, "imagine if some citizen were plucked up, and you had shirked your duty."

"Ooh," admitted Simone. "You're right. Adira would hang us from a yardarm in the harbor 'till we rotted."

"Balls of Bolas, but it's dark out here!" grumbled Badger. "It never gets this dark at sea. I say, being a pirate's tougher than being a sailor. You can push a navy captain overboard when no one's looking, but—*Opp!*"

"It's here!" Jaeger's warning roared in the night.

"Where?" shouted both women.

Badger couldn't answer. One foot snagged by a rope, he crashed on his face, barely throwing his cutlass wide lest he fall on the blade. Pained, winded, he kicked viciously to free his feet, but another noose cinched hard, and he was dragged backward by both ankles. Skidding on his belly and flopping like a fish, Badger backslashed with his cutlass and felt steel bite flesh. Then a rasp like porcupine quills raked his hand and sawed flesh to the bone. Losing his cutlass, he settled for yelling.

"Help! This way!"

By slapping the cobblestones and kicking wildly, he flipped over and snatched a fish knife from his right boot. Bucking upward, Badger jabbed at the night and speared flesh. A wet clawed foot kicked him in the teeth and laid him out flat. As his head struck stone, sparks skyrocketed in his brain.

A dogfight erupted in the dark.

Through his ringing ears, Badger heard snarling, snapping, and growling. Inhuman screams and gibberings set Badger's hair on end. Worse was a fearsome roar from Jaeger. Punches, wet slaps, and gurgles resounded. Simone shrieked a pirate charge that ended in *Oof!*

Wilemina shouted "Hola!" her bowshooting battle cry, but Badger heard no strike.

The rope on Badger's legs twisted until he spun like a dogfish on a hook, then abruptly he dropped free and flicked shorn fibers off his ankles. The ghastly gibberings receded into the night. The docks fell quiet except for the murmur of water beneath their feet.

Simone lit a candle stub. In the tiny light, eye-smarting after hours of darkness, three humans peered around with bulging eyes. The women helped Badger rise.

"What in the name of seven benighted seas was *that*?"

"There were ten or more," gasped Sister Wilemina, "whatever they were. I made out their silhouettes against the moonlight on the lake."

"They bleed," said Simone. "I sliced one before it cold-cocked me. Damn near split my liver with a hammer blow."

"I cut one." Badger still held a scrap of ropes in one hand. Queer rope, he found: rough-woven but as tough as iron wire and impregnated with slime. "What was hunting us?"

"Where's Jaeger?" asked Wilemina. "He—oh!"

"I'm here."

Jaeger's immense white-bellied frame loomed in the candlelight. They hadn't heard his approach. The tiger man showed empty paws. "They escaped."

"What were they?" asked the three.

"Not men. Not fish. They live in the lake."

Silence reigned as everyone stared at the glittering water.

* * * * *

"What do you mean, they live in the lake?" snarled Adira. "It didn't even exist three months ago! It's brown and churned-up and no deeper than the belly of a bireme!"

Adira paced before a brazier of crackling scrap wood and dried camel dung. Palmyra's town hall, once empty and neglected, was crammed with tables, writing desks, podiums, chairs, and benches, while the walls were festooned with maps, charts, lists, and notices, busy even in the dead of night. The hall reminded Adira of Hazezon's bustling city chambers in Bryce, and she was irritated by the comparison.

"We followed tracks to the lake," said Badger. "Feet with claws, like a fish's foot, if fish had feet."

"Jaeger smelled them," added Simone. "His nose is as good as his eyes, and he can see in the dark. They're—"

"Merfolk?" Adira waved two brown hands. "Sea sprites? Naiads? Water nixies? On the ocean I'd believe in a trice! But here in the desert? We're two hundred miles from blue water! And why seize anyone? What could they want with land dwellers? And where do they flee if the lake's a puddle? It's daft!"

No one replied. Adira looked to Jaeger, but he lay in a corner and napped.

Pacing again, boot heels clomping, Adira drew one of her matched daggers crisscrossed at her lower back and idly flipped the blade from hand to hand.

She muttered as if alone. ". . . never suffered this bilge before . . . I've half a mind to let Johan seize the city, and good luck with it. . . . Palmyra was *my* town, not a playground for every pumpkinhead with no place to drop anchor. . . . Lightning strike me blind if I like *this* nonsense. . . ."

Fuming, Adira suddenly whirled and threw her dagger overhand. It turned once in the air and struck the wall inches above Jaeger's head. His amber eyes popped open, huge and round. They flicked to the dagger quivering just above his whiskers.

"Brace and bail, you baggy sack of stripes!" The pirate leader hooked a thumb south. "Take these fumble-fingered pie-thieves aboard the pinnace. Sail to Bryce, if you can find it, and tell Lard Bottom we need his noodle-slicing to solve a mystery."

Slinking out from under the steel blade, Jaeger stretched so his elbows brushed the roof beams. "Mean you, that I should beseech his honor, the Tetrarch of the Free Realm of Bryce, Lord Paramount, and Suzerain, His Lordship Governor Hazezon Tamar, that we humbly request his magical expertise?"

"Aye," frowned Adira. "Tell my bloated ex-husband we'll pay in jam tarts and lemon ices. That'll bring him running."

* * * * *

In the highest chamber of frosty Krieghelm, a whining voice droned.

". . . Strongheart returned earlier than expected. With only her Circle, though the bulk of her mercenaries are bound to follow. She toured the new fortifications with Declan and suggested improvements. She's learned of the disappearances along the docks and sent out patrols. . . ."

The spy rattled on while Johan paced his chamber. A plain woman draped in desert robes fidgeted on her ample bottom, for broad daylight washed in the long line of square windows. All spies, like cockroaches, shied from daylight. Johan was too busy these days to accommodate a peasant's wishes. He hadn't slept in three weeks, and worked noon to noon. Johan asked a few questions that made the spy wrinkle her brow, for they seemed aimless and petty. She couldn't know Johan's questions were to cross-check reports from other spies, for he trusted none of his invisible eyes. He paid the woman with gold coins minted in Bryce.

"Keep your eyes open. Send word immediately if Adira leaves Palmyra, and when Hazezon departs Bryce for Palmyra, providing he goes at all."

As usual, Hands the chamberlain let a few minutes lapse before he announced the next petitioner.

Amid a steady stream of supplicants, one stood out. A short dark officer entered in a newfangled uniform: gray tunic tailored tight to her body, a sheepskin jacket, tall boots, and a metal helmet with a curious visor of smoky glass. Painted against the red star on her chest flew a sharp-shinned bird with a hooked beak.

"Marshall Udele, Your Majesty." She carried the helmet under one arm, very military, but her cheeks and lips were chapped as if lashed by arctic winds.

"Progress, Captain?"

"We forge ahead, milord. Nine drakes flying. Six smashups, but we're learning. No lack of volunteers since you spoke to the army, a great help. Our company sends thanks."

"Still only one aloft at a time?"

"Yes, milord." No excuses, which pleased Johan.

After a few more questions, the emperor promised more magic-users for her force, then dismissed the captain.

Hands leaned back as in walked a trailblazer from the far north, a hulking barbarian with sharper eyes than usual. He wore leathers and strapped boots and a full brown bear pelt draped so the empty head sat on his shoulder. He lugged a leather sack and, with Johan's permission, dumped it on the floor. Out rolled three heads, two male and a female, their features distorted into masks of horror.

The barbarian gargled, "Y' Majesty. Heads of three chiefs of Blue Mountain tribes. All Ærathi berserkers. Only un-underlings rule now."

"Do they send warriors?" asked the emperor. "When? How many?"

"Many." Barbarians had trouble with numbers. "As many . . . as leaves on small oak tree. To depart at full of Mist Moon."

"Good." Johan didn't pay the barbarian, since his ilk mistrusted money, but scrawled a chit by which he could redeem food and supplies in the marketplace. Johan mused, "Doubly good. . . . With Ærath finally subjugated, the north is ours. Now we turn all our attention south. Eh? Yes, go. But chuck these out the window."

Hands clicked his heels to announce the next visitor, but Johan raised a blood-hued hand.

"Let them wait. Summon my generals. Tell them dawn breaks."

"Y—Your Majesty?"

"Just repeat it, Hands. They'll grasp its meaning."

Chapter 11

"I've never seen it, nor sign, but some have." The water seller whispered with head down so Hazezon had to crane forward. "The secret ocean below the Sukurvia. The Sunken Sea."

"The Buried River, some call it," said his companion, a maker of brass pots. "The Toloron is but one-tenth of the mother of rivers, a mere shadow of the real waters, as thin as shadow is to a man."

"Yes? Please, tell more." Hazezon Tamar waited in vain. All around voices echoed off the stone walls in the tavern, half-cellar, half-cave, etched by time into Palmyra's rocky knob. Craftspeople sipped cool drafts over a lazy midday meal. Hazezon was also working, asking about merfolk. Few would talk, as if water spirits lurked in corners.

"That's all I know," said the water seller.

"And I," said the brass worker.

Thanking them for their time, Hazezon left a gold coin on the table to pay for their drinks and climbed the worn stone steps to the street. Squinting in the spring sunlight after the dark cellar, he tugged his keffiyeh low over his bushy white eyebrows.

Questioning erg dwellers took an eternity, for custom considered it bad manners to broach a subject without first sharing small talk and news. He'd wasted much of the morning in marketplace hangouts. Never talkative or intrusive, Palmyrans became clams when the Sunken Sea was mentioned. Time and again Hazezon had heard, "They don't like it talked about," or "Bad luck to anger the hidden ones," or "Some that ask are took by night and ne'er seen again."

Scratching his beard, Hazezon decided to fish elsewhere. Alone, for lallygagging servants would stifle tongues, he strode down to the waterfront.

The docks were both old and new. The old ones had been uprooted and floated higher to meet Palmyra's new shoreline along the lake, and new ones were built to handle increased traffic. Barges and pinnaces and smacks and drows rubbed gunwales three-quarters around the town like a floating forest. Seeking anyone his own age, Hazezon finally approached an old man and woman who soaked up sun against a south wall. Their threadbare clothes suggested they might accept a coin or two, but Hazezon knew a desert dweller's innate dignity might prefer hunger over insult, so he adopted his most humble manner.

"Good noon, venerable ones, and a thousand pardons for disturbing you. You look to possess the wisdom that assuages advanced years, and this miserable child would beg a crumb of your hard-won knowledge. But may I first send for tea and honey cakes, for I missed my morning repast and hate to dine alone?"

"Tea and cakes would not be remiss." The crone's voice was scratchy from years of breathing sand. Bundled in a dun robe so only a hawk nose and black eyes peeked, she nodded as nobly as any queen to Hazezon, so he might sit on a nearby crate. The old man's eyes were rheumy with cataracts, so likely he saw only Hazezon's silhouette, dark against light. The governor of Bryce signaled a shop girl. When the elder couple wolfed and gulped their portions, Hazezon ordered more. Mild and patient, Hazezon introduced himself as "a minor clerk from Bryce," let drop his desert origins and wanderings, cited some known but not famous ancestors, slowly wending a circle toward the Sunken Sea.

Oddly enough, mere mention sparked the woman to talk.

"Aye, it's true, Lord Governor." No fool, she'd guessed the mage's identity. "A secret sea underlies Sukurvia. Desert dwellers know of it, though few have dipped their fingers."

Hazezon walked with care, as if stalking a timid deer. "Having lived so long and fruitfully, and traveled so far, have you *seen* the hidden waters?"

"I have." The old man's voice rasped like steel on stone. "I've drunk them. Legends say the waters are purer than any well or mountain spring, and they bring wisdom, and long life, and sexual potency. Maybe so, for I've outlived everyone I know but Sheba here. Sweet water, and cool, I can taste it still."

"Where?" blurted Hazezon, then sipped mint tea from a tiny cup to cover his blunder. "Is it such a place a man can still reach?"

"A man could journey from sun to sun, but never to this spot, for it no longer exists." Robes barely rustled as the elder shook his head. "Years gone, with me barely in my beard, my tribe camped near an ancient well in a hollow called the Blue Blanket for the color of the stones. Not near the mountains. A shallow dish out of the wind. Dry, where no flash flood could overtake us. We pitched our tents and rolled in our robes. As the stars watched o'er us a giant walked by. The desert quivered like an animal in a trap. We woke and waited, but nothing happened, so slept again. Then came a curious thing, I dreamed I drowned, and woke to find it true!"

"Drowned?" asked Hazezon.

A husky chuckle. "Water threatened to smother me. Shouting for fright, I arose in a pool a furlong long with water rising by the second. Frightened, we grabbed our goods and splashed to dry ground. The ancient well overflowed like a fountain. The water lapped our sandals as we sat and watched, for it was truly a miracle. Though warned not to, I drank some. By sunrise the water had vanished, leaving no trace. Some claimed it a dream."

Said the old woman, "Once from a high pass in the Flint Mountains we glimpsed water far away, no mirage. When we arrived there was nothing, except fish."

"Fish?" marveled Hazezon.

"Fish. Little brown fish no longer than my fingers. More than we could count. Lying on rocks as if rained from the sky. As dry as old leaves, but real."

After a respectful silence, Hazezon asked, "So these unseen waters come and go, a whim of the land, yet leave no path a man might walk?"

The man's robes shifted, a suggestion of a shrug.

"No doubt paths descend to the waters, but to tell of one entry point would be to write on the wind, for tomorrow it may be gone. The Buried River shifts in its bed. Holes that lead downward are soon closed."

"You mean, by quakes?"

"No, by those who dwell below."

The last had an air of finality, and Hazezon didn't pry. Instead he eased, "May I ask, worthy grandfather, why you talk freely of that which frightens others?"

The woman's black eyes sparkled like agates. "Ancient as we are, and poor, what can we lose? What fear but the long last leap into the dark?"

More tales were told of desert oddities, but eventually Hazezon rose, for he had other waters to fish. He wished to reward these helpful souls, but to offer money would insult and shame them. Thinking, he drew from his wrist a bracelet of silver wire wrapping tiny emeralds, a trinket to him, but worth enough to feed these nomads until their suns set.

"Thank you for enlightening me, milady, 'lord. I say, ma'am, you remind me of my own sage grandmother, who has already walked to the next world. She once gave me this bracelet to hold for her. I hate to impose, but if you visit her tent in the future, could you give it her?"

A wizened hand accepted the bracelet. "I expect to visit many old friends soon. If I see your grandmother, I will give her this bauble and compliment her for siring a well brought-up grandson." The bracelet disappeared inside a fold of robes as she added, "Do not fret. All things come in their time."

Mulling mystic wisdom, Hazezon climbed into the heart of the town as if floating up into a cloud. Dizzy by the time he reached the busy town hall, he found only Jaeger present. Asleep as usual, the tiger sprawled on the floor with one foot stuck through the rungs of a desk and one arm coiled around a post. Scribes stepped over him. Hazezon noted how, like a common house cat, Jaeger slept large parts of the day, no doubt the source of his savage energy. Yet at his approach, one amber tiger eye opened.

"How fared your search for knowledge?" Jaeger uncoiled from the floor, not sleepy at all.

Hazezon stood back lest he develop a crick in his neck looking up. "I . . . basically learned nothing."

The tiger man licked a paw and smoothed his whiskers. "The prey comes to the hunter who waits."

Feeling boyish under this rain of elder advice, Hazezon nodded. "True. If nothing else, I've spread word. Perhaps the circles that scribe the desert will swirl to me. . . ."

So it soon proved true. The next morning, as Hazezon and his manservant and two scribes walked to the town hall from their inn, a tiny girl in ragged robes reeking of sheep stopped him at the door.

"Milord Tamar," she piped like a mouse, "I can lead you to the Sunken Sea."

* * * * *

"Down."

The child pointed into a dark arroyo, a scar amid desert hills. Hazezon Tamar leaned and peered. Pebbles disturbed by his boots dribbled into darkness.

None of the humans spoke. Jaeger's voice startled them.

"Water. I smell it."

Hazezon looked at his companions, Adira Strongheart and her Circle of Seven. Treetop the dwarf, Badger, Simone the Siren, the archer Sister Wilemina, the pale Heath, the scruffy Virgil, and Jaeger. Hazezon's new manservant Seabrooke and a female scribe named Echo had also volunteered for adventure, which the lord thought foolish. He peered at the sky, overcast, roiling like boiling lead. Their bedrolls this morning had worn frost. This crack in the bosom of the land lay twenty miles from Palmyra. Hazezon marveled that news of his search had coursed through the desert grapevine so quickly. The waif of a shepherdess had walked all that night to tell her secret.

The child shivered in her ratty robes, big dark eyes staring like lamps. Hazezon asked, "How found you this sally port?"

"I didn't," piped the girl. "My ram found it. He followed the scent of water. I went after and tried to drag him back, but they caught him and took him!"

"Who?"

"I know them not." The quaint old-fashioned phrasing of the desert. "But they took my ram, and I've lost him forever. My flock will dwindle, and I'll be bereft."

Hazezon counted the scrawny sheep cropping thornbrush and buffalo grass. The girl was seven sheep away from poverty.

"Where is your tribe?"

"Dead."

No regret, just fact.

"Daughter, you've done us a great service. If we come out of this crevasse alive, you'll have a new ram, new robes, and a tent to sleep in these frosty nights."

"I shan't need all that." The girl bore her paupery with dignity. "But I need a new ram."

"We waste time." Adira Strongheart was all business. "Do we descend or not? It's a dubious chase. We're seven leagues from Palmyra. How can anyone raid our lake at this distance?"

"We'll descend," stated Hazezon.

Wilemina and Heath unsaddled the horses and entrusted them to the shepherdess. The rest shucked their cloaks and tightened sashes, and donned "dwarven helmets," as the joke went. In Smith's Lane Hazezon had ordered copper headbands with polished dishes and candleholders to light their way, for the depths would be inky. Simone honed her cutlass. Virgil shucked his heart-shaped shield, reckoning it too clumsy for close passages, but tucked his long-beaked axe in his belt. Wilemina and Heath wrapped their bows in blankets and left them, feeling naked without the wood in hand. Treetop donned horsehide gloves sewn with cestus punching spikes in the knuckles. Adira shucked her many jangly bangles and gave them to the shepherdess. The scribe Echo juggled a new short sword. Seabrooke, knowing his limits, eschewed a weapon and instead wriggled on a pack stuffed with supplies. Each explorer carried a coil of rope with an iron grapnel at each end. Jaeger simply waited, wearing only his goathide harness and the bronze dagger that he never drew in a fight, with double coils of rope looped around his shoulders. The tiger man waited, sniffing the cool breeze welling up from the ravine.

"Ready?" asked Adira. "I'll lead. Jaeger, back me. The rest of you string out. Haz, keep to the rear with your ink dabblers. Don't get in our way."

"I can take point, if you allow," rumbled Jaeger. "Venturing in the dark—"

Adira bounced her knuckles off his white belly.

"I lead. And if you question my authority again, best grip that crooked dagger in your hand. Paw."

On that cheery note, strung in a ragged line, the explorers slithered and skittered down the ravine and into darkness. In a last look, Hazezon watched the shepherdess to see if she waved goodbye. She did not.

* * * * *

Unending, dreary, and irksome went the descent. No path, just a steep drop like a mountainside. The party fell, skidded, jumped, and dangled from ropes. Their heads clunked on knobs and spurs and jags, but most wore keffiyehs to dampen the blows. At times they had to squeeze through cracks barely big enough for their ribs. Other times ceilings were lost in darkness. Often the tunnel split, and Adira chose the way, twice butting into dead ends. Doubly irritating, sometimes they had to surmount a knob to wend down again. Scabbards, and belts, and haversacks were hooked a thousand times until people were ready to shuck their tackle and hurl it into the depths. Darkness was absolute. It was only kept at bay by the tiny candles flickering at their greasy brows. They lost track of time. Eventually, starving, with candles burned to nubs, they stopped to rest.

This cavity was typical: dirt, mildew-stained rocks, black shadows, a jagged wall at their right hand, nothing to their left, a ragged shaft up and down. They gulped their water and sipped from wineskins and munched rations, and watched the darkness squirm before their eyes as if alive. The air felt chill as they cooled down.

"If I'd known there were so many tight squeezes," puffed Badger, "I'd'a volunteered to stay home and scrub bilges."

Adira told him, "If you spent more time training and working instead of building a potbelly in bars, you'd think this a lark. Best you burn some suet. Soft pirates are no use."

"You blokes are too big, is your problem." Treetop the dwarf thrived, feeling at home, though he had to traverse twice as many steps. "Underground's the only place to live. Cool and dry and cozy all year 'round. Never rains nor snows, nor blinds you with sun. No painting or brickwork or shingling or thatching. And if you need more room, you just burrow where you will."

"Same as being buried alive, says I." Seldom happy, Virgil refused to admit any terror of the depths, though he glanced about constantly. He drained his wine and tossed the skin.

The eldest, Hazezon suffered short breath and strained muscles, but stoically denied his discomfort.

"To answer your earlier question, Adira, we might have started twenty miles distant, but we trend steadily toward Palmyra." His voice echoed faintly.

"I believe it," said the pirate leader. "The direction is true, but with all this up and down I can't tell how far we've come."

"Four miles and a bit," said Heath, who never got lost.

"I still can't believe there's an ocean down here," said Simone.

Muscles yelping, Hazezon plunked on a rock, glad he could contribute something, if only information.

"Not so queer. The sands of Sukurvia are a giant sinkhole. Tirras is mountainous toward the north. The western reaches are bluffs hundreds of feet high, nomads say, and even the sands to the east rise from the river. The Toloron slopes only gently to the sea. So the Sea of Serenity might trickle fingers under the desert. If so, you'd need not descend far to find salt water."

"Far?" objected Badger. "We've fallen down so many rock faces we could'a crawled into some fiend's purse!"

Jaeger purred, "Legends say underworld waters run to the jungles in the east. Water with no source sometimes bubbles from the ground. And I smell a great quantity of water not much farther below."

Like most of the tiger man's quiet announcements, this news stunned the group. Adira said, "Finish stuffing your gobs. I want to find the monsters who drag my citizens into the drink."

Tugging harnesses aright, fixing new candles to their copper headbands, the group staggered up on stiff legs and fell into line. Rope and grapnel in hand, Adira skidded down another rock face onto a wide shelf cracked in a thousand places. Jaeger let his rope trail, mostly relying on his claws to descend, and plunked beside Adira.

Who immediately whipped her elbow into the tiger's brisket. "Shove off, Stripes! Give me room! Love of little fishes, how you loom! I feel like a mouse in a woodpile! And your breath would blow a buzzard off a dead camel!"

"You're scarcely finer." Jaeger still loomed over Adira. "Know you stink like a dog? I can barely bear your odor for gagging!"

"You moth-eaten rag-eared carpet!" Adira jabbed a stiff finger into Jaeger's chest, her hand sinking in white fur. "Why do we tolerate you? Bad enough to drag sawed-off dwarves and pointy-eared—"

"Hoy!" Treetop and Heath objected as they dropped onto the shelf.

Adira was just warming up. "— now we're saddled with you, a crooked-back mongrel mad mage's mistake!"

One by one the party members gained the shelf and immediately took sides. Cacophony echoed and fragmented against the stone walls.

Badger urged Adira, "Aye, tell him his claws scar our decks!"

Simone slapped his arm, "Jaeger's worth twenty of you, you mossy-bottomed bait barrel!"

Echo shoved Hazezon's manservant over some dark obstacle so he crashed and skinned his hands. The girl shouted, "That's for giving me orders! You're not Lord Governor, you bootlicker!"

Wilemina and Virgil traded punches, then gouged for each others eyes, grunting with the effort.

As Adira drew both daggers and Jaeger flexed flinty claws, Hazezon clutched an aching head and wished they'd all shut up. He couldn't resist screaming at Adira, "It's all your fault we're trapped down here, you brainless scut! You'd led us into the jaws of death so you can spit in the eyes of nine devils—"

Yet even as he bellowed aggression, Hazezon analyzed his actions, as was his wont. Weary and wobbly, he should be resting, not bickering. But he felt compelled to vent his rage—

"Compelled?" he blurted aloud. "No, that's wrong! It's Adira's blundering—No, wait! We shouldn't—Ach, my head!"

Gripping his skull, Hazezon fought to think clearly, but mad notions whirled in his brain like dust devils. Why? What could—

Forcing his eyes open, he looked around—and grunted in shock.

Scuffling, gesticulating, folks had dropped their candle headbands, so only a few lights flickered on the ground—and that was wrong too. The chamber would soon go black. By the waning light, Hazezon saw his servant Seabrooke stayed on hands and knees, oddly cursing and berating Echo as she hammered his back. Very queer, thought Hazezon, then saw Seabrooke's hands and knees were mired in—black tar?

Sneering, Hazezon called, "Serves you right, Seabrooke! You're a precious poor valet! Conal must spin in his grave—*What am I saying?*"

Clamping his mouth, squeezing his head tightly, as if in a vise, Hazezon struggled to think while his brain throbbed fit to explode. Seabrooke was being swallowed by a noxious ooze, yet he carped at him like a fool. Echo's feet had also sunk in black bile, while Hazezon—

Mashing his head between his hands, Hazezon roared, "*Eront, canta, cabessia!*"

Jolted, Hazezon dropped to both knees. "Where am I? Why so dark? Who shouts? And what's this vile fungus creeping up my legs—Aha!"

Remembering, the elder mage lurched free of the greedy black fingers. He slapped at his clothes, but the filthy stuff stuck fast. Wiping grimy hands on his embroidered tunic, Hazezon stamped to Adira, clapped both hands on her head, and before she could whirl and gut him with daggers, yelled, "*Eront, canta, cabessia!*"

"What?" Adira shook her head, blinking. "Haz! Get your hands off me! What are—"

"Look at your feet!" Hazezon moved on to lay hands to heads and purge the spell of madness overtaking the party. People trembled and swayed as their last few memories burned away, then hollered as they discovered tendrils of primordial ooze crawling up their legs like giant leeches.

"Down!" Hazezon shoved people headlong. "Get down, down to the next drop-off or whate'er it be! To stay will see our bones picked clean!"

Arguments ceasing, the explorers pried free of the ooze, which now smothered the shelf past their ankles, as thick as dung in a stock market. Jaeger urged Adira along. Echo and Treetop hacked Seabrooke and the others free.

In a short tunnel with a steep-sloped floor, the pirates struck candles alight and scraped ooze off their boots and legs with the backs of their knives. Many shivered as if freezing. Virgil and Heath were white with fear. Chagrined, Adira frowned at her ex-husband.

"So that black ooze infects the mind with disharmony so travelers argue and never see the danger until too late. They're overrun and suffocated and eaten, I suppose. Why didn't you succumb, Haz?"

"I'm not certain." The mage's hands shook so badly his knife sliced his hand-tooled boots. "Beard of Ragnar, what a vile way to expire! A scimitar is mercifully quick, but to be smothered and digested slowly—*Ugh*! My mind swirled with madness and hatred, but to improve your magic steadily you must observe how it works. I saw—"

"Never mind." Adira raked back her curls. "It's done. We'll avoid it on the way up."

Miffed, Hazezon chided his wife. "You might thank me for saving our lives, O most-high mighty empress of Palmyra."

Adira only snorted, then caught a fresh grip on her rope.

A mile beyond and half a mile deeper, they found it.

In the darkness, Adira scaled a cliff face. The tiger stated they were very close, and even the humans could smell water and salt. Now they waited for their leader to goad them on. Badger called her name. Then her boot heels clopped on rocks. Adira's voice rose as if channeled up a well, "Come down. It's here."

Silently the adventurers crept down a slimy slope to where Adira stood poised, staring outward. At first it seemed a flat shelf of slate, or even a sheet of ice, but one by one the seekers knelt and touched the surface. Gentle ripples dimpled. Heath touched his lips. "Not pure sea salt, but a taste. This must indeed be an arm of the Sea of Serenity."

"Not necessarily." Hazezon himself tasted the water. "It could be fresh water from the mountains that's leeched salt from the sands."

Awestruck, the intrepid eleven stared, some tiptoeing to make the light extend. The placid water spread past the firelight, its far side unknowable. Crags pocked the surface like islands, but the echoing darkness suggested a huge vaulted chamber.

"Hel-lo!" called Wilemina, to test for echo.

"Quiet!" snapped Adira. "No one must know—"

Everyone jumped as a *ker-plook!* resounded. The impetuous Badger had lobbed a rock into the distance. Adira's backhanded fist smacked his chin and knocked him sprawling. Skidding on slime, he slid half into the chilly water before Treetop arrested him.

"You idiot!" Adira hissed like a wildcat. "If you bring an attack down around our ears, I'll kill you first!"

Massaging his bruised chin, Badger husked, "Sorry. Didn't think. But what's next? We can't—*ulk!*—can't go any farther."

"He's right." Heath pointed in both directions along the craggy shore. "There are stone walls on both sides and water before us. The only way to proceed is by raft or swimming."

Tense silence. No one had thought to bring a boat or raft. And recalling the vicious webbed-footed night stalkers that attacked Palmyrans, no one dared swim.

"Then we're stumped." Adira planted her fists on her hips and glared at the water as if personally insulted. "We'll turn back to one of those forks higher up. Likely the damned holes will dead-end or just lead back here—"

"Look!" bleated the scribe Echo. "I-in th-the—"

Everyone grabbed his or her weapons.

The placid water suddenly boiled. Almost before the searchers could drag their blades from their scabbards, five, seven, a dozen, a whole army of sinister wet figures burst from the water in a sheet of spray.

* * * * *

Tirras celebrated.

". . . I had a dream last night, my children, a dream that foretold victory!"

Johan's booming tones bounced off the cliff walls behind and reverberated outward toward plain and desert. At a great cleft in the rocky bosom of the north the River Toloron dropped a hundred feet in a shimmering cascade that boiled into mist that occluded the sun. At the waterfall's foot yawned a large lake etched in bedrock, and on this sunny day the water glittered as blue as the unsullied sky. The lake was crammed from shore to shore with huge barges and smaller watercraft. Crowds jammed the lakeshore and the stony rims of high balconies. Many more people were packed behind. Almost the entire populace of Tirras had come to watch the first wave of the army launch into their southern journey. Fire drakes and whalebone gliders circled and kited in the sky, masters of the treacherous updrafts that sucked and slobbered about the rocky cliffs. Every man, woman, and child hung on the emperor's words.

Johan stood on a stage erected on a barge so everyone might see. Today his ruddy face and black tattoos were muted to a pale pink with dark creases, and his horns were hidden, so he looked like any average citizen. His purple lizard-skin robe draped like cloth of pearl-gray, another illusion to make him appear a common man who'd risen to dominance by hard work, not by devious and nefarious machinations.

"I had a dream," Johan droned, hypnotizing with his voice, "where the Sea King himself, Oligarch of the Oceans and Sovereign of the Sea of Serenity, blessed our mission! Tall he was, higher than the tallest pine, and broad of brow! Naked but for a white beard and jeweled crown like a cathedral steeple! He spoke not a word, but when I, in all humbleness, asked if Tirras might free itself of our rocky realm, the Sea King nodded like a great sage of old, and vanished! Then did I know we would succeed!"

Arms in the air, Johan paused as twenty thousand throats cheered. When the noise subsided, he rattled on, noting that very few listeners fidgeted. He lectured about years of nonexistent oppression by desert dwellers, of ancient and manufactured grievances that must be put right, of fabricated insults that southern folks heaped upon doltish northerners, and of impossible crimes by which southern spies undercut Tirras. The crowd ate up every word.

Finally, bored, Johan wrapped up his rally, pausing for deafening cheers. ". . . No longer will we be poor neighbors scrabbling for crumbs amid rocky wastes! Today is a new day, a day of triumph! With the fates themselves on our sides—What?"

As if struck by wonder, Johan stared skyward. Twenty thousand heads rose to see. At first there showed nothing. Then, as if blown from the clouds by a sky god, circling fire drakes and whalebone gliders suddenly tumbled end over end. Drakes clawed for air, squawking, while their riders hauled on the reins. Two gliders suffered. One flipped like an arrow-shot bird, but righted and skimmed to a hasty halt on the grassland. The other glider, soaring too low, strained to rise but smashed nose-first into a cliff. For a second, broken bones and crushed pilots clung to stone, then they plummeted to splatter on rocks below.

Ignoring the stricken ships, Johan held his skull-tight hood as if it might blow away, causing thousands to emulate him. The emperor wailed, "Oh, the pity, our most daring fliers snuffed out! But see, my children, what this means! The wind blows from the north stronger than ever before! Winds of change! An omen! Our doughty northern creators urge us southward with all speed, to crush our enemies and take our rightful place as rulers, of all Jamuraa!"

Raising his hands, Johan pointed south. Hundreds of bargemen and watermen hoisted oars, paddles, and poles. "Go, without delay! Invade the south! So speak the spirits and your emperor!"

Paddles dipped, poles bent, and oars creaked as hundreds of barges jammed to enter the throat of the Toloron. Men and women sang, laughed, hugged, cried, and cheered as the great expedition got underway.

Unaffected by his winds of change, Johan watched with a cynical smirk. The northern winds blew eternally in these parts. All he'd done was invoke some wind gusts to send his captains cartwheeling. A spectacular display his empty-headed followers would recite for years. As the first boatloads turned a bend in the river, laughing and hurrahing, Johan was reminded of sheep, as easily led to the greenest pasture or the grimmest abattoir with only blind obedience in their hearts.

Yet even sheep could think, corrected Johan. These people,

empty-headed, were mere puppets who did nothing until their strings were pulled. In a way, Johan gave them purpose and life. Soon he'd control all the denizens of land, sea, and air. Jamuraa would become a puppet theater.

Johan the puppet master.

Chapter 12

Ultimately, the darkness did them in.

Adira's explorers only glimpsed the enemy who burst from the secret sea. The party witnessed human shapes with chiseled faces, eyes that shone a ghostly shimmering green, pointed ears, and hair like kelp. Claws adorned their hands and feet. The fins along their forearms threatened razor cuts. They were armed with barbed tridents or serrated copper swords, and some nets to entrap a victim for the thrust.

Yet before any human could act, Jaeger leaped from the shore like a ballista bolt square into the raiders' midst. He jumped with his arms outspread, a span eight feet or more, and smashed into ranks of merfolk before they set foot on shore. His striped hide struck pale-green flesh, and a dozen assailants were knocked underwater. Jaeger was up in seconds, streaming water from his fur. His long arms windmilled to snag merfolk or send them spinning and stumbling.

"*Avast!*" Guided only by the candle flickering on her headband, Adira Strongheart plied a cutlass and dagger, swiping deadly steels arcs in the air to drive the merfolk back. She wanted seconds to gather her wits and gather her troop if possible. Better they clustered back to back then be picked off singly. Naught would do but kill or be killed. Half-crouching to keep her footing on the slimy stone, she alternately hacked with her cutlass and jabbed with her dagger. The merfolk were almost as inconvenienced, crowded elbow-tight. A merwoman with a long-beaked hatchet chopped two-handed, but a companion jostled her elbow, and Adira struck. Her cutlass crashed on the sea-woman's shoulder, a crippling blow that made her reel back in pain and shock. Adira flicked her dagger and pierced the merwoman's breast below the ribs. Her heart punctured, the woman dropped and slid back into black water. Exploiting the hole the woman left in their ranks, Adira slashed a merman above the hip. He tilted and sank, but Adira couldn't follow with a killing blow because too many enemies charged. Twisting her blade to free it, she stepped close to the falling man for a partial shield, then lunged at a merman behind, but he saw the thrust coming and dropped. Off-balance, Adira kicked for footing, skidded as she'd feared, and sprawled on her bottom. Before she could scramble back up, a trident haft spanked her head. The glancing blow knocked off her copper headband and plunged her into darkness. Her cutlass clashed against the brass shaft while she poked at the dark with her dagger. A pipe whanged her in the head, clipped her again, and laid her flat. Within a second she was hauled into the water to sink like a foundered ship.

Jaeger romped and bounded in the shallows like a tiger batting fish from rapids. Everywhere his black claws rent flesh. Where possible he hooked his claws to dig deep and yank a merwarrior off his feet. With his cat's eyes he saw every shadow and silhouette by the wan light of candles and eyelamps. Time and again he hooked warriors and upset them, flicking them to their knees or facedown or tumbling them into the depths. Any attack helped his companions fight or run, but more merfolk kept leaping from the water until even Jaeger was overwhelmed.

The land dwellers fought valiantly, but not for long. Treetop was smothered by sopping nets that slapped down on him like a ton of seaweed. Only one hand remained free, and the dwarf hammered his legs and feet with the spikes in his gloves. Twin tridents stabbed and pinned the net. Then a merwarrior pounded a brass hammer atop the nets until the dwarf's flailing hand fell still. He too was pulled into the silent lake.

Simone was literally swarmed over by bodies as hard as hickory and slick with slime. Spun around and slammed on her face, her arms were pinned and wrapped in codline that cut her wrists and numbed her hands. Cursing her captors got her a cold wet net wrapped around her head. Hoisted by her arms and legs, she kicked and struggled, then floundered frantically as cold water embraced her, but she soon fainted for lack of air.

Wilemina and Heath, bereft of their bows, banded together for protection as they were surrounded by nine cool-headed merwarriors. Heath lunged with his archer's short sword only to have it tangled in a sopping net. His dagger was similarly snarled when a trident butt flicked past Wilemina's head and bonked his. Stunned, he sank to one knee and had it kicked out from under him. Then his head was stomped against stone. Wilemina hacked two-handed with her sword, but her attackers defended themselves with tridents. The Calerian archer was pierced in the chest by two cruel barbs. Bowled back, she tripped over the prostrate Heath and was stomped unconscious. Both were pitched into the sunken sea.

Badger and Virgil were put out of the fight before it began, for a merman surging from the water snapped his net and flung a gallon of water over them. The candles at their brows extinguished, and the men were blind. A foot crashed in Virgil's brisket, Badger was booted in the groin, and the two fell together. Fishhook claws caught their hair and both men were dragged into the water to be pinned and submerged by cabled hands until their breath ran out.

Hazezon learned, as he'd feared, that he was too old for

adventuring. Before he could utter even an aura spell, a sword pommel thudded against his skull. Dizzy and pained, he fell and was caught by ice-cold hands to be tossed headlong into the water to drown.

Hazezon's manservant Seabrooke, unarmed, was tripped by a trident and flipped into the brine. The scribe Echo, screaming in her first real adventure, barely lifted her new sword before it was slapped from her hands to clang on stone. A whipping claw smacked her throat. She dropped gagging and retching. Panic made her gargle as chilly hands pulled her underneath.

Half-drowned, half underwater, Jaeger battled on. Sopping wet fur made him as slippery as any fish-man, but he was eventually buried under flesh as the mermen and women clutched and hung on. Dragged down, he clawed and bit viciously, knowing he was the last defender. Then dark water closed over his snarling roaring head, and he knew no more.

* * * * *

"This is all your fault, Haz. It's insane to follow a fat-butted merchant into a hole in the ground."

"I'll agree with that, honey."

"And don't call me honey."

Badger groaned, "Bad enough—our plight. Now we must—listen to lovebirds bicker while we—await the axe."

"Shut your gob," snapped Adira.

The explorers shivered and coughed in the icy darkness. They'd awoken one by one in a stygian pit heaped deep with garbage. Many of the bones in the offal were human, an unpleasant touch. They huddled for warmth. Badger couldn't stop coughing, and others hacked as harshly. Dumped in the sunken sea, they'd been towed on the surface, then submerged and ferried through black tunnels of water. Some held their breath, some pinched their mouths and nostrils until they nearly burst. Everyone pulled through except the dwarf Treetop. Too small to hold much air, he'd drowned along the route. The merfolk had kept his corpse.

"Damn that—dwarf for dying." Badger hacked up water. "He owed me nine—gold. He could'a kept it if I'd known."

"Small in stature but great in heart," said Heath.

"As feisty as a wildcat," sniffled Simone, teeth chattering. The explorers had been stripped of their tackle and bracelets and half their clothes. Badger's shirt hung in shreds. Sister Wilemina, gored across the ribs, had none until Hazezon gave up his voluminous embroidered vest. Their few rags were sopping wet, never to dry in this dank pit. People huddled against Jaeger, but even the big cat seemed defeated, and his fur smelled rank.

"He had clever hands," said Adira, "and a nimble brain. We won't see his like again."

The eulogy petered out. Silence fell as the survivors contemplated their own grisly fate. Echo quavered, "These merfolk snatched people from the streets of Palmyra? To eat them?" Her words choked in tears.

"Be brave, my child," cooed Hazezon. "We're not dead yet. Adira, can you do something for light, please? It's the dark that shadows our spirits. My magics are pitifully far from desert in this drowned world, else I'd levitate some of us upward, if not out."

"*Ah-shisht!*" Adira's hands and face glowed in a cold nimbus of blue fire. "This makes me a target, Haz, but it's fair they take me first."

"We won't linger long," grumped Virgil, always gloomy. "There must be scores of fish-folk to feed."

Adira's magic glow painted queer shadows on the slimy walls. Bones clad with moss, and newly chewed, littered the pit, and the pirate leader wondered if being able to see really improved to their mood. "Before I die, can anyone tell why the fish-men suddenly prey on land dwellers?"

"They're hungry," droned Virgil. "I am too, but maybe starvin's better. Skinny folk might get et last."

"Hush your dreary dripping and think, Wooden-Noggin!"

"I ken your thinking," said Hazezon. "The river's run since the glaciers. Palmyra's hundreds of years old, and these caves are surely not new. So why only in recent months would merfolk fish for men aboveground?"

"There's more bait dangled in Palmyra these days," carped Adira. "The populace has grown tenfold since we bought your infernal bargain."

"That bargain dammed the river and moated the town," returned the mage.

"And built a lake." Adira's eyes seemed to glow. "Is that why we suffer raids from underwater?

"For whate'er reason, the merfolk can't be happy . . ." mused Hazezon. "My fat-bottomed merchant skills might come in handy."

"How so?" sniped Adira. "Will you sell our skins to save yours?"

"Still your shrilling, woman," said Hazezon. "Leave me to ponder. . . ."

Hours dragged in the dark underground. Adira had let her magic glow lapse so they again huddled in blackness, resting and biding their time. Under Adira's orders, fighters had plucked and twisted leg bones from the hideous midden around them, then labored to grind them into spikes on the rough rocks, though most guessed it was busywork. Adira had others scour the fetid trash for any weapons accidentally tossed below, but they found none. Finally she ordered her mates to form a human pyramid, and she scaled the high sides of the pit. Stealth availed her nothing, for as she groped for a handhold, a trident haft whistled and crushed three fingers, tumbling her back in the pit. The unseen guards had no qualms about breaking bones, Adira noted bitterly, as long as the meat was not spoiled.

Eventually the prisoners heard a patter-slap of finned feet, and everyone stiffened, wondering who'd be chosen to die. Sea-green lamps of eyes hung in the air as merfolk gazed down. Iron pinged on stone, and Badger muttered, "Grapnel." The merfolk must intend to fish for their supper, the land-dwellers guessed, hooking some poor sod like a pike on a line.

"Friends!" The unlucky explorers jumped as a familiar voice boomed in this evil alien den. "We bring you greetings from the upper world! And presents such as you've never imagined!"

If the prisoners were confused, so were the guards. Green-glowing eyes swiveled above the pit's edge. The iron grapnel pinged once again, then stopped.

"What is your wish, my friends?" Hazezon forced a jolly tone, though he didn't know if the fish-men understood or not. "Swords of copper and brass that never rust? Jewels that sparkle like foxfire? Sharp chert and flint for cutting tools? Glass baubles and tankards? Chains of brass to, uh, fasten? Sweetmeats—uh!" Adira elbowed his ribs at the touchy subject of food. "Uh, these things and more, whatever you wish we can get, my fellow nomads of the waves! Yet to bring you treasure, I, Lord Governor of, uh, Palmyra, must address your chief. Your leader? Shaman? Do you fine folk speak our language? For surely I'll be son to a spavined donkey if my words utter gibberish. A meeting with your—Oh."

The lamps winked out like candles blown by a breeze.

"You scared them off, you windbag," said Adira. "You used to pronounce speeches in your sleep too."

"I tried my best, and my best skills are negotiating, though some call me a crass and petty pennymonger." Hazezon added, "At least they withdrew their iron hooks. And I recall we did more romping between the sheets than sleeping. I often dozed at my desk because you kept me busy from dusk till dawn."

The darkness made it easier for the old lovers to talk of past intimacies, no matter if it embarrassed the unseen listeners. Adira retorted. "Your memory's as faulty as your eyes and ears.

You suffered aches in your fingers from stacking silver in your counting house."

"And head and jaw from you hurling pitchers, platters, carving knives, and whatever else came to hand."

"I never threw a carving knife," countered Adira.

"My mistake. A cleaver. It flew out the window and cut a swathe through my hyacinths."

"What kind of man fusses with flowers for hours a day?"

"You didn't mind dousing your rum with honey from my beehives!"

Badger interjected, "That's more like it. I missed the bickering."

"Belt up!" said both exes.

"Somebody is coming," rumbled Jaeger. Everyone looked up.

A single pair of green eyes floated over the dark edge of the pit. Then a bright sphere of cold fire flared. A white conch shell glowed as if filled with fireflies. The shell seemed to be balanced in the hand of a lone merwoman. Bangles and beads of coral and bone rattled on both her skinny arms, as did layers of necklaces and belts and ankle bracelets. She bobbed the conch shell, then lobbed it. Fumbling, Virgil barely caught it before it crashed.

A squeak like a dolphin's startled the prisoners. "You of-fer pre-sents?"

* * * * *

"Beck-on-er is my name," squeaked the shaman. Some of her words were whistled, some sung. "I au-ger for my peo-ple. We are the tribe Born of the Beck, a ri-ver folk, a fresh-et of the Lu-lu-ri-an Clan."

The accent was antique, similar to Jaeger's, noted Hazezon. The prisoners, now perhaps visitors, still huddled for warmth guarding their backs against sudden attack. One by one they'd been hauled from the pit, except for Jaeger, who'd climbed the stone with strong claws as easily as scaling a ladder, to his companions' consternation. They'd been escorted through passages dry and wet, once wading in water up to their knees, to this single chamber or throne room. The ceiling was tilted, and the floor was uneven. Water was ankle deep in spots. Beckoner perched on a rock etched with crude runes, but nothing else about the chamber seemed significant. Hazezon tried to keep a level head, knowing his bargaining position was weak. Chilled, hungry, and waterlogged, he'd promise anything just to gain his freedom to the warm dry desert.

"We spear the char-fish and the sal-mon," fluted Beckoner, "as they swim up the river to spawn. Your new dam blocks their course, and my peo-ple hun-ger."

Hazezon and Adira had agreed to share the negotiations, as long as Adira agreed to stay civil. She said, "We understand, Your Grace, Beckoner. The salmon and char gather in the lake. Our fishermen have prospered."

"At our ex-pense," bristled the shaman. Everyone gaped at the queerest blend of fish and woman imaginable. Beckoner's face was as thin as a hatchet, though her eyes loomed as large as bullseye lamps. Her skin was pale ivory tinged green, and her hair laid flat in ripples like kelp. She went naked, though her legs and torso were encased in layered scales like armor. Gills gaped at her neck as if her throat were cut. All sea-folk were short and scrawny, the women flat-chested and lean-hipped, but the humans had felt their hard-shelled hands. From a lifetime of swimming, these creatures were as tough as wired whalebone. As shaman, Beckoner was hung with more bangles of bone and coral then they could count. The gawkers could only guess whether the jewelry constituted her office vestments, the tribe's collective treasure, magical charms and amulets, or served some other function. Beckoner gave a musical jingle with every gesture of her webbed three-fingered hands, reminding Hazezon of the jangly Adira.

"Your fish-er-men cull our schools," explained Beckoner, "and we go hun-gry. We cannot ven-ture into sun-light for long, so we work at night to seine the sal-mon. But not e-nough can we trap due to your dam, so we fished else-where."

"On shore?" asked Hazezon.

"Yes. Sheep we would take, and dogs, but when none could be had, we sought o-ther meat."

"People," grunted Virgil. Jaeger prodded his ribs with a claw like a shark hook.

With his old ears, Hazezon strained to grasp Beckoner's high-pitched squeals until his head ached. Struggling against a shiver, Hazezon said, "We beg a thousand pardons, Your Grace. Our water-dwelling neighbors should never go hungry, and we'll rectify our failing."

"You will de-stroy the dam?" asked the hatchet-faced shaman. Sea-green eyes bored as direct as lighthouse lamps.

As Hazezon groped for an answer, Adira Strongheart spoke just as directly. "No, Your Grace, we cannot. We laid the dam to blockade the river against an army of invaders from the north. Our village, and Bryce, and all the sea cities, will be conquered without that dam."

"We care not for your vil-lage," said Beckoner. "We shall de-stroy the dam."

Both headstrong women began to fume. Hazezon jumped in before sparks flew. "Ladies. I see no reason why we can't compromise. The lake is now full and serves to block the river. The fish are a bonus but not necessary. Why not widen the gaps in the spillway, or install a crooked stile so the fish can escape? Both races benefit."

"What about Treetop?" growled Virgil.

The Governor of Bryce turned to Adira's frowning Seven. "Like any early death, Treetop's loss is regrettable. He was your boon companion. But we seek to avert a war that threatens many deaths. I'm sure the Beck tribe will pay blood money for Treetop's, uh, inadvertent death. Will you, Your Grace?"

The water-witch stared with wet, unblinking eyes. In the magical glow of the conch-lamp, her skin glowed with a luster like mother-of-pearl. "If you free the fish, and pay pre-sents for our aid, we will send blood mon-ey to the lit-tle man's kin."

"What money?" asked Virgil.

Hazezon could have throttled the stubborn fool but bit his tongue. Adira Strongheart heaped on coals. "Verily. We sacrifice salmon and charfish and give you weapons and goods. What gain we?"

"Your lives." Beckoner's squeaks were not at all funny. "And these, which your peo-ple val-ue."

Beckoner pulled a necklace from her neck and draped it across Adira's palms. Hazezon gulped. What he'd assumed were bone and coral beads were pearls!

"Matched whites," gasped Adira, "and some black! And these are rubies polished round!"

The spokesman of the underwater race shucked bracelets and anklets and lobbed one to each of Adira's cronies. "We har-vest the sea bot-tom. Accept these pre-sents from the tribe Born of the Beck in re-grets for your friend's death. You stole our food and in-vad-ed our realm. Now let us be, if not friends, al-lies from two spheres."

No one had an answer, which the fish-folk accepted as assent. Hazezon Tamar grinned. He told Adira, "Our successes are hard-won, but even a tortoise reaches home eventually."

"Then use your vaunted powers of persuasion to get us back to the surface," said Adira. "I'm freezing."

* * * * *

Beckoner and others escorted the new allies to the surface. An unpleasant journey, for thrice the visitors were plunged in icy ponds and towed underwater. Beckoner explained this route was deliberately circuitous, for a straight run would require the air-breathers to be towed too long underwater. They splashed in and out of lakes and ponds, climbed slippery rocks, and bumped their heads a thousand times. Hazezon shivered uncontrollably, sure he'd die of chill before he saw daylight. Others were just as miserable.

Further, the mage's hopes of traversing this under-desert kingdom, or even tapping its resources, were dashed. Yes, Beckoner explained, more than half of Sukurvia was undershot by craggy wet caverns. Whether they reached rumored oases in the east, she couldn't say, for the sea's outer limits were unexplored. But water followed its own twisted path, more often than not trickling between crevices too small to let even merfolk pass. Lakes and ponds were rare and small, a few acres at most, far apart, and connected only by narrow submerged raceways. The merfolk had also, over centuries, constructed their own secret dams so only trickles were tapped from the River Toloron. Extensive travel for an air-breather was impossible. Hazezon agreed as he beat chill water from his ears.

Unless, he thought, Beckoner lied to protect her race's secrets.

Adira asked about egress to Palmyra's new lake. Beckoner described a double-cleft cliff in the rocky hills along the River Toloron. The shaman explained that the Born of the Beck tribe didn't inhabit the sunken sea year round, but only wintered to spawn in spring, as seals migrate to ancestral coves. Hazezon recalled how Bryce fishermen saw mermaids and mermen only on rare occasions in high summer. He wondered too if fisherfolk who saw too much were dragged overboard and drowned, but kept that thought silent.

"All said," Hazezon muttered through chattering teeth to Adira, "this water is too deep to draw from wells, unless we employ some magic pumping engine that I can't fashion. And the water's saturated with salt, so it can't be drunk. Still . . ."

"Still what?" asked Adira, for her ex-husband's mind had drifted off.

"Eh? Oh, nothing."

They trudged on wrinkled feet galled by salt, suffering in silence the gloom of endless tunnels. Finally they reached a familiar spot: the first sunken shore they'd found. They'd been given their clothes, weapons, climbing ropes, and grapnels, the lot sodden and ragged and rusty.

"Time to part," announced Beckoner. "As a-greed, we shall meet you at mid-night on the docks three nights hence to ex-change tools and jewels. See your fight-ers lay down their wea-pons."

"And your tridents and nets," added Adira. "But we're agreed. Let's hope this misadventure launches a new era of peace and prosperity between our two races."

Beckoner only nodded. Turning as one, like fish in a school, the merfolk dived headlong like dolphins into the sunken lake with barely a ripple.

"Good riddance," grumbled Virgil.

"You want to bitch?" asked Badger. "Imagine the bloody great climb back to sunshine."

Everyone groaned except the tireless Jaeger, but they straightened their slimy tackle and looped on their ropes.

Hazezon's heart fell, for the climb would half-kill him. He vowed, once aloft, to shy evermore from adventuring.

And yet, he had to get back for he had other adventures to explore. In his mind he drew a triangle with three sides: the big desert sky one world, the sand the second, and this watery realm the third. Magic ran in threes, the same as the enigmatic prophecy of None, One, and Two. A mage who could grasp three disparate elements and forge them into a whole, might garner great power.

"Power enough," whispered Hazezon to himself, "to be hailed throughout Dominaria as an archmage without peer. The stuff of legends. . . ."

* * * * *

Miles to the north . . .

"We've surrounded the hollow, Your Majesty. But since these are the first southrons we've encountered, we consult you as to our course." Gold-encrusted helmet under his arm, Johan's general waited, irritated by vague orders that forced him to beg like a boot boy.

"I'll come." Rising like the great purple lizard whose skin he wore, Johan set down an antique grimoire and left the cabin of his royal barge. Outside three more generals convened, helmets almost touching, but they ducked their heads as the master passed. The general who escorted Johan puffed his chest up with importance, though his role and duties were still unclear.

Johan glided slowly down the gangplank and up onto night-time dunes, oblivious to the sharp shale under his bare feet. The emperor gazed at his army. On both sides of the river glittered thousands of campfires, as many as stars in the desert night. Johan would have smiled at the might and power they represented, but to smile was to celebrate, a possible jinx at the outset.

A mile, then two they went, the general retarding his steps to match Johan's plodding pace. The emperor went slowly everywhere. He seldom slept or ate, believing that a steady gait was the key to a clear mind and long life. Finally, ahead they saw a ring of soldiers with upright spears and shields set on the ground, who gazed into a hollow.

At the rim, soldiers shuffled aside as Johan peered with his agate eyes. A circle comprised ten tents, oblong where walls could be raised or lowered to catch or block a breeze. Nomads in dun robes sat around fires, eating, talking, two women singing. Children played hide and seek among boulders.

Johan asked his general, "You spoke with them?"

"Yes, Your Majesty." The general stood rigid. "I asked their mission. They claimed to travel, that they've camped here for centuries and always will."

"What made they of our invasion?" Johan watched the

hollow. If the nomads knew they were discussed, they gave no sign. The ring of soldiers might have well been thornbrush to them.

"They saw our armada, of course." The veteran general shivered now, for death hung in the air, though he didn't know whose. "They claim the invasion is not their concern. Their tribe springs from the desert, they said, so is eternal. 'Old as the erg,' whatever that be. Uh, what shall we do, milord?"

Not answering, Johan looked at the sky and saw only stars. Raising his chin, drawing back his lips, the mage blew air that whistled through his yellow teeth.

A soldier grunted. High above the nomad camp, silhouetted against twinkling stars, fluttered a clutch of black rags as if wafted on a breeze. Johan again puffed through his teeth. More rags fluttered. Then more, a black cloud.

In the camp, the nomads noted this phenomenon. People stopped talking and gazed upward. From their perspective, the stars were blotted out.

The cloud descended, and screams ripped the night.

Johan's troops hissed as the nomads were smothered by flapping fluttering shapes that clung to their hair, faces, and hands. The nomads ran shrieking, colliding with tents and collapsing them and stumbling into fires igniting their robes. Some rolled on the ground, clawing at their faces. Some tried to dig into the sand. A few raced to escape the arroyo, but Johan calmly ordered them shot down. Frantic soldiers peppered the refugees with spears to keep away the flapping menace.

Finally the death wave subsided. In the hollow, only a few twitched or kicked. Most lay still. The black swarm crawled like maggots over rotten meat.

"What *are* those things?" asked the general, visibly shaken.

"Vampire bats." Johan showed yellow teeth. "A virulent breed from the tropics with razor incisors. The first bite paralyzes the victim's muscles. Their eyelids droop shut, mouths hang open, arms and limbs go slack. Then can the bats peel the skin open to suck blood, which continues to flow, for the heart still beats. Fascinating creatures, masters of their realm. You should emulate them, General."

"Y-yes, Y-your Majesty."

They waited a while longer. Some soldiers, sickened by the grisly slaughter, staggered from their posts to retch. Finally Johan sucked the air back through his teeth and the hideous bats vanished.

Turning away from the corpse-strewn arroyo, Johan said, "Now the nomads are truly one with the desert. To answer your earlier question, General, treat every southron we meet as a spy and act accordingly. Is that clear? Good."

Chapter 13

"Would you *look* at it?" muttered Badger.

"Farther than the eye can see," whispered Wilemina.

"Thousands," said Jaeger. "More than can be counted."

Three scouts wedged in a pocket in a promontory nine leagues north of Palmyra. They kept their heads down and off the skyline, for no doubt Tirran scouts prowled both sides of the river. The three wore drab desert robes, stained and ragged to blend with the background. Keffiyehs covered their heads and necks, and rags wrapped their hands. Sister Wilemina had daubed brown paint on her beautiful horn and ivory bow: she was religious but not fanatical. They knew captured scouts would be executed as spies.

"It's frightening," said Wilemina, "but too, it's history, isn't it?"

"Aye, if history is tales of dead people," said Badger. "Which everyone in Palmyra will be once this lot arrives. I wish I'd volunteered for something safe, like mucking out dragon dens or ditching volcanoes."

What the trio watched was Tirras's invasion of the southlands.

The River Toloron was swollen from spring rains, and Johan's army plied it as a highway. Barge after barge after barge drifted two abreast in the turgid current. A simple box of wood, each barge was packed with forty or fifty soldiers and poled by ten or more watermen. Sculls like water beetles preceded the barges as watermen watched for snags. Floating behind the infantry, the trio noticed barges laden with knocked-down siege towers, catapults, and ballistas. Along the shore clopped regiments of cavalry, hundreds of men and women on high-stepping horses that kicked up yellow dust. Patrols eager for action spurred up every gully and rill, hunting spies. Next marched more infantry, too many for barges. Then lumbered war elephants draped with red mantles sporting swaying howdas. Columns of camels were kept far back because they spooked horses. Then came yokes of oxen and strange brutes with high shoulders and sloping rumps. The twin columns ran out of eyeshot. A million hooves and feet kicked up a pall of yellow dust that twisted miles into the desert sky.

Badger squinted, for the haze blew south on the eternal north winds. "Palmyra only needs to look up. That dust announces this army like trumpets and drums. Look at all of them! Everything from Æerathi berserks to whirling dervishes. What's them queer backward-leaning beasties?"

"Monoxes," said Jaeger. "Sixteen in that herd. Then thirty-two camels, then—"

"Belay. Perishing saints, with them eyes you could track a butterfly over a rainbow. You'll be handy if you're not killed in the first day's fighting. You count livestock. Wilemina, tote up the siege weapons, anything that can breach walls. That includes dwarves 'cause they must be sappers, or I'm a sunfish. Too bad we can't write nothing down." If they were caught, fast talking and quick lies might save them, but not if lists of enemy numbers were found in their pockets.

"Remember to salute."

"Salute whom?" asked the two.

"Ach. Children let out to play," sighed the old sailor. "S.A.L.U.T.E stands for size, acts, location, uniforms, time, and equipage. It's not enough to count numbers, the size. You must note what your foe does to guess his next move, his actions. Mark his location and the direction he goes, then you'll know when and where to expect him. Uniforms tell a soldier's job: horseshoes mark cavalry and those yellow torch crests might be provosts. Time tells how long you can prepare. Equipment shows their intent: shovels and picks for digging, combustibles for burning, ropes or chains for trussing slaves, lumber and carpenter tools to build bridges, and so forth."

Dutifully the scouts counted numbers and gathered facts and committed all to memory. Badger licked chapped lips. "I got questions won't get answered today. Does Johan travel with his army or did he stay home like a sensible despot? If he is down there, how do we spot him? Will he have a headquarters tent and private pack train, or a gold-leafed barge? Does his bodyguard have special uniforms, or a standard on a pole, or any foofaraw that makes him easy to spot? Or not?"

"And how do those constructs stay aloft?" Jaeger pointed a black claw at dots in the sky.

"Osai vultures," said Badger. "They follow an army like sharks after a slave ship."

"No," said Jaeger. "Men fly them."

"What?" The old sailor squinted. "No. Must be condors or drakes."

"Man-made, wire and bone." The tiger's great striped head shook stubbornly. "Men fly like birds."

Badger didn't argue. "Even so, what good can they do Johan? Keep counting."

Years of experience let Badger sit and study and calculate odds. New to organized warfare, Jaeger was content to watch and learn. Sister Wilemina was young and yearned for action.

"The riders come close." Juggling her bow, Wilemina leaned from their hidey-hole to track the cavalry squads. "Shall I slip forward and pin them down?"

"No, you twit." Badger grabbed her hem and plunked her back in the hidden pocket. "Why kill a handful and bring the whole army down on our necks?"

"What if the entire squad disappears?" asked Jaeger. "An ambush that killed the lot but captured an officer would bring priceless information."

"It's my head's priceless. Besides, no one knows nothing in an army except the commander, and usually not him, even." Badger pulled his robes aright and checked their exit path. "And Adira said no. We count numbers and scurry home. You'll get a bellyful of fighting soon enough. Now shift south before you tots foam into a berserker rage."

Heads down, the scouts slid down the back side of the promontory. But Badger went last, pausing for one last look at the vast army and armada wending into the distant hills. He muttered, "What do nomads call the Great Feathered Serpent? Makou? Well, here he comes, larger than legend and bound to swallow Palmyra. Guess I needn't fret about growing old and feeble after all. . . ."

* * * * *

"We're not ready!" wailed Adira. "Half the fortifications are unfinished! We've not enough food for a siege, nor soldiers! Even the water supply is iffy—"

"No matter how long we might prepare," said Hazezon, "t'would never be enough."

The two leaders braced a table strewn with lists, charts, letters, sketches, notices. The town hall was now a war room where scribes dodged every whichway, scraped and chalked vellums, shouted for runners, and otherwise organized the town's meager defenses.

Adira Strongheart shoved back her mass of chestnut curls and retied her headband. She was drawn and pasty and baggy-eyed while Hazezon was creased and seamed like a prune. The erstwhile mayor of Palmyra flung out a hand. "Your first suggestion?"

"Call out the militia and hope for the best." Hazezon shrugged, exhausted by weeks of decision-making and dismayed at the extent of Johan's army. From spies' earlier reports, Hazezon had expected three thousand soldiers and that many camp followers. But if Badger's scouts didn't exaggerate, nine thousand armed Tirrans might march upon them.

"Oh, rare advice!" Adira rubbed her eyes. "Ring the bell and shove the townsfolk to slaughter. Fortifying is asinine! I must've been insane to listen! We're pirates and mercenaries, by the suffering of Sunastian! We should cut our cables and run!"

Again Hazezon shrugged. "But you won't. Though I shall."

"What?" Adira's red eyes narrowed.

"Recall? We agreed that when Johan's five leagues away, I zip to Bryce to summon the bulk of our militia. Certainly you don't need one burned-out magic-user."

Adira shook her head to clear it. A scribe cut in front of her, and she batted the man's head in irritation. "Frankly, I forget what I've signed on to, so needn't keep my word. How do I know you'll fetch your militia? It'd serve Bryce best to let Johan beat on Palmyra alone while you fortify to save yourselves!"

"'Dira," chided Hazezon in a soft voice. "You know better."

Relenting, Adira flicked a hand over lists and maps and plans. "What's the first defense again?"

"What's the best bargain? The cheapest. In this case, one that costs neither lives nor money."

* * * * *

"I know it's a bit late," Adira told her city engineer, "but perhaps we should have built the dam north of town."

Blind Declan chuckled. "You 'mind me of my late wife. No sooner would I move the bed against the wall and the rug by the door, then she'd want 'em back again. No, the dam below the town fills the lake bed, as we surveyed. North, the water would just overrun the banks and carve a new channel. Besides, if we had penned all this water north, think if Johan's sappers destroyed the dam. Palmyra would be whisked away like a sand castle."

"As you say." Weary, Adira nodded, then agreed aloud because the blind man couldn't see her gesture. "That would probably please our fishy neighbors down in their sunken sea, wherever it lies. They've been precious use in preparing, I merit."

"Right queer, that lot." Declan tilted his head, white eyes staring at nothing. "I met 'em by moonlight and give 'em tools of copper and bronze and even some steel prybars and hammers because they asked, though they'll rust in no time underwater. Not talkers, they. Barely a word and back into the lake, says my granddaughter. I never heard a splash."

"Who can blame them if they slip out to sea? I'm just sick of giving orders. Some blade work'll be a blessing."

Adira stood atop the North Seawall, as the locals insisted on calling it. All of Palmyra, a knobby peninsula, was now girded by stone walls above water. North walls overlooked a bend in the river and two stone jetties. The west walls overcast the lake. The south view was the dam and newly gapped spillway that let salmon and charfish escape. To the east lay the thinnest defense, a wall above a moat a mere thirty feet wide.

At Adira's feet bobbed a small boat with eight oarsmen.

The mayor was accompanied by Declan, city engineer, and his dutiful granddaughter Celeste. She was also accompanied by other town officials for moral support: the tax collector, pindar, clerks, and Cole's widow standing as Palmyra's new sheriff. With her were deputies in yellow smocks and red crescents. Strongheart's Circle of Seven was strung along the seawall: Jaeger, Badger, Simone, Heath, Sister Wilemina, Virgil, and Hazezon's ex-scribe Echo, who refused to quit and was allowed to stay. Most of Palmyra's citizens waited too, all facing north, anxious and frightened to see the force that would change their lives forever. Wilemina murmured, "Everyone senses, this day history is written."

"Bards will call this the Battle of Palmyra," said Badger.

"Or the Siege of Palmyra," said Simone.

"Most likely the Palmyran Massacre," said gloomy Virgil. "If anyone survives to sing of it."

Adira turned to her cohorts, wanting to smile, but unable. "I wish Treetop were here to tell us a joke."

"He'd say the joke's on Johan," laughed Simone, and the rest chuckled.

"There!" Echo pointed upriver with her short sword. "Pickets!"

First came three Palmyran cavalry riders who'd trotted upriver. They galloped home, pennants on lances flying. Hard behind charged twenty Tirran cavalry in gray and red, hooting and hollering at the first ignoble rout of the enemy. The Tirrans clattered and passed the new stone jetty, then circled the town eastward, careful to stay out of bowshot. Seeing them venture that way, Adira hoped Hazezon's entourage had gotten away south.

A collective gasp arose from the multitude as two war elephants strode into sight like great gray land-going ships. The beasts stopped, and their howdas swayed as the riders studied the town. Two more elephants plodded up to form a wall of flesh. Tirran infantrymen marched in perfect time to brace the elephants, and to their sergeants' shouts, they slammed their spear butts on the dusty roadway along the lazy river. A Palmyran scull like a peapod with three rowers skittered into view. Then a barge crammed with Tirran soldiers nosed between the stone arms of the jetties—and bumped into their first obstacle in the conquest of the south.

Where the river narrowed at the bend, Declan's masons and laborers had piled two jetties extending from either bank, a stone mound a dozen feet high and wide. Anchored deep within the guts of those jetties were the ends of an enormous anchor chain, the biggest Bryce could provide, so the fifty-foot span of river was closed by iron links as thick as a man's wrist. Logs stapled to the chain kept it afloat just below the rippling surface.

Palmyra's first defense was small, almost an afterthought, and wouldn't slow Johan's army for long. Yet when the barge bumped the giant chain and halted, the citizens of Palmyra gave a spontaneous cheer as at a great victory. Waiting along the stone wall, Adira Strongheart shook her head ruefully but smiled.

To the eight rowers bobbing in the boat below her feet, she said only, "Make way."

"Out oars!" called the bosun. The pirates dipped their blades and pulled in perfect time. Paddles dribbled trails of sparkling water as the boat scooted a hundred yards and twirled in place just below the log chain. The bosun called out merrily, "Good day, gentles! Our mayor and militia leader, Adira Strongheart, bids our worthy visitors from the north all welcome, and asks that Johan, if in attendance and not too busy, will parley on the bosom of the waters."

Palmyran laughter floated over the water at the ironic message. Tirran soldiers frowned, but an infantry general passed the message up the line.

Where the Seven waited, Simone asked, "Adira, what if Johan's stayed in Tirras?"

"He wouldn't." Adira gazed upriver. "A power-mad maniac like him will need to toast his victory. Lo and behold."

The Palmyran rowers were given a message. As they puttered back to the seawall, the bosun bellowed, "He comes!"

Time lagged as more invaders clustered just by the stone jetties to stare at their target. Palmyrans stared back, or called rude jests. Adira looked to the sky and wondered if future bards would note the late-afternoon sky wore a high haze that made the sun a brassy tarnished disk. Finally Tirran heads turned, and the first barge scuttled back so a bigger barge might pass. Watermen climbed onto the log-and-chain boom to muscle a jolly boat over the barricade, then waited. A regal figure with ruddy, tattooed skin, and wearing a thick purple robe walked a plank to the jolly boat. Sitting on the center thwart, Johan, Emperor of Tirras and Northern Realms, was rowed across the new lake, probably ignorant that the water's roguish name was Johan's Joy.

With less ceremony, Adira Strongheart tripped down the siege wall and vaulted into her boat. She admonished her followers, "Wait for my signal. Don't twitch an eyebrow before. Out oars, you wharf rats. Let's beard the purple dragon."

As the boats bumped in midlake and a thousand people looked on, Adira Strongheart studied Johan's crew for signs of treachery. They seemed simple soldiers or sailors without spears or crossbows in neat gray tunics painted with a queer red four-point star.

For the first time, Adira Strongheart beheld the notorious Johan. He was a shock, if human, with his red skin and black tattoos and horns like some efreeti or djinn from Rabiah and his purple lizard-skin robe that seemed to crawl over his body. She wondered if he'd grown the horns deliberately to frighten children, or had suffered a mystical mishap playing with bad magic. The horns seemed familiar, until Adira realized the army's puzzling four-point blazon mimicked Johan's red face with its downturned horns, chin horn, and black vee tattooed between his brows. Typical of a despot, she thought, to make every soldier wear his lord's face.

Most loathsome were Johan's eyes, as baleful and dead as a shark's, as if the owner had seen everything and despised it, and only existed to conquer for the sheer embrace of power. She wondered, *But does he enjoy the chase?*

"Adira Strongheart." Johan's voice was deep and mocking, more alive than his face. "You've dammed the Toloron and fortified Palmyra. Why?"

"I'd think even a troglodyte from your scabby mountains could guess that." Adira goaded Johan to gauge his reaction. "It's not I alone who thwarts your invasion. Bryce, Kalan, Enez—all the coastal cities have pledged to stop you on this spot."

Johan's black-hooded eyes surveyed the citizens crowding the seawall. He demanded, "Do you jest? We journey to invade Bryce. Palmyra is barely a way station. I could divert six bargeloads of the greenest infantry to sweep your village end to end and put every man, woman, and child to the sword before sundown."

Tilting her nose in a cocky way that so irritated Hazezon Tamar, plunking one boot on the gunwale, the pirate chief fluffed her curls. "You'd be surprised at the toll we exact. Altogether, you'd best row home. Invest your time in farming the uplands. The southlands are too prickly a thorn to seize. Our defenses here are but the tip of the sword forged for war."

"You mock?" Black eyes bulging, Johan shook so hard his boat jiggled, his first sign of emotion. "Carve this date on your tombstone, Adira Strongheart. I planned only to enslave Palmyra. Now I'll snuff it like a guttering candle."

Adira spread both arms wide as if stretching, an action that pressed her breasts tight against her husband's old shirt. "At last, the adder's tongue spits venom. Your threat ends our parley."

So saying, Adira clapped arms to her side, squatted, and kicked mightily off the gunwale.

Johan's eyes flew wide as the pirate leader back flipped over the far gunwale and swan dived into the lake.

Immediately, two arrows sizzled through the air where Adira had stood. The first whizzed by Johan's head, close enough to nip his purple hood. The other smacked his breastbone, the impact so hard he flopped and crashed at his oarsmen's feet.

Atop the seawall, Badger yelped, "Sins of our fathers, what a shot!"

Heath, the pale archer with the mysterious past, piffed without pride. "He flinched, else I'd have split his heart."

"I missed!" Sister Wilemina, devotee of Lady Caleria, greatest of hunters, banged her bow crossways atop her head. "I missed! I missed! The Lady punish me! I am not worthy to bear her bow!"

Jaeger had screened the two archers as they nocked. Now he cocked an ear to the wild cheers of the Palmyrans. "No shame in missing that shot, daughter. To even skim a moving man in a bobbing boat at that range was a miracle."

The Circle of Seven watched as the Palmyran rowers frantically scuttled away from Johan's boat. Adira Strongheart stayed in the water clinging to the gunwale of her boat lest one of Johan's thugs raise a hidden crossbow. Bobbing in the lake, giddy as a schoolgirl, she chattered, "My easiest victory! I near bashed my head on the gunwale with that back flip, but it stunned Johan! Wonderful! With Johan dead, I suspect his entire army will dissolve in chaos! His generals will likely squabble—"

A babble from the shore made Adira prick her ears. Cheering had turned to gasps. Her head streaming water, Adira asked her rowers, "What is it? What transpires? Turn this damned boat so I can see!"

Paddling like maniacs, Adira's oarsmen swiveled the boat. Towed through the water by one hand, Adira saw.

Johan was alive.

Propped by his boat crew, the emperor of Tirras swayed but stayed upright. The arrow still jutted from his chest, but as thousands watched, the master mage grabbed the shaft with a blood-red hand, gritted his teeth, and yanked the shaft from his breast. Tossing the bloody arrow in the lake, he pointed across the water at Adira Strongheart, whose heart skipped a beat.

Blood streaming down his breast, Johan roared, "You die last!"

* * * * *

"So much for diplomacy." Trailed by her Seven, with Jaeger in the lead to part the crowd, the sopping-wet Adira jogged toward the town hall and war room. "Hazezon won't be happy."

Badger called above the bustle, "It's a bad sign if villains don't die when you kill them."

"He'll die." Adira was shaking, and not ashamed. Perhaps Johan wasn't human and couldn't die. "You lot, get to your battle stations—Where's Heath?"

Simone nodded toward the lake behind. "He rowed into the lake to retrieve his arrow. He reckons it's lucky."

"Bad-lucky!" objected Virgil. "It didn't kill him first time, so it never can!"

"Naw," said Badger. "The arrow's got a piece of his soul, if the bastard has one. It'll seek out his heart next time. What we need's a charmed arrowhead."

"My luck's poisoned!" wailed Wilemina. "I missed the greatest shot of my life!"

"People make their own luck!" pronounced Simone.

"Children." Adira Strongheart paused at a crossroads. Palmyrans, Kalans, Enezites, and others surged in all directions. "Let's not argue. We have a city to save."

"We weren't arguing." Badger's tone was wounded. "We were just—"

Adira's finger twirled a circle. "Tell it to the Tirrans. Git!"

At the town center, Adira dashed to the stables and ordered horses. As stablehands scurried to bring out the beasts, a young female scribe rushed to Adira with a fistful of lists. With one flick of her hand the mayor sent the parchments sailing around the plaza. "Time for plans and talk is done, daughter. Find a sword and strap it on."

Ignoring the scribe and a hundred others, Adira mounted as her horse was led outside. Virgil and Wilemina as bodyguards, mounted too. Adira ordered, "Stay close but don't trample any citizens. That's the Tirrans' job. *Hya-ah!*"

Despite her disdain for clerical details, Palmyra's mayor knew she needed first and foremost a good picture of Johan's siege. Correct information would save lives in the long and short run. So, as leader of the militia, she set out on a rapid tour of the defenses.

First they rode east to the thinnest wall. Adira stepped straight from the saddle onto a fixed ladder that rose to a flat rooftop. Several buildings throughout the village had been reinforced as observation posts. A Palmyran guard with a spear let Adira and her bodyguards pass, but any citizens would be denied the vantage point. A new adobe parapet ran around three sides of the rooftop. Screened by its protection, the mayor assessed the invaders' approach. War elephants and cavalry guarded the infantry as they marched in squares to seize the neck of Palmyra's peninsula. The only land escape from the town was cut off. Framed by soldiers, sappers like gray ants raised picks, and shovels, and began digging trenches, and throwing up barricades. Tirran archers eager for glory scaled rope ladders dangling from the elephants' sides and crammed together to shoot. Adira Strongheart watched the first flock of arrows soar into the village and disappear in alleys and streets.

Behind the Tirran front lines, verging on pebbly hills, quartermasters and engineers laid out lines of string to mark guard posts, kitchens, latrines, and other army edifices. Virgil droned, "This's no one-night stopover in port. Wait till they get serious about besieging."

Below her feet, inside the new siege wall, militiamen and soldiers of Palmyra, Yerkoy, Enez, and elsewhere clustered elbow to elbow and took turns to peek at the foe. Sergeants bellowed last-minute instructions and warnings, but in the time-honored tradition of armies everywhere, the soldiers could only hurry up and wait.

Sister Wilemina fingered her bowstring. "Shall I send a test shot?"

Whirling, Adira snapped, "Wil, if you waste a single arrow, I'll snip your bowstring and strangle you with it. Then I'll tell Lady Caleria that you ran off to the hills with a one-eyed goblin because you were pregnant with triplets!"

"Don't do that, please!" wailed the young woman.

Quitting the eastern observation post, Adira saddled up and chugged for the north wall through buzzing crowds half-eager for battle and half-frantic. She gained another parapeted rooftop just in time to see the log-and-chain boom shorn. With an infantry barge pushing the barricade tight, archers erected movable shield walls to screen errant arrows from Palmyra. Dwarves with metal-cutting saws attacked a single link. Within minutes the heavy chain snapped, and the logs floated free. Packed with cheering, jeering soldiers, the big barge entered the lake called Johan's Joy. Another followed, and a third, then more as dusk descended. When twenty-five barges had passed, the next three were jammed abreast and wedged against the stone jetties. Engineers roped the barges together, then hulking barbarians overlaid them with planks. Immediately Tirran cavalry clattered over the jury-rigged bridge.

"It's official," moaned Virgil. "Palmyra is surrounded."

"That's what 'besieged' means," said Adira tartly.

Wilemina said, "I know what happens next."

"The dam."

Mounting and trotting through town, they saw people still scurried every whichway, though many just crouched behind seawalls and watched the invaders entrench. Climbing a rooftop post into the cool spring night, Adira cast her gaze south.

The Tirran's progress was easy to track, for torches were propped on poles throughout the lake armada. The flickering lights reflected in the dark water. At all points of the compass, Palmyra sat amid a sparkling sea of lights like fairy fire on the ocean while a million desert stars winked overhead. Adira said, "It's a shame we're in such deadly danger, for this's the most beautiful vista I've ever beheld."

Then Adira's pirate eye took over, and she studied the foreign fleet to grasp their intentions. "Wil, ride and fetch Declan. You know where he lives."

Amid shouting and torch-waved signals, twenty barges were slowly clustered at the west, out of bowshot and catapult shot from the town. Sailors sank anchors and tested their bite by cranking hard on capstans. Engineers busily roped and chained the barges together. Meanwhile five barges crowded against the dam, wood grinding against stone, with only the spillway left clear. Close to town, these barges were lined by more movable shields, called mantles. Adira grudgingly approved, for she'd employed mantles often in boarding operations at sea. From behind the screen came a grinding of rocks moving, and muffled thuds. Some soldiers staggered off the far end of the dam to pitch stones.

Soon Declan limped up the ladder with arthritic hands and feet. His brawny daughter Celeste led him as gently as a kitten. Greeting the blind man, Adira sketched a picture for the blind architect and engineer.

"See if I guess right. Five barges press against your dam. To add weight, they shift rocks from the dam into the barges. Other teams lug excess rocks away and dump them. The twenty barges yonder are prepared to storm our siege wall if called upon, but the leaders are smart enough not to bring all the barges on the lake. If the dam suddenly bursts, all this lake water would surge through the gap and the barges might be sucked into the vortex and crushed, or even block the flow. So they anchor at the western arm of the lake and bind the barges into a floating island of wood. The rest of the fleet waits upstream where a sudden drop in the water level won't endanger or beach them."

"That's not how I'd proceed, but t'will suffice." Declan's white eyes stared at nothing. He asked a few questions and mulled the answers.

Virgil mused, "It's hard toil to erect something, but devilishly quick work to tear it down. With all those blokes hauling rocks, that dam'll breach before dawn."

"They can't toil underwater," corrected Declan. "It takes a coffer dam planted upstream to work dryshod. Once the water begins to spill over the dam, the current'll be too strong to take off rocks. For a day anyway. And it's still a barrier to barges, so what will they try then?"

The seafarers and city engineer pondered and estimated and devised a dozen defenses, though most were discarded as either too costly in lives or too trivial in execution. Having archers slip downstream to cross the river and snipe the rock-looters seemed a worthwhile delaying tactic, and Adira sent Virgil to convey orders. Lobbing mystic fireballs or burning arrows at the barges might ignite them, but they wouldn't burn long with water so close to hand. Fashioning a Palmyran barge into a blazing fireship might serve, and Declan sent Celeste to round up junior engineers. Wilemina suggested sending canny scouts to capture Tirran soldiers and don their uniforms, then infiltrate the landward camp. More city defenders gained the rooftop to join the discussion. Plans were proposed and fell by the wayside as night wore on and Palmyra settled for a long haul. Prowling the dim streets, Jaeger climbed the rooftop and listened to the war council as he watched the busy machinations with glowing amber eyes.

"What galls," said Adira, "is our efforts matter so little. Johan originally planned to bypass Palmyra, and so he does.

Our log boom and this hard-won dam won't bog him down for two days! He can leave one green regiment to pin and whittle us while his invasion of Bryce and all the southlands forges ahead. We're barely a bump in the road. Our preparations and sacrifice will come to naught—"

"Mother of Night!" Wilemina pointed her bow like a finger. "Look! On the water!"

Down the line of the rock-filled barges, torches suddenly upset, soldiers yelled, and blows were struck. A wooden mantle tilted and splashed in the lake. Sword and spear blades flashed in fire-lit darkness.

"It's—I can't see!" chirped Adira. "Who's attacking?"

"Friends we forgot we had." Jaeger's rumble startled the humans. His superior cat's eyes could distinguish the combatants. "The merfolk rise to our rescue."

Chapter 14

"Just like them, the fishy scoundrels!" carped Adira. "Never send word nor hope, and then spring an unsupported attack! Fyndhorn's fish, we must—Virgil, ride to the plaza and ring the alarm! We can counterattack across the dam—"

"Sooner," rumbled Jaeger. The towering tiger man leaped onto the roof's parapet, swung his long arms for balance, and launched into space. Adira and her escort gaped as Jaeger vaulted the street below, bounced off the stone seawall, and soared in a high curving arc that struck the lake with barely a ripple. The last leap seemed thirty feet, and the humans rubbed their eyes, scarce believing.

"Look how he swims!" chirped Wilemina.

By starlight and torchlight they watched Jaeger cut the water like a marlin, sweeping arm over arm toward the nearest barge. Virgil breathed, "Never saw a cat take to water before."

Treading water, Jaeger listened and decided the first barge was deserted. Fierce fighting resounded farther on. In the darkness swords and daggers clashed, steel on bronze. The battle was punctuated by screams and shrill pipings like dolphin whistles. Surging through the water, Jaeger caught the barge gunwale to pull himself from the water when two Tirran soldiers plunged headlong beside him. One enemy soldier floundered, unable to swim. Jaeger helped by snagging his bare head with flexed claws and slamming his skull against the boat. The other paddled in a circle, unsure where lay the barge in the dark. Jaeger whacked his head with a paw that crushed bone. The victim sank without a burble. The tiger man boarded.

Sniffing and peering in darkness, his nose telling as much as his eyes, Jaeger discerned that the fight, or rout, was almost over. Merfolk had swept the Tirrans from four barges and now battled to clear the last. Racing along a gunwale no wider than a man's hand, Jaeger hopped down in the last barge and jogged over loose rocks. As he neared the brawl, two merfolk whirled with copper-tipped spears.

"Friend!" growled Jaeger. "Palmyran! Friend of Adira and Beckoner!"

One merwoman recognized him and turned back to the fight. In the bow of the barge, some stubborn veterans of Tirras refused to give up the ship. The merfolk, strong and wiry from a lifetime of battling oceans and storms, valiantly thrust and hacked at the nine men. Covered with a scaled coat of leather, steel helmet, shield, and long sword, and flanked by eight soldiers, the Tirran officer was almost impervious to attack. Copper and bronze banged off his shield, and he returned every blow. Five merfolk lay crumpled at his feet, and now he shouted encouragement to his squad.

"With me, lads! Sweep them into the bay!"

Reckoning his bronze dagger and claws were inadequate against such armored might, Jaeger searched for a weapon and found many under his feet. Squatting, the dripping tiger man hoisted a boulder as big as a bushel basket, poised it a second overhead, and heaved.

Hampered by darkness, the officer barely saw the oncoming missile and flung his shield up as if flinching. The stone smashed his shield into his face and crushed his nose. As he skidded and fell, the great rock smashed his leg. Spitting teeth, the man tried to shout orders but only gargled blood. By then Jaeger had pitched another boulder and knocked a man clean off the barge. Another rock soared as if from a catapult and mashed a man's leg, so he tumbled and tangled his partner. The next stone hit no one as terrified soldiers dropped swords and shields and vaulted the gunwale to land in the lake, anything to escape that terrible rain of death. Those who remained were stabbed and hacked. Jaeger had hoisted a stone but lacked a target when a merwoman whistled, "They rush!"

A patter and clatter of feet along the stone dam announced a charge. Twenty Tirrans had formed their famous wall of shields and spears. Sergeants at either end carried torches to light the way. They trotted fast, eager to impale anyone in their path.

"Jump!" yelled Jaeger. "Over the sides!"

Splashes sounded as merfolk bailed over the gunwales, for it was suicide to oppose that steel dragon. Two wounded merfolk were plucked from the barge's bottom and chucked over the side. Then their rescuers dived. Jaeger sat poised on the gunwale.

Like clockwork toys, the phalanx merged a wide rank into two columns. Covered by comrades, pairs of soldiers hopped down in the barge atop rocks and immediately raised spears to defend. Jaeger watched the evolution, precisely done but woefully late, then kicked and dived over the side. Orienting with the barge, for he didn't wish to rise alongside and be gored, he stroked through water teeming with naked, scaled bodies.

Thirty feet from the barge, he surfaced. A merwoman with streaming seaweed hair paddled close, barely moving as she trod water, as graceful as a sea snake. Jaeger spat lake water and asked low, for sound carried across water, "Have your people another plan?"

"This is di-ver-sion. Come, see."

Dipping, she disappeared. Jaeger reflected ironically how merfolk forgot land dwellers needed air. Cleaving the surface, Jaeger veered in her direction and hoped to catch up.

The merfolk congregated near the stone jetties, Jaeger learned, where the bulk of the Tirran armada waited. The merwoman had crawled upon the slanting rocks, almost within arm's reach of the barges. She hung more in the water than out, and signaled Jaeger close. Beckoning silence, she bid him listen upriver. The tiger shook his head to fling water from his furry ears.

A thousand sounds stippled the night. Bored soldiers dozed and snored. Sergeants counted heads. An officer posted sentries, laying out their circuits. Guards paced. A provost barked at two miscreants. A camel gargled. A squad trotted off jingling toward some engagement.

Then he heard a yell and another. Jaeger heard shouts and yelps and bellows all along the unseen river. Over the shouting rushed a gurgling and gushing, and kegs, and boxes thumping sodden bulwarks.

"The i-ron tools," explained the merwoman, luminous eyes like green lamps. "Our people pry the bel-lies of the boats."

Now Jaeger recognized the gurgling, like a hundred casks emptying at once. Men and woman shouted uselessly. The tiger man wondered how many ships could be sunk before the Tirrans organized a defense, if possible. Fighting foes who struck from underwater would test the savvy of any veteran.

Always curious, Jaeger slipped off his rock and paddled against the lazy current. He swam under the three barges that were roped together. One listed by the nose as men struggled to shift supplies to stop the leak. Even as Jaeger paddled underneath, the barge gave a giant *cloop!* like a fish sucking in a fly, and slipped beneath the surface. Almost dragged under by a ceiling of wood, the tiger dived, bounced off the river bottom, and squirmed free. With a gasp he gained the surface, panting, letting himself float, and thought, I'm not a cub anymore.

Behind, planks splintered and grated as ropes snapped. On the water's surface bobbed broken boards, blanket rolls, canteens, parchments, and other flotsam. Jaeger thought it an ironic joke of war that barges converted into a bridge were now a major obstacle to be raised to clear the way. Watermen labored to save the other barge, catching sacks of cornmeal or rice and stuffing them in the tilting stern to plug a missing plank. That barge they might save, the tiger noted, if the carpenters and boatwrights were brave enough to enter the water. A better plan might have paired the merfolk to pry loose boards and steal them entirely. Both armies were new to this queer warfare, Jaeger reflected. Tactics changed hourly, and once a trick was exposed, it wouldn't work again.

At the next pair of barges, one barge floated high and dry. Tirran spearmen leaned far over the side and jabbed deep under the boat's flat keel. A soldier's spear shivered, and he barked, "Got one!" Jaeger tasted blood in the water. Treading water, the tiger hooked the man's brawny arm and jerked. His shoulder dislocated, and his ribs banged the gunwale as he was plucked off his feet and thrown in the drink. Jaeger left him to drown or be carved by merfolk. The remaining spearmen shied from the gunwales.

Jaeger stroked upriver. Some barges bubbled and gurgled while laborers pitched supplies on the riverbanks. Some barges had been saved by lashing to rocks. Others bobbed untouched. Archers shot uselessly into the water, their arrows jetting deep but then floating. Jaeger slipped along, nose and ears nearly submerged, but his breath whistled through his nostrils, and he feared discovery. Swimming was hard work, and he was too old to pursue it all night. Best he slink ashore and slip into the hills, or simply drift downriver with the current. Aside from catching the odd soldier like a bass snapping a dragonfly, he could aid little here—

Not far upriver, light revealed the emperor. Johan's barge was twice as wide and as long as the rest, a palace of wood, lit by iron-cage lanterns on poles and hung with banners. A cabin hunkered amidships. Low in the water, Jaeger could see only the flat roof like a stage. Generals, retainers, and clerks bustled aboard, but the tiger man didn't see the tyrant. Jaeger wanted to rest and observe, but the shore was packed with soldiers and livestock. He swam to a deserted barge whose stern tilted in the air. Gripping with flint claws, he scaled the tarry wood and perched like a seagull, banking on furor and darkness to disguise his silhouette. He wondered what Johan made of the underwater sabotage, for barges continued to be holed farther up the river.

Johan's staff jittered around the barge. Generals shouted orders, scribes scurried, serving women rushed hither, and so on. At their center, like the eye of a hurricane, worked Johan. The mage poked a brazier on iron legs in a sandbox that rendered it fireproof. By the cherry-red glow Jaeger watched sweat roll down the mage's ruddy hide and black stripes. His ensorcelled horns gleamed like pewter.

Jaeger wished for a bow and arrow to punch a hole through the mage, then recalled Heath had shot the man dead center. Idly Jaeger wondered what might kill Johan, and if he, agent of omens, was the instrument. Certainly it was queer how similar they appeared, black stripes on red or orange. Surely more than coincidence had set Jaeger in the desert on the eve of Johan's invasion. An ancient prophecy had lain waiting like a spider. Some dueling deities, perhaps, had driven horned man and tiger man into opposition. How the contest would end, no mere mortal could know. Yet the tiger knew, as clearly as if the message blazed across the sky in clouds of fire, that Jaeger and Johan would clash, and only one would walk away.

Johan reached some result at his flaming forge. He plucked up a ram's horn, touched it to his forehead, invoked some spell, then quickly scooped flaming coals into the horn's bell. Unaffected by the fierce heat radiating from the horn, Johan paced to the edge of his huge barge, held the horn high, and pronounced, "*Stahl fallah nok stune!*"

The horn of glowing coals plunked in the river.

Thirty yards off, Jaeger witnessed a miracle. The horn hissed like an angered dragon as it sank, but never extinguished. Rather, the fierce fire grew hotter, as if stoked by river water. The sunken horn burned yellow-red, then white-hot, and finally as blue as a morning star. The glare was so bright Jaeger had to avert his eyes a hundred feet away. He worried the light would reveal him like a rat in a hen house, but soon a greater worry consumed him.

Perched on the tilted barge, the tiger man's toes dangled in the water. Now he winced and jerked them clear. A wave of heat pulsed upward, as hot as summer rocks at noon. Hot steam tickled Jaeger's nostrils, and a queer whiff of cooking. Easing a foot over the water, the tiger flinched, and gargled in astonishment.

The river boiled.

Human screams tore the night. Tirrans who labored to save the sinking barges, knee-deep or waist-deep, shouted as they were scalded. Comrades hauled out shrieking victims. Along both shores rippled questions and shrill warnings. Canny officers called to brace with spears, guessing what would happen.

Jaeger's heart fell. Up and down the river, merfolk plying sabotage were boiled like lobsters. Frantic merwarriors broke the surface like porpoises and tried to vault ashore or into boats. Some fell back, scalded too horribly to survive, eyes and brains and guts boiled like eggs. Others who struggled ashore or into boats, dying or half-dead, were butchered by angry Tirrans. The hot copper stench of blood mingled with steam to create a gruesome fog.

Johan had boiled the river and his own men, thought Jaeger, but he'd scotched the merfolk's vandalism. The emperor was callous and cruel, but clever and quick. A deadly foe. Again Jaeger pondered if he must kill Johan, and how, and whether his reward would be everlasting favor or an ignoble death, or both.

For now, he had to save his hide. The Tirran army goggled at the river, fetching torches to slaughter merfolk. Perched like a shag on a bollard, Jaeger would be spotted and made a target for archers.

Guessing the eastern bank held fewer enemies, Jaeger crouched and leaped twenty-odd feet to plunk on pebbles. A squad of Tirrans saw his flight, and ran shouting to intercept the spy. Four, Jaeger counted, with no other soldiers close by. Rather than dash off, he dropped to his knees as if exhausted, hunkering to appear defeated and defenseless.

"You!" shouted a sergeant in a helmet with down-turned horns. "Stand fast! We need—"

At ten feet, Jaeger leaped. His claws crushed the sergeant's throat, tearing flesh, veins, and arteries. The man's head flopped backward like the lid of a box, only his spine holding his head on. Hooking one hand into the gory corpse, Jaeger threw it sideways. The body bowled over one soldier and made another stumble. That unfortunate soldier waved a sword-bearing arm for stability. Jaeger whicked claws and severed tendons and veins. Blood spurted as the man flopped. The one man left standing gaped. Crowding close, the tiger gripped his sword hand, dislocating the wrist. His free paw crushed the man's breastbone, so ribs pierced the heart and lungs. The man collapsed like a scarecrow.

The only soldier unharmed lay pinned by his sergeant's body. Jaeger clawed the corpse away and aimed to spear his throat with four iron digits. But as the young soldier's eyes snapped opened in shock, the tiger man paused. He'd used every kind of brutal assault against Tirrans, but now thought of one more.

Snagging the man's tunic and plucking him up like a chicken, Jaeger jerked the victim so close his whiskers brushed the man's eyes. Stinking of water and blood, the tiger growled, "Tell your comrades I am but the first. Soon a hundred tiger folk will stalk your army and capture unwary men like crippled goats. No one will be safe. Those with sound judgment will flee for the mountains. Or die like these, in agony and sadness."

Crooking his arm, Jaeger flung the soldier onto rocks fifteen feet away. By the time the man crawled upright, aching and stunned and terrified, the tiger man was gone.

* * * * *

"Get down!"

With the dawn came threats from the air, or at least pests. Soaring on a morning wind, flying fiends buzzed Palmyra, and made Adira Strongheart and her Seven flinch atop the rooftop post. A whalebone glider swooping overhead dropped a bottle of flaming pitch that shattered in the street below. The rulers craned to see where the fire had struck. Adira guessed, "The market. I hope the clean-up crews scoured all the burnable garbage. Virgil, ride and see."

Adira watched the strange contraption bank away south. The southrons had grown accustomed to Johan's quirky flying engines. The pirate leader, who had some small magical ability, had even begun to understand the concept: a light framework of whalebone and shellacked wings mimicked a stiff-winged bird. She mused aloud, "But that's not enough. Some incantation must boot it aloft. It's something Hazezon should study, and quick. We need our own flying gimcracks."

Badger shielded his eyes with one hand to squint into the sunrise. "How d'ya reckon? They only drop fire bottles or darts. The worst someone can suffer is a burn or a punctured skull. They're just paper kites, really, that ride the wind."

"Think, you mossy turtle! The bird things are mobile observation posts. Spies in the sky. Their missiles might be nuisances, but the knowledge they can drop is worth diamonds."

Badger only shrugged. Sister Wilemina, quick to spot trouble, ventured, "Adira's right. We need to study flying warfare. Imagine the damage I could inflict from above with long arrows—"

"Another one comes," said Adira.

"Flying against the wind!" added Simone.

An even stranger sky-soarer came creaking along, tacking against the breeze like a drow with lateen sails. The construct looked like a giant dead falcon: a desiccated shell of dried bone and flesh rehung with the bird's own feathers and patched with stitched linen where flesh was lacking. It carried not one, but two riders. By doggedly rocking their feet side-to-side on a crude seesaw to a monotonous *creak-flap* like a lop-sided windmill, the flyers made the wings flap in a grotesque parody of life. Cutting diagonally against up- and downdrafts let them fly in any direction.

Echo bleated, "They're coming this way!"

Pointing, shouting to her passenger, the captain aimed the dead bird into a dive straight at Adira Strongheart. The unending *creak-flap* grew louder, menacing. A crock was poised in the passenger's hand.

"I don't want to find out—" began Badger.

"Jump!" ordered Adira.

Pirates scrambled to quit the rooftop. Despite his years, Badger vaulted the parapet after his leader, who bounded as fleet as a doe. The two thudded atop sandbags on the next roof as the ghastly glider zoomed overhead with a shadow hurtling before it. Tossed a second too soon, the menacing crock exploded on the parapet. Adira and Badger covered their faces with sleeves as a foul pea-green glob dribbled down the wall. Brown smoke roiled and adobe sizzled as the glob ate the mud wall. Evil smoke wafted away over the dead lake that had been Johan's Joy.

Wincing at a bunged knee, Adira said, "If the Tirrans send up any more toys, we'll have to avoid the rooftops. Tell me that's not a significant handicap. Song of the Damned, those captains are learning to aim."

"The wonders of regular practice," agreed Badger.

Brushing up her clothes and again mounting the rooftop, but watching the skies, Adira groused, "I hate being cooped up in my own town! And this piddling potshootting is a farce."

"You'd rather the Tirrans put more zest into their efforts?" Simone shielded her brow as the rising sun stabbed her eyes. "I fear they're just warming up."

Adira Strongheart peered eastward. For days the Tirrans had burrowed like demented moles. Row upon row of dirt berms protected headquarters and troop tents, temporary forges, pit latrines, outdoor kitchens, and workshops, and a hundred other activities. Industrious dwarves had brazenly tapped the town's moat to feed water to the invaders, so a small livestock pond glistened in a hollow. Elephants hobbled on chains to graze. Cavalry clattered over shingle. Greasy smoke marked trash fires.

With the dawn, catapults began in earnest to hurl boulders into the besieged town. Sappers and engineers steadily assaulted the eastern wall and moat, aiming especially at the twin towers guarding the massive gate. Catapults, and ballistas, mangonels, and onagers were cranked tight, loaded with stones, and loosed. Boulders as big as cauldrons crashed amid the adobe and stone houses of Palmyra. Firepots and stinkpots started fires and spread clouds of putrid gas that made residents cramp and vomit. Bucket brigades and cleanup crews of auxiliary militiamen labored to eradicate the fires and messes, but more boulders and pots fell all the time. The men and women flinched whenever a flying contraption blotted out the sun. Even average citizens began to grasp that the sky assaults were not just distractions, but real dangers.

"It's still small beer," pronounced Badger, the old sailor. "Johan's not wasting his conscripted sods to no purpose. This battering we get is just practice for his sappers, a bad neighbor knocking at our door."

His last words were lost as a stone whistled overhead and smashed on the docks. By now even the Tirrans had pinpointed Adira's observation posts, and knew she mounted every dawn to scout the enemy. Soon the six catapults would be shifted to rain stony death on the building, so Adira peeked while she may. Yet little had changed in six weary days.

"This is worse than puking in the scuppers from yellowjack," said Adira. "*It's boring!*"

"It's not seafaring, that's certain, where fates change with the wind." Gray-striped head down, Badger shrugged. "Siege warfare is an endurance contest. The insiders huddle and hope their food and water hold out and reinforcements arrive. The outsiders bombard and dig and hope reinforcements don't come."

"Damn all Tirrans and their two-tone tyrant! I hope takklemaggots devour their bully beef and fleas infest their armpits!" Adira cursed the enemy colorfully as stones rained from the sky. "And damn you, Badger, for being right! Maybe!"

For six days Palmyra had awaited for an attack that never came. Cranked by tireless dwarves and northern barbarians, the catapults rattled and slapped night and day to pitch boulders. Near thirty Palmyrans had been crushed or maimed, though Adira knew the toll could be worse. "Damn Johan for a craven coward! *I'd* attack in a trice! He's got three-four times our number! One big sally from all sides and our heads would feed flies on the parapets!"

"We've got walls and a moat. Johan's clever, but he can't walk on water." Badger was tired of trying to educate Adira, a woman of quick action and faint patience. "It'd cost Johan dear to sack this town, and he'd net only us minnows. The army keeps us pinned down. Once Johan repairs his barges and bursts the dam, he'll skate down to Bryce, the real prize. If he rules that, who cares if Palmyra still holds out?"

"I care." Adira swore as a stone smashed a corner of the house. The parapet was buffered with sandbags, but they wouldn't protect her if a boulder dropped from the heavens. "We're skunked either way. If Johan controls Bryce, Palmyra must sue for peace. The price of that would be our scalps."

"Cross the western wastes, scale a cliff, walk to Buzzard's Bay, steal a boat. If Bryce does fall, Johan will gain a lot of suckerfish friends. Best we depart or suffer a slow death."

"I'd grow dizzy totting up the jackanapes who've tried to scuttle me." Creeping to the north wall, Adira peeked upriver. "Maybe Johan'll act today. Heath and Jaeger report most of the barges are repaired."

The elf and tiger man, as silent as thistledown, had regularly infiltrated the enemy camp. Adira had joined them twice, casting herself invisible, yet the dangerous reconnoiters netted scant information. The mayor could as easily track the enemy from rooftops. The Tirrans, after all, had no need to hide.

In the last few days, some stalwart hotheads had rushed breaches broken by catapult stones, but always the Palmyran militia or volunteers from Bryce or Enez or Yerkoy pushed them back. Scarce a hundred had been hurt on either side. Raids sparkled in the night as daring defenders chipped at the enemy, a drop in the bucket. Meanwhile, Johan's carpenters and boatwrights cannibalized a few shattered barges to fix many. The merfolk's fishy bodies had been hauled to the desert as a feast for vultures. Otherwise, no swimmers had been seen.

"It's not fair." Adira plunked on her butt and rubbed her red eyes. "Our biggest danger is some foolish Palmyrans might get fed up and rush out to slaughter. My people are plucky but flighty, pity their petty ways. Before Johan crawled up our cable, I couldn't force a soul in this rathole to haul water, bury garbage, militia drill, or even vote. Now they risk their lives and fight like fiends to defend a place tumbled around their empty heads."

"Nothing sparks a bloke's interest like being denied his due." Badger ran his eye over the town's roofs. Most were smashed full of holes as if from a meteor storm. "Scarce a house can't boast a brand-new atrium. Good thing it never rains—Hello!"

"What?" Adira sprang to the northern parapet. "It's Johan. What's that bilge rat got up his slimy sleeves?"

His shadow slanting long in morning sun, the emperor of the north strode the far side of the river, braced by fifty archers and cavalry. Wrapped in purple, the distant figure paced regally as the troop slowed to match their master. The parade circled the lake, passing the twenty bound barges with a few token guards. Adira and Badger shifted south as Johan's entourage approached the dam's far end. Having boiled the merfolk, Johan commanded the river. By night his Tirrans labored to demolish the dam behind stout shields. The spillway was gone and the stones awash, but the dam still penned a six-foot difference—and still blocked any barge.

Adira Strongheart and Badger watched the mightiest mage of Jamuraa order the archers to part like a sea of grass. Twenty feet shy of the dam, amid a rubble of displaced stone, Johan fit a ring to a lean finger. Even the two pirates could see the huge ring covered half his hand. Chanting a long while, Johan lifted linked hands towards the heavens, faced each point of the compass, and finally knelt to touch the ring to the soil before his bare toes.

Nothing happened.

"Piddling fool," chortled Adira. "He's wasted—"

The land jumped.

High on their rooftop, Adira and Badger were staggered. Around rang a grinding, grating, and moaning as stone churned against stone. Adobe crumpled and peeled in sheets.

Dust spurted from the parapet wall. A crack opened big enough to pinch Adira's boot.

Too stunned to speak, the mayor clutched the quivering wall and watched her town sway sickeningly. "Gr-gr-groundquake!"

Badger didn't hear. He sprawled on his belly, holding the roof. The cacophony of shifting stone was deafening and painful.

Water rushed.

Eyes jiggling in her skull, Adira gaped as her town's hard-built dam disappeared.

Where the dam had bridged the riverbed, a cleft opened big enough to swallow an ox train. Into the newly made gorge dropped most of the stones from the dam. Slamming and banging roared like a hurricane in crashing waves, shock and aftershock punishing the town. Each jolt shook Adira's spine, rattled her jaw, and made her brain quiver like jelly. She clutched the wall and danced in place to keep her feet.

Where the land had torn, muddy water swirled and eddied as if stirred by a giant hand. Water was sucked down only to spit forth in frothy geysers. Brown waves crashed and collided, vomited into the town and spurted arcs of spume onto Johan's entourage. Yet gradually, in minutes that dragged like hours, the churning water settled, sucking and backfilling, and finally flowed onward toward Bryce.

As would Johan's armada.

Badger spat rock dust. Adira's voice sounded tinny as a girl's. "The dam's gone."

"So is—*Ptah!*—Johan's need to stay. Look, as smooth as a baby's bottom."

Though the river still churned and kicked like a panicked seahorse, nothing more obstructed safe sailing. A few wet boulders marked each bank, but the dam was gone as if never even planned. Johan's spell had tapped some remote region where the land curdled, constantly unsettled, perhaps some volcanic portion of the great unexplored north. He'd shifted this foreign soil underneath the dam, and it plummeted into the void.

"And there," sighed Adira, "see."

The Emperor of the Northern Realms never lingered long. Already barges crept in a string through the stone jetties. To the west, beyond the twenty moored barges, the lake jubilantly named Johan's Joy was already receding. Adira saw rich brown mud at the far west gleam in the sun. By noon the lake bed would again be desert. The barges on the river crept slowly, roped together like a waterbound centipede, each poled by twenty watermen. Soon the first barge reached the dam site. Adira and Badger crossed their fingers, but the boat passed without a bump. Soldiers cheered and jeered as a second, then a third barge passed Palmyra. When the first three were safely through, a boatswain bellowed. Axes severed cables, and the first barge of Tirras floated free on the gentle current. Soldiers waved gaily at Adira Strongheart, who stood fuming on her rooftop.

A man with leather lungs cupped his hands. "We're bound for Bryce! But we'll be back!"

"May gannets pluck out his eyes," muttered Adira. "He's right. And there's not a damned thing we can do."

* * * * *

Johan felt no joy, no thrill of victory. Obstreperous Palmyrans had slowed his invasion eight days, and he disliked mortals interfering in his plans. Adira Strongheart and her cronies would pay in pain for their trifling. Perhaps he would work them to death rebuilding the dam, for creating a lake at Palmyra was a good idea. He imagined revenge. If he magically infused Adira's crew with giant strength and the inability to sleep, then dulled their senses to pain, he could make them toil for weeks until their bodies broke. Then he'd reverse the last spell, enriching their pain until even the brush of a fly's wing brought agony. That done, he'd impale them to die slowly and publicly in the village plaza.

The master mage's ruminations veered as a general bumbled up. Johan spotted two scouts slumped on foam-flecked horses, dust still settling on their leather helmets. The grizzled general trembled as he presented bad news with a frozen face.

"Em-emperor, m-my apologies for disturbing you. Our scouts report from the south. H-Hazezon Tamar leads an army toward us, a day's march south. Four thousand foot, nine hundred archers, hundreds of cavalry, camp followers and pack trains to support them. S-sir."

Johan's hooded black eyes bored into the general's soul. For a moment, the emperor considering killing the man, immolating him into a burning pyre, but killing a messenger was an act of petty tyrants.

"So war finally finds us," droned Johan without emotion. "Do our infallible scouts recommend any worthwhile terrain to fortify or entrench? Yes? Then urge our army dig in. And stop shivering, you dolt, else I turn you into a quaking tree rooted amid these rocks."

As his generals convened, Johan gazed across the swollen surging river and flotilla of barges to Adira Strongheart's observation post, but the rooftop was deserted.

Chapter 15

"The desert ain't s-supposed to be c-cold," Virgil's teeth chattered a whisper.

"When we were stuck in Albatross Alley, and the pitch dripped off the standing rigging, you complained it was too hot." Badger flicked his fingers to conjure flame on his thumb. By the meager light, and one-handed, he inspected his last four crossbow bolts. The party was isolated in the hills far from Palmyra and had to harbor their supplies with care.

"Douse that light. You spoil our night vision." Wilemina's voice was muffled by a keffiyeh against the night chill.

Adira Strongheart grunted in disgust. "Hush, the lot of you, or I'll carve out your flapping tongues. Next time we go adventuring, I swear I'll recruit only simpleminded children. Less bickering and better order-following. Tend your weapons. We move when those lights die down."

"Cavalry!" hissed Heath.

In the starless desert night, where frost made every surface sparkle, the guerrilla party hunkered in the shelter of what they'd thought was a shelf of rock. Now the "rock" quivered and flapped, writhing in pain, then settled in resignation. The creature was a desert ray, sand-colored skimmers that mimicked manta rays of the ocean. Forty feet on a side, the beast had been girded about its bulging head with a leather harness that let six of Johan's soldiers hang on and ride. In today's running battle, the ray had been peppered by Yerkoy archers. The poor creature had crashed here, snapping arrows shafts and driving the barbs deeper, then was abandoned to die slowly.

The dying ray was not the only battlefield litter. Arrows, broken spears, dead soldiers and horses and war dogs, sacks of salt, bits of armor, a fur cape, and a smashed glider had scattered across this dish among the pebbly scrubby hills four leagues south of Palmyra. Where it seldom rained, the land was tangled with grass, scrub, and thornbrush. Poor country to fight a classic tactical war, Johan had found to his dismay. Wonderful country to wage guerrilla war, except that raiders had to constantly breast brush and briars. Adira's Circle of Seven had hit and run behind enemy lines for nine nights straight. Their leather trousers and dun-colored robes and sheepskin jackets and head scarves hung in tattered strings that blended with the forbidding landscape.

Now the Seven crouched under a wing of the dying ray and listened until their ears rang. Heath was picketed north and Jaeger south, so the desert-bundled squad was Adira Strongheart, Virgil, Badger polishing a heavy crossbow, Sister Wilemina with a double quiver of long arrows, Simone honing her cutlass, and Echo, who these days scribed in blood. Above the distant clatter and calls of both armies in the distance, they heard iron-shod hooves clop and skitter on shale. Mostly the Seven strained to hear the snuffle of hounds. Dogs, whether trained for war or hunting, were their biggest bane, because none but Jaeger and Heath could sneak up on dogs.

As they strained to hear, Wilemina reached for Adira's arm and walked fingers down to her wrist: *They come this way.*

In turn, Adira poked the archer's callused fingertips: *How many, do you think?*

A moment's hesitation followed as the young woman attended the night. Then her fingertips tapped Adira's palm four times: *Twenty*.

Adira pushed Badger and Wilemina to circle the desert ray. The cavalry would keep to the flattest path. With Heath on the slope above, and the others at two points around the dying ray, they'd box the horsemen without any danger of shooting one another. Silently the Seven scuffled into place and lifted weapons.

The cavalry was hardly silent. Experienced scouts would have wrapped the hooves in rags and tied down loose gear lest it chink, even cut off iron rings and snaffles. Sabers clashed on belts and bridles jingled. Still, these Tirrans were smart enough to send a point man down the rude path. By starlight Adira saw the man's painted leather helmet glisten, and the cocky horsetail crest swish rhythmically, as if timed to his mount's sway. His horse whickered at the smell of strange humans, but the tired cavalryman assumed it disliked the dying ray and only booted its belly, eager to rejoin camp. Half a mile behind Tirras's front line, even a cautious soldier might think it safe. At the bottom of the slope thirty feet on, the point whistled once, signaling for comrades to follow.

Adira Strongheart breathed slowly and waited. Plodding, four cavalry topped the ridge and minced down the dicey shale, spread out lest a horse sprawl and slide. Just as Adira drew a breath to shout the signal, a sky-burning fireball soared overhead. Garish blue-white light revealed five of the Seven hunched with weapons, not ten feet from the line of cavalry.

"Strike!" shrieked Adira, too hurried to curse. "Cut 'em down!"

From three directions arrows whistled and whacked flesh and leather. Heath stood up, as skinny as a scarecrow against the fire-lit sky, whisked arrows from his back quiver, and sent them winging into the cavalry. Four times he shot, and four times killed. He dodged as a cavalrywoman loosed a crossbow with a sharp *pung!* The elf archer ripped his ragged cloak loose of the shaft that pinned it to the stony soil even as he fished for another arrow.

From the far side of the crippled ray, Sister Wilemina shot low, as she'd been trained, to hit the torso. The eerie light of the arching fireball had caught the bulk of the cavalry troop still over the ridge, so her arrows struck the same men Heath killed. Seeing her error, Badger slapped her hand down and booted her butt up the slope, then hurried after. If they were lucky, they could flop in high thornbrush as darkness returned, and to get clear shots at the riders over the ridge.

Lanced from two sides, men and women screamed and tumbled from saddles. Horses reared and kicked. Shouts echoed. Events happened too fast for most folk. Only Adira, long used to keeping a cool head in a fight, pictured what happened next. Believing they'd stumbled into a full force, the Tirran captain over the ridge ordered a charge. Cavalry drew sabers and spurred their mounts viciously to breast the ridge, shouting to disorient and dishearten the foe. Adira could have laughed at the lopsided brawl—and instantly she formed a plan, and acted.

Upward she yelled, "Badger, kill the hindmost!" and down the dark slope, "Hit the point man!"

Loosing a crossbow bolt at a looming cavalry soldier, not sure if she struck, Adira tossed her bow atop the dying ray. Dashing in darkness, she vaulted a horse scrambling to rise, then drew her cutlass just in time to meet the first maniac who bounded over the ridge. Facing windmilling hooves, she leaped aside, slashed hard, then staggered as the keen blade walloped the horse across the breast. Shocked, the beast shot out four feet so its hooves slithered in shale, blood spraying from the fearsome wound. At the abrupt stop, the rider pitched headlong from the saddle. If Adira hadn't ducked, she'd have cracked skulls with the flying rider. The man's flailing saber kissed her shoulder.

Shouting, "Get him, Echo!" Adira snagged the horse's flapping reins and dragged her body's weight. With feet locked and a hundred pounds dragging down its nose, the dying horse keeled over and crashed. The huge body blocked the path, accomplishing Adira's goal.

The next idiot slammed square into the downed horse, and this woman also quit the saddle with a squawk as her mount broke both front legs. The crippled animal added to the barricade. Adira scurried alongside the desert ray to avoid flailing hooves.

"Virgil, get up here!" Crouching to keep a low profile, Adira hoisted her bloody cutlass and raced up the rude path to intercept the next rider. Either by the sputtering light of the disappearing fireball, or by sheer luck and instinct, this woman sensed something amiss ahead, and she jerked her horse's head to the right to crash amidst thornbrush. Quick thinking gained her little, for the horse immediately became mired amid the briars. Hacking thorns with her saber, the rider failed to see Adira Strongheart slither up the horse's rump, grab the saddle cantle, and shove her cutlass straight-arm. Steel pierced wool cloak, leather armor, white skin, then lungs and heart. The rider was dead before she spilled from the saddle onto thorns.

Directly atop the ridge, Virgil crouched as another rider charged. Careful to stay low, he economically chopped one leg out from under the horse with his long-beaked axe. Three-legged, the beast stumbled and crashed as its rider spilled backward over the cantle. Virgil's axe slammed down and missed in the newly returned darkness. Steel sparked on flinty stones, but his next hasty chop split the man's forehead and spattered brains across the path.

Just the other side of the ridge, the cavalry troop quit their charge as Badger, Wilemina, and Heath sent arrows slamming amidst them. A calvaryman yelled a retreat, and the survivors spun on their iron-shod heels to clatter up a gully and vanish in the night.

Echo used a dead man's hem to wipe her short sword after slitting throats. Sister Wilemina skipped down the slope, straightening her twin quivers and leaf-blade sword. She reported, "Badger dispatches the wounded."

"Go back and watch his back," commanded Adira. "The cavalry might feel so shamed they grow backbones and come back. But be ready to move. We can't linger. This fight made noise, and someone'll come trotting."

Sliding his axe in his belt, Virgil flipped a cavalryman off his dead horse and rifled the saddlebags. "I hope they carry rations. I'm sick of raw horseflesh."

"Search for crossbow quarrels too. We run low." Adira inspected her crossbow. "When next I see Hazezon, I'll chop off his fingers for sending fireballs streaking overhead. Why can't the thick-headed bastard remember we hunt out here?"

"Purse." Virgil squeezed a velvet pouch to make silver jingle. By pirate custom, he had to report all booty, so it could be shared. Cheats who hoarded were marooned at sea or, on dry land, blinded and abandoned to the desert. "A dagger with a hilt that looks like silver wire. Spyglass."

"I'll take the spyglass for my share," said Adira. "Strip 'em and slash 'em and let's get going."

Quick and efficient, the guerrillas looted the dead of money, rations, and supplies such as blankets, crossbow bolts, and spare bowstrings. Virgil tried on leather helmets until he found one big enough to fit his head, but he sliced off the horsetail crest lest a Palmyran archer peg an arrow at it. Wilemina found a blue cavalry cloak not daubed with blood, then reversed it to the dull gray lining. Badger hefted a cavalry saber and kept it. With too many weapons to carry off, they shattered the lances on rocks and chucked sabers and daggers into the thickest thorn lest the enemy recoup them. They cut reins and bridles and saddle cinches, then left the rest.

Adira wrapped Heath's skinned ribs and then counted noses, careful never to leave anyone behind. "Good night's work. We'll squeak through their lines, then hole up and sleep. I need to ask Hazezon as to where he wants our lines fixed next."

"What difference?" asked Virgil. "The Tirrans push south and we harry 'em and push 'em back. The lines change by the hour."

"Virgil." Adira had picked up a lance, and now she rapped Virgil's ribs, so he sat down abruptly. Slinging her crossbow across her shoulder, she said, "Save your bull head for breaking rocks. The day I need your advice, I'll grab an anchor and hop overboard. All done shopping? Then get up the slope and down. We'll find a cave. In the morning I'll learn if we're winning or losing this war."

* * * * *

"Hard to say," replied Hazezon Tamar. "Still, that we slow Johan's army even a trifle is partial victory."

The Governor of Bryce ran a hand down his face, which looked thinner and more seamed, the cheekbones pronounced. Adira peered at her ex-husband and discovered he'd gone completely gray.

The allies' headquarter camp was quiet just before dawn. Scouts would await the sunrise to see the foe, then report in. Hazezon sipped honeyed mint tea from an ornate brass mug brought by his manservant Seabrooke. Adira noted his hands trembled as if palsied.

"I hate land warfare," chided Adira. "At sea you either capture a ship, or it gets away scot free."

"Or burns to the waterline, and you gain nothing. Which may happen here. I, unmilitary cluck that I am, grind our allied armies into powder against the Tirran grindstone, but the wheel slows. We might die, but Johan will be thwarted." Hazezon grinned over the rim of his cup. "Would that outcome suit you?"

Munching, she groused, "Nothing suits me. And I suggest you refrain from giving recruitment speeches."

Hazezon's manservant Seabrooke brought a breakfast tray of figs and pita, but before the master could reach, Adira grabbed them. Even eating was hard work, she was so weary. Adira cast about the camp as sunlight sparkled on frost already evaporating. Just for an instant, the air smelled like spring rain and fresh greenery. Otherwise the camp was dismal. This gully was a jagged scar hemmed by stark walls of broken shale. Tents sagged, scattered higgledy-piggledy amid bushes and pockets of sand. Picket lines of horses trailed haphazardly. Exhausted dirty servants rolled in blankets under tables and bushes, desperate to ignore the dawn and steal a few more minutes of sleep. Horse and dog manure, piles of bones and feathers, and other trash were dotted about. On the lip of the arroyo, vultures squabbled over a camel carcass. The bulk of the allied army camped up there on the flats.

"What are the day's orders?"

"The same, only different." Hazezon rose, swaying on his feet.

"That's helpful."

"Oh, 'Dira, must you ape your mother so well?" Mopping his face, Hazezon sighed, "I can turn only part of my attention to command. I've been researching a spell on a huge scale that might stop Johan in his tracks."

"Oh, my, my. Will you dazzle him with your brassy and stupid fireball spells?"

"No, this trick is grand. It should—Never mind. It's bad to discuss magic aforehand." Hazezon stepped to a table and shuffled sketched maps. He pointed out Johan's line, made educated guesses as to Johan's objectives and how best to counter them. Hazezon took time to explain his guesses so Adira might have the whole picture. Sabotage behind enemy lines was incredibly dangerous, and information saved lives. He concluded, ". . . He's also roped three barges in a line and encamped a force on the river's west bank, no doubt to give his men a moment's respite from these pestiferous guerrillas." He grinned at his ex-wife.

"The Tirrans are cranky," said Adira mildly. "They must not sleep well. Perhaps it's guilty consciences, or else it's finding a sentry's throat slit, scorpions in their food, or a dead goat dropped down a well. Their pickets' lines are cut so camels and horses wander. And two barges collided when their anchor cables were slashed. Too bad they didn't fetch up with the fleet, for they burned like tallow candles."

Hazezon Tamar rubbed his sagging face and slurped tea. "I'm glad I'm not your enemy."

"Who could be your enemy, O gracious and generous Lord Tamar?" Adira gave a simpering smile, then added tartly, "I'd think any girl would throw herself at your feet and beg to be your sweetheart."

The ex-husband just stared as Adira straightened her tackle and marched off. Seabrooke said, "It's none of my business, milord, but were I you, I'd take her in my arms and smother her with kisses until she wilted."

"I tried it once," said Hazezon. "She kneed my plums up past my liver. I was sick for three days and still don't think they've descended. But I'll admit: I've few regrets in my life, but letting her slip away is one."

"You didn't tell her your plans for a last-ditch defense if Johan gets too far."

"She wouldn't listen." Hazezon watched his ex-wife sashay away. "And I still get distracted talking to Adira, even after all this time."

* * * * *

Late in the afternoon, within a shallow cave shielded from sun and overhead fliers, Adira Strongheart watched a battle. Beside her sat Jaeger, as silent as usual, witnessing everything. Some of the Seven slept in the cave while others sheltered under brush on the next hilltop. Whenever vulnerable to sneak attack, Adira split them into two parties. If one half were captured or killed, the other would be alerted and carry on the fight.

Adira watched Tirrans and southrons tussle on the plain below, a scowl creasing her bronzed face.

Jaeger asked, "What troubles you?"

"It's nothing, and everything," frowned Adira. "Look at them. Armies scuffling like red ants versus black. This whole war, this campaign to stop Johan from seizing the southlands seems so pointless at times. What does it matter, really, if Johan enslaves the south? True, he'd gain absolute control over peasants and farmers and merchants, but so what? If he crushes them under his thumb, they'll starve but so will he, for it's farmers and tradesfolk that produce food and goods, the lifeblood of civilization. He might conscript their sons and daughters into his army and navy, and send them to war across the Sea of Serenity, but some pompous ass is always stirring up war. People who dislike his rule can leave, probably. And the higher Johan climbs, the farther he'll fall. Some schemer in his cabinet will knife him in the dark or poison his plate. Or he'll die of old age. In the end, his empire will crumble. That's the history of mankind, toys of destiny that we be."

Jaeger nodded, not arguing, and watched the fight. This morning Johan's army tried to bring his siege engines forward to punish temporary entrenchments of the allies. Elephants and mule teams labored to haul some catapults and ballistas across the plain while engines in the rear hurled boulders and arrows as long as trees. Brycers and Palmyrans and other southrons scrambled in retreat, but regiments of allied cavalry crisscrossed the plain to slice at the laboring Tirrans. As one Tirran crew scattered and the mule team was thrown into confusion, hee-hawing in dismay, southern infantry ran forward and chopped the traces to free the animals. A skirmish flared around one catapult before the Tirran artillerists were chased off or killed, and Kalan sappers quickly planted a fire in the framework. Before it could ignite the thick beams, twin fire drakes with leather-clad riders swooped low and chased off the sappers with fire breath. One rider tilted his drake to perch atop the wobbly catapult as a defense as Tirran infantry rushed to encircle the machine. Everywhere within eyeshot, similar life-and-death duels crackled across the drab desert. Johan's army inched, southrons struck, sparks flew, the duel dragged on.

"See?" said Adira. "Fewer than ten Tirrans killed, and the catapult still stands. At this rate Johan won't reach Bryce before fall, but we'll have precious few soldiers left with four sound limbs. I'd argue it makes no sense, but . . ."

"But humans defend their homeland, the same as ants?" rumbled Jaeger. "Perhaps the lesson is simply that, sometimes one must think, other times act."

"I suppose." Adira rubbed her nose where skin peeled and itched. "Hazezon Tamar is not a bad man, you know."

Jaeger tried to decipher the sudden change in topic and failed. "No, he is a fine man."

"Who?" Adira stared big-eyed at the tiger man.

"Hazezon?" Jaeger was thoroughly confused.

"What of him?" snapped the ex-wife.

Realizing he'd made some error, but ignorant of what it might be, Jaeger moved on. "I'll relieve a picket so they might sleep."

"Yes, do." Adira was peevish and suspicious. "We've more work come nightfall."

* * * * *

"It's the river that worries me," Adira told her Circle of Seven. "It gives Johan dual mobility. He can march overland or skim down the river, and leapfrog himself or us. So tonight, we go after boats again."

The Circle huddled in brush atop a high riverbank that had been undercut and collapsed sheer. Invisible in dun robes and sheepskin jackets, they studied the torches strung along the far riverside like fireflies.

"They'll be doubly guarded after we burnt them last two," said Badger.

"Which means the guard details are doubly tired," retorted Adira. "They fight our army by day, remember, and we give 'em nightmares by night."

"The river looks busier," said Wilemina. "Aren't there too many torches?"

The scouts weighed that observation, listening hard and trying to pierce the pools of light. Adira grunted, "You're right. More work crews than usual."

"Maybe they shift supplies," said Virgil. "But to load or offload the barges? That'd tell us a lot."

"Aye. Let's find out." Adira tolled, "Badger, Heath, Echo, Jaeger. Move up along this bank, cross the river, and find out what they're doing. And no, Badger, I don't care if you get wet swimming the river! I'll take Virgil, Wilemina, and Simone and scout south. Find out what they're loading and which way. Report back here when the Cyclops toes the horizon."

"Can we sink 'em?" asked Badger.

"On your way out, if you don't get caught. Everyone got tinder and flint? Good. Go."

An hour later, having half-swum, half-waded the river, Badger's squad touched two barges on the far side of the river. Badger was partnered with Heath. Jaeger and Echo gripped the hull of the next barge down. They'd agreed to investigate every boat in opposite directions. Clamping a dagger in his teeth and shivering in chill water, the old pirate reached high, gripped the gunwale, and hauled himself slowly from the water.

Hanging by his fingertips, Badger and Heath eased their noses over the side. The barge was sixteen feet wide and sixty long, and packed with sacks of foodstuffs. Men sweated under the harsh tongue of a corporal to heave sacks to their shoulders and stagger up a plank out of the barge.

"That answers the first question. They unload." Badger whispered to his dripping companion around the dagger in his teeth. The crew toiled twenty feet away in the waist of the barge. Fortunately Badger needn't climb aboard to learn more. Hanging by one armpit, the pirate nicked a bag with his blade, then stuck his hand in the rent. Sliding back overside, he licked the powder on his hand. "Sweet. 'S corn meal."

Heath nodded, face pale and eyes bright in the darkness, long hair dripping. He nodded that he'd check farther along. In a few moments he returned, hissing low, "The aft holds barrels reeking of salt. Pork or beef. They're being unloaded too."

"So the barges'll sit empty. Wonder what Adira and Hazezon'll make of that." Leaving the plotting to others, Badger urged, "Move along. Spot-check the other barges—Suffering saints!"

Men hollered, and the barge bobbed as a great weight crashed from the sky atop sacks and barrels. Badger and Heath got a blurry glimpse of dark-red scales glinting in torchlight. A hot desert wind blew as a beaked mouth as big as a shark's opened above them. Flame flickered deep in the fire drake's throat. The two scouts let go of the boat, pointed their feet, and sank to the bottom. As bubbles streamed from their noses, a flash of light illuminated the surface of the water like a thousand diamonds.

Thumping the rocky river bottom, Badger kicked off at an angle to slide under the barge. Through a watery blur he saw Heath do the same. Badger's trajectory smacked his skull against the barge's tarry bottom. For a second he saw stars and almost lost his breath. Then he clawed and hand-walked desperately along the bottom to reach the end of the barge and open air.

The fire drake that had dropped from the night was waiting. Barely did Badger's head break the surface and he gasp air than a sinuous neck coiled and a beaked mouth stabbed at him. The heavy barge rocked, sending ripples across the river, as the drake shifted its grip to snap again. Claws like pickaxes scarred the gunwales that creaked in protest. Bobbing in the water, Badger felt like a minnow pounced upon by an osprey. Sacrificing more air, he again sank, back flipped, and tried to dive away from the barge.

Surprise made Badger burble air as a pile-driver force smashed the water and nabbed his leg like a bear trap. The drake wasn't afraid of water, and the old sailor was yanked half in the air by the crushing beak. Badger had time to scream "*Helllppp!*" as he dangled by one leg. Then he yelped and almost blacked out from pain as the bony beak ground bone and flesh in his calf. His tackle hung at odd angles so he couldn't draw his knife or cutlass. No matter, for the fire drake shook him like a puppy, then bashed him against the barge's tarred sides. Dunked and slammed, Badger worked to sip air and prayed his companions swooped to the rescue.

Tirrans shouted as the fire drake fished its prey from the water. The creature's rider, a lithe woman chosen for her small size, wore leather breeches, boots, a jacket, and a leather helmet with a poured-glass visor that dropped over her eyes. Her only weapon was a long-handled goad with an iron hook to drag the drake's head in whatever direction. The captain sat in a tiny saddle held by rope netting that passed over the drake's breast and between its wings. For reins, she clutched a loop handle threaded between its short horns. Her shouts did little to direct the beast, for it harried its prey and wouldn't let go.

Badger was dangled by one leg, head down in the water. For all its size, the drake wasn't strong enough to lift the man's weight, so it slammed its catch against the barge's bluff bow to stun it. Its rider cursed, and Tirrans shouted as they ran in all directions. Some dashed close to see the drake's quarry, some slunk away to avoid the wildly flapping leather wings. Badger was knocked windless and drowning.

Forgotten for the moment, Heath swam the length of the barge underwater and surfaced by the stern. He hauled on the gunwale to see what happened. He witnessed the scene clearly, for soldiers brought torches to watch the fire drake tussle. The beast was less like a flying lizard and more like a featherless bird, scrawny and bony, ribs and hips and spine protruding through the wrinkled leather hide dappled with spots. Its color was dark red, or reddish brown, and its tall veined wings were almost black. Oddly, Heath noted one wing membrane showed a circular bite, where apparently another drake had snapped. He marveled the beast could fly at night and pounce on an enemy unheralded. The drakes were a bigger threat than Adira had reckoned. As soldiers hollered and dashed hither and yon like madmen, Heath watched two craggy claws tear sacks as the creature shook Badger like a terrier breaks a rat.

Seizing opportunity, Heath clambered aboard the stern. He yanked his bow off his shoulder and drew an arrow. Everything was sopping wet, and water sloshed in his quiver, but the bow was ebony with a silk string and though the arrow fletching was sodden, a range of thirty feet didn't matter. Hauling string to chin, he aimed forward of the drake's ribs and hoped his arrow didn't spank off bone. He loosed. The shaft smacked deep into the flying wyrm's chest.

Yet, as if archer and target were mystically linked, Heath was stabbed deep into his vitals. Knocked sideways by the blow, he felt his hip and found a crossbow bolt jutting. With professional interest, already shocked and dazed, Heath figured the quarrel had been shot at very close range. Picking up his head, suffering another jolt of agony, he spotted a crossbowman standing stock still on the riverbank. A woman with short fair hair held an empty crossbow to her shoulder and squinted down the stock. Her eyes bulged. Very young and new to soldiering, she was amazed she'd shot a stranger and likely killed him.

Other Tirrans spotted Heath. Crouched on the barge, near fainting from the pain, Heath abandoned his post before the soldiers hacked him apart. Gasping, almost crying, he inched backward over the stern. He tried to clutch his beloved bow, but his hand wouldn't grip tight, and the half-twist seared his guts like a flaming iron poker. His last words were, "Elves, hosts of harmony, hear my plea!" Then he tumbled in the water and sank like an anchor.

Two barges away, Echo clung to a barge. Swimming was new to this daughter of the desert, and she hadn't mentioned the fact to anyone. Adira Strongheart and her companions heard the commotion and saw torches cluster, heard a great squawking, but were too low in the water or on the shore to see. Adira swore to herself, "That's torn it! Don't get killed, you misfits!"

Only one of the Seven could attack. Tirrans along the riverside gasped as a huge manlike tiger bounded from one barge to another, soaring in great leaps across space. Light flashed on a wet hide of black and orange stripes—

— then Jaeger pounced with teeth and claws upon the drake's neck.

Chapter 16

The squawks and screeches of the fire drake were drowned out by roars and coughs as Jaeger raked with his claws and bit with his bone-crushing jaws. Having been first shot in the side by an arrow, and now cruelly pounced upon, the drake's first instinct was to drop its prey and escape skyward. The feeble Badger plummeted into the river. The weight of the drake's leather-clad rider was already a burden and now borne down by the heavy tiger, the drake might as well have been chained by iron.

Jaeger shredded scrawny flesh as he tried to sever the drake's spine. His claws gouged into the drake's throat, and his feet ripped at its breast. The drake was cousin to the great flying wyrm, and it twisted powerfully, squirming like a snake in slime. Loose leathery skin bunched around its neck. Jaeger slipped and slid half-around and hung under the drake's beak. The fire drake had two sturdy legs of its own, and its claws raked Jaeger's head. The drake's claws found little to grasp in wet cat fur, until talons hooked around the tiger man's head and gouged at his eyes. Jaeger was forced to let go his toothy death-grip or go blind. In that second, the fire drake kicked to launch itself into the night sky, but Jaeger clung like a leech.

Soldiers scrambled along the shoreline but found little they could do. Sergeants and officers bellowed, "Fetch crossbows! Lances! You there, shoot, damn your eyes! Yes, shoot the tiger! Never mind the drake or the rider! Kill that warrior!" A few crossbows were brought into play. Strings punged and quarrels sizzled. Two bolts whacked through the leathery membrane of the drake's wings. One spanked off Jaeger's white breast, cutting a furrow. Another split two of his toes and hung like a giant thorn. Cavalry afoot trotted up with long lances trailing pennants, and sergeants shoved them onto the barge to lance both battling animals.

Hearing the commotion, Jaeger knew he stood in grave danger, yet he clung to the drake, determined to kill it. He'd attacked to free Badger from its scaly grasp, and should abandon the fight, plunge into the river, and escape. But the fury of bloodlust clouded Jaeger's mind. One of them had to die, regardless of future fates.

In the water, Echo dog-paddled alongside the barge with her head down. When she reached the end, where Jaeger and the drake grappled inches overhead, she found Badger clinging to the rudder by one hand. Half-drowned and beaten, the man mumbled, "Go. Get free."

"Where's Heath?" hissed the girl.

"Heath? North—under the barge."

"I can't swim under the barge! I can barely swim at all!" Yet to desert a comrade was unthinkable. Echo drew a deep breath and dived. She bumped her head twice on the boat's bottom and swore the vessel would sink for all the mad thrashing above it, but after an eternity of no air she reached the end and rose spluttering. Squeezing water from her eyes, she couldn't find Heath hiding in the stern's shelter. Hissing in fright, she bobbed and caught the lip of the barge and watched. Jaeger and the fire drake tussled, soldiers danced gingerly with lances atop sacks and barrels of foodstuffs while a forest of torches lit the shoreline. Echo spotted a familiar object: an ebony bow. Immediately she was struck by the importance of her discovery, for Heath never went anywhere without his blessed bow. Snatching the weapon, Echo splashed back in the water and slithered under the barge. Hot tears spilled down her cheeks. She knew they'd never find Heath alive in this surging river.

Still in a frenzy, Jaeger refused to be left behind as the fire drake batted him loose and flapped to take off. The tiger man thumped down on the barge, then leaped again and snagged a bony leg with a roar of triumph. The jolt brought a squawk from the drake's rider, who spilled from the saddle and crashed painfully atop iron-rimmed casks and barrels. Lightened of its burden, the fire drake beat its long tattered wings and groped for air, but the tenacious tiger trapping one leg made the bird tilt and thrash, so its wings slapped the barge, water, and attacker. Jaeger slit his eyes, flung out his free hand, and hooked his claws into the nape of the drake's neck. His questing hand snapped off the iron head of Heath's arrow where it jutted from mottled skin.

The Tirrans closed in, growing confident the drake couldn't slash them nor blister them with flame. Pushed by sergeants, they jogged around the windmilling wings to stab the fabled tiger man they so feared. Yet flailing wings and whipping tail knocked two men flat. One soldier, angered and terrified, rammed his lance through the drake's wing to where he reckoned the tiger man clung. He got satisfaction when the lance bit flesh.

Jaeger yelped as the iron-headed lance rammed his armpit and ground against his shoulder blade. Screeching in outrage, he swiped his elbow hard and snapped off the lance. The cruel iron head twisted deeper into his shoulder muscles as wood splinters were dragged out in a gout of blood.

Squawking at the alien stink of cat blood and the pain of its speared wing, infuriated at the world, the drake dipped its bill, hawked up a wad of gas, and belched fire.

The ball of flame rippled over its own leg, blistering but washing over the unforgiving assailant. Yet while the fire would have charred a man's flesh, Jaeger's sopping-wet fur protected him. Hairs on his ears and jowls and paws singed and curled, and his nose and muzzle were scalded. Blood flowing down his side dried instantly with a sulfurous stink. Yet the stabbing and burning attacks only stoked his fury. Hanging by one clawed hand from the drake's neck, Jaeger balled his great fist and smashed the drake square in the breastbone, pounding again and again like a sledgehammer.

As its ribs caved in, the lizard-bird keened. Agonized, with lungs and organs maimed, the creature flopped on the barge like a collapsed tent. Its long jaw smacked the gunwale. Jaeger already dangled half in the water. Refusing to release a kill, he kicked clawed feet against the barge's side and arched his back, yanking with all his might on the drake's head.

With a great thrash and splash, tiger and drake disappeared under the water.

Silence fell over the river and shore. Soldiers jogging to the barge's side made it dip. If they expected to see the water boil and churn into froth, they were disappointed. Ripples and a few bubbles broke the black surface, but that was all.

* * * * *

Across the river in darkness, Echo struggled to drag Badger onto gravel and gorse bushes. The girl was hampered by Heath's bow slung over one shoulder and digging into her neck, but she refused to chuck it, as if keeping the bow would keep Heath alive, wherever he was. Adira Strongheart had abandoned the boat-burning expedition and crossed the river. She helped haul the sodden pirate onto dry land. With her strong hands, Simone flipped Badger on his stomach lying downhill. Then she pounded his back to force water from his lungs. Shuddering and vomiting, he came alive. Echo had flopped on her face, spent.

Sister Wilemina's sharp eyes spotted the bow on Echo's back. "Where's Heath?"

"Lost!" The girl retched water. "Only . . . found . . . his bow."

"Keep your voices down!" hissed Adira. "We don't want the whole Tirran army on our heads! So Heath's dead or captured. Where's Jaeger?"

"On the—bottom?" Echo gulped and cried with exhaustion.

Against her wishes, Adira Strongheart cried too, damning herself for a show of weakness and anger. "This is fine! We're stuck in a war we didn't want, and I have to t-take up the fight, killing and hiding day and night, just to get my friends killed one by one, all for n-nothing! May Johan be damned to a thousand painful resurrections, and damn Hazezon for opposing him, and d-damn me—"

Crumpling to the ground and rubbing her eyes viciously, Adira held her breath to quell her blubbering. She was aching, soaked, freezing, wrung out, and so tired she could have slept for a month. If only, she lamented, someone else could take command for just a day—

"They're up to something," warned Virgil. He pointed where torches clustered at a high-ridging barge. "That boat's empty. They'll pile in and scull over here, is my guess. They know we're here."

"I want Heath back, and that tiger." Rising, Adira cursed colorfully and uselessly. "I'm sick of losing good people to Johan's drones, but we must retreat. I don't know—Heart of a hart!"

Adira and her Seven jumped back as Jaeger burst from the shallows. Flinging his long arms to the stars, the tiger man shook mightily like a great dog, spattering the party with cold river water. Whipping his shaggy head, Jaeger batted water from his ears and blew spurts from his black nostrils. Blood flowed from his armpit, and now he clamped one hand tight to the wound. As calm as a corpse, he rumbled, "The drake drowned."

"Damn you!" At the end of a frazzled rope, Adira smacked a fist on Jaeger's white breast. "You gave us a fright! And where's Heath? He was under your captaincy!"

"Heath." The tiger man recalled finding Heath's arrow jutting from the drake's neck. Dimly, reconstructing the scene, he recalled glimpsing the elf from the corner of his eye, the man tumbling, curled in agony. "Heath . . . dropped off the stern. Pierced in the side? I'm sorry."

"Sorry . . ." Adira Strongheart shook her head in vain to clear it. Jabbing fingers, she commanded, "Go. Get up the slope. Drag this baggage along. Virgil, Simone, come with me. Wilemina, take post atop the ridge and peg any Tirrans as they step ashore. Pin them down. We'll hunt downriver. If Heath survived he'll be swept downstream. Meet in Haz's camp. Move, you lazy blackguards, 'ere I lash you with a cutlass!"

So saying, Adira stormed into the darkness to find another lost lamb.

* * * * *

"Offloading those barges can serve only one purpose," said Hazezon. "To make room for Johan's only other commodity: soldiers."

"I guessed as much," replied Adira. "His army didn't push hard enough yesterday to take that valley. They were only fighting for show. The question is, how to prevent it?"

Silence fell. The rulers of Bryce and Palmyra huddled around a snapping fire, for the night was cold. Hazezon still occupied the same camp: With Johan's army not advancing, there was no need to relocate. In the predawn chill, only the whimpering of a war dog suffering bad dreams was heard over the snapping of the pitchy fire. The only ones in sight were picket guards and Virgil, who threw dice with some teamsters from Yerkoy by candlelight. Jaeger and the rest slept in a cold camp among scrub on flats above. Heath had been found far downriver. He had crawled ashore with a crossbow point lodged in his hip. Clerics had drawn the arrow and administered potions both magic and herbal. Then Heath was lugged aboard a packet boat bound for Bryce. There Keepers of the Faith in a temple dedicated to the Archangel Anthius would nurse him back to health—or bury him. The clerics thought if he'd survived this long he'd live forever, and Heath was a stolid man, with or without elven blood. Adira hoped so. Her Circle of Seven was reduced to four. Badger coughed constantly from lung rot, and even the unkillable Jaeger had slumped from his shoulder wound.

A brass pot bubbled over, and Hazezon poured fresh mint tea. The mage thought aloud. "Yes, it's what I'd do. Johan bangs heads with our army by day and your guerillas by night to no purpose. He wants revenge on Palmyra, but it's just a gnat in his ear. Bryce is the prize. Since he controls the river, and we have no fleet to oppose him, why not dump his supplies ashore, cram most of his army into barges, and sail through us to sack Bryce? He could leave five hundred green troops here to guard his supply train and keep us busy. I don't know why he didn't try this earlier."

"He's stubborn, is why." Adira sipped tea and massaged her aching forehead. After finding Heath, she'd raced here to report the mysteriously empty barges to Hazezon. "Johan fancies he's the monarch of Jamuraa. He marched downriver and expected Palmyra to roll over like a puppy. We didn't, so he's offended. Against better judgment, he's lingered to throw rocks when he should have continued his conquest. Owning Bryce would put the wealth of the Sea of Serenity in his hands. But he's too conceited to divert from a plan or listen to a council of generals or advisors. Lucky for us. Our two heads may defeat his one."

"Two heads and ten thousand veterans would serve better." Hazezon sat back on his stool. "The only hindrance I see is to blockade the river. If we stuffed six caravels with rocks, say by dismantling one of Bryce's jetties, and they could tack upriver, which is unlikely since heavy ships would scrape the river bottom, we could sink the caravels and barricade the river."

"And Johan would do that land-shifting trick again and drop them into a magic well." Gazing at the quiet camp, Adira wondered where all the fighting had gone. "Or he'd simply beach and march overland and take Bryce in the rear. Better use your fleet to evacuate Bryce. Board your populace and sail them to Kalan or Shaibara. Burn the city so Johan gets nothing."

"We've not that many ships." Hazezon Tamar shook his gray head. "And it's a miserable option. Impoverish my people. Render them orphans without a state. Maroon them to the mercy of our sister cities, if their rulers even allow the ships to dock, for who wants a ton of poor relations dumped on their hearth? And what a betrayal. Bryce has fielded three thousand fighters, and the auxiliary militia trains daily at home. My people would crucify me if I surrendered, and I'd deserve it."

Adira sighed in assent. "People bred on rocks and saltwater are too stubborn for their own good. If only we could block the river permanently, some dodge that Johan couldn't subjugate. You hinted of some trick up your sleeve. What was it?"

"To arms! To arms!" A cavalry rider, pennant flying from her lance, drummed recklessly close in the darkness. "Tirrans converge on this camp, a thousand or more!"

"Up!" bellowed Hazezon, and was joined by a score more. "Rise, my children! We are attacked!"

"I'll fetch my Seven!" Adira raced off.

Quickly the pirate leader and Virgil panted up a twisting path through gorse. Adira's cold camp was hidden on the back side of a low hill, out of sight of Hazezon's. She booted blankets and rumps, then snatched her crossbow and quiver. As people yanked on cloaks and jackets and tackle without question, Adira yelled, "Grab bows! A thousand Tirrans race to capture Hazezon!"

"I thought she hated him," huffed Virgil, sliding his heart-shaped shield on his arm. "What's she care if Hazezon is crucified?"

"It's not how she really feels." Sister Wilemina donned two quivers and added Heath's, then kissed her bow for good luck.

"So women say one thing and mean another?" Virgil tugged on his pilfered boiled-leather helmet.

"Exactly," snapped Wilemina, "Same as men!"

"Belt up and gear up!" called Adira. She counted Wilemina, Virgil, Simone, and Echo. She'd need new recruits for her Seven, if anyone among the allies was foolish enough to join her suicide squad. "Everyone have bows? Then let's go."

Rather than descend, Adira sought high ground to scout the enemy. As they spiraled up the goat trail, Adira explained Johan's strategy of dumping supplies and cramming onto barges to bypass the southrons and besiege Bryce. "This push is another diversion, I'm betting, just to harass Haz and his generals and keep them away from the river. Look!"

Cresting the hill, they stood higher than the lip of Hazezon's arroyo. Surrounded by rolling hills of pebbles and gorse lay a valley split by switchback arroyos carved by a recent flash flood. Hazezon's arroyo, one of many, was an excellent hiding place, deep in a maze behind jumbled rocks that prevented a cavalry charge. Even friendly visitors had to be guided into its heart. Now an enemy force on the valley floor sought to decipher the maze aided by eyes in the sky.

"Damn it," said Adira. "I told Hazezon those flying engines were dangerous! But did he listen?"

Aloft, leather-clad riders steered a fire drake and a whalebone glider above a regiment of quick-stepping Tirrans flanked by platoons of cavalry. The glider was a flimsy framework of baleen bound with wire and wide wings of lacquered parchment or deerhide. The flier soared on the north wind that gained strength as dawn broke. He or she, muffled in leather and a scarf and visored helmet, pointed which switchback the regiment should follow. Circling, not bound to a breeze, the fire drake and rider skimmed low to watch for spies, archers, scouts, or other surprises.

"It's not right, spying from the clouds like angels," groused Virgil. "It goes against nature."

"It's not safe, either." Nocking an arrow, begging help from Lady Caleria, Sister Wilemina sighted on the fire drake as it spiraled around the sky. The drake hung its head like a hunting dog, beak partly open as if tasting the air. Doglike legs were tucked under its belly, and the scouts on the hill heard a distinct whistle as it neared. Its rider looked back to chart the regiment's progress.

As the drake soared near the hill, Wilemina loosed. The arrow impaled the rider with a vicious slap of wood against leather. Despite the arrow lodged in her ribs, she retained a grim grip on the single loop rein, with her legs pedaling uselessly. Her dangling weight yanked the drake into a downward spiral. Frightened, the beast bit instinctively. Either the drake's beak clashed on the woman's arm, or the arrow wound weakened her, for she lost her grip. Grabbing air, she plummeted into a dark canyon. Seeing that, the whalebone glider soared up and out of sight.

"Good shooting, Wil!" Adira already dashed down the hill. "But they're alert to us! Run!"

The fire drake squawked as it soared without direction, loop rein flapping against its mottled brick-red hide. Below, the Tirrans pointed out the scouts on the hill. The infantry kept up their punishing quickstep to thread between gullies, but a platoon of twenty gave a shout and kicked their mounts.

Descending the hill, Adira Strongheart dashed onto the plain of sand and pebbles, steering to circumvent yet another arroyo. The Tirran cavalry drummed toward them, less than a quarter mile off, but more gullies separated them from their quarry. As the five ran, Virgil called, "That ain't a thousand head! 'S more like six hundred!"

"Enough to wipe out Haz's camp!" yelled Adira.

"We'll be cut off before we reach the hills over the river!" puffed Simone. "And hunted like rats!"

"We'll risk it!" called the leader. "That's the only way Haz can escape! We must prop the back door open!"

Saving their breath for running, the quintet scurried around an arroyo and doubled back at a slant. Adira's goal was the broken hills along the River Toloron, for they afforded a thousand sheltering caves, clefts, rockfalls, and byways, and the river itself, if necessary. Simone was right: Six hundred soldiers goaded by anger could comb the hills and find five scouts.

If the scouts ever reached the hills, still a mile off. From the north came, "*Troop, at the gallop! Hut!*"

Glancing that way, the Seven saw the intrepid cavalry captain ordered his troop to jump a yawning ravine. Horseflesh launched into the sky like eagles, tails and crests flipped, hooves strained to find solid footing. Two beasts spilled downward to broken bones, but eighteen horses plunked down safely. Adira's eyes bugged, for she hadn't counted on that daring maneuver. Secretly she gave the officer credit for heroism.

Virgil called, "They'll catch us for sure!"

"Right! Halt and nock!" Planting her feet, Adira whipped an arrow from her hip quiver, stamped into the stirrup of her crossbow and yanked the string, then nocked and aimed. Wilemina, Simone, and Virgil lifted bows and crossbows. The pirate chief called, "Echo, find a descent that won't kill us! Hurry!"

The cantering cavalry spurred to a gallop and lowered lances. In the early dawn light, the long steel heads, as wicked as needles, glinted like quicksilver. Adira swore at how fast the horses had caught them, thundering within spitting distance inside a minute. Her miscalculation might get her followers and herself killed.

"Aim for the horses! We need a barricade! Spread your shots left and right! Aim. . . . Loose!"

Four arrows slammed horseflesh. As practiced, they'd spread their shots to match their stances, so leftward Simone shot left and Virgil shot right. The first horse ran on despite an arrow in its chest, hard-pressed by a spurring rider. Then it misstepped and crashed full-length on its jaw. Its rider skidded in gravel ten feet beyond. A second horse swerved at the sting so its bony skull clonked another's. Both riders tangled atop their tumbling mounts. The third and fourth horses stumbled and slowed, blood flecking their muzzles. Yet the other cavalry riders merely steered around the victims, kicked again, and aimed their stampede straight at the scouts, eager now to lance the foe.

"Here!" Echo called from fifty feet along the ravine's lip. "It's still high, but there's sand—"

"We'll take it! Go!" Adira batted her crewmates toward Echo. She nocked string and flung another quarrel, hurrying the shot as her vision filled with brown and black horseflesh and sparkling lances. Her arrow struck a rider high in the shoulder, slinging her back in the saddle. Then Adira was surrounded by stamping hooves and lances striking like adders' tongues. Three horses boxed her in, and she swerved by instinct to dodge a stabbing lance.

"Hold! Pin her! Capture the bitch!" One rider hoisted his lance high at the last second. He called over the jingling stamping grunting cacophony, "Don't kill her! That's Adira Strongfellow!"

"Strongheart!" yelled the pirate leader. Skipping away from a lance point, she swung her crossbow and walloped a rider. As the man reeled and struggled to keep his seat, Adira dropped the weapon and scooted under the horse's belly, getting clunked in the head by a boot and stirrup.

For a second, no horses milled in her way. Not looking back, she pelted across pebbles to a fresh break at the edge of the ravine. A drumming from behind filled her ears. Then a lance point whisked her flying curls. Half a dozen feet from the crumbled lip, Adira jumped feet first without looking. Her back slammed the edge, scraping skin off her spine. Then she was falling, falling, falling—

—and *slammed* on her backside into a sandpile, her breath knocked from her body.

Gasping like a fish, head spinning, through a gray haze Adira saw Virgil, Wilemina, Simone, and Echo sand-speckled as hedgehogs, for they'd also jumped onto this sandpile crumbled from the edge above, but they hadn't landed on their lungs. Two grabbed Adira's shaking hands and yanked.

Virgil called, as if down an enormous tunnel, "Don't lallygag! They carry crossbows!"

Dizzy, shaken, Adira toppled to her knees, unable to walk or even breathe. Cursing, Virgil lobbed his crossbow to Simone, then scooched and slung Adira across his shoulders like a lame sheep. Echo led the way into another dark cleft adjoining this ravine. The party stumbled into dimness just as crossbow quarrels spanked the rocks by their feet.

* * * * *

Once they'd regained their breath, the Seven circled around to play cat-and-mouse with the Tirran infantry. Popping from cover like wolverines, for three hours they pegged all their arrows at the hard-trotting troops. Skirmishing but creeping steadily southward, for Adira Strongheart always followed a plan, they mounted a rocky outcrop overlooking the allied hideout. For the first time since yesterday, Adira slumped on a rock to rest, chuckling despite her fatigue. "My, my. It worked."

The hidden camp was abandoned. Tent flaps hung open, a cart lay overturned, a forgotten or balky horse grazed on nearby grass. Hazezon's breakfast fire still smoldered. Tirran foot soldiers and pikemen clattered into the camp but netted nothing. Raiders slashed tents and kicked the fire and even hacked down the horse in frustration. A panting lieutenant whipped off his feathered helm and hurled it at the ground, then jerked an arm at a troop of cavalry on the ravine's lip. A bugler blasted a dismal note announcing failure. It was echoed by another musician far to the north. Then a different note sounded, and the nearby bugler repeated it. Evidently it was the call to withdraw, for the Tirrans tramped away north, heads down, shoulders slumped, a night and morning of hard marching wasted.

"What now?" Virgil munched dried apricots and washed them down with the last of the water, for dodging all morning had been thirsty work.

"Haz must have pulled back to the riverbank. We'll top this hill and find out." Adira finger-combed her greasy curls, hoping she'd get a bath sometime soon, and groped for her crossbow, then remembered she'd lost it. Standing, her world spun and dimmed for a moment, so she grabbed a handhold. If her Seven noticed her near-faint, they said nothing.

Hours along, scouting the riverbank, Adira and her crew saw Tirrans by the thousands ranged along the opposite shore, most just waiting. Each bore a spear, backpack or blanket roll, a haversack of rations, and a canteen.

"They look ready to travel," hedged Wilemina.

"Where are the barges?" asked Virgil. The party couldn't see upriver here, where the Toloron coiled around a hill.

"They'll arrive," said Adira, "and that army will float like autumn leaves into the heart of Bryce to make it their new home."

A mile on they found Hazezon and other allies packed in a dark cleft not far from the river. It was no camp, just a rest stop. Threading a bevy of clerks, servants, horses, pack mules, and camels, they found Hazezon consulting two generals, a dark sullen man from Yerkoy in gold-filigreed green, and a slender white-haired woman from Kalan in brown. The generals' staffs sharpened swords or counted arrows, or ate as much as they could, for more fighting would break soon. Sitting back against a rock wall, as big as a horse but more gaudy in black and orange and white, Jaeger listened. A bulky bandage wadded in his armpit and cloth wound around his shoulder was the only sign of a wound.

Flouncing into the meeting, Adira plunked on a folding stool and told Hazezon the Tirrans awaited transport across the river. The generals frowned. Hazezon said, "We know. I dispatched a fast boat to Bryce to bring up rock-laden sloops to block the river, and ordered every archer stationed in the hills to rain arrows upon them as they pass, but those're our only defenses."

"There must be something else." Slumped on her stool, Adira scratched between her ample breasts indelicately. Her Circle of Seven, or Four, sat and awaited her command. "Something we can do."

Hazezon and the generals waited patiently, but Adira said no more. Curious at her silence, Hazezon said gently, " 'Dira? What—"

Without a sound, before anyone could catch her, Adira Strongheart flopped forward into the dirt. People twittered and waved their hands, but Hazezon squatted by her side first. Rolling her over, he gently brushed dirt from her face and thumbed back an eyelid. "Just fainted, I think. But summon my leech."

"Her spirit waxes stronger than her heart." The rumbling voice from the shadows made everyone look up. Jaeger loomed against the rock face. Shaking his great shaggy striped head, he scooched and lifted Adira, lightly as he would a lamb. He said to Hazezon, "She has no plan, I fear. Do you?"

"No." Hazezon waved a sweating face, feeling faint himself. "I wish Adira hadn't fainted like that. It rent my heart. Uh, I have one, possibly two, last-ditch spells, but they won't aid us in this case."

"So we've exhausted our resources." Jaeger cradled Adira to his massive white chest. "Unless we have . . . one more?"

"What?" asked a dozen.

"The river endangers our cause," rumbled the talking tiger. "Let us then visit the river and beg for aid."

Chapter 17

"Sure this is the place?" Hazezon's voice hushed as he peered into damp darkness.

"Beckoner claimed egress to Palmyra through a double cleft cliff a few miles below the village," explained Jaeger. "This is the only such vent."

Four paddled a tiny pram: Jaeger, Hazezon Tamar, Sister Wilemina, and Adira Strongheart. Johan's soldiers lined the riverbank, as numerous as cattails, so the questing party had only dared venture out by night. Yet the humans were helpless, for the cave was stygian, a cloying suffocating blackness. With only Jaeger's cat's eyes and nose as a guide, it took all their nerve to keep paddling deeper under the cliff.

Hazezon was amazed that Jaeger had remembered a tiny phrase dropped in passing, and his estimation of the tiger man's intelligence rose yet again. Squinting uselessly, hunching his neck in anticipation of clonking his head, for the risen river left only three feet of air under the stone ceiling, Hazezon talked to comfort himself, but in whispers, for sound carried over water and Johan's army was not far. "I hope they're still here. Beckoner said the tribe only winters here, then spawns in spring, like migrating geese, then slips back to the Sea of Serenity. Spring is half advanced."

"They're here." Eschewing a wooden paddle, Jaeger dipped great furred hands. "I smell them. There."

Humans caught their breath as paired green lamps glowed under black water. With no more noise than rising mist, three heads broke the surface. The eldritch glow, like fairy fire far at sea, lit faces as pale as corpses, with pointed ears and eyebrows, and dripping hair like seaweed: a sargasso of drowned dead. A voice piped, "Why do you come?"

"We seek the counsel of Beckoner." Jaeger's rumble echoed and reechoed from stone walls and still water.

No answer from the merfolk. They simply sank, and their eye-lights winked out.

"Chatty bunch," said Adira. "I could use a few in my Circle. Oft-times my ears ache from drafty babble."

"Adira." Hazezon turned but saw nothing. "Are you sure—"

"If you ask," warned the pirate, "if I'm all right one more time, I'll dump you and drown you, Haz. Even a war dog's allowed a nap."

Unseen, the ex-husband smiled. Returning to business, he asked, "Do we paddle on or just wait?"

"Wait," said Jaeger.

Sister Wilemina broke the silence. "I know a soldier from Yerkoy. He was promoted to sergeant after six months because he executes orders well, and can think. He can read too. I could approach him about joining the Circle, if you wish."

"He's not your lover, is he?" jibed Adira. "I don't want starry-eyed romantics mucking up my orders because they're spatting."

"N-no!" Everyone heard the Calerian archer blush. "No, he's not—We don't—He's a friend! It's a tenet of our faith—"

"Chastity, charity, and devotion, yes, and three hours of archery practice a day." Adira left off teasing. "I might bespeak him, but it's no recommendation to follow orders like a pet pony. I need folks who jump in blind because they like it, not because they're ordered. But we'll see."

Silence reigned in the dark. Jaeger tensed, making the boat bob. The humans saw lamps ignite underwater, a dozen pairs of eyes. A narrow face split the water. Beckoner, shaman of the Born of the Beck clan of the Lulurian Tribe, treaded water. No taller than a child, skinnier than a plover, she wore bangles of coral and bone and pearls at neck and wrists, and her ankles looked like clusters of barnacles on anchor hawsers. She hovered in the water, absolutely still.

"What do you seek?"

"Your Grace." Hazezon did the talking, salting in flattery, but he wished fervently for some light other than the merfolks' eyes. "Johan's army will sail downriver to enslave Bryce and all the Sea of Serenity. He—"

"Not the sea," interrupted the shaman. Her voice piped and squealed, some notes sung, hard for Hazezon's old ears to grasp.

"What? Oh, well, no." The ruler of Bryce thought fast. "But if he captures our seaport, we can't send your people anymore presents."

Beckoner considered, staring as eerily as an owl. "Tell me more."

Hazezon sketched events of the past few days, leading to this moment where Tirrans mustered on the riverbank to embark. Upon finishing, there came no reply. The fishwoman only stared.

Adira cut in. "Beckoner, those bastards boiled your people alive and slaughtered the wounded who crawled ashore."

The big eyes blinked, so momentarily the merwoman vanished. She asked, "What would you have us do?"

Hazezon stifled a sigh, supposing dwelling underwater soaked one's brain. "What can you do? Our force can snipe at barges but not stop them. I've ordered ships to block the lower river—not so you folks can't pass—but time grows short. If you could attack the barges from underneath, perhaps again prying boards—"

"We did that and died."

Well, yes, thought Hazezon. As many Brycers and Palmyrans and other southrons died on land. He curbed his tongue. The southern cause needed these prickly people. "Any help, or suggestion—"

"One thing," said Beckoner, "but great hard-ship for my clan."

"Uh, hardship?" asked the governor. "If we can ease your burden—"

"You can-not. We dwell-ers of the depths shall suf-fer, as we always do with your kind. Yet we shall sac-ri-fice for the sake of our dead kin. You shall not see us a-gain."

With that, the merwoman sank beneath black water. Dozens of luminous eyes swung about and retreated in the depths, then were gone.

Humans and tiger bobbed in the boat. Adira asked, "What will she do?"

"I have no idea," muttered Hazezon. "But her word is bond, I'll merit. *Brrrr*. . . Let's quit this damned cave before we ice over."

Guided by Jaeger, they paddled out the cave mouth and sighed with relief to see stars. The party gritted their teeth for silence, for voices carried clearly from upriver. Tirran officers tolled off units to board. Sergeants called muster rolls of soldiers already packed into barges. Watermen cursed as boats were sculled or poled into procession.

They'd depart soon, Hazezon knew. In the darkness, even sniping from above would do little harm. Whatever Beckoner planned, she'd better—

"Hark!" hissed Adira.

Sister Wilemina broke silence in her surprise. "Someone . . . sings?"

Over the water, from no source they could place, came an eerie singing. The words were ancient, unknown. The music rose and fell in an uneven pace like wind through a forest. Some notes piped high and hung, impossibly long. Some gurgled down a foreign scale, warbled, and faded. Long rests left the ear hanging. Then a low keen would rise and sink. Repeating like bird song, the tune varied in parts so the mind lost the thread. On and on caroled the inhuman chant.

"Something's—" Hazezon gasped, "something's happening to the river!"

The song trilled like a lost bird's, infinitely sad, but gradually a new sound masked the singing spell. Water seethed like a rapids, rushing and gushing, yet at a distance. Hazezon dipped his hand in the river, cold and wet. "I don't understand."

"The current runs backward!" said Adira. "North! That's never happened before!"

"Impossible!" Yet Hazezon knew his ex-wife was right. The party had to paddle south, away from Palmyra, to keep their place, lest they be towed near the Tirrans. The enemy had sensed trouble too. Hired watermen, even though long used to the River Toloron's quirks, moaned at its wicked behavior. Officers who'd orchestrated the boarding conveyed contradictory orders, some commanding the force to disembark, others to stay put.

The rush and gurgle of water grew to a roar like an unseen waterfall. Hazezon half-expected to feel spray on his face. Again he dipped his hand. Current curled around his fingers.

Through the hair-raising chaos, the eerie song of Beckoner, shaman of the Lulurian, trilled on and on. The swirling of the river was a steady roar, like a thunderstorm surging around their boat. Hazezon's party paddled frantically. Frightened by an unknown menace, the mage called, "Beach us! On the east shore! Quickly!"

Paddling frantically, they jolted when the boat smacked a rock. Adira said, "That's wrong! The riverbank is another ten yards!"

"Not anymore." Jaeger's voice was calm, partly because he could see in the dark. On sure feet he balanced in the pram to hold the rock. "The water level has dropped an armspan or more. Best we quit the boat."

The roar was subsiding, the gushing degraded to a rude gurgling.

"The river drains away? Where could the water go?" Sister Wilemina climbed the rock, crouching low, scuttling backward to let her companions step up. "It can't return to the Tirran mountains, can it? No shaman could possess such power!"

Last out, Adira Strongheart abandoned the pram. "Jaeger, lead the way. Everyone tail on. The river must have drained into those underground caverns we visited. Miles of them could contain this river ten times over. Remember the merfolk blocked the river from below with rocks and magic? Perhaps Beckoner sang the magic to extinction."

Hanging onto Jaeger's pelt, the four slid off the rock, then waded muddy pools and crossed sandbars to reach shore. Howls rose now from outraged Tirrans. Nature had betrayed them. The invaders were beached.

"Now I know," mused Adira. "She claimed never to see us again. With the river gone, the merfolk can't venture this far north. They can't winter over. Fyndhorn's fish! They've sacrificed their ancestral spawning ground!"

Jaeger watched the opposite bank and reported. "Their barges have bottomed out. They're grounded on gravel banks, pointing every whichway. As helpless as turtles."

"It's uncanny." Awestruck, Hazezon Tamar stared at the dark riverbed. "The river is gone, whisked away! I've never seen any such spellcasting in my life!"

"Johan's army is stopped," said Wilemina. "He must march a hundred sixty miles to Bryce. Can his supply train stretch that far?"

"No," said Hazezon.

"Yet it bodes ill for us." Adira Strongheart sounded grim. "We're trapped here with Johan. And since he can't move downriver, he'll turn his full attention upon us."

White blobs of faces turned in the dark. Adira said, "The desert will finally see all-out war. Us against Johan's army, three or four times our size. . . ."

* * * * *

From a high pebbly hill, morning showed a dirty ditch studded with slimy rocks as far as the eye could see, the grave of the dead River Toloron.

"Great Defender, the Toloron was the lifeblood of Palmyra!" Still astounded by the night's magnificent display of power, Hazezon Tamar wondered aloud, "How far north do you think the river ceases to exist? I mean, are the headwaters in the mountains still flowing, so we'll see a trickle that builds until the river is restored to its glory? Or has Beckoner's enchantment banished the river forever by breaking its back?"

"I can't know, Haz, and neither can you." Adira Strongheart stared not at the dead riverbed, but westward where Johan's army covered the scabby plains of scree and sand. A tidal wave of humanity and livestock, a deadly force that could sweep Jamuraa from one sea to the other.

Mumbling to himself, Hazezon abandoned the river question. Curiosity must wait. Perhaps for eternity, for the allies' chances of survival dimmed daily.

No one planned to roll over and die quietly. Already scouts sniped at Johan's larger force, like ants biting the toes of a lion. Unthinking, Adira drew and juggled one of her matched daggers. She asked, "What do you reckon, it's eight miles to Palmyra?"

"Or less. We might fare well. I still have a few spells in my grimoire." Hazezon mopped his face, tired by a night of boating and walking. Now he faced a hard day's work conjuring on the scale he'd never dared contemplate.

"Is that your magic manakins?"

"Them," the mage admitted. "And something else. Big. I just hope I've the strength for what I attempt."

"You've got it." Adira didn't look at her ex-husband, but Hazezon appreciated the vote of confidence. Sheathing her dagger, Adira tripped down the hillside between patches of stiff gorse, as nimble as a chamois. Below waited Wilemina and Simone with horses. "Start twiddling your binnacle, Haz. I'll try some last-ditch delaying tactics!"

Skipping like a girl, Adira reached the bottom and vaulted into the saddle. Booting her horse, she swung westward. Hazezon wished his ex-wife might have wished him luck, or blown him a kiss, but the time for pleasantries was over. Now would come blood and pain and sorrow. Sighing, the wizard trudged down the hillside to find his servant and mystic accoutrements.

* * * * *

Still flushed from riding, Adira dismounted and scaled yet another steep hill of skittery rocks. Wilemina and Simone braced her with bows and nocked arrows, ready to pick off any sniping archers. The sun lifted in the east, and the desert stirred.

Rugged country, this desert. Hills were heaps of rocks with precious little soil. Gullies and ravines crawled like broken-backed snakes toward the rapidly drying stripe of mud and gravel that had been the River Toloron. Johan's army retraced their steps, advancing north toward Palmyra, but the broken land slowed them where every rock afforded a hidey-hole for an archer or crossbowman, or an entire party of daring scouts. Soldiers could thread the hills easily, but cavalry horses found the stony footing dangerous for fragile legs. More importantly,

Johan's supplies had been stranded on the nearby riverbanks when the river vanished. The invasion force had to either stay close or ferry supplies with them. Johan had some pack camels and mules and elephants, but never enough to move all his war materiel. Creating a supply line or splitting the army were organizational nightmares that had thrown his high command into turmoil.

From her stony peak Adira Strongheart assessed the elements she could see. Regiments of infantry mustered in squares and waited while junior officers called the roll. One force that Adira recognized made her curse. Men dressed in short robes of dark brown and turbans of blue silk were dervishes, half-mad hotheads from the wild steppelands of the west. They danced around a fire to a frantic drumbeat, soon to be feverishly crazed for action. Tirran archers practiced shooting at a blanket draped between poles. Cavalry riders kicked out fires, cinched saddles and tied down blanket rolls.

"What are they up to?" Intrigued by one activity, Adira pointed. In a pocket between hills carpenters swarmed over two agitated gray-black elephants yoked side by side. Drovers jigged and jogged to calm their animals without being crushed or smacked with a trunk. Across the beasts' broad backs stretched a pair of padded braces from which hung a gigantic beam three feet thick. The butt of the beam was capped with iron and painted an angry red, just as the elephants were daubed down their foreheads and trunks and across their ears with red and blue war paint. The beasts fidgeted and shied as large rolls like carpets were unrolled. Drovers yanked on the goads hooked behind their ears to keep them steady while workers hung stiff woven-grass mats down their gray sides.

"That must be primitive armor against arrows," offered Sister Wilemina.

"That's a walking battering ram!" said Simone. "It'll shatter Palmyra's walls to crumbs."

"That unit, and they, and they," said the pirate captain, "will move soon. They'll march the morning and likely break at noon. Still, given that an army moves slowly, they could begin breaching Palmyra's walls before sundown. Tomorrow at the latest."

"One day left to live, Virgil would say." Wilemina could be as gloomy as their grumpy companion sometimes.

"One day for someone, but not us." Adira took a last look, then skidded down the hill. "Come on, you codfish! Tail on and mount up! We'll fight 'em right here!"

Clattering up and down nearby streams and gullies, Adira and her Seven gathered a jumbled force of Palmyran militiamen, Robaran Mercenaries, dwarves from Yerkoy in green and gold, Bryce fisherfolk. A cavalry patrol from Kalan in brown found their morning meal interrupted as Adira kicked their fire into sparks and ashes. "Everyone grab weapons and fall in! We'll show Johan what's a fair fight!"

Leading her troop at a trot, a mile farther on Adira found what she'd spotted from above. Two low flat prominences, crumbling cliffs of sandstone, met a shallow valley split by treacherous gullies. Just what Adira needed. Hopping off her horse and smacking it toward the rear, she called, "We'll make a stand right here! Get busy!"

Shouting and punching anyone who dallied or questioned, she first ordered the cavalry, some sixty-odd, to split up and find Johan's army, especially the war elephants, and lure them hither. They were also to find any defending Palmyrans and bring them to this position. Everyone else she put to work rolling rocks off the slopes and stacking them into a rude wall between the low cliffs. The dwarves fell to, for building was their meat, and they sang a growly monotonous song to speed their capable hands.

Three hours they labored as more Palmyrans and allies trickled in. Adira wasn't certain Johan's army would come this way, but the odds looked good. Since they spoiled for a fight, they'd probably chase the cavalry Adira dangled as bait. When the rough wall reached her chest, the pirate leader quickly outlined maneuvers. She sent Wilemina and Simone and fifty other archers ranging up the slopes with strict instructions to stay hidden. She put the dwarves of Yerkoy in front with their axes and mallets. The second rank, militia and fisherfolk, were to sheathe their hand weapons and ply spears and lances—

Time ran out.

"Here they come!" With a thunder of hooves the Kalan cavalry pelted up the valley and leaped the wall. An officer called, "Right behind us!"

From beyond the next hill resounded a bellow from humans and animals. A troop of infantry tramped into sight. Cavalry flanked them, and in the forefront trotted the whirling dervishes, so antsy they danced in place. The defenders from Palmyra, four hundred at most, fell silent in the face of a thousand veterans. From the center, Adira raised her cutlass and hollered, "Stand fast, sons and daughters of the southlands!"

Still, her knees jittered as two dark gray masses as big as thunderclouds loomed into view. The war elephants swayed clumsily, unused to the yoke and bridge with a huge beam hung between, and their itchy armor of grass mats. To all eyes, their sheer massive power would carry any battle. As the Tirran cavalry and infantry paced alongside, handlers towed the elephants forward with hooks behind their ears. No doubt the handlers wanted to practice smashing walls with the untested battering ram. As the huge beasts plodded forward, the southern force stepped back, and even Adira's presence couldn't stop them. To a tremendous roar of encouragement from the Tirrans, the blood-red painted iron beam struck the wall of stone.

Rocks hurtled through the air around the Palmyrans' and allies' ears. Adira ducked as a stone as big as her head sailed by. A man beside her crumpled as a rock creased his forehead. Stone rattled on iron-rimmed shields and steel spear points. Dust swirled so thick for a moment Adira couldn't see the elephants. Perhaps that was best, for she filled her lungs and bawled, "*Bide, me hearties, and stand by to repel boarders!*"

With screeches and war whoops and weird warbling wails, the barely controlled dervishes charged the gap. Shrieking, they scampered over rubble still tumbling and launched into their mad attack, spinning in place to lend power to wide-sweeps of their twin scimitars. The first forty through the breach planted and spun, yipping like coyotes, and plunged into the militiamen, uncaring if they died so long as they bought glory. A dwarf lost an arm, the stump squirting blood. Another dwarf lost his head as matched blades slashed his throat. A dervish whipped twin swords in a frenzied figure-eight that chopped a fighter's shoulder—

Then dervishes died. Urged by Adira's shrieking commands, the second rank of allies shoved hard with their lances and spears even as the first dwarven rank recoiled from the vicious suicidal attack. Teamwork took its toll as the allies acted in concert against the individual assaults of the madmen. A dervish spun wildly only to impale his throat on a spear. Another danced sideways, slashing circles in the air, but split his liver on a lance with its butt wedged in the ground. A Yerkoy axeman, initially staggered by a slashed forearm, whacked his heavy blade through a dervish's skull. A dervish was tripped by a spear as a partnered sword punctured his groin and guts. One fiend dived headlong amid the dwarves, but the spearman behind hooked his robe and hauled hard. The dervish spilled on his face and was pinned through the back to the ground. Up and down the line the dervish attack faltered. Mad ferocity meant to terrify and scatter suddenly fired the ire of home-grown soldiers backed by the unstoppable will of Adira Strongheart.

The great war elephants, yoked in tandem, again swung the battering ram against the erratic wall to send stones flying. Hooked by their handlers, the elephants halted, for they were valuable creatures and not trained to attack footmen. Clumsily the elephants were backed from the breach, carefully, for cracks in the ground had split wider under their weight, so they had to turn in tandem to skirt a crevice.

A bugle pealed. Arrows suddenly rained from heaven amidst the Palmyrans, puncturing chests, arms, throats. Tirran archers in gray and red, with gay red caps with pheasant feathers, had climbed the rocky slopes to loose a withering rain of arrows into the defenders' ranks. Arrows smacked and whapped wooden and leather shields, ricocheted off rubble, shattered against the ground. Too many thudded home in flesh.

Sensible men and women would wither and fade under such an iron hailstorm, but these Palmyrans and allies were led by Adira Strongheart, whom many believed led a charmed life. She called, "Wait! We've got our own surprise! Look!"

As Adira had laid out, the signal to the enemy archers had also signaled her side. Led by Wilemina and Simone, Palmyran and Yerkoy archers and others rose from concealment atop the heights and sent arrows sizzling into the Tirrans. Overconfident, the Tirrans hadn't sent scouts ranging ahead to flush snipers, and now they paid a pitiable price. Since the Tirrans occupied the extreme ends of the heights, they had no place to retreat but down the slope. They did, but many collected arrows in their backs and tumbled the hard way. Once they were scattered, the allied archers sent arrows winging at the Tirran infantry and cavalry, who'd crept to the broken stone barrier to protect the elephants and swarm into the valley.

Seizing opportunity, Adira shouted to her troops. "Will we just stand here? Let's kick 'em in the teeth! They want war, the scurvy rats, so have at them! Charge!"

Adira scooped up a fallen lance, flipped it sideways against the backs of wavering troops, and shoved to stop their backsliding. Screaming foul pirate curses, she leveled the spear and raced at the foe. Men and women blinked and, rather than be branded cowards, charged after.

Some Tirrans who'd gained the valley floor nocked and loosed arrows at the foe. An arrow kissed Adira's cheek, another parted her hair, then she reached the breach to drive her spear into the brisket of a huge redheaded archer before the man could draw his sword. Palmyrans and allies braced her at both elbows. Enraged, they hacked and chopped the archers and infantry, who quickly fell back. The Tirrans had expected mayhem and slaughter, but not on their side. The astonished elephant handlers, slowly turning their beasts, now smacked gray flesh frantically with their goads.

"Drop them!" shrieked Adira. "Cripple the elephants! Kill the monsters!"

Vaulting the shattered wall, the charging southrons swarmed around the elephants and their guards and handlers. Dwarves and militia and mercenaries jabbed thirty bloody spears, gouging the loose gray skin of the besieged elephants. Terrified out of their wits, the poor beasts staggered sideways in panic. One stepped on his keeper's leg, then crushed the woman as she fell. The stinging spears made both elephants bolt. Yoked, unable to sheer aside, one brute stumbled in a crack. The weakened edge crumbled, and the elephant tumbled, dragging its squealing companion after it. A snapping like trees falling resounded as bones broke and the elephants plunged half into a collapsing ditch in a pained panicked pile.

"Retreat!" shrilled Adira. "Handsomely! Slow! Don't give 'em an inch! That's it! Split port and starboard! Move!"

As clumsy as a drunken centipede, the force of defenders backstepped behind the sundered wall. Panting and puffing, they were grateful for even a tiny rest, and fumbled to slurp from canteens. Whapped by Adira's cutlass, the southrons split left and right to clear the way, though they didn't know why.

Adira knew. Jamming fingers in her mouth, she whistled shrilly and croaked, "Bear down and board!"

From two hidden arms of the rill thundered the Kalan cavalry, whom Adira had secreted as reserves. Sixty brown-clad cavalrymen and women, forgotten in the chaos, champed at the bit for action, barely able to keep their prancing horses in ranks. Iron hooves rang on rocks as a bugle pealed and the shout went up, "For King and Kalan!"

Like dancers in a play, the twin ranks merged into a phalanx four abreast. Cavalry sabers whisked from scabbards and were poised upright, a shining hedge of steely death. *Clop-clop jingle-jingle clank-clank* rose to a crescendo as the force kicked to a canter within heartbeats. Over rubble, spilled weapons, and bodies drummed the cavalry for the breach. The horses almost balked at the alien smell of wounded elephants, who struggled feebly in the cruel embrace of crumbled dirt. The foremost riders were handpicked for ability and agility, and the brown-wrapped riders locked their reins in iron fists and kneed the beasts into compliance. Without a word, with one thought, the first four riders and mounts jumped the sundered wall like a single sixteen-legged creature taking wing. Thumping on the far side, the cavalry confronted a boggled mill of infantry, archers, and a few cavalry. The pride of Kalan grinned as they raised their sabers and shouted, "*Yaaaaa-ha!*" A final kick gave the pent-up horses their head.

A tornado couldn't have consternated the Tirrans more. One minute they were bursting a flimsy wall with war elephants and killing with dervishes and archers, and the next minute the elephants were down, the dervishes wiped out, and the archers blown across the hills. Then laughing cavalry rammed full into their faces. Despite the cries of their officers, the infantry ranks shuffled back, fractured, broke—and died.

A man on a horse might as well be a dragon to a footman. Rearing against the sun, mounted on a half-ton of horseflesh with four stampeding legs, a cavalryman can swing a saber from the sky and split a soldier to the crotch. The Kalanites did just that.

Flying together in teams of two, veterans hacked left and right as their horses rode roughshod through the Tirran ranks. Men were clobbered by iron hooves and bulled aside by muscled flanks. Many sprawled and crashed, tripped by their own feet or the treacherous pebbles of the desert. Some blundered into clusters and tangled.

Everywhere infantrymen died. A saber cleft the back of a man's head. A heavy blade chopped a shoulder. A running man looked back to see a saber slam in his face. Another man running, hands in the air, felt a sudden tug and marveled as his arm flopped to the ground before him. Two friends whirled to make a stand and had their skulls split as one. Through the scattering ranks drummed relentless hooves like thunder while flashing blades struck like lightning. Tirran archers hoisted bows and let loose and shot their countrymen in the confusion. Some hotheaded Tirran cavalry threw their lives away in brief clashes, sliced to ribbons from two sides as teams crisscrossed like dancers.

Within five hellish minutes sixty Kalan cavalry massacred nearly two hundred foot soldiers. Then a Palmyran bugle pealed retreat. Without missing a step, teams wheeled as if yoked and rocketed toward Adira's wall. Urged by red-faced sergeants, some Tirran regiments had locked shields shoulder to shoulder—the infamous shield wall. Yet the windmilling cavalry had kept an escape route clear as the bugler urged them back. Four, six, nine riders fell, shot from the saddle or dumped by wounded horses. Pairs of Kalan riders bent low in the saddles and hooked companions under armpits as superbly trained mounts vaulted the rubble wall to safety. Cavalry cheered and southrons yelled because they'd left death and despair and anger in their bloody wake.

Adira was ready with the next command. "Handsomely now, haul together and retreat!" Adira Strongheart's flamboyant clothes and chestnut hair were dusty and disheveled and streaked with blood. Her old shirt was soaked with sweat. Yet she grinned through a mask of dust at what her ragtag force had accomplished. "Up the valley, all together or they'll break us! We've bought Palmyra and the southlands another day or two, me hearties, so give 'em a cheer as we go—Oh!"

Disaster.

Adira swayed on her feet, struck by a queer lethargy. At first she thought it a dizzy spell, one of many these days, but then found she couldn't move her feet. At all. As if they were rooted to the ground.

Wilemina and Simone ran to her side, alarmed by her sudden silence. Tirrans regrouping beyond the wall noticed too.

Staggered, her vision swimming, Adira Strongheart glimpsed a pair of hands pointing at her from the Tirran infantry ranks.

A *stinking magic-user*, she thought. Some hand-waver's bewitched me. Johan's got many mages in his army. This one strikes from the shadows like a coward, causing mischief.

Despite grasping her predicament, Adira couldn't lift either foot. The southron allies had begun to retreat in lockstep, unassailable except by the odd arrow, going slowly, encumbered by wounded hoisted on shields and shoulders. Now Wilemina shrieked for them to stop and aid Adira.

The Tirrans heard too. To an officer's roar, they charged the broken wall to kill the enemy commander.

"Leave me!" Adira barked, hopelessly stuck and mind-blasted besides. "Shove off!"

"Never!" snarled Simone. Slashing a figure-eight in the air, she hollered, "Kill the Seven if you can!"

"Hola!" screamed Wilemina. "For love and Lady Caleria!"

Southron allies clattered to join them just as the Tirran line struck. Adira and her valiant guards were smothered by a tidal wave of shields, swords, spears, axes, and screaming shrieking warriors.

Chapter 18

"Adira's what?" blurted Hazezon.

"Wounded, is all," Simone assured him. The black woman pressed a hand to her bleeding scalp, caking blood in her kinky hair. "We were overrun but got away. Adira was bewitched, glued to one spot by a sneaking sorcerer. She's fine. Well, not fine. A bit bashed up."

Hazezon Tamar didn't hear anymore but left his servants and generals, mounted his new horse, and galloped for the hospital tents. Southrons were scattered through the hills, most going in different directions. On his way, the mage passed dwarves, archers, muleskinners, Keepers of the Faith, and other factions of the patchwork army. As he reached the hospital, a hollow between hills, he saw tents being struck and loaded on travois behind mules and donkeys. Cooks and cooks' helpers stuffed carts full of pots and pans. Keepers of the Faith in oyster-colored robes with sleeves rolled up helped dying and wounded into more carts. The field hospital only patched the wounded before sending them back to Palmyra, but now the entire operation had to retreat or be overrun by oncoming Tirrans.

Hazezon saw Wilemina, Simone, Virgil, Echo, and Badger, still hobbling from his fire drake pounding, clustered in a circle. Dismounting, dropping the reins, he pushed amid the Seven.

Adira Strongheart was unrecognizable. Her face was battered, swollen, and turning blue against skin deathly pale. Hunks of her gorgeous curls had been ripped out. She was tucked by a blanket dappled with blood and lashed to a board stretcher. Still, one eye peered at the ex-husband as he fell to his knees.

"Haz." A raspy croak. "I bought us one day—maybe two. No more. It's time to spring your big trick—whate'er it be."

" 'Dira!" Hazezon sobbed the name, and the Circle of Seven turned away in embarrassment to give them privacy. Afraid to touch his ex-wife, the mage let his hand hover in the air. "Simone told me—"

"I'm fine. Hurt—is all. Broken arm—leg. My bonnie braves saved me. I should pay them more." Her mashed mouth smiled.

" 'Dira." Gingerly Hazezon took his ex-wife's hand. "I've always loved you. I still do."

"I know." The smile quavered. "Makes it hard to avoid you."

"Governor!" A voice from outside the circle got Hazezon's attention. The general from Kalan. "There you are! Governor, how shall we cover the retreat? We need your council!"

Torn between love and duty, Hazezon hesitated, until Adira squeezed his hand.

She whispered, "Go, Haz. There's still . . . lots to do. I'm . . . Ah! . . . out of the fight. It's up to you. Luck."

"Thank you." Leaning forward, Hazezon planted a kiss as tender as the brush of a butterfly's wing on Adira's bloody brow.

Rising, he ordered Wilemina and Virgil and the rest, "See that she's safely ensconced in Palmyra. Gather as much water as you might and hunker down."

"What?" Temporarily in command, Simone demanded, "Adira said you planned to sic your sand warriors on the Tirrans. What's that got to do with hoarding water?"

"Just do as I say. It's what Adira would want." That sounded ominous even to Hazezon, as if his ex-wife had died.

Militia generals and lesser officers had arrived and waited, fidgeting in silence. Hazezon asked them a few questions in an impromptu war council as the hospital was carted away along with his ex-wife. He learned the Tirrans' advance had stalled due to Adira's frenzied counterattack, and the enemy rested and repaired and regrouped for the remainder of the day, with only hours left until sundown. No one doubted that, first thing on the morrow, the army would march to Palmyra—unless they were balked. One woman put it, "The Tirrans can sup tomorrow eve in Palmyra's central plaza."

"We're ready to defend, milord," said a militia leader. "So are Bryce and Kalan and Yerkoy. No one shirked before, and now Adira Strongheart, may she live a hundred years, has shown the Tirrans are vulnerable to a canny plan."

"No." Hazezon shook his head so his keffiyeh whisked his white beard. "We're done fighting. Our only tactic is a headlong retreat straight to Palmyra. There will be no engagements, no skirmishing, no ambushes. Make sure no ally is left stranded. Is that clear? Get to Palmyra, gather water, and get undercover."

A general began, "Governor, can't you tell us—"

"Not without provoking the wrath of the desert's protectors, and we need their help. Once you reach Palmyra, bolt the doors and stop the windows with rags. Bring spades into the homes. Will you remember all this?"

"Remember?" A frustrated Yerkoy officer demanded, "What is this blither, sir? It's rumored you'd conjure sand warriors! You can't keep us in the dark, Governor!"

"Hist!" Fingers crooked, the mage sketched a sigil of protection in the air. Officers gaped as if Hazezon had snapped. "I dare not speak, lest the magic leak away like water through a sieve. Now I go."

Ignoring pleas and questions, Hazezon mounted his horse. At the brow of a pass Adira's Circle of Seven carried her stretcher. For a moment, Hazezon Tamar offered a heartfelt bargain to any spirits that might take pity on men. *I'd give all my power and the rest of my years, and yes, turn all the southlands over to Johan, if only Adira would survive.*

Pausing, wondering if he really could strike such a devil's bargain, Hazezon shook his head, better not to learn.

"Ho, Belladonna, let us ride! When dusk descends, our work begins!"

Hauling reins, Hazezon clattered away south as the southern allied army plodded north. Rounding a hill, he turned east, toward wasteland.

* * * * *

Dismounting, Hazezon made sure Belladonna's reins were tied firmly around a rock big enough for the horse to move. He poured water from a skin into a leather wallet and let the animal drink its fill. Then he tied on a feedbag. "You'll need strength for the morrow, Belladonna, as shall I. If we see the morrow."

Turning a full circle, Hazezon Tamar nodded. He was alone on a flat plain of the Sukurvia desert. The sky soared overhead in a dizzying dome that made the man feel small. He muttered, "A goodly comparison, I an insect under the eyes of gods."

Taking from a saddlebag some oddments and pouches and a small prayer rug, Hazezon brushed away rocks and smoothed coarse sand, laid his rug, and knelt on creaking knees. He faced east, from whence he hoped for succor. He lined the magical implements on the sand. A small ball as heavy as lead sharply incised with crossed grooves. A fluff of goose down that he weighted with a rock. A dried pit scorpion, very brittle. A milky crystal. A lock of black hair said to be an efreet's. An eggshell sucked dry. A purse of fine sand like diamond dust. A tuft of Belladonna's tail, for the horse was a fine runner.

Lastly he drew in the sand a mystic sigil of destruction: an inverted **V** crossed by jagged lightning. He cringed under the sky while drawing it, hoping not to invoke real lightning.

"Now," he mumbled, "we learn if the fates can be swayed from their course."

Hazezon was well read, and a good listener to antique tales, so could name at least thirty desert spirits. Talking to the air, he invoked them all, name after name. Gybo. The Phoenix. Lustra. The Sea King. Wullab. Many others. Etiquette worried him, for spirits were jealous creatures with strict hierarchies, but Hazezon did his best not to offend. At every name, he heaped on praise until his tongue began to twist.

Having gotten the spirits' attention—he hoped—Hazezon spent a roundabout time identifying himself, humbly, as a servant of the people. "Always, in my own small way, have I toiled for the good, for stability, and for peace." He reminded the unseen ones of his sacrifices over the years. "This sorry son of the desert has spent many lonely hours singing your praises." He talked of how an invader from the formidable mountains wished to enslave the desert's nomads, erg dwellers, shepherds, even the sacred Citanul druids. Pointedly he explained that only eternals could rescue the desert's citizens now, for they had shot all their bolts, exhausted all their energies, and shed much blood.

The mage whispered to the wind for hours. For good measure, Hazezon invoked all the spirits he could name, even visitors like Lady Caleria and borderline spirits like Makou who delighted in mischief. Gybo the Galloper, the double-headed phantom horse, he begged for speed. From Wullab the flood-spitting fish he asked sky-sailing. Of Ash-May-Ruf, Mother of the Erg, and Ash-May-Aran, Mother of the Night, he asked protection for her myriad children. The Firestorm Phoenix, he hoped, could lend heat and updrafts.

One-eyed Phanal-Unorg he asked to blow wind from his cave. Lustra, mistress of the south wind, he asked to lean west. Of the Sea King, Oligarch of the Ocean and Sovereign of the Sea of Serenity, he asked only for no conflicting maelstroms that might hurt his cause. Of Makou, the Great Serpent, he asked to whip with his feathered tail. And to Sethrida, he apologized profusely for burying her river. On and on he rattled.

For himself, Hazezon asked nothing. For years he'd craved great power, a single peek into the heart of magic. Now he banished all self-aggrandizing notions from his head. The times needed humility, not greed. If his thoughts strayed at all, he thought of Adira, wracked and beaten so harshly. He might have included a plea for her welfare, but refrained. A blessing for one woman might distract the desert spirits, who were notoriously flighty.

As he talked, Hazezon constantly shuffled the oddments before his prayer rug. He switched the purse, the feather, the crystal, the leaden ball, the dried scorpion, and the rest back and forth, like a marketplace gambler playing Find the Pea.

Occasionally he opened the purse of fine sand and trickled a pinch to the night air. This was the hardest part, for as he released each pinch, Hazezon sent his thoughts winging high into the overarching firmament. To reach for the upper atmosphere while staying anchored in his frail body was no easy task, and time and again the mage felt his soul quivering within him, as if determined to burst free like an uncaged bird. That idea made Hazezon sweat despite the cool night air.

Time passed. Hazezon grew hoarse. The night swam before his tired eyes in crazy swirls like oil on water. It crossed his mind that, exposed to the night, on his knees, in a mystic daze, he'd make a splendid tidbit for hungry hyenas or lions. A fanged brute could snap his face off, and he'd barely see it. But he shoved gloomy thoughts aside and concentrated on coercing the fates, hoping their marvelous protection would extend to their supplicant.

Talking, begging, pleading, promising, Hazezon's voice gave out. Perhaps he dreamed he talked. In his stupor, the squirming darkness began to take on shape in the form of visions.

Apes beat a drum and danced around a fire. A mountain howled in a hollow voice that drove men mad. Fearsome sand worms burrowed through soil like maggots through cheese. A crippled monster scarred with stumps shrieked in darkness. People with feathers peered from snowbanks. Dark tigerwomen sharpened knives for sacrifice. Vicious horned beasts burned in silhouettes of fire. A fire drake fluttered like a falling leaf. A shooting star scorched the night. A headless mossy monster hooked claws like tree branches. Jaeger lay trampled, soaked in blood and sand, then a red-soaked Johan reared to the sky, rejoicing with arms uplifted. Sailing carracks skimmed off the water and took flight like birds, sailing amid clouds on the eternal north wind. A yellow-skinned vampire curled in a robe and dreamt of blood. Stones and the men who dug them soared into the air. Johan hung in a tree and glared with eyes like red glass. A ghost sobbed and could not be consoled. Adira Strongheart's hard eyes melted into black pearls that grew brighter and brighter until they seared Hazezon's vision and he was forced to look away. . . .

Grunting, Hazezon rubbed his eyes, but the light persisted. A thin crack reached from horizon to horizon. What was it? Then a yellow eye winked.

"Ah!" The groggy mage muttered. "Dawn breaks! But have I—?"

Hazezon Tamar blinked as the thin slit of sun, flaring like the unwinking evil eye of Orms-By-Gore, passed upward into a cloud bank.

Or maybe. . .

Pushing upright, swaying on his feet, Hazezon peered east. It was true. The clear desert dome of sky was occluded by a long low bank of dirty brown. The brief sunrise had been immediately eclipsed by substance in the air.

"That's it! I've done it!" Hazezon hoarsely croaked.

"Congratulations."

Hazezon Tamar jumped two feet in the air and sprawled on his broad rump on his prayer rug. Looming against the western sky stood Jaeger in bold stripes of orange and gold, as bright as a sunrise himself.

"Wullab's whiskers!" gasped Hazezon, clutching his chest. "You gave me a fright!"

"Apologies." Jaeger bent and lifted the mage as easily as he would a child. "I spent the night nearby, but you were oblivious. You are indeed a miracle worker. Men will sing your praises for ages to come!"

"Nay, don't jinx me!" Feeling giddy and drunk from lack of sleep, Hazezon tried to remember what came next. He touched the tiger man's white belly, found it soft and warm. "Jaeger. Perhaps I imagined you. I saw you—I had visions. Wild weird images. Are you real?"

"As real as memory," replied the tiger man. "I thought it fair to accompany you. After all, we began this adventure together."

"And so shall finish together? Very well." Hazezon was cheery and agreeable. Rolling his prayer rug, picking up his oddments, he admitted, "This spell, if I risk boasting, is a mighty deed. My mightiest ever, and probably my last great one. It took months of research and preparation. I could never duplicate it."

"What have you ensorcelled?" The tiger padded silently on long legs.

"You'll see. They'll all—Thunder and lightning!"

Walking after his horse, for Belladonna had dragged the reins and rock far, Hazezon halted at a blonde mound streaked with red. A dead lioness, her throat slashed and belly ripped open. She lay not twenty feet from where Hazezon had sat, her head pointed his way. The wizard looked at Jaeger. "Your doing?"

The tiger man glanced. "She must have cut herself on shards of flint."

Hazezon's hands trembled so hard Jaeger had to help him mount. Belladonna shied from cat odor. From the saddle, Hazezon said, "If the fates truly sent you, it wasn't just to save me, but all the southlands."

Jaeger's muzzle crinkled, a tiger's smile. "If the fates sent me."

* * * * *

Bombombombombombom. . .

Belladonna stepped gingerly to the edge of a sandstone bluff. Below, a drum pounded an unending rumble. Other drums picked up the beat until the rattling throbbed in the dry desert air and thrummed against the breastbones of the high observers.

The head of Johan's army assembled on the flats. Regiment after regiment of infantry flanked by troops of cavalry with bright pennants mustered into ranks to sergeants' bellows. Attached to each regiment were archers with their gay red caps and pheasant feathers and tall bows upright. Teams of elephants or monoxes or mules waited patiently with carts or wagons of supplies, or else knocked-down siege weapons. Phalanxes of dwarven sappers made last-minute preparations, cinching ropes and hammering pintles. Generals and their staffers trotted on jingling horses up and down the line, eager to move on and reap rewards and promotions.

Like a giant colorful snake, the rest of the army twisted away between hills. Somewhere toward the end, well protected by a rearguard, would be Johan's private pack train, with a sheltered palanquin carried by sixteen guards. Ahead of the forward columns lay only a few small hills and one long ridge, a mere eight miles. Then they would knock on the gates of Palmyra.

"Just in time." Hazezon Tamar slid from the saddle. Part of his mind was distracted and hazy from overwork and lack of sleep. The part he needed could see his goal with crystal clarity.

"Or perhaps not." Jaeger pointed a black claw at a troop of cavalry who'd spotted them. As one, the troop kicked to a canter and vanished up a vale to reach the bluff. To capture Hazezon Tamar and the fearsome talking tiger would be a brilliant coup on this day of victory.

"Maybe ten minutes before they arrive," Hazezon agreed. "Perhaps enough. If my trick works."

If the threat of twenty armed cavalry troopers worried Jaeger, he didn't show it. A breeze from the east shivered his whiskers and short mane. He glanced that way, for an east wind was rare. For once, there was no sun to see. Rather a high thin overcast like a gray gauze curtain shifted before his keen eyes.

The tiger asked, "Is this queer weather your doing? Hazezon?"

The mage didn't hear. Having tied Belladonna securely, he skidded on his heels and plump rump down the sandy face of the bluff. Amber eyes alive with curiosity, Jaeger bounded after his friend.

Halfway down the slope, Hazezon dug his heels in coarse sand to stop. Johan's army stood not a mile off, and now another troop of cavalry detached to intercept the intruders. One rank unlimbered crossbows from their saddle cantles.

"This is their big push. Hear the drums?" The mage babbled, and knew it. His head buzzed and roared, and his eyes kept slamming shut. He'd been awake for two nights, preparing and then supplicating the desert spirits, begging for every crumb of mana he could amass. Below, drumbeats shifted from a ruffle to a march. As one, the first regiments picked up their feet to distant shouts and tramped, slowly but steadily, for Palmyra.

While Jaeger watched, Hazezon drew from an inner pocket his short dark wand with the double pop-eyed faces. Jamming the end in sand, he twirled the stick between his palms until they grew warm. Magical verses hissed between his teeth, little ditties that aided concentration mostly, and every verse ended with, "Stand, sons of the sand!"

A long time Hazezon twiddled, until sweat trickled from under his keffiyeh and ran down his hawk's nose into his white beard. The hum of horse hooves drummed on his ears, and he imagined he felt their impact through his wand. He'd never conjured on this scale before. Nor was he sure he'd amassed enough mana for the job, for he asked a lot of thin desert soil and wispy air. Nothing might result, in fact, for his magic sometimes failed, and he might be hacked to pieces by Tirran sabers, as would Jaeger, but he spun his wand and hissed, over and over, "Stand, sons of the sand!"

"Ah," was all Jaeger said, but it meant Hazezon's life and homeland might be spared.

In a half-circle radiating outward from the wand, humps broke upward from the sand. Within seconds they rose to man-high mounds like termite hills. Those closest to the source formed first. Sandy heads took the shape of kerchiefs. Lines cleaved down sandy breasts to outline robes and tunics. Hems broke free of the soil to reveal boots. Lumps flowed into hands, and from hands sprouted scimitars.

All the simulacrums were fashioned in their maker's image, so a dozen sandy Hazezons faced down the cavalry riders. Those gallants stopped as their horses shied from the queer apparitions. Riders kicked them to circle around and vault the slope, but twenty sand warriors formed a living hedge, so the cavalry captain yelled for ten troopers to dismount while ten held their reins.

Bumps as numerous as fallen apples in an orchard stippled the sand, row after row after row spreading outward from Hazezon. Jaeger purred in amazement, for the bumps never stopped forming. Forty, eighty, a hundred-sixty, and more. Still Hazezon drilled at the soil, red-faced, puffing and panting. Hundreds became a thousand, then doubled, then doubled. The forest of sand men continued to arise until they reached the first ranks of Johan's army.

Still bumps arose even between soldiers' feet. Men and women cursed and stomped on the bumps, but they were as hard as rocks, and the soldiers had to give way. Drums beat frantically as orders rang out to shift ranks away from the sand warriors. Only a few minutes had passed since Hazezon invoked the spell, but homunculi filled the valley, almost threatening to crowd out Johan's force. Yet not one of the sand warriors stirred an eyelash, but stood like statues.

"How—many?" Hazezon still knelt and drilled, his breathing ragged. "How—"

"Numbers?" murmured Jaeger. "I know not well. One for every enemy soldier, if not more. And yon cavalry would bid us halt with naked blades."

"*Gahh!*" Hazezon's strength gave out. He slumped, heaving for breath. Far off, where Johan's army wended through hills, hundreds of ankle- and knee-high lumps stopped growing, never to take the shape of man. Hazezon saw more soldiers were running to the forefront to lend support. The dismounted cavalry advanced, less then thirty feet away, threading a course through unmoving statues of sand.

Breathing heavily, Hazezon rose, for his task was in some ways just beginning. Raising one fist made a thousand sandy scimitars reach for the sky. Taking a mighty step, swinging his arm boldly as in his old pirating days, Hazezon blared, "Go, my children!"

At the command, more than four thousand land-born brethren plucked sandy feet from the desert floor and marched forward, upright scimitars of sand sweeping down with a silent roar.

Chaos.

Living soldiers and magic mimics clashed like stampeding herds of wild bulls. Tirrans hot to prove their prowess whanged at the sand warriors, expecting them to shatter like sand castles, only to discover the simulacrums were as hard as marble statues. The clanging of steel swords on ensorcelled sand was terrific, a wicked din that rang from horizon to horizon. Far behind the army, Hazezon Tamar chugged forward and slashed his empty fist up, down, across, in stabbing motions forward, and any other way he could think to inconvenience the enemy. Not as fast as humans, the sand warriors got in only a few swipes of their scimitars compared to humans, but in the milling confusion many Tirrans were killed, slashed overhand or gored through the guts. Enchanted blows spanked off Tirran shields, denting iron rims and scarring wood. A Tirran stumbled and was decapitated. Another lost an arm. One man was pushed as if by an implacable wall and crushed between opposing sand men. Men and women backed into companions' swords to avoid the whisking scimitars. With the sand army coming to life to that one command, it seemed as a hedgerow had suddenly sprouted thorns and thrashed to impale intruders.

Nor were humans the only casualties. Drovers grabbed reins and wrapped jackets around the eyes of terrified mules and horses, but nothing could shield the elephants and monoxes from panic or damage, for sand men swiped at anything that moved. Elephants were sliced down their flanks, monoxes were gored, horses had legs chopped out from under. Animals rebelled and bolted, but everywhere sand men whipped steely swords like scythes. Beasts that weren't stabbed blundered into soldiers and trampled many.

Sand men on the outskirts of battle surged toward the enemy, grinding together with a harsh grating noise. In some places they were packed too tightly to move and slashed empty air or clashed scimitars together in imitation of the magic-wielding master.

Huffing and puffing on the sandy slope of the bluff, Hazezon Tamar saw the results of his magic firsthand. Half dismounted, the cavalry troop found itself surrounded by acres of sand men that in the next instant sprang to life. The ten dismounted soldiers whacked at the nearest sand men, their sabers bouncing off stone-hard heads and blades, but they were surrounded by dozens of homunculi intent on killing.

The troopers afoot went down in gouts of blood. Those on horse had their mounts assailed from all sides. Screaming horses bolted and crashed headlong into scimitars, or toppled sideways and fell under magical blades. Thirty feet off behind an advancing field of statues, Hazezon and Jaeger flinched at the hideous screams of the tormented troops. Still Hazezon scuffed forward, slashing and hacking as if driving his homunculi troops by sheer iron will.

Down in the vale, bugles pealed erratically. A drum began a ruffle, then quit as a general countermanded an order. Tirrans strived to regroup and form their famous shield wall, but they bulled in vain against the unstoppable sand men. Wounded soldiers were trampled into pools of gore by the massive weight of the living statues. Hazezon grimaced at the thought, as if he crushed men under his own feet, but he pressed on, though now Jaeger helped prop him lest he fall on the shifting slope.

Watching the frenzied and one-sided battle from afar, Jaeger said, "I recall these sand warriors have one weakness."

"Correct, my friend." Hazezon puffed, red-faced from all this magic sword swinging. "Their flaw was exposed in Bryce during the last raid. A shame. I shouldn't have wasted the spell then and tipped our hand. But even sorcerers can't foretell the future. I expect that any moment—Ah, word carries from the rear."

A single bugle call split the morning air, and it carried a note of triumph. Officers shouted themselves blue. Jaeger and Hazezon saw when the secret was broadcast to the front of the army. Soldiers dropped swords and squatted to heft rocks of any size and pitched them hard. Hazezon was almost glad, for soon he could drop all this infernal playfighting before his heart cracked.

Homunculi hit by rocks instantly crumbled to heaps of sand.

Other soldiers heaved rocks, some men squabbling over who should seize a stone. Whether a sand man was smacked in the head or merely brushed on a sword tip, the magic dispelled and they slumped immediately. As fast as Tirrans could scrounge and heave rocks the army of sand men collapsed. The wave of resistance rippled outward from the valley floor. Some soldiers grown reckless dived amidst the collapsed heaps to snatch up rocks, only to be stabbed by sand men still fighting.

Huffing, swinging, Hazezon explained, "Sand comes from stones worn over ages into crumbs. My 'sons of the sand' are therefore 'sons of stone,' and any touch of their father-stones banishes the magic. In that raid on Bryce, Johan's mage Xira Arien inadvertently stumbled on the secret when she summoned stone-throwing imps. Likely she rushed forward from the rear once she heard of the magical attack."

The invading army crushed sand warriors by the hundreds. Only a precious few battled on. Glancing up the slope to the bluff, Hazezon said, "Our proud army of manakins will soon be good only for making mud pies. You'd best crest this bluff before the Tirrans recall our presence."

"I'll wait for my friend," said Jaeger quietly.

Hazezon grinned, sweat coursing down his face, then suddenly quit as the last sand warriors were bashed to dust. With a gasp, Hazezon unclenched his sword hand and worked his arthritic fingers. "Come. No time to dawdle."

Clambering on hands and toes, helped by Jaeger, Hazezon gained the bluff and swung astride Belladonna. Then Hazezon twisted in the saddle to look east.

Unnoted during the short furious battle, the desert sky had darkened like dusk at midmorning. Pointing at the angry sky with a shaking hand, Hazezon said, "In truth, I didn't expect much of my constructs. A diversion, no more. There comes my real threat to Johan's supremacy."

Jaeger's white eyebrows arched at the sight of the eastern sky roiling a turgid yellow-brown. "So that darkling dome is your doing?"

"My small effort and hope." Always superstitious, Hazezon didn't tempt fate by boasting. "In long hours of study and meditation I've harvested the few driblets of mana the desert will relinquish. Last night I asked the desert spirits for help, and offered a suggestion. A good worshiper should make his deities feel needed, after all, and I've asked for little in past months."

"But what have you, or your cantankerous spirits, done?" Jaeger stared eastward, fascinated as the sky was steadily occluded, until the darkness reached overhead. A chill as of sunset or an eclipse settled on the desert.

"I've drawn the wind." The old mage's voice held a hint of boasting. "Perilous work. Tracing currents of air, trying to gather the very breath of storms in your arms, then seeking to move it, while all along you can neither see nor touch this enchanted wind is no small chore. Damned hard, in fact. Many's the time I felt my soul slipping away to remote reaches of the heavens. Had I failed to keep my spirit, you'd have found my corpse an empty husk lying on my prayer rug."

Hazezon tugged off his keffiyeh, revealing a head of cropped white hair. The eastern sky was occluded from northern horizon to southern and far overhead. Roiling clouds like a dark brown curtain ate the landscape. Jaeger blinked as a hilltop no more than three miles away disappeared behind the curtain. Hazezon tasted the wind, then touched fingertips to his lips. "Taste it?"

The tiger licked his muzzled and spat grit. "You've conjured a *sandstorm?*"

Smug, Hazezon grinned. "Almost cost my soul, and might haunt me yet. But yes, I did. Not bad for a decrepit and fat-bottomed pot-peddler, eh?"

Shaking his head in wonder, Jaeger said, "I think you've assured your place in books of legend."

"Perhaps." Hazezon stared down into the valley. The army of sand warriors was gone, leaving no more than heaps like anthills. A few hundred Tirrans had been killed or wounded, but thousands now reformed ranks and marched on Palmyra. Still, a few raised arms and pointed to the eastern sky. "I don't know if I'll be proud of how the legend ends. Those poor bastards will suffer for Johan's ambition."

Jaeger watched eastward, toward his homeland. He wanted to lean back from the oncoming curtain of storm, millions of tons of sand swirling at cyclonic speeds. Black birds streaked overhead, wings pumping to escape the unnatural fury. The tiger man purred, "Best we get to Palmyra."

"Agreed. We mustn't linger. Our route lies diagonally across this bluff, a straight run." Hazezon screwed his keffiyeh on his head, wind flicking the tails. His eyes twinkled with mischief, as if he were suddenly sixteen years old. "Tell you what, Sir Stripes. Shall we race to Palmyra? Or rather, shall you and Belladonna?"

Grinning toothily, Jaeger blew a kiss at the horse's muzzle, hunched, and sprang a full twenty feet in one gigantic bound, off and running.

"Hoy! Wait up!" laughed Hazezon. "Tower of the Tabernacle, stir your stumps, you plodding glue pot! *Yeeee-hah!*"

Chapter 19

Six days the storm raged.

Even in Palmyra, where they buttoned up stout houses and were forewarned to gather water, people suffered. Houses with thatch lost their roofs in the first few hours, so that home dwellers had to stumble, blind in the whirling grit, and seek succor with neighbors. The roofless houses filled with sand within hours. The few wooden houses found sand trickled in every crack and sifted from the ceiling like flour. As the winds increased, wooden houses creaked and groaned and shivered. Soon they tilted against the fury of the storm, as if giants pressed with horny hands. In the first night, gale winds knocked wooden houses down, and the occupants were crushed. People who lived in stout adobe houses with flat roofs were safe, but even they discovered by candlelight that sand crept around the doors and shutters, heaping ominously.

No one could venture out against the blinding skin-searing grit. The wind was a banshee, a monster without pity that sucked and slobbered and shrieked and scoured the town like an army of berserk fiends. It was dark during the day and pitch black by night. Ships beached on the dry lake filled with sand. Some rolled end over end and smashed into other ships. Everything not nailed down was carried away: banners, flowers, leaves from trees, carts and haystacks and woodpiles and more. Everything standing was smothered in sand and pebbles as big as pearls. Public wells were drowned in sand.

The Palmyrans, mainly former desert dwellers, had prepared by fetching water and filling every vessel, but after a few days even that supply ran out. The people suffered from thirst, unable to eat salt rations and dried fruit. Parents taught children to suck pebbles to wet their mouths.

Candles guttered and extinguished. Every man, woman, and child, hunkered in stuffy dark houses squashed knee-to-knee with neighbors. At first they joked and told old stories to keep up their courage, or sang, but after the third day, no one spoke, for their throats were raw. The elders had nothing to say, for never before had the sands of Sukurvia blown so fierce. Fear etched peoples' nerves like acid as they grew more terrified the storm would never end. Jammed together in fetid rooms with poor air, folks huddled in misery and listened to the howling winds that sought to obliterate life from the desert, never abating.

Trapped in the open, the Tirrans fared much worse.

As the storm descended, generals commanded and officers ordered and sergeants shouted. Treating the interruption like an early dusk, orders circulated to make a cold camp. In sand that stung the eyes and rattled the ears and caught in the throat, the army dragged the big tents off the pack train and fought to pitch canvas against the rising fury. Pegs failed to hold in sandy soil, wind whipped the cloth folds like mares' tails, poles teetered and toppled. The few tents erected were soon blown flat. Giving up, soldiers huddled shoulder-to-shoulder and tried to kindle fires. Sand in their faces became an irritation, then a real danger as they snorted it continually. As hours passed and the winds increased, they stumbled or crawled to their collapsed tents. Unable to see, they wriggled under the heavy folds, scooped a space under their rumps, packed touching knees with the canvas draped over their heads, then struggled in the dark to keep sand from whisking inside. They listened to the hissing wind, still rising and bringing ever more sand, and they began to worry.

Wranglers and drovers shoved and smacked balky mules, camels, horses, elephants, and monoxes flank-to-flank in picket lines, which in the stinging sand they secured to wagons or siege engines. The animals grew frantic as the wind peppered them with pebbles and their hides began to bleed. Wranglers tied kerchiefs and rags over the animals' eyes lest they be blinded, but that kindness only made the beasts kick and mill worse, and there was not enough cloth. Horses tried to break and run, yanking on picket ropes so smaller animals tumbled and were trampled underfoot. Small herds of animals roped together blundered downwind and fell into crevices that split the desert floor. Animals suffered broken legs, shattered ribs, and cracked hips. Tangled in twitching suffering piles, one by one they died in misery.

The humans lasted awhile longer. A few soldiers without shelter crawled under wagons and dragged down the canvas covers, but these were eventually blown off by the wind or rent by its fury. Desperate enclaves of sappers tipped over wagons as makeshift barricades, working blind in darkness, but sand filtered in and around and heaped to their shoulders, then higher. Some took refuge amidst pack animals, slitting the throats of horses and mules so men could huddle between carcasses. These pitiful mounds were soon buried.

Slow-witted barbarians from the north were first to rebel. As the hours dragged and the screaming winds grew worse, barbarians and a few women recruited into Johan's army blindly struck out of improvised shelters. There was no escaping the storm, and they blundered into crevices, bodies broken or hopelessly wedged. A few found caves or clefts in rock walls, and crawled in and slept, some to be buried alive by sifting sand. Some barbarians stumbled across soldiers sheltering under humped canvas. They tried to crawl in but were driven out by humans with knives. Enraged, the barbarians dragged off the tents and fought back. Canvas was ripped and blood spilled while sand sizzled around them.

Some soldiers familiar with the desert took their chances and deserted. Wrapping in blankets and rags, a few staggered west to find the dried riverbank, where they knew caves abounded. Some found shelter, but others skidded on rocks and were lamed, or else toppled into the dry riverbed and couldn't climb out. Slowly the dead river was smothered by sand. Others strode northward, hoping to surrender and beg shelter in Palmyra. They were unable to see the sky to navigate by stars, and they were soon lost and took what shelter they could find to wait out the wind.

One conclave of six veteran sergeants sensed the magical intensity of the storm and the hint of the spirits' displeasure. Conspiring in secret, they drew knives and slew their inferiors, then collected canteens and robes. Roping together, they trudged what they guessed was south because even the northern fates seemed to have surrendered to Palmyra. They blundered into a conclave of veterans staggering north. Angry words were exchanged, swords drawn, and men died and were buried.

A group of elephant drovers recruited from the southern seas tried to bull to safety. Chaining the beasts in a line, they climbed to the howdas and goaded the elephant's backs with iron spikes. Angry, panicked, the encumbered elephants soon struck a rock outcrop, and immediately they rubbed the irritating howdas against the cliff until only red smears were left, and those were soon erased by sand.

Johan's huge army had been strung out five miles, from the flats to the serpentine passes and valleys. Working together, some squads improvised shelters in rocky gaps or crevices and shared and harbored their water. One quartermaster ordered wagons toppled and tied together, and supplies stacked at the center: her soldiers survived muzzily on diets of beer and wine. Mages sprinkled through the army helped by summoning walls of shale, thorns, bramble, and even in one spot, tombstones. One mage exhausted her power summoning fresh fruit from a distant jungle. One day, then two, the invaders huddled in misery while the screaming unending wind shredded their sanity. Some endured, some lashed out, some lived, some died.

Johan's personal entourage fared well, despite the horrific circumstances. With many hands, a single huge tent was erected and supplies gathered within. Working with his lesser mages, the archmage invoked a spell to encase the tent in a protective bubble. Sensing that the storm was both natural and magical, Johan ordered his servants and cooks driven outdoors. Sheltered within were his generals and their highest staffers, his scribes and money counters, his mages, and a few others.

As the first fierce day drew to a close, Johan enjoyed a sparse meal and wine by candlelight, while his guests listened uneasily to the wind. Everyone wondered, without speaking, why their leader didn't stop the storm. A few guessed the truth: that Johan was a wizard of the mountains, and he'd met his match against an experienced desert mage.

As the second day dragged, the winds grew so powerful Johan's tent bulged and shivered, its magical bubble distorted. Generals rendered impotent by nature's fury paced and watched the thin canvas walls and talked in low voices about how to reform the army after this debacle eased. Johan ignored all his followers. He sipped water and studied an ancient grimoire of arcane lore. That evening, before dinner was served, the tyrant ordered his scribes and minor mages pushed out of the flaps of the tent at sword point. None of the visitors slept well that night, for the tent rocked like a ship in a typhoon.

As the third day dragged, no one spoke of how to reform the army, for no one believed it still existed. Johan ordered the generals' staffs driven out. A swift and bloody sword fight ensued, which Johan settled by blasting the participants into charred ruins. The acrid stink of burned flesh lingered in nostrils as the lucky chosen few passed an uneasy night.

Finally, late in the sixth day, the winds began to lessen. Generals and mages, faces haggard by strain and worry, pleaded with them, so they might live to see the sun once more. As night neared, the wind settled to a low moan, though days before men would have called it a stiff breeze. Huddling at the tent flaps, the survivors recoiled as Johan waved a red hand and banished the magical bubble. With a simple gesture of that ruddy hand, Johan shooed everyone out.

Only Johan remained within, parting the tent flaps with red hands. In the new eerie silence, he instructed, "Generals, assemble your troops. Mages, ready spells to aid them. Find servants to ready my pack train." Then the tent flaps flopped into place.

Squinting in the faint light of dusk, the remnants of Johan's staff peered about and saw only sand. One, bolder than the rest, parted the tent flaps and croaked, "Your Majesty, there's nothing—" He stopped. Others gawked.

Johan had vanished.

* * * * *

In Palmyra, at the town hall, a solid door wedged in its frame by waist-high sand was battered from the inside repeatedly by a heavy table. When the door finally splintered, eager hands yanked the remnants inside, along with a dune's worth of sand. People crawled over it: anything to get outside. They scaled a low dune onto the roof of the town hall.

And gaped in awe at a changed world.

Here and there throughout town, Palmyrans dug out to stare around. In the light of a setting sun, as far as the eye could see, Palmyra contained only the upper halves of thirty or so stout houses, and a few bedraggled treetops stripped of leaves or fronds. All else was gray-brown sand from distant hilltop to hilltop. Even the scar of the dry riverbed was unrecognizable. The sands of Sukurvia had washed over the town like a deluge. Palmyra had almost ceased to exist.

Adira Strongheart, Virgil, Echo, Simone, Badger, Wilemina, Jaeger, and other citizens who'd been crowded together for days, all looked at Hazezon Tamar as if beholding an angel of deliverance. Even their blurry shadows, stretching long across new sand as the sun set, seemed afraid to approach the archmage. Finally the brash Adira waved a bandaged arm in its sling.

"Haz, you're one remarkable wizard!"

Hazezon Tamar was thunderstruck at the change he'd wrought in the world, or had coerced the desert into making, but he tried not to show it.

Nodding idly, as if eyeing a painting he'd daubed or a leather belt he'd woven, he said, "Yes, a fine piece of work, if I may so boldly compliment myself. I'd thought my powers had waned. But I don't mind, if this is a testament to my greatest work. The fates have smiled on me, and I'm content."

"What about the Tirrans?" rasped Virgil.

"Never mind them," said Simone. "We need water and quickly. The wells must be buried, but the cisterns will be safe, once we dig them up."

"I have a water-dowsing spell that may suffice." Hazezon couldn't stop smirking, as smug as a fox. "We won't suffer."

"The Tirrans must have suffered. They must be dead." Limping a circle, Adira saw only sand stretching in all directions with distant hilltops like islands. Her mind kept rebelling, for the map in her head wanted to see a river and sheep pens and green-topped palms and scrubby hills, but all sights were new and frightfully desolate. "Unless they summoned a miracle or shifted away. Johan can't do that, can he? No, of course not, else he would have earlier. Still, once we replenish the water supply, we need to alert the militia. Or do we?"

Adira's Circle of Seven glanced at one another, never having heard their leader sound uncertain. Still, it was a new world out here, and changes were expected.

Hazezon gazed south over naked sand. "Johan's army must be buried to a man." The import of the fate he'd dumped on thousands of soldiers was just sinking in.

"Johan is not buried." Jaeger's rumble made some shiver, an alien sound in a silent world. The tiger man went on, "Even should his army perish, he would survive, drinking their blood if need be. Johan is out there, no doubt already scheming. I smell him in the wind. I must hunt him down."

"Because you're the only one left?" Adira took a step toward the tiger but lurched on her splinted leg. "Because of the prophecy?"

"Yes. It's my destiny to bring him to ground." Jaeger curdled his muzzle, showing fangs, the tiger's smile. His human friends looked somber, with puzzled stares. " 'When None meets One, only Two shall remain.' I have long pondered this omen and decided I am the None."

"Because you're unique?" asked Hazezon. "A mage's construct, so the only one of your kind?"

Another smile, shy, then Jaeger admitted, "That was a lie. My race are the tiger folk who inhabit a vast oasis named Efavra in the eastern desert. I claimed to be alone to protect them, lest intruders seek them out."

"Then why tell us the truth now?" asked Hazezon.

"It's time. For you and them." Jaeger's eyes grew misty, either recalling the past or glimpsing the future. "I came west because . . ."

"Yes?" prompted Adira.

"Because someone had to." Jaeger shook his head, whiskers flicking. "But I'm of no race in this portion of the world, hence None named in the legend. My coming brought the ancient prophecy to the mind of the desert druid, hence the desert itself. No one can walk without leaving a footprint. I am None, who shall clash with One, who must be Johan, leader of lonely Tirras in the north. Two shall remain: Palmrya and Bryce, or else Hazezon Tamar and Adira Strongheart."

Into this stunned silence, Badger opined, "That's the problem with prophecy. It can mean any damned thing you want."

"Some sayings ring truer than others," said Jaeger.

"But if only Two remain," objected Wilemina, "neither None nor One will survive the clash."

Jaeger only bobbed his great striped head, a tiny nod or shrug. "A small sacrifice." He took a step as if alone.

"Here." Adira Strongheart signaled, and a trusted townsman who'd guarded the water supply in the hall gave the last two canteens to Jaeger. A breechcloth and bronze dagger and two canteens seemed pitifully inadequate to brave a new and unknown desert.

Hazezon Tamar licked dry lips. "I—Uh, we—It's not easy to say—"

Jaeger raised a broad paw. "Among my people, it's considered bad luck to say good bye."

Whirling, the tiger bounded away. Striking on all fours, Jaeger soared, sometimes on two legs, sometimes on four. In an amazingly short time, he reached a distant hill and was lost in the shadows that shrouded the landscape.

"We'll never see him again, will we?" asked Wilemina.

Hazezon stared at the gathering gloom and saw nothing. "That's the problem with prophecy. . . ."

* * * * *

Johan had not vanished. He had magically donned the disguise of a minor mage who'd been driven out in the storm to die, a short, bearded man in gray robes with red sleeves. In the aftermath of disaster, none of his generals or mages noticed. The survivors staggered away from Johan's tent to seek the remains of their army before night returned. Johan plodded toward the nearest hill, feigning weariness like the other mortals.

His mind seethed with plots of recovery and revenge. Hazezon Tamar, Adira Strongheart, and that tiger man Jaeger had outwitted, outfought, and outspelled him, and they would suffer as they died. But not today or even this season. Shattered and scattered, his army could never conquer the continent. Best let the broken remnants of the army crawl back to Tirras like a bear retreating to its den to lick its wounds. Johan always had plans layered on plans, but the spirits of this desert disfavored him, and he could never subjugate it. Nor need he. He'd seek new horizons, new tribes, new magics, new schemes. Where, he didn't know, but as superstitious as ever, he reckoned he'd receive a sign as clear as the Mist Moon soon. Such was his luck, never to lack for ambition or plots for long.

Rounding the hill out of sight of his befuddled generals, Johan found life. A writhing brick-red mass scrambled to claw free of the next hilltop. Johan ventured that way. With a squawk and squeal that split the dusky air, a fire drake squirmed like a snake to free its wings from a rocky cleft. A leather-clad flyer tugged on the drake's reins while three soldiers scooped sand under the drake's feet. Johan grabbed the reins and helped pull, and the drake popped loose. The beast shook sand from its ears and flapped its wings, glad to be free.

"That's better!" The flyer, a small woman, stroked the drake's muzzle while the soldiers sipped from a canteen. Smiling at the fat little mage, the flyer said, "We flew in just as the storm descended. I'd spotted this cave from the air, but it was high on a hillside then!"

She laughed with relief and the sheer joy at being alive, as did another flyer and three grimy soldiers.

One said, "Lucky we'd just filled our canteens and could grab waterskins off the wagon."

Another added, "We should have grabbed spades too!" They laughed together.

"You were in that cave?" Johan peered at the narrow cleft they'd crawled from. "You were lucky you didn't blunder into takklemaggots. Oh, my, you've one on your boot." He touched the flyer's leg as if to show her.

"What? *Ahh!*" The flyer's face paled as a forked tail as white as bone suddenly jutted from her boot top. The maggot was huge, as long as her hand, and like an arrow it burrowed into her calf as if digging into cheese. Falling in her fright, the woman jerked at the boot only to see a pair of rust-red eyes peek from her leather sleeve. Pain struck, and she whapped her arm, then pounded her body to still the searing burn of the maggots infesting her skin.

Backing away from the shrieking flyer, Johan bumped into the three horrified soldiers. They screamed, suddenly infested with takklemaggots boring through their skin, guts, necks, and legs. Johan moved again, catching the fire drake's reins to lead the beast away. Two hundred red-eyed takklemaggots greedily devoured the stricken soldiers. By the time Johan looked back, only one strong man still kicked feebly in the sand. Johan saw white snaky shapes breaking free of his flesh, then burrowing back down.

As he walked the hot sands with bare feet, Johan shed his disguise with every step like a snake its skin, so the short bearded mage became a tall gaunt man with red skin, black tattoos, and three horns jutting from his head above a purple robe. The tyrant felt no remorse at killing his own troops with takklemaggots. He needed the fire drake to further his plans and didn't want anyone to report where he went, lest his enemies learn. His subjects lived and died to serve him. And any who died probably deserved to, for likely they were sluggards who neglected their duties and failed to build Johan's empire. Properly motivated soldiers would not die but would succeed for their emperor's glory.

So too, this fire drake would serve. Once aloft, Johan would let the beast seek water. The direction it flew would reveal the signpost that fate intended as Johan's next step.

Snapping the reins, he forced the fire drake to drop its head. Johan stared into the smoky, dark eyes of the drake to cow the beast, to show who was master. Yet something spooked the animal, so it tossed its head, and the compulsion spell broke.

"Curse you, son of a wyrm! You will obey—"

From the corner of his eye Johan saw movement as the fire drake's nostrils flared in fear.

Glancing, Johan panicked.

Bounding across the sand came a thunderbolt of stripes in orange, black, and white, aiming straight for Johan.

For once, Johan moved swiftly, clambering into the tiny saddle so his bare feet dangled below the fire drake's sinuous neck.

Jerking at the reins and loop handle, he screeched, "Up! Rise, you miserable monster! Fly!"

Creaking and slapping and flapping, the fire drake clawed toward the sky. Leather wings scooped air like a kite. Unused to so much weight in a rider, and stiff from being cramped for days in a cave, the beast floundered. Johan uttered a levitation spell, and instantly the drake's body lifted a dozen feet higher. Still chanting, Johan leaned over to find Jaeger, then recoiled.

With a tiger's coughing roar, Jaeger leaped after the enemy of the southlands. Clawed hands gripped the cinch strap netting across the drake's breast. Instantly the winged creature sank toward the ground.

"Begone!" The emperor was enraged. "Banish yourself, beast-man! You're not fit to sully your superior's hem!"

"I'll sully—your bones—and scatter them to the winds!" The fire drake scrabbled with its claws to dislodge the tiger. Jaeger struggled to hang on. He hoped the drake didn't spew fire, for he wouldn't survive another such blast. Constant fighting for months, searing wounds, and the harsh dry desert had taken their toll on the tiger man. Now, after his frantic run across the desert, he found his breath short and his recent arm wound seeping blood. Jaeger's strength was hollow and fading.

Slashing to sink his claws in the drake's neck, the tiger growled, "Johan! Your quest for glory ends here!"

"Never!" Johan was hissing to preserve the levitation spell keeping the drake aloft. He couldn't invoke another enchantment without quitting the first. So he ripped a dagger from his belt and leaned to cut at tiger claws. "I'll not be defeated by a bastardly mistake like you!"

Jaeger's feet touched down, but the reduced burden just made the fire drake flap and fight harder to escape. Hooking his claws deeper in the drake's hide, so the animal shrieked and writhed, Jaeger slashed his talons at the emperor's legs. Yet the drake dragged him, and he twisted and spun dizzily, before he could grip—

Leaning in the tilted saddle, Johan stabbed. Aiming for the tiger's wounded shoulder, the emperor's dagger punctured the tiger's leather harness square through the buckle. The blade sank deep in shoulder muscle.

Jaeger hissed and squirmed at the pain, yet he refused to let go even as Johan twisted the blade.

The archmage growled like a tiger himself. "You'll stop no one!"

"Even if I fail," Jaeger's eyes glowed as he pronounced his own prophecy, "there will come another—"

His last words.

Smooth new-laid sands suddenly dimpled under the fire drake. Sand caved in a perfect circle nine feet across. From the depression vomited a column of gray flesh as big as a waterspout.

Looking down, Johan recognized the thing. A sand worm, a denizen of the frightful barren eastern desert, but never seen this close to the River Toloron. The soil was thought too stony to support the monsters. The mage understood. The sandstorm had dumped countless tons of new sand soft, enough for the fearsome worms to burrow in. In their eternal quest for food, they'd instinctively followed the sand. Here came the first, alerted by the thumping of life on the surface, for anything living was fair game to a sand worm.

As fast as a galloping horse, the worm burst from underground. Its mouth was a ring of shark's teeth. Obscene pink tentacles rimmed the teeth, as did straggling hairs or filaments and a rudimentary pink-gray fin like a ragged sail. Remnants of elder land wyrms, legend made them, forlorn dragons that had lost their will to dominate. Stripped of their names and memories and magic, the sky-soarers had been cast underground to burrow in dirt like true worms.

Johan recalled this ancient lore in mere seconds as the yawning pit of razor teeth engulfed Jaeger. One second the tiger man dangled from the harness. Then only his head and one arm were visible. Jaeger's eyes bulged in surprise, and blood spurted from his muzzle as he was crushed like a beetle.

Then he was gone, as was the worm, humping its immense body and dropping like a rock down a pipe, back into its underworld tunnel to digest its prey.

Given strength by terror, the fire drake clawed into the dusky sky until it flew alone under the stars. Johan wiggled his bare feet as if surprised he still had them. So close had the sand worm come that one tentacle had whipped his dirty feet. He could still feel the tingle and sting.

"Yet I'm alive to continue my quest," he said aloud.

Tilting back in the saddle, Johan shoved his dagger in its scabbard, but it wouldn't fit. Fingering the dagger, he found Jaeger's shoulder buckle impaled on the blade. The curious bronze sigil was curled like a ram's horns. Johan puzzled, having never seen the sign. Prying it off the blade, he pocketed the buckle, all that remained of the tiger warrior from the mysterious east. The wizard muttered, "So I acquire another good luck charm to aid my quest. . . ."

Looking about, Johan discovered the fire drake flew east. That seemed appropriate. He sought new tribes, new lands, and new magic, and the east was unexplored. The tiger man had come from the east, an agent of destiny and a test for Johan. Though his army had been defeated, the emperor had triumphed in a larger way, for he'd beaten a legend and outwitted prophecy itself. None and One had clashed, and only Two remained: himself and the continent of Jamuraa to be conquered. The tiger man had even spoken as if prophesizing, foretelling that another would follow. So eastward must be more tiger men.

"Mine for the taking," the emperor proclaimed to an invisible audience. "As I defeated one, so shall I enslave all. And gain revenge on *all* my enemies."

Booting the fire drake with his bare heels, the emperor rode alone, high in the starlit sky, to conquer the unknown east.

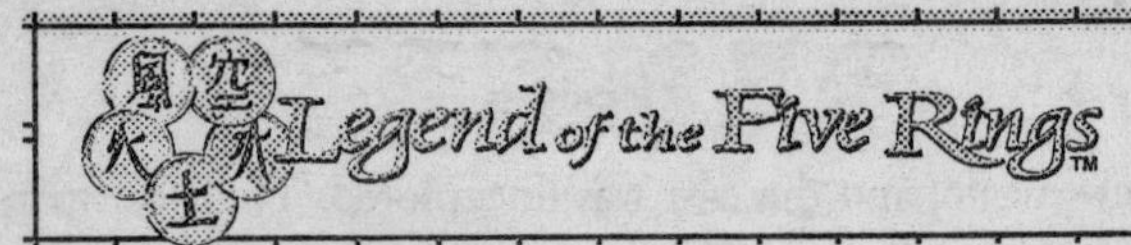

The Phoenix

Stephen D. Sullivan

The five Elemental Masters—the greatest magic-wielders of Rokugan—seek to turn back the demons of the Shadowlands. To do so, they must harness the power of the Black Scrolls, and perhaps become demons themselves.

March 2001

The Dragon

Ree Soesbee

The most mysterious of all the clans of Rokugan, the Dragon had long stayed elusive in their mountain stronghold. When at last they emerge into the Clan War, they unleash a power that could well save the empire . . . or doom it.

September 2001

The Crab

Stan Brown

For a thousand years, the Crab have guarded the Emerald Empire against demon hordes—but when the greatest threat comes from within, the Crab must ally with their fiendish foes and march to take the capital city.

June 2001

The Lion

Stephen D. Sullivan

Since the Scorpion Coup, the Clans of Rokugan have made war upon each other. Now, in the face of Fu Leng and his endless armies of demons, the Seven Thunders must band together to battle their immortal foe . . . or die!

November 2001

Tales from the world of Magic

Dragons of Magic

Ed. J. Robert King

From the time of the Primevals to the darkest hours of the Phyrexian Invasion, dragons have filled Dominaria. Few of their stories have been told—until now. Learn the secrets of the most powerful dragons in the multiverse!

August 2001

The Myths of Magic

Ed. Jess Lebow

Stories and legends, folktales and tall tales. These are the myths of Dominaria, stories captured on the cards of the original trading card game. Stories from J. Robert King, Francis Lebaron, and others.

The Colors of Magic

Ed. Jess Lebow

Argoth is decimated. Tidal waves have turned canyons into rivers. Earthquakes have leveled the cities. Dominaria is in ruins. Now the struggle is to survive. Tales from such authors as Jeff Grubb, J. Robert King, Paul Thompson, and Francis Lebaron.

Rath and Storm

Ed. Peter Archer

The flying ship Weatherlight enters the dark, sinister plane of Rath to rescue its kidnapped captain. But, as the stories in this anthology show, more is at stake than Sisay's freedom.